MO' DIRTY:

STILL STUNTIN'

DARRELL KING

URBAN BOOKS

www.urbanbooks.net

Urban Books, LLC
78 East Industry Court
Deer Park, NY 11729

Mo' Dirty: Still Stuntin' Copyright © 20 Darrell King

ISBN 13: 978-1-60162-291-4
ISBN 10: 1-60162-291-0

First Trade Printing
First Mass Market Printing December 2010
Printed in the United States of America

10 9 8 7 6 5 4 3 2 1

Distributed by Kensington Publishing Corp.
Submit Wholesale Orders to:
Kensington Publishing Corp.
C/O Penguin Group (USA) Inc.
Attention: Order Processing
405 Murray Hill Parkway
East Rutherford, NJ 07073-2316
Phone: 1-800-526-0275
Fax: 1-800-227-9604

MO' DIRTY:

STILL STUNTIN'

Chapter 1

"Hood-rich Niggas"

Leon McBride had long since left the comfort of the witness protection program after the 1994 arrest and conviction of Marion "Snookey" Lake and the other members of the infamous Dirty South Syndicate. He originally had been given a new identity and was sent packing out west to New Mexico, where he spent three bittersweet, homesick years before returning to the Deep South in '98. There he spent another seven years down in Jackson, Mississippi, and enjoyed a successful run as the minister of a local Baptist church.

Now it was 2005, and the pastor had returned to his beloved Savannah, Georgia, to live for good. He'd even managed to open up a brand-new church near Bull Street, called Spaulding Baptist. The new white-and-blue house of worship boasted a large raucous congregation of 788 loyal parishioners and a forty-five-man choir, arguably the best in all of Savannah.

During the humid summer Sundays the fifty-two-year-old preacher could still deliver the word with force and vigor, causing the parishioners (especially the lovely young women) to swoon in the spirit. He still had a hidden lust for flesh that bordered on obsession and simply couldn't resist the temptation of bedding down the sanctuary's choice vixens, be they married or single. He wasn't married himself but shared a luxury cottage with his long time fiancée, Collette Briggs, in the exclusive Kingsford Plantation, an expensive gated community. Yet the skirt-chasing pastor often rented costly rooms at the Marquis de Sade Inn out on Fripp Island, where he could find adequate time to fully indulge in all his sinful fantasies.

Still, McBride knew that without the armed protection of the feds, he had to be extra careful traveling the streets of Savannah. Though Snookey Lake was currently serving time and Mafia don Alberto Cellini was said to be overseas, he realized that criminals had long and keen memories, and that neither prison bars nor thousands of miles of ocean could prevent them from extracting revenge if they chose to. He, however, continually convinced himself that as long as he kept a low profile and stayed away from drug dealers and their wares he'd be just fine.

Besides, he had his trusty armor-bearing brothers, Luke and Wallace, to watch his back, even to kill for him if need be. And with the convictions having been well over a decade ago, there was little chance that any hoodlums loyal to the old Dirty South Syndicate would be left on the streets of Savannah or anywhere else. For this reason Pastor McBride could often be found cruising darkened streets of the city with one or more of his girlfriends, dining at the top eateries, or catching a play or two at the civic center every Wednesday night after Bible study.

Either of his two armor bearers would secretly bring one of the pastor's young lovers to his chambers well after the other members had left the building for the night. They would then chauffeur the amorous couple to their Fripp Island love nest, with its huge oak shade trees, bubbling fishponds, and well-mowed courtyards.

The inn's exterior property provided a touch of vintage Southern charm to the gorgeous hotel. On Wednesday nights, a live jazz band entertained smitten couples out on the enormous patio, where they sat cuddled together at candlelit tables or danced cheek to cheek in the open courtyard below the silvery light of the full Georgia moon.

There, beneath the dark shadows of the oak limbs, Pastor McBride sipped on White Zinfandel and dined on fried catfish, okra, and Spanish rice, stealing a sultry kiss or two between bites. The pastor and his lover, the beautiful eighteen-year-old elder daughter of the choir director, became increasingly more passionate with their kisses every time their lips met. Surely in due time they would leave the patio to retire to their appointed room to enjoy a night of lovemaking.

By 10:30 the next morning, McBride and his teen sweetheart showered, dressed, and left the Marquis de Sade Inn cuddling and caressing in the back seat of a white limo driven by Brother Wallace as they left their dirty little secrets behind on Fripp Island.

Little did Pastor McBride know, he wasn't the only one heading back to Savannah from the island hideaway.

Trailing the long white limo, about two cars behind, was a Silver Volvo S80. The well-groomed driver picked up a small black cell phone and pressed TALK. Almost immediately, a female voice answered at the other end.

"Ms. Briggs, it's Detective Lionel. I've got a lead on your fiancé. At this moment he's leaving Marquis de Sade. We're crossing the Stonewall Jackson Memorial Bridge. I have over twenty photos for you to look over also. Yeah, he's been up to no good, I'm afraid."

Without speaking, Collette Briggs gently flipped her cell phone shut and walked slowly to the front door. She paused briefly in the doorway, sighing deeply before making her way down the stairs and to the navy blue Jeep Grand Cherokee that awaited her in the circular cobblestone driveway out front. She reached down into her purse to remove a large wad of cash, passed it through the driver's side window to the scowling, cornrow-wearing youth sitting behind the wheel immersed in the throbbing tunes of T.I.

The young man politely took the money from the church lady's outstretched hand and counted it to be certain that it was all there. Then he put the Jeep in DRIVE, after replacing the T.I. disc with Trick Daddy, and slowly cruised past the gigantic wrought iron gate and disappeared down the street into the traffic beyond.

As Ms. Briggs stood in the driveway dressed in her flowing satin nightgown, she felt both guilt and supreme satisfaction for what she'd just done.

The Spaulding Baptist Church would be the pastor's first stop after dining on a light breakfast at the Old Country Buffet restaurant just before placing his playmate in a taxicab to take her home.

The young man pulled up on Bull Street around 1:45 PM and waited patiently outside of the church entrance. He let the Jeep idle gently as he put it in park and rolled up the windows, blasting the interior air conditioning units because the June heat was a blistering ninety-five degrees outside. He opened the glove compartment and removed a sturdy chrome 9 mm Glock handgun with a fully loaded clip that extended slightly beneath the handle. Smiling, he slowly attached a silencer onto the muzzle of the weapon and reclined his seat as he surfed through his cell phone's stored number settings to decide on which girl he'd settle down with later that night after he'd taken care of the day's business affairs.

There were few pedestrians out and about on this particular day, which was ideal, because daylight shootings often brought witnesses, at least those bold enough to testify.

The young man behind the wheel was no stranger to murder. He'd killed many people before—male, female, young, and old. It didn't matter one way or the other to him, and he had no problem offing witnesses. Today, however, everything seemed to be working out perfectly.

By 2:26 PM, Ms. Briggs received the phone call she both dreaded as well as impatiently awaited. Her would-be husband, Pastor Leon McBride, was dead. He and his chauffeur, Brother Wallace, had been shot multiple times as they stepped out from their parked limousine and climbed the steps toward the entrance of the sanctuary.

Many people wanted the womanizing preacher dead for one reason or another, but Peter "Whiskey" Battle had done it for the money. Both the incarcerated druglords as well as the pastor's very own betrayed fiancée had paid him handsomely to have Leon McBride eliminated.

A day later Whiskey drove back home to Peola to pick up the prison gang's portion of the money for the McBride hit. The two-and-a-half-hour drive from Savannah to Peola seemed like mere minutes, the way Whiskey was balling up Interstate 44.

First order of business was to meet up with David Ambrosia at West Peola's posh and popular nightclub, 95 South. Ambrosia had taken over the club after his brother, Lee, was murdered in '92. The nightclub was a favorite weekend hot spot for Peola's young adults and drew multitudes of celebrities, especially hip-hop stars. Ludacris, Jay-Z, and Snoop Dogg were just a few of the luminaries who could be seen there on any given Friday or Saturday night. And local up-and-coming Peola lyricist, ATL Slim, was a fixture at the club and often performed live before sold-out audiences on summer weekends.

Whiskey knew how much his niece, Peaches, enjoyed live shows featuring rappers, so he stopped at his older sister's house to scoop her up. Peaches enjoyed the atmosphere of the lively nightclub, especially when her favorite entertainers walked about the VIP section and mingled freely with the little people like herself.

Whiskey, close friend and business partner of David Ambrosia, was a frequent visitor of the club and always received food and drinks on the house whenever he stopped by, but he'd recently limited his visits because he didn't particularly care for the place that much anymore. The clientele had become much younger, with more patrons in their late teens than years earlier, and their rowdy behavior brought about the need for more bouncers, which slowly eroded the easygoing surroundings he had become accustomed to. He also disliked the new manager Ambrosia had hired to oversee the weekly activities of the facility.

Leona McIntosh, a recently divorced forty-six-year-old mother of three from Brooklyn, New York, poured all of her energy into her young daughters and her career. After graduating from New York University with a master's degree in business, she managed the world-famous Apollo Theater and Radio City Music Hall, making her no stranger to the world of entertainment. Leona was a shrewd, oftentimes cutthroat employer. She brought 95 South a sixty-five percent increase in total revenue, and an eighty percent increase in patronage since given the position a year earlier.

But it was the cold, unforgiving methods Leona used to handle her staff that Whiskey disliked. She was an absolute asshole as a boss and ran the club like some third world dictator, firing even long-term employees for infractions as minor as missing a spot of dust on the bar counter. Whiskey didn't feel her one bit and wasn't planning on staying long.

As Peaches mingled with a few of her college friends near the crowded bar, Leona, with an out-stretched hand and bubbly smile, approached Whiskey from behind the doorway leading to the VIP section. "Hello, Mr. Battle? I'm Leona McIntosh, the manager here. Mr. Ambrosia unfortunately can't be here to meet with you this evening due to a pressing business matter he had to attend to out of town. He sends his apologies and promises to phone you as soon as he returns later in the week. However, if you cannot wait until then, he suggested that you take a flight out to LA. He also asked that I tell you he'd be more than happy to pay for a round-trip ticket for you. If that's what you decide, he would like for you to catch the 12:30 AM red-eye flight out to LAX. Be sure to fly Southwestern. A first-class ticket will be waiting. Is that satisfactory for you, or no?"

"Yeah, that'll work." Whiskey swigged down a shot of tequila and lime.

"Great," Leona squealed. "Mr. Ambrosia will have a limo waiting for you at the airport when you arrive. Check it out. If I'm not mistaken, he'll be at the roast for Eddie Murphy, so you'll be riding with Gabrielle Union and Halle Berry. Now ain't that a blip? Afterwards, you guys are staying in Beverly Hills with one of Mr. Ambrosia's business associates."

Whiskey could tell that the manager was exaggerating a bit, but it didn't matter to him. This trip was nothing more than a business trip, a journey to receive monies due, not a vacation. "A'ight then. Let me take my niece home 'cause she ain't got a ride," he said, rising up from the barstool.

"What? Are you kidding me? You're like family to Mr. Ambrosia. I'm certain he'd want to see your niece safely home after we close for the night, and so would I. Besides, look at her and her girlfriends out on the dance floor. The place is jumping, and there are cute guys all over. She's having a ball. You'd totally ruin what's turning out to be a wonderful night if you took her away now. I'll make sure she gets home right after we shut things down, I promise."

"Yeah, yeah, yeah. You just make sure she don't get too happy ordering all them apple martinis, a'ight?"

Whiskey left the club, while his niece, oblivious to his silent departure through the packed dance floor and right out the front door, danced the night away.

Later that night, he caught the red-eye from Peola's Burrell National Airport to the bustling LAX. After a light meal and a few glasses of champagne, he dozed off comfortably in his plush airline seat for most of the cross-country three-hour flight. When the plane finally landed, he was a little upset because he'd just missed the best part of Martin Scorsese's *Casino*, only catching the part when Joe Pesci's character, Nicky Santoro, was beaten to death by baseball bat-wielding wiseguys. He sighed out loud as he rose from his seat to remove his belongings from the overhead luggage compartment. He never could finish watching that damn movie. Something always prevented him from seeing it to the end.

Around 4:45 AM PST, the limousine, by no means occupied with Hollywood hotties, drove into the curved driveway of an enormous Beverly Hills mansion. Once Whiskey stepped out from the rear of the elegant vehicle, he could literally see the entire expanse of La-La Land, its lights twinkling in the distance. The Hollywood sign glowed like a lone sentry on top of a hill, as helicopters fluttered across South Central, shining their searchlights in an attempt to apprehend wanted gang members.

As Whiskey walked toward the front door, a smiling David Ambrosia, flanked by two scantily clad dimes and with a half-empty bottle of Moet in his hand, approached him.

After a brief reunion of laughter, embracing, and playful banter between the two, Ambrosia welcomed Whiskey into a magnificently furnished mansion, leading him along an intricately designed, winding staircase that spiraled nearly three floors up from the bottom foyer, and showed his weary, jet-lagged homie his room. Then he gave his goodnight daps and returned to the lower regions of the manor to his female companions.

In the spacious, Las Vegas-themed bedroom was

a full-size refrigerator filled with several cases of imported and domestic beer and dozens of packaged frozen TV dinners. An actual miniature kitchen area held a microwave oven, and a large chestnut table with a metal bucket filled with ice and a large bottle of California Merlot.

Right before he turned in for the night, Ambrosia text messaged Whiskey to meet him at 1:30 PM downstairs in the main dining room for lunch.

It didn't take long for sleep to overcome the exhausted Georgian, who slept soundly past one.

It was 3:25 PM, and his host had long since dined and left the premises by the time Whiskey showered and dressed and came downstairs to an empty dining room, except for the housekeeping crew tidying up the area for dinner later that night.

The house chef, a spry old Venezuelan woman around sixty or so, prepared him a turkey breast sandwich that quickly proved to be filling. Afterward he proceeded to the outdoor pool area in the back, where sounds of splashing water and the giggle and laughter of bikini-clad beauties drew him like moth to a flame.

Once there, he wasn't disappointed with the bubble-butt sistas mingling with leggy blondes and buxom Latinas poolside. Some tanned themselves while stretching their taut, young figures along colorful pool chairs and reading the latest gossip mags behind dark sunshades. Others splashed about playfully in the clear, turquoise water of the pool as they hit a big, bouncy inflated ball back and forth between them.

Whiskey smiled devilishly as he took in the scenery, stroking his strong chin in expectation of a sexually gratifying night. Only a suitcase filled with neatly stacked benjamins could top fucking the shit out of a sexy-ass broad, especially the raunchy, no-holds-barred nymphos from Southern California. He'd had one or two in his day, and their bedroom skills proved to be among the best he'd experienced.

As he stood in the rear of the pool area dressed in silk Bermuda shorts and a Versace shirt, he sipped on a tall glass of Long Island Iced Tea he'd been given by a voluptuous, caramel-complexioned life-guard he'd engaged in a brief, flirtatious discussion. When she relinquished her post atop the diving board, an equally stunning female took her place in the white chair overlooking the pool.

While mesmerized by the sheer number of hot-bodied beauties surrounding him, a hand fell upon his shoulder, breaking his lust-filled daydream. It was none other than his boy David.

"It's a whole lotta bad-ass bitches out here today, huh?" Ambrosia said in his cool Georgian twang. "If you ain't careful, you might fall in some pussy. Know what I'm sayin', Whiskey?"

As always, the baller was looking fresh in a khaki Phat Farm short set, matching Nike sneakers, and a glistening platinum herringbone chain that adorned his neck. The pleasant aroma of his $500 imported Italian cologne hovered in the dry Californian air around them like an aura of sweet-smelling raisins. The boy was still a boss player.

"Don't worry 'bout these hoes. They'll be ripe for the pickin' later on. You already know bidness befo' pleasure, playa. I need fa you ta meet some of my folks, a'ight?"

Four thugs in their twenties, all wearing black-and-white checkered bandana shirts, creased khaki pants, and black-and-white Chuck Taylor sneakers, raised up off a tastefully remodeled 1964 Chevrolet Impala.

"DiVante, Du-Loc, Snatch Man, and G-Loc, here is my man, Pete. We call him Whiskey back home."

As they clasped hands and embraced with the usual brotherly affection shown to one another in the hood, Whiskey could tell that these cats weren't fake, wannabe gangstas. They'd put in work.

"Wassup, pimpin'?" DiVante said. His father was the late DiAngelo Lovett, the former South Central leader of the Reapers street gang who'd become a well-respected civil rights and anti-gang activist before being brutally gunned down by the very hoodlums he'd once helped organize. Everyone who was anyone in the hustle game knew the Lovett family, especially out West.

The other three bandana-wearing gangstas wore scowls on their hardened young faces and bore prison tats on their neck and forearms. Surely they had seen their fair share of violence and death. Whiskey could tell a true soldier from a fake dude by the way he walked, talked, and carried himself. Game recognized game, and both parties showed one another respect after the brief introductions.

The six young men smoked two thickly rolled blunts and discussed which woman each of them wanted to sleep with that night.

"You tryin'-a hit dis shit, dawg? Dis right here is a *sherm*. Ya know, a sherman stick, it'll go nice wit' da chronic."

Whiskey noticed through reddened eyes that everyone else was smoking the PCP-soaked cigarette. "Naw, I'm a'ight. I don't fuck wit' dat sherm shit. Plus, I gotta stay focused, ya know. Got dat bidness thing ta handle, feel me?"

"True dat," Ambrosia said, choking slightly off the acrid-smelling sherm stick before passing it on to Petey, who stood next to him. He wrapped his sinewy arms around Whiskey's shoulders. "You still tired from da flight, bro?"

"Not anymore. Took a good long nap, ate a li'l bit. I'm good for right now."

"My girl Bianca can cook her ass off, can't she?"

"Well, all I got from her was a sandwich and some fries, but hey, if she's a professional chef, I guess so."

"Dawg, ol' broad can burn," DiVante said. "I've eaten mo' than a little bit of her meals. She da bomb."

Du-Loc said, "Yeah, 'specially her chicken fajitas an' shit. Dem joints is good as a mufucka."

Whiskey stomped the remainder of the roach underfoot. "I don't really give a fuck 'bout no ol' Spanish cook an' all dat bullshit. I took a plane all da way out here for one reason and one reason only—to get my money. Feel me, Davey boy?"

"C'mon, baby, you know how I roll. I got you, dawg," Ambrosia said in his usual laid-back manner. "I got ya paper right here in this duffle bag, but my mans an' dem got a slight problem, a'ight? A problem dat dey needs yo' help to get handled, feel me? Dey got an ex-employee who tried to get outta their gang. He skipped town a li'l while ago, an' now his bitch ass is snitchin' to the feds."

"Fa sho," DiVante added.

"DiVante had this cat runnin' thangs out in Long Beach for 'bout four or five years, slangin' rocks outta at least six stash houses. Dat nigga was doin' it big, pushin' beamers, flippin' dollars like it wasn't nothing, and livin' in a four-bedroom beach house overlooking the Pacific Ocean. Then, behind some shit he fucked up, he got busted. You know what happened next, right?"

"The nigga snitched, right?"

"Bingo. But it gets deeper, 'cause that fool got roots down in da Carolinas. The feds set him up wit' a trailer down in Beaufort, South Carolina and changed his identity an' all dat type secretive bullshit, just as long as he brings down the major playas in the South Central, LA crack game. Which includes the whole Reapers gang, which, of course, is run by none other than my man, DiVante Lovett. You know good an' damn well dat we can't let my man DL go out like dat behind some fuckin' dumbass snitch, right?"

Whiskey took a deep gulp of Long Island Iced Tea, wiped a diamond-encrusted hand across his moist lips, and belched loudly. He stared intently at DiVante Lovett.

The handsome, rugged-looking youngster with the long, braided hair and smooth, sandy-brown complexion stared back at him through unblinking hazel brown eyes that women adored and men feared, silently awaiting an answer.

"This mufucka is due to go on the witness stand

this comin' fall, around October or November. The feds gonna have him call everybody an' their mama out. Ain't no goddamn way we gonna let dis punk bitch last dat long."

"You gotta peel his cap back, homie. David done told us dat you da man when it comes ta deadin' niggas. We know da dude's livin' down in y'all's neck o' da woods an' shit. So can you take care of this light work for us or what?" Petey puffed on the powerfully narcotic sherman stick.

Whiskey finished the glass of iced tea and sat it down on a small patio table near him and turned toward DiVante. "Ya know what, cuz? About five years ago this dude named Nathan robbed a credit union in West Peola and got away wit' somethin' like two to three grand. He had his two cousins as his flunkies. He never did fully pay them cats what he owed dem an' even turned around an' ratted on 'em when he got his dumb ass busted a year later. Shit, da nigga even brought my name up in it, 'cause he had bought the getaway car from me before he'd pulled off the robbery. I was fuckin' pissed off and hurt at the same time, 'cause I thought Nathan was my man an' shit. But I ain't even had to get at 'im, for real, 'cause his cousin Topp shot 'im in da face comin' out of da police station on St. Patrick's Day two thousand. I'll never forget that day as long as I live. I was lucky I didn't get locked up my damn self behind dat stupid shit."

"What does that gotta do wit' anything?" DiVante asked.

"Well, what I wanna know is, why you gotta get me ta dead dis dude? I mean, y'all got thangs on lock out here an' shit, right? Everyody knows dat da

Reapers run almost all of the Pacific Coast and can touch folks even in other states, so why you need me to handle ya bidness for you?"

"You gotta hear me out, playa. We got things pretty much airtight out here on our end, that's true. An', if necessary, yes, we can reach out an' touch a nigga anywhere in da country if we have to. But that would take way too long to get done, know what I'm sayin'?"

"I dunno. I guess if y'all cool wit' my man David, then we pretty much family, right?"

"Bet. David's always talkin' 'bout you, dawg. He been tellin' war stories 'bout you for so long, we feel like we know every damn thing 'bout you. An' from everything that DA been tellin' us, you a straight G, no doubt, an' we want you ta do dis nigga for us, cuz."

Whiskey snickered. "Well, I'm pretty sho dat you done stretched a coupla niggas out in da streets befo' ya damn self, ain't dat right?"

Snatch Man dragged deeply on yet another cigarette that he'd just soaked in a small container of PCP, exhaled a cloud of smoke, which hovered in the air above his head, then spat a thick clump of phlegm onto the ground below. "Sheeet, nigga, how I feel 'bout dat bitch-ass nigga, I'll murk his whole mufuckin' family, cuz, believe dat shit."

Du-Loc took the sherman stick offered to him from Snatch Man. "I'm wit' my man Snatch on dat one. I'm 'bout ready to ride on dat mark myself, for real."

Whiskey took the army-green duffle bag that Ambrosia gave him, knelt down, and quickly began flipping through the twenties, fifties, and hundreds.

Once he was satisfied with the amount there, he stood and addressed the group.

"A'ight, what's dis nigga's name, and how does he look?"

"His name is Larry, but da streets know 'im betta as Gimp. He a short, fat, dark-skinned nigga wit' a pot belly and a thick-ass beard an' shit." DiVante flipped open his cell phone and scrolled through a series of photos featuring himself and other members of the Reapers, including Gimp, posing gangsta-style, brandishing weapons, forty-ounce malt liquor bottles, and wads of money spread out fan-like within their grasps. "He used ta be one of my most hard-core enforcers, handlin' business for me whenever bustas got outta line out here in da hood. He almost single-handedly kept da Bloods and Crips sets out in Watts. He'll dead a nigga without hesitation an' won't give a fuck who dey is—I'll give da nigga dat much. Since da age o' twelve he been out here on da streets grindin', an' da boy know how ta flip dem dollars, as you can see from dese here pictures an' shit. He know how to network wit' da game's biggest ballers."

"Beaufort, huh? I wonda why da feds would send a nigga all da way across da country? Well, I guess it would be understandable though," Whiskey remarked.

DiVante nodded in agreement. "The feds know dat leavin' Gimp anywhere on da West Coast, he's as good as dead. Ya know they can't afford to take dat risk, so quite naturally they gonna place him somewhere far off where they feel he won't ever be found. But, see, two things Gimp's fat ass can't resist—Naw, make that three—pussy, money, and food. We both got da same coke connect, a Mexican cat outta Houston. Ya see, obviously Gimp been hittin' 'im up for some weight over the past two or three months. I heard 'bout Gimp's new place o' residence by just kickin' it on da phone one night wit' my man Chico. I bet he don't even know how much of a favor he did a nigga dat night.

"Listen to me, Whiskey, there ain't no fuckin' price dat I won't pay or can't pay so I can stop dis nigga from testifying against me an' shit. Ya heard what I said, cuz? I'll pay whateva to shut Gimp's mufuckin' mouth for good.

"Da feds must not know that Gimp's been buyin' a couple o' kilos o' pure Colombian flake through one o' his new little country girlfriends that make all o' da phone calls and pick-ups for him. Da nigga's too smart to get hisself caught up a second time. But, anyway, his main girl works at a restaurant called The Toddle House. Supposedly he picks her up from there around 11:30 PM every Monday, Wednesday, and Friday night. Feds be checkin' up on him a lot, though, so you gonna have ta watch ya back. When you get back down South, hit me up on da cell and lemme know after you done peeled his wig back, and I'll wire you da cash. Ya know I'm good for it, or else David here wouldn't o' introduced you to me, right?" DiVante reached out a clenched fist and gently pounded his with Whiskey's.

Whiskey sat down on a nearby pool chair and blew kisses at two curvaceous beauties, who smiled brightly as they passed the young men en route to the opposite side of the busy pool. "I ain't got a problem wit' bustin' a cap in ya man an' all. It's all in a day's work for me, you know, but I'm gonna have to ask for thirty grand, fifteen gees up front befo' I fly back, an' another fifteen after I murk dis Gimp character for you. Is dat a'ight wit' you?"

"Like I said earlier, it's whateva, dawg. My pockets stay on swole, so money ain't an issue for me, cuz. I just want da nigga dead, that's all."

Whiskey liked what he was hearing. All the stories he'd heard about DiVante and his now dead pops DiAngelo being gangsta and boss playas must be true if he could just come up with fifteen thousand dollars in such a short amount of time. This was surely not some weak nigga wit' short money.

"Y'all ain't gotta worry 'bout ol' Gimp fa too much longa, 'cause once I get back down South, his ass is grass." Whiskey placed the duffle bag near his chair and smiled with the realization that his best friend had set him up with a top-dollar-paying murder job with the added perk of having access to a major West Coast drug trafficker to boot. He would have to show David Ambrosia how much he appreciated his looking out.

DiVante gave Whiskey his personal cell phone number, which the Southern bad boy placed into his own cellular menu.

"Whiskey, if you complete this work like we ask you to, and mind you, I already know you will, we can have a real long business relationship makin' moves dat make money, okay? Before you leave for Georgia tomorrow night, I'll have Du-Loc drop off da fifteen gees for you around noon. I got a bitch I fucks wit' who works security at LAX. She da head o' da airport security an' shit, so she can have her staff let you slip through wit'out all da fuckin' questions as to why you travelin' wit' so much cash. 'Cause, dawg, you carryin' a li'l over twenty-seven grand, wit' the fifteen I'm puttin' up, plus da twelve you already got in ya duffle bag. So you know dem rental cops gonna trip."

"That'll work. If everything goes as planned, this fool should be long gone by the end of da week, I promise you dat much."

"I bet you he will." DiVante grinned. "After you confirm dat Gimp's dead, I'll wire ya da second payment by Western Union ."

Snatch Man eyed a thick, big-booty redbone clad in a skimpy two-piece, who blushed bashfully as she pranced by. "I know you niggas like talkin' 'bout peelin' dudes' caps back, an' money an' shit, but I'm 'bout ta hit dis pool an' fuck wit' dese bitches right now."

Whiskey rubbed his palms together in anticipation. "Shit, nigga, you ain't gotta tell me twice."

"We gonna have a lotta fun out here wit' dese hoes dis evenin', homie, so let's go on over to da bathhouse over here to da right. I already got da joint stocked wit' a bunch o' swim trunks o' all different colors and sizes, ready to wear. I even got Speedos, but don't wear dem faggot-ass joints. They strictly for da Jacuzzi action, you feel me?" David said.

The five young men followed Ambrosia along the water's edge toward the beige, stucco-colored bathhouse at the far end of the pool, nestled in between a clump of pygmy palm trees. As they entered, each one chose a spacious fitting room, where they found shelves stacked from top to bottom with neatly arranged swimwear.

DiVante playfully nudged Whiskey as they emerged from their individual dressing rooms. "Ya first time visiting LA seems ta be turnin' out quite nicely, huh, Whiskey? You been paid pretty good, an' now you 'bout ta getcha mufuckin' brains banged out by one o' dem sexy dimes out there in a minute or two. Now that's gangsta."

DiVante wasn't lying. Whiskey would never forget his first trip out West. As he walked out to the edge of the Olympic-sized pool and sat down casually at the edge of the thirteen-foot area of the pool, dangling his muscular legs into the cool, clear water, gorgeous females swam below his feet, while the other cutie pies chatted away continuously as they laid back comfortably on their poolside chairs and smiled at him flirtatiously.

A deejay began spinning a medley of West Coast gangsta hits featuring the aggressively sick tracks of Ice Cube, Snoop Dogg, and Doctor Dre, and the beauties began to sway seductively as they broke out dancing to the ghetto jams blaring loudly from the thumping bass speakers spread out around the pool. Within minutes the boys were surrounded by curvaceous, bikini-wearing sex kittens grinding on them to the West Coast classic, "California Love."

The young revelers partied well into the night, a steady flow of twenty-somethings from all around the Beverly Hills neighborhood eagerly joining in the wet and wild festivities.

Next morning's sunrise, Whiskey arose smelling of expensive imported liquor and the funk of the unbridled sexual marathon from the night before. He crawled out from under the naked, cum-stained bodies of two snoozing beach bunnies sprawled out

across his broad chest and snoring loudly in a sex-
and booze-induced slumber.

As the Georgia-bred enforcer stood beneath the
tepid spray of the above showerhead in the luxurious
mahogany-tinted marble bathroom, he could now
focus solely on the job ahead—murder.

June 27th, 11:40 PM Beaufort, South Carolina

"Dey dat fucka go, dawg!" Lil' Shane quickly
started up the engine of the rust-colored 1981
Monte Carlo, which rattled to life with a loud gut-
tural roar. The cocaine-sprinkled marijuana blunt
filled the interior of the classic vehicle with a
strange, sweet-smelling psychedelic aroma, bringing about a dreamy, surreal atmosphere that briefly
masked the very real drama that was about to un-
fold.

"Calm yo' ass down, dawg. I got dis." Whiskey
placed the last three hollow-tip slugs into the magazine of the TEC-9 and stuffed it into the stock of the
gun.

He'd done this type of thing many times before,
so he wasn't nervous or jittery in the least. In fact, he
seemed rather eager to carry out his deadly assign-
ment.

Then he positioned himself on the passenger's
seat, so that he might have leverage enough to blast
his target from the open window as they cruised
from across the street to the other side.

Medium in height but built like a beer barrel,
Gimp was recognizable not only from his rotund
form, but also from his slight limp, as he made his

way from his parked SUV toward the dimly lit restaurant before him. Onward he hobbled, puffing on a smoldering Black & Mild cigar and observing the messages on his cell phone, which glowed a fluorescent green in his palm in the dark South Carolina night.

From his expensive urban wear ensemble accented by sparkling diamond jewelry upon his hands, wrists, and neck, and classic Chuck Taylor sneakers, Whiskey could see that this cat continued to rep his West Coast roots even now while deep in the heart of Dixie. He almost admired the man he was to soon kill. He smoked the blunt he held down to an insignificant roach before flicking it out the window into the darkness beyond.

Lil' Shane shut off the headlights and put the engine in neutral, letting the big car drift along the street silently, except for the softly humming engine.

As the Monte Carlo cruised down the street toward Gimp's parked truck, Whiskey stuck the muzzle of the TEC-9 out the passenger side window. The TEC-9 had incredible firepower. A mere pull of the trigger could squeeze off over a dozen murderous rounds of hot lead into some poor fool or unsuspecting crowd, always guaranteeing three or more kills and multiple injuries.

The Monte Carlo seemed to take forever to pass Gimp's big-bodied Yukon. However, once they rode past the front end of the Yukon, Gimp's corpulent form came into view. Whiskey leaned forward, allowing his upper body to protrude out the window slightly. His finger on the trigger, he steadied his gaze on the heavyset man standing a mere twenty paces away, where he'd suddenly stopped in order to scroll through his phone's digital menu more closely.

Lil' Shane whispered, "Blast his fat ass, Whiskey. He done stopped. He's standin' still for you, man."

The assault weapon held by Whiskey began rattling off a barrage of deadly shots, splitting the silence with a deafening series of *rat-a-tat-tats* accompanied by bright orange flashes of flame that erupted from the barrel.

The ex-gangbanger-turned-informant screamed out in shock and agony as dozens of hollow-tip bullets zipped through and around his wide frame. He fell backward onto the cobblestone path with a blubbery plop, his cell phone tumbling a few feet from his hands into the grass along the side of the pathway. Gimp's left leg and his right arm twitched with rapid herky-jerky movements, and as his blood pooled out onto the cobblestone, his breathing came in short, gurgling gasps.

By the time his girlfriend and her coworkers raced to the scene, he was already staring ahead, eyes wide open in death. While his lover cupped his bloody head into her arms and weeped hysterically, the other witnesses could do little but dial 9-1-1 as they caught but a brief glimpse of the fleeing Monte Carlo's red taillights speeding away down the dirt road, down the hills, and past a dark grove of palmetto trees beyond.

Chapter 2

"The Ways of a Ryder"

July 13th, 2005, 10:22 PM

Whiskey was just leaving North Peola's affluent Sorrell Dunes gated community after dropping off more than a few bags of blow to several of his well-heeled coke clients. He'd spent a little over forty minutes making rounds and came away with twelve grand. He then hopped in his Jeep Cherokee and got onto the busy Madison Highway outer loop, en route to South Peola's Hemlock Hills project.

He hadn't fed his pit bull terriers at all that day, so that his fighting dogs might be ornery and game for the bloody contests of the coming midnight hour. The controversial and brutally violent blood sport attracted dozens of ghetto youth from all over Peola's projects with their best-bred fighting pedigree canines—American pit bull terrier, German

rottweiler, Japanese Akita, and English bull mastiff.
The featured combatants fought oftentimes to the
death, while the yelling mob bet hundreds on the
outcome of the savage battles.

Dogfights were usually held on the weekends,
out near Geneva Projects through the Sundance Forest and on the property of an old, abandoned farm-
house, reputedly said to have once been a part of
Harriet Tubman's legendary Underground Rail-
road. Peola's upper-crust residents would often
send associates down to the hood with several hundred dollars to place side bets on the area's top
dogs.

Whiskey had learned to breed, raise, and train
dogs for the pits from his older brother, Leon, for six
years, just before he was shot to death by Peola's police during a routine traffic stop—They mistook his
reaching for his car's registration as attempting to
grasp a weapon. Though Whiskey had raised a variety of fighting dog breeds successfully, he special-
ized in the rearing of pit bulls, with which he rarely,
if ever, lost matches. People came from as far away
as Florida to breed their dogs with his or to buy
newborn puppies from his champion fighters, and
paid top dollar for these services, which could run
anywhere from $800 for a puppy to $15,000 for stud
services. Whiskey usually never fought his own
pets, except for a select few that he would bring out
to fight, to advertise the elite fighting prowess for
business as well as bragging rights.

The pathway leading up to the pitting areas themselves was well guarded by armed lookouts, who
only allowed walk-ins with a single ace of spades
playing card with a hole punched through the

middle as a part of the process to gain entry, along with ten dollars and the secret password, which would change with each passing month. Vehicles were not allowed entry, nor could any car, truck, or motorcycle penetrate the dense surrounding under-growth of Sundance Forest anyway. Elaborate escape routes were developed, in case of a surprise police raid, which was virtually impossible for the cops to launch.

Spectators who attended these bloody affairs mostly came to bet on the dogfights alone, yet it wasn't uncommon for certain individuals to approach the presiding hustlers to solicit drugs. In fact the dogfights were, in large part, a veritable bazaar for all sorts of illicit activities. So when Paul Ballard nudged Whiskey to converse with him privately outside of the barn, away from the fierce action of the pits, he wasn't the least bit surprised.

Paul had just recently gotten out of Akron Correctional Facility after doing a six-year sentence for an armed robbery beef back in 1999. He, like most others who came home from doing time behind bars, had become noticeably larger, especially in the upper body area. He now wore thick, curly hair in long, tightly knotted dreads that flowed down to nearly a quarter of his wide, well-muscled back. His white wife-beater stretched tightly, revealing powerfully built pecs, and tapered down to display a solidly chiseled set of six-pack abs. Numerous crudely stenciled prison tattoos covered his dark, brawny arms, and his baggy jeans hung well beneath his narrow waist, showing nearly the full measure of his gray-and-black boxer shorts, and exposing the glossy, black stock of a Beretta 9 mm.

"Sup witcha, baby? Looks like the grind been treatin' you well, cuz." Paul grinned through diamond-encrusted gold teeth.

"Hey, you know how we do it down here in da Hills, dawg. Ain't nuttin' change since you been gone."

"You brought dem two pits up next, right?" Paul took a wad of rubber band-wrapped bills from his shorts and peeled off seven hundred dollars.

"Yeah, Buddah is da black-and-white male wit' da white spot in da middle o' his forehead. He fifteen an' 0, with seven kills, and dat brindle joint is Daisy. She ain't got but one eye, but she done been in over forty fights an' she ain't lost one yet. She done kilt over twenty-two dogs. Da last dog she fought an' kilt was a one hundred-pound rottie. She tore his big ass up in less than three an' a half minutes flat. Buddah's a bad mufucka, but Daisy ain't no joke. Put ya money on her."

"I know dat's right." Paul handed Whiskey seven hundred-dollar bills and turned the bottle of malt liquor he'd been drinking up to his lips for a quick swig. "I'm side-bettin' wit' you tonight, pimpin', 'cause everybody from da Hills know dat you breed da rawest dogs in Peola, for real. If they don't know—fuck 'em—they'll soon find out. Ain't dat right, Whiskey?"

"I'm always willin' ta teach a nigga a li'l som'n-som'n."

"A'ight, bet. Let's go back in an' make a li'l bit o' money, shall we? But befo' we go back in," Paul said in a more serious tone, "I gotta let you in on some shit dat's been jumpin' off out here in da hood, a'ight?"

Whiskey nodded, and both men walked back into the old, decrepit barn.

Just as they entered, Lil' Shane released Daisy into the ten-foot-wide caged-off pit. The air was filled with the sickly smell of blunt and cigarette smoke mingled with liquor and blood. The sandy floor of the baiting area was raked for several minutes after each battle, to allow the blood of the wounded or dying dogs to sink in, to prevent the upcoming canine warriors from slipping.

Daisy sprang immediately at her opponent, a powerfully built, white English bulldog, and fastened her mighty jaws with a vise-like grip onto its throat. Both mongrels tumbled about in the sand of the pit, thrashing around, snarling, yelping, and growling ferociously, while dust and blood-flecked froth flew across the miniature arena. The raucous shouts of the betting crowd grew louder as the canine combatants twisted and turned, each one trying to gain an advantage over the other to deliver a final death bite.

Paul turned to Whiskey and whispered into his ear, "I been out here hustlin' for a minute just like you, Whiskey. 'Cept, I done hooked up wit' a new connect dat's got me on a whole other level, playa. I'm 'bout to put you on to some deep shit, my nig, but only if you think you ready for it."

"It ain't a helluva lot dat can shock me, Paul. Talk to me."

"A'ight, you asked for it. Since I got out in January, I been meetin' wit' my parole officer twice a month, the first and last of each month, right. Okay, although I'm on papers an' shit, dis bitch I'm s'pose ta meet wit' each month is cool as a mufucka. Plus, she got me workin' wit' a coupla dirty cops in da department. They some down-ass dudes though. I done peeped 'em, an' they legit. They pullin' in mo' money than Snookey and dem back in da day, 'cause dey da ones bustin' all da dealers. They got our backs, though, as long as we split the dope profits fifty-fifty down da middle. Now I know dat da amount seems a li'l bit high, but hey, whatcha gon' do? Argue wit' da po-po? We stand ta gain a whole lot mo' than what you might think in da long run. Plus, dem pigs got access to da crystal meth business. Dat shit right dere is hotter than *E* pills used ta be, ya heard? We gotta get dis money, dawg, an' I know dat wit' ya help we can make even mo' than ever."

"I dunno, Paul. I don't too much trust no cops, dawg, 'specially not these dirty-ass fuckas down here in Peola. You know what dem people think 'bout us po' black folk in da hood, don't ya?" Whiskey whispered back, sneaking looks at the two dogs grappling in the swirling dust of the pit.

"Yeah, well, don't you go worryin' 'bout no sneaky ol' cracka cops, a'ight? I got things on lock wit' dem boys dem. Oh shit! Look, Daisy done got a death lock on dat bulldog's throat. Look like we gonna be 'bout a thousand dollars richa in a few, huh?"

"I told you, I don't breed losers, an' don't you ever forget it, a'ight?" Whiskey lit up a half-smoked blunt he'd just removed from his baggy denim shorts. While enjoying the slowly, creeping buzz delivered by the potent sour diesel bud, he began to reconsider his previous decision to not associate with Pete's police pals.

"Yes!" both men yelled out with joy as the pit judge forcibly removed Daisy's blood-soaked jaws from around the badly torn neck of the lifeless bulldog.

Whiskey quickly moved through the densely crowded, clamorous, and smoke-filled aisle toward the pit area, where he secured his victorious, yet battle-scarred pet and returned her to his personal dog handler, who fed her a juicy treat of raw venison before placing her in a roomy holding cage. He then met with the losing dog's owner, who reluctantly shelled out a wad of cash totaling a grand, and returned back through the liquored-up throng to his rickety bleacher seat next to Paul. Whiskey folded a knot of five hundred dollars and placed the cash to his pursed lips and kissed it gently before stashing it down into his exposed boxers.

"Thank you, my man. I can get used ta dis dog-fightin' shit, 'specially if I'm winnin'. Check it out, Whiskey. Ya know who dem pigs tryin' ta get at though? Dey own boss, ol' punk-ass Mickey O'Malley an' shit."

Whiskey's eyes went wide with disbelief.

"Oh yeah, dat Mickey O'Malley been fuckin' it up for a whole lotta folk, dawg. Da only baller he even fucks wit' out here on da streets is David Ambrosia, an' ever since David moved down to Daufuskie Island, he been shittin' on every fuckin' body, cuz. Even members o' his own police force want his bitch ass dead, 'cause can't nobody make no money wit' him comin' down hard on dope dealers all over da city. Know what I mean?"

"I feel you, partna. I know how dat redneck Irish mufucka can be. He damn sho don't play fair."

Whiskey shook his head. "When a man starts fuckin' wit' ya chedda, you gotta bleed his ass, no doubt."

Suddenly the clamor of the betting horde caught their attention, as a fierce Presa Canario and a vicious Japanese Tosa raged violently down in the dusty pits below.

"Now dat's da Whiskey I used to know, a straight soldier who would dead a nigga on sight. So wassup? You know you and I used to be two o' da baddest enforcers ta bust guns in all o' Peola. Remember when we used ta run wit' Dawn, Shawn, and Rae-Kwon? *Sheeet*, nigga, we use ta strike fear in bitch niggas' hearts, dawg."

"Yeah, I know, I know. It's jus', you know, a whole helluva lot different. You talkin' 'bout takin' out a fuckin' chief o' police, playa. You just can't walk up an' peel a cop's wig back like talkin' 'bout it, pimp, feel me? 'Specially not a goddamn chief o' police. C'mon now."

"Whatever, nigga. I done seen you pop plenty o' so-called high-profile cats befo', dawg. How 'bout da pastor you jus' took out over a month ago? Yeah . . . didn't know I knew 'bout dat shit, huh? Word gets out fast on da streets, you should know dat." Paul looked his friend straight in the eye without blinking, searching for some sort of reaction from him.

"Looka here, Paul," Whiskey responded with a slight tone of irritation in his voice, "I'm a hustla an' a thug wit' a gun who'll do whatever it takes ta make a dollar, an' if it means I gotta kill a mufucka, then guess what? He's as good as dead, as far as I'm concerned. 'Specially if da paper's lookin' right. I don't give a fuck who it is or what occupation da mufucka claims. Dat ain't my concern. I'll deal wit' da Lord when I go ta glory. Until then I'm gonna do me all day long." Whiskey took out yet another pre-rolled blunt and fired it up, to soothe his suddenly frazzled nerves.

"Hey, calm down, baby. I ain't comin' down on ya, dude. I'm just tryin' ta help both o' us make a little bit o' money by workin' wit' dese crackas, dat's all. Just like ol' times. 'Cept we'll be smokin' a cop dis time around. C'mon, Whiskey, don't nobody like O'Malley's fat Irish ass, no mufuckin' way. He ain't nuttin' but a white racist any ol' way. He ain't never done nuttin' for da hood or us black folks, like you said earlier. Plus, a whole lotta white boys out in West Peola losin' a shitload o' cash as we speak 'cause o' dat fat, roly-poly bitch. An' dey want his ass taken care of just as bad as da crack-slangin' niggas down here on da South Side, feel me? Besides, like I said, dem peoples done promised me over sixty grand for da hit. Shit, we can split it thirty-thirty if you want, I don't care. I'd be happy to give you fifty grand, you know dat. I'da done it my damn self, but like I said befo', I'm on papers an' shit."

Paul motioned for Whiskey to come closer, and when he did, gave him a beige-colored envelope that seemed somewhat bulky and overstuffed. "Go on, open it up. Shit, I'm dyin' ta see what dem cops blessed you wit' myself."

Whiskey slowly ripped it open and twelve hundred dollars in cash spilled out into his waiting hands. "Goddamn! Yo' li'l badge-wearin' buddies uptown really want ta off O'Malley, don't they?"

Whiskey flipped the benjamins through his fingers one by one.

"Ya damn skippy, they do. An' when you pull off da job, there's plenty mo' green waitin' for ya. So is it on an' poppin' or what?"

"Tell ya boys in uniform their retainer fee is fully accepted and ol' man O'Malley should be given a nice twenty-one-gun sendoff in about a week or so, a'ight."

"How 'bout two weeks, just to be on the safe side, cuz? We don't wanna rush nuttin' unnecessarily."

"That'll work too."

"Lemme give you my cell phone number, a'ight. It's 737-324-6116."

"Cool. I got it logged into my menu. What's a good time ta holla at ya?"

"I'm always on da move an' shit. I start my day earlier than most, usually around eight. But I always check my messages throughout da day, so you can expect a call back even if you don't get me right away."

"You ever race ya bike?"

"Naw, but I'll drag race da shit outta my ol' '65 Ford Mustang. I calls her *Mustang Sally*, after the old Wilson Pickett song. I been workin' on her for over five years. She got an eight-cylinder cam, an' she ain't been beat yet. I done took hundreds of niggas out on Century Boulevard in Pemmican. Ask David, he'll tell ya hisself."

"Okay, I heard dat. Well, maybe I gotta bring my old '72 Roadrunner out da garage an' shit, so I can get some o' dat action on Century Boulevard some time. When y'all drag?"

"Mostly on Saturday nights at around one or two in the mornin'. A whole lotta cats be out there wit' their whips and their bitches. Races be 'bout a quarter-mile to a mile, but I prefer da shorter one-block races myself, you know. Lotsa money out there ta make, fuckin' wit' dem spoiled, rich kids. Dey ain't got shit else ta do but throw away dey parents' dough."

"How many races you won?"

"I'd say around 'bout six or seven. Now I'll tell you dem white boys from Canterbury Arms wit' their Ferraris and tricked-out Porsches ain't ta be fucked wit'. Sleep on dem crackas, an' you'll lose da shitty drawers off ya ass, dawg. Bring ya A game if an' when ya come out—Just a warnin'."

"Who's won da most races out on da West Side?"

"Jeremy Lattimore, da mayor's son. He drives a lemon yellow 2004 Dodge Viper. He hasn't lost a race yet."

"How many races has dis cat won altogether?"

"Shit, who knows, dawg? It's gotta be over a hundred or mo'. Now, dat I do know."

"Hmmm . . . I see. I do gotta bring my A game when I come out ta dat joint wit' da whip an' shit, huh?"

"Shit, yeah. Unless ya jus' tryin' ta throw away a couple o' hundred dollars an' whatnot. If dat's da case, shit, jus' hand da shit over ta me. I'll spend it for ya."

Whiskey grinned and threw mock jabs at his friend's ripped abdomen.

Whiskey believed in his heart that David Ambrosia had to be the one to discuss the killing of Pastor McBride with the recently freed jailbird. He wasn't necessarily upset about the whole thing, because they were all longtime pals. However, with Paul's connections caught up in the mix, he figured that discretion would be in order, until he proved that they could be trusted.

"The best car I ever raced was an '81 Ford Pinto. Man, that li'l whip could ball, you hear me?" Paul smiled as he reminisced. "My li'l brother Marion and me pimped it out and souped da engine up, and boy, we was dustin' niggas out on Madison Highway, 'specially da outer loop an' shit. You shoulda seen us. We burned a cop or two back in da day wit' dat joint. Dat ride was da shit."

"Sounds like it coulda been a winner. What da fuck happened to da joint?"

"My brother fucked around an' totaled it comin' back from South Carolina one night. I guess it was around ninety-six or ninety-seven, one o' da two. I can't quite remember now, but he jus' broke his wrist and had a couple o' scratches on his face and shit. But, other than that, he was a'ight."

The bestial growls coming from the pit caused the throng of cheering spectators to break out into a resounding roar as the great Tosa, bloodied but undeterred, pinned the equally monstrous Presa to the gore-splattered dirt of the dusty arena and delivered a fatal bite to its exposed jugular, bringing the bloody combat to an abrupt and merciful end. The Tosa's owner, along with several others who'd placed heavy wagers on his dog's odds of besting the Presa, cheered loudly and embraced each other in victorious celebration.

Paul peered down at the cell phone clipped to his denim shorts and answered the chirping device. He conversed briefly before hanging up.

"Whiskey, I gotta get up outta here, dawg. I gots dis bad-ass bitch out on da North Side, right? She jus' moved here 'bout two or three months ago from Brazil. Bitch is fatta than duck butta an' fine as shit, an' peep dis, she can't get enough sex, no matter how much dick I gives her. Believe me, I breaks da bitch back, ya hear what I'm sayin'? Plus, she got plenty money, 'cause she lives right on Sorrell Dunes Beach in da fancy li'l condos an' shit. Yeah, a freak bitch wit' long dollars. She's a keeper, for now anyway. So I'll holla at ya sometime dis week, probably Wednesday or Thursday, so we can go over dis bidness shit we discussed, a'ight?"

"Aw, c'mon, nigga. Fuck dat ho. We ain't seen each other in a minute, an' I got two more pits I'm 'bout ta put in da ring, playa. If you stick around for a while, you'll be walkin' outta here wit' well over a grand."

"Maybe next time, baby boy, but dat pussy callin' a nigga right 'bout now, cuz. An' da wood in my drawers is tellin' me dat I gotta answer dat call, so I'll holla."

"Yeah, whatever, nigga. Get ya pussy-whipped ass da fuck on." Whiskey chuckled lightly.

Then he and Paul Ballard walked outside into the humid night, complete with a hazy but starry sky hanging above the dark silhouettes of tall Georgia pines and old moss-covered oaks.

"You got my number, so I'm gonna expect a call by midweek, Whiskey, for real though, 'cause we gotta take care o' dis, seriously."

Whiskey waved his hand nonchalantly as he watched Paul walk with the flashlight-wielding sentry toward the dark forest trail and into the inky blackness of the woods ahead. He smiled and slowly returned to the din of the raucous crowd within the barn to renew the series of dogfights he'd come to bet on earlier.

Chapter 3

"Family Reunion"

Tasha had just finished preparing breakfast for her four children when her younger brother stepped through the front door a little after eleven. Whiskey's nephews, Ron, Kelly, and Barry, raced over to embrace him excitedly.

Whiskey returned the love and followed the trio into the living room, where they were busy playing video games on the PS2. He observed the violent game play of the pixilated figures on the wide-screen television and grinned as his nephews pressed frantically on the handheld controllers while intently viewing the screen.

"What y'all li'l niggas playin'? *Grand Theft Auto*?"

"Yup. And I'm already on da fifth level right now," Ron said proudly.

"Yeah, y'all gonna put up dem damn games an' clean up my living room too. I know dat much.

Now wash y'all hands and get ready ta eat breakfast."

"Pete, you want some'n ta eat? We got plenty."

"Maybe a li'l later, sis. I'm gonna just catch up on a li'l sleep an' shit 'cause I had a long night an' I'm beat dis mornin'. Where Peaches at?"

"She spent da night over at her girlfriend Ramona house. It's like dat's her second home now."

Whiskey's sister, LaTasha Battle, was a thirty-three-year-old administrative assistant for the Jefferson Davis accounting firm in Burginstown, an upstate college town populated by primarily young white-collar types. Tasha, as she was more widely known, had been a hard-working homemaker since the tender age of eleven when her mother, Maureen Battle, first began to exhibit signs of chronic substance abuse. She'd raised her two-year-old brother, Peter, while her pregnant mother ran the streets with various lovers in search of a good time in the form of a bottle of cognac, a bag of coke, or cheap sex in the backseat of a Cadillac.

Tasha and her younger brothers never knew who their biological father was, nor did their neglectful mother release information of his identity to them. But it was widely rumored among relatives as well as casual associates that the infamous New Orleans drug lord, Marion Snookey Lake, had indeed fathered the Battle trio.

The story was that during the early reign of Snookey Lake, he often visited the low country regions of South Carolina and Georgia to establish a target drug trafficking network, as well as a quick escape route out of the Crescent City when and if the ever-present FBI closed in for the kill. During one such interstate trip through southern Georgia, the Louisiana kingpin was introduced to the svelte, ruddy-complexioned knockout sitting alone cross-legged at the bar in a nightclub known as Da Juke Joint by the late Wallace Minter, who at the time was a local town pimp and petty dope peddler that Snookey would use as an important marijuana and heroin connect between South Carolina and Georgia's low country communities.

There was a strong and immediate attraction between the two, which developed into a full-fledged love affair spanning eleven years of bittersweet interaction, with Snookey Lake traveling back and forth between states to visit his illegitimate family when away from his wife and children down in New Orleans. He only referred to himself as Maureen's "friend" when in the company of mutual friends or family and demanded that his girlfriend do the same. But once his Georgia-born mistress became pregnant with their third child, Snookey became less loving and more distant, while Maureen's behavior was the polar opposite, being increasingly possessive and insecure and often sparking heated arguments between the couple.

Eventually Marion Lake left Maureen for good after one particularly violent row.

While Snookey Lake would return to his wife Melissa and their twins, Dawn and Shawn, Maureen would bear a second son, whom she'd call Alonzo, yet still loving the man who'd left her with three children, a cocaine addiction, and a broken heart that never completely mended afterward.

"I got a shitload o' work to do today for the job, so I'm gonna need you to watch the boys for me for 'bout three or four hours. I'm a li'l behind on some paperwork that my boss needs when he gets back next week, so while he's away on vacation, I wanna catch up on it."

Whiskey waltzed over to the fridge and bent low into the open door amidst the frosty mist billowing out. He eyed the neatly stacked rows of foodstuffs for a beer. "A'ight, man, whatever. You just hurry up 'cause I got places to go and peoples to see, so bring yo' butt back here ASAP," he said jokingly, plucking a cold bottle of Corona from between a container of leftover meatloaf and fruit punch.

"Nigga, please," she retorted with a sly grin, while preparing the plates with steaming-hot breakfast chow. "Ron, Kelly, Barry, get off that game an' wash y'all's hands for breakfast."

"A'ight, Mama, we comin'!" Ron yelled. He dropped the game controller and bolted toward the bathroom door, and his two brothers quickly followed him.

Whiskey helped his sister set the dining room table for breakfast. Homemade grits laden in butter sat steaming beside thick slabs of country bacon and stacks of buckwheat pancakes slathered in maple syrup.

The mouth-watering aroma brought the three boys racing from the bathroom and into their awaiting seats with freshly washed hands, which their dutiful mother stopped briefly to inspect before continuing on with her morning meal preparation.

Tasha was a wonderful cook, a skill she'd learned from years of experience as a teen whose mother seemed to prefer all-night parties to responsible parenting. She'd graduated from peanut butter and jelly sandwiches to full-course turkey dinners on Thanksgiving and had seen to it that neither she nor her younger brothers ever went hungry. It got to a point that even when their mother was sober or at home long enough to attempt cooking, her bland dishes were left mostly untouched in favor of Tasha's more savory meals, which she herself greedily devoured.

After finishing up at the dinner table, Tasha left her sons behind eating heartily as she returned to the kitchen to prepare her own plate of Southern-style victuals. She then spotted a plain white envelope lying on the green marble tile of the kitchen countertop.

"Didn't I ask you to stop bringin' dis shit in here for me?" Tasha flashed the wad of cash she'd just removed from the envelope. "I don't need it, and I don't want it, okay?"

"That's over a thousand dollars right there. Don't tell me dat you don't need it 'cause I know better." Whiskey took a quick swallow of beer and belched loudly as he leaned up against the kitchen wall and faced his big sister.

"Look here, li'l boy, don't come in here talkin' that ol' bullshit to me, a'ight? You gonna respect me, and you damn sho' gonna respect my house. I work for a livin', an' don't you forget it! Every two weeks

I bring home a nice paycheck that lets me take care of me an' my kids, so I don't need any of your dope money to take care of my needs. Now just take ya li'l twelve hundred dollars back, 'cause we ain't hardly hurtin' for nothin'!"

"A'ight, a'ight, my bad, sis. You know I would never disrespect you or your house. I just wanna do my part to kinda help out some 'round here an' show my appreciation for everything you've done an' still continue to do, dat's all." Whiskey looked up at Tasha sheepishly. "You're always workin' so hard, and ever since Ma got locked up two years ago, you been workin' harder than ever. So I just wanna do a li'l somethin' for you an' my nephews 'cause dey daddies don't do shit for 'em no way."

Whiskey finished the bottle of Corona and placed it gently into the kitchen garbage pail and folded his well-muscled arms across his broad chest as he awaited a response from his sister, who stared at him in front of the refrigerator, hands akimbo on her wide hips.

"First of all, Ma was a deadbeat parent way before she got hooked on crack and decided to rob that 7-Eleven. She didn't do shit for none of us, an' you know this. An', yes, the fathers of my boys ain't worth shit either. Both of 'em ain't nothin' but sperm donors. I know this better than anybody, but that's my problem, not yours. I appreciate your concern, but mind your business. I got this. An' as for you helpin' out around here, you my brother, you ain't gotta do nothing but take out the trash, keep my car runnin' good, and babysit every now an' then, and that's all. You're my little brother, not my man, so I don't expect for you to take care of me. But

I do wish that you'll leave all o' dem li'l hoodlum-ass friends you hang around alone, 'cause I don't want you gettin' yourself caught up like our mama or our criminal-ass daddy, Snookey."

"Ain't nobody gonna get in trouble, you trippin'. An' our father got snitched on by our cousin Rae-Kwon an' dem. If it hadn't been for his bitch ass, our pops would be out right now."

"Don't even go there with me, boy. Snookey left us high an' dry a long time ago, an' he even got our sister Dawn killed, fuckin' with that hustlin' lifestyle. What kinda role model dad is that? And don't you dare blame Rae-Kwon for Snookey's arrest. Hell, I woulda helped bring him down myself, 'cause he was nothin' but a cancer to this whole community. His own wife left his tired ass, and Shawn ain't been right since Dawn was killed. He's the reason our mama got strung out on that shit. Fuck Snookey Lake wit' a sick dick, an' I mean that shit!"

"A'ight, sis, calm down. I'm sorry I brought dat shit up. My bad." Whiskey gently came over and planted a kiss on his sister's rosy cheek before returning to the fridge to fish around for another bottle of beer.

He found one, closed the door, popped the top on the cold brew and took a deep swallow. "I'm always gonna be on yo' side, no matter what, even though I don't fully agree with you on everything you say, just like I know you don't agree with me all da time. But dat's life, an' it's all good. I just want you to know how much I love you, sis, dat's all."

"Yeah, yeah, I guess you a'ight." Tasha smiled as she embraced her younger sibling, warmly kissing him on his forehead as they hugged. Tasha felt more of a maternal bond with Whiskey than that of an older sister. After all, it was she who had changed his dirty diapers and burped him when their mother was away, which was most of the time.

After the brief expression of love and sentimental feelings between the siblings, Whiskey backed away and emptied the Corona bottle of its golden contents in one huge gulp, belched out loudly, and tossed the empty bottle in the trash.

"A'ight, Tasha, go ahead an' do what you gotta do 'cause I gotta holla at Alonzo at seven o'clock out Badlands Manor an' shit. So you gotta hurry back, okay?"

Tasha sighed with disgust at the mention of her youngest brother.

Alonzo Battle was by far the most volatile of the three siblings, causing mischief throughout his tender twenty years. He'd been arrested multiple times since the age of fourteen, the latest arrest landing him in the Peola county jail for a year and a half for violating his parole. He strongly resembled both Snookey Lake and his late half-sister Dawn, and also possessed their hair-trigger temper.

Tasha had kicked Alonzo out of her home twice in the past for repeated infractions. She had to constantly warn him about smoking marijuana in the apartment while her boys were present, or packages of drugs stashed in closets and dresser drawers, not to mention guns and the unopened boxes of ammunition that went with them. Alonzo also, unlike Whiskey, could be belligerent and rude to his older sister, especially when he'd been drinking.

"So what's his li'l no-mannered ass doin' with himself now?"

Whiskey shook his head, trying to think of a way to skip the subject of Alonzo's chronic life of crime, which had become a tired source of debate between them over the years. "C'mon, Tasha, you know Alonzo gonna do what he do. Ain't no changin' dat cat. But, hey, he gotta live his life for himself, not us."

"Yeah, you're absolutely right. I just hope that he gets himself together one of these days, 'cause I ain't ready to bury him just yet."

Whiskey nodded in agreement, though he wished deep down inside that his two siblings could finally let bygones be bygones and come together as a family again.

As soon as Tasha returned home, she arrived to a well-vacuumed, neatly arranged home that smelled of fragrant Khush incense. Her three young boys were all fast asleep in their beds, snoring lightly. Tasha apologized to her brother for arriving home so late.

Whiskey shrugged it off, though, because he felt that babysitting was the least he could do for a sister who'd done so much for him. Besides, he greatly enjoyed spending time with his rambunctious little nephews whenever he could.

Twenty-year-old Alonzo Battle sold illegal narcotics such as cocaine, heroin, ecstasy, and crystal meth out of his three-bedroom apartment he shared

with his girlfriend and her two-year-old son out in
Badlands Manor. He also worked as a bouncer at
the 95 South nightclub in West Peola, where he got
most of his drug clientele, which many times included undercover cops. On weekends, he and
Whiskey would hook up at the club or at one of
North Peola's sports bars to flirt with the sexy wait-
resses, watch the big games, or simply talk business.

Alonzo usually bounced on Friday and Saturday
nights, and occasionally during the weekdays whenever he provided security for personal events like
bachelor parties, card parties, or pool parties. But,
on this particular evening, he'd phoned his brother
from the famed restaurant, Big Mama's Kitchen, out
in West Peola.

Big Mama's was hands down Peola's premier
eatery. Located in the posh Pemmican County of the
city's elite West Side, the beloved restaurant had
been serving the residents of Peola and the surrounding area with fine Southern cuisine since 1922.
Everybody who was anybody dined there, and
many locals boasted that it was the single best five-
star restaurant in the entire state of Georgia. On
weekends there was live music, jazz and R&B performances on Saturdays, and on Sundays, the soul-
stirring renditions of the various local gospel groups,
their Southern Baptist spirituals bringing a bit of
church to the patrons as they dined.

Of the three siblings, the tall, sturdy Alonzo
physically resembled Snookey the most, with similar handsome facial features and dark, curly hair. In
fact, he was the spitting image of his father. He wore
his silky locks in long braids that hung loosely
down his broad back and wide shoulders. Like

many ex-cons, he boasted a post-prison physique, which was magnificently buff and adorned with homemade tattoos.

Rocking an army-green South Pole cotton tee, a pair of baggy Rocawear denim shorts, a sparkling 24-carat white gold herringbone chain with a brilliant diamond-cluttered Jesus charm, he was covered with the scent of weed and Issey Miyake.

And from the look of his reddened eyes, he was well beyond just a simple buzz.

As he embraced his older brother, his breath screamed of one too many Hennessy and Coke.

"'S up wit' cha, big brotha?" Alonzo said, smiling broadly through his diamond-studded grills. "Whatcha been up to, nigga?"

"Just tryin' to maintain out dis bitch, dat's all. What 'bout you?" Whiskey said, hugging his baby brother tightly against his chest.

"Bouncin', hustlin', fuckin' bad bitches, you know how we do it down in da South Side. Da blocks been kinda hot lately since bitch-ass O'Malley done cracked down on da coke shipments out on da Gosa Harbor, so cats ain't been pumpin' dat 'girl' like dey used to, ya know. But, hey, real niggas know how ta switch dey game up in order ta get dat work regardless, feel me?"

Whiskey nodded in agreement and took up a menu, while a cute waitress stood patiently in the background. "Sup wit' Paul Ballard an' shit?" Whiskey asked, briefly peering over the leather-bound menu in his hands.

"You askin' me? Shit, dat's yo' boy. I should be askin' you what's up. He got shit locked down on da South Side. Been dat way since ninety-four, you know dat yaself, dawg."

"No doubt." Whiskey ordered a pitcher of Corona Extra and a forty-dollar fisherman's platter.

After Alonzo wolfed down every bit of his expensive meal, he eased back in his seat, wiped his greasy mouth with a cotton handkerchief, and ordered yet another glass of Hennessy and Coke, flirting with the blushing waitress the whole time. "I ain't really hollered at too many cats since I got outta da pen a while back, you know, but you know Paul got juice like a mufucka out on dese country-ass streets and dirt roads 'round here. So everybody know dat half-white mufucka got shit on lock. Shit, he even got da chief o' police kissin' his ass."

Alonzo flirted even more when the attractive waitress returned with both of their orders. She smiled bashfully and returned to her duties as the drunken young hustler spewed catcalls and wolf whistles her way.

"Yeah, he got shit on lock wit' da hustlin', but I done heard he stepped his game up by fuckin' wit' da po-po, similar to what you doin'."

"Well, da old sayin' goes, if ya can't beat 'em, join 'em. I guess dat's what da boys in blue is doin' now, 'cause you got a coupla crooked-ass cops, crackas, and niggas alike makin' plenty money, rubbin' elbows wit' us hot boys, ya know?"

"Paul been locked up wit' me too for 'bout four months befo' he got out. He said he been in contact wit' Snookey through some Black Gangster Disciples in Akron. He told me our daddy gon' be transferred to Akron in September of this year. Once dat happens, shit gon' be pumpin' like old times back on da streets."

"Paul oughta know 'cause he done been locked down way longer than me, an' he got connections in da pen dat reach all over da whole country."

"Dat's all gravy an' everything, but I believe shit when I see it for myself an' not befo'." Whiskey sighed as he poured himself a tall glass of brew. "I done talked to Paul myself 'bout his dealins' wit da po-po, but da part 'bout him doin' bidness wit' Snookey, I still gotta see for myself."

Alonzo shrugged off his brother's skepticism as he sipped on his sixth round of Henny and Coke. "Yeah, Paul got it goin' on. He had a nice li'l bit o' money comin' to 'im back when we was both locked up down in Akron too. He was pretty well connected wit' da gangs inside, like da Geechee-Gullah Nation and da Black Guerilla Family. He sold lotsa weed and more than a li'l bit o' powda. He even slung some smack whenever he could get it from da Latino cats."

"I know, 'cause I helped 'im sell a lot o' da dope myself," Whiskey said.

"Yep. When he graduated high school, he musta served dope to the whole fuckin' senior class, teachers included."

Whiskey nodded. "Yeah, him and David Ambrosia's brother, Lee. They was pumpin' a whole lotta weight through school back in da day, an' when Dawn, Shawn, and Rae-Kwon came to Caymon High and hooked up wit' 'im, it was on an' poppin' for real after that."

"But crackhead-ass Jason Dombrowski fucked everything up when he snitched on niggas after

O'Malley arrested his dumb ass for breakin' into his house, tryin' to boost shit." Alonzo paused to glance lustfully at the plump backside of a passing waitress as she bent over to retrieve a crumpled ten-dollar tip she'd just dropped.

"But back to da matter, when I was in da pen, I used to fuck wit' a whole lotta Jamaican niggas. Now I know back in da day, when da South Peola homies was beefin' wit' dem dreads in Badlands Manor and Geneva Projects, shit was ugly 'tween us an' dem boys. But I got to know dat dem dreads ain't so bad in da joint. As a matter o' fact, I did bidness wit' dis one cat from Kingston name Richard Olson, but cats in da pen called 'im Deadeye Dick 'cause he lost his right eye back in da day in a knife fight as a teenager in Kingston. He was da head o' da Trenchtown Posse up in Akron, and dey controlled fifty percent of all da dope comin' in da pen, while da 'eses' and skinheads split da rest. While I was locked up, this dude became a fuckin' legend up in da pen. Niggas inside was sayin' ain't nobody made da type o' paper nor had da juice like Deadeye since our cousin Rae-Kwon and dat ol' Jewish pimp, Lionel Kurtz, was doin' it big back in da eighties. I know for damn sho I musta pulled in over five grand a week when I was pumpin' for 'im while we were both inside a while back. He had da C.O.'s on lock. Da warden and even cops on da outside was workin' for 'im.

"He bought the Lion's Den nightclub after Big Gabby got sent to da pen, and he done opened up three more nightclubs. Plus, he got a big recordin' studio in North Peola where wannabe rappers an' amateur singers go to audition and lay down tracks while sellin' dope outta dem joints da whole damn time on da low.

"Right befo' I got outta da pen, some hatin'-ass niggas got wit' some dudes on da outside who was beefin' wit' da Trenchtown Posse, and befo' ya know it, da feds had a sting operation dat shut da whole program da fuck down. 'Round 'bout twenty-five prison guards got convicted on federal drug charges. Dat included da warden too. Cats wit' as little as two years left got hit wit' ten mo' years for being part o' da ring. I was real lucky, 'cause I'd stopped sellin' shit six months befo', 'cause I got wit' dese Muslim dudes an' called myself 'goin' righteous' for a hot minute. Turns out dat Allah musta saved my black ass for sho', 'cause if it wasn't for me reppin' Islam, I woulda gotten caught up wit' da rest o' dem po' bastards. Deadeye was da ringleader o' da whole thing, so da feds hit him wit' da kingpin statute, and a federal jury up in Atlanta found him guilty on all counts, from drug trafficking and murder to blackmail and extortion. He was nailed wit' a hunit an' ten years in federal prison. I don't know where he's at now. All I know is dat he's locked down in supermax. Cats say Deadeye is somethin' like one hundred feet underground all alone in a cell by himself, watched by closed-circuit cameras, and armed guards are his only human contact. He never sees daylight, and no one can call, visit, or write him—He's fucked for life."

The cute waitress came back with Whiskey's pitcher of beer and Alonzo's Henny and Coke, while a baby-faced waiter, no older than eighteen, gently placed the steaming fisherman's platter in front of Whiskey.

Alonzo hastily drank down the potent, syrupy elixir, grimacing as the warm rush of Hennessy opened like wings in his chest. "Niggas was gettin' on da map like a mufucka when dat one-eyed cat was bossin' up. Dude put hustlas on, rap niggas on, fly-ass bitches on. *Sheeet*, nigga, even da po-po got on. Nigga, my man brung a lot o' paper to a whole lotta folks, inside da joint an' out. I know for damn sho I was one, so da hood gotta show son some love.'

Whiskey nodded, biting into a succulent piece of baked salmon then shrugged his shoulders, making eye contact with his younger brother on the opposite side of the dinner table.

The waitress again approached the pair as they sat conversing in the back of the restaurant in the secluded VIP section of the entertainment-themed eatery that was their usual dining spot. "May I bring y'all anything else, gentlemen?" the blushing girl asked, presenting a bright, dimpled smile.

The boys, now engrossed in hustle talk, waved her away politely and continued on with business.

"Dat's all good, an' I feel you on my man's hustle an' everything, but what da fuck he gotta do wit' yo' hustle? A'ight, bet, Peola's police chief, O'Malley, been runnin' five-O round dese parts for years. Since our daddy been locked up, niggas ain't been gettin' dey money right. Dat's been for a minute now, so niggas from Peola, and Savannah hustlas too, done hooked up wit' Cackalacky niggas out in Beaufort County, an' we been bringin' dope from New York and Miami to Hilton Head Airport. Snookey and da Fuskie Krew brings da shit on a boat to Daufuskie Island, where dudes load 'em and start drivin' packages back to da stash trailer down on Haig's Point ta weigh an' bag up, proper like. Snookey's at Bloody Point prison puttin' in work an' makin' moves from inside an' outside. Dat's been gettin' fuckas rich. Niggas been makin' so much money, dat now da police wanna get in da game?" Whiskey asked.

Alonzo took a swig of his drink. "Now some o' dem boys in blue want money just like cats in da game, an' dey approached us wit' a deal. Dey watch our backs, and we'll watch dey's, so I'd say 'bout a hundred cops, black an' white, 'specially white boys, though, is makin' sho dat da coke money comin' in from Daufuskie is greasin' all o' our palms 'cause Daufuskie coke is servin' da whole Souf Cack and Georgia low country. You know how much money dat is, Whiskey? *Sheeet*, nigga, we bring in somethin' like five million dollars a year or more. I really don't know for sho, but I do know dat it was four million plus. Anyway, we got one small problem," Alonzo said in a thick Gullah accent. "We need you ta get rid o' Mickey O'Malley's bitch ass 'cause jus' as ol' bitch-ass Rossum, former New Orleans' police chief, had set him up in top-cop status here in Peola, he was invited to spend two months on Daufuskie Island to help train and prepare the Daufuskie police to handle the growing drug trafficking they'd faced for da past three years. Now you know dem gutta-ass niggas out here ain't gonna let dat fat-ass Irish mufucka fuck dey money up no longer."

Whiskey nodded and continued eating his seafood meal.

"So what's up? You down, or what?" Alonzo reached across the table and grasped the half-filled pitcher of Miller Genuine Draft to pour himself a glass of the golden brew. "Da cops I'm workin' wit' is willin' to give you fifty grand for da hit. O'Malley is currently rentin' out a townhouse on Melrose Plantation. I can have his whereabouts to you in a day or two, a'ight?"

Whiskey stared down into his half-eaten meal and rubbed his tired eyes slowly, contemplating this latest offer of murder-for-hire. "Alonzo, I dunno 'bout dis one here, playa. If I do take yo' cop buddies up on dey offer, I'm-a get a coupla li'l young cats I know to do da hit, and then I'll pay dem afterward. Don't worry, dese youngsters is some junkyard dawgs when it comes to pushin' niggas' wigs back, 'specially if you payin' 'em for it an' whatnot."

"Good, man. Dat's da deal, pimpin'. Anyway, on a different subject, how's Tasha and da boys doin'?"

"She doin' good. Da boys, dey a'ight too. She just stay worryin' and thinkin' 'bout yo black ass most o' da time. Dat's 'bout it."

"I dunno what fo'. She treated a nigga like a stepchild when I was stayin' dere an' shit."

"Anyway, I been helpin' David at the studio, layin' down tracks for his fiancée Godiva, for her upcomin' album this winter."

"You mean, *the* Godiva? Ambrosia's 'bout ta wife that fine-ass thang? Dat's one lucky-ass mufuckin' dude."

"Luck ain't got shit ta do wit' it, baby boy. David got game, dat's all, an' da good sense to know a good bidness move when he sees one."

"So you think she'll win da *Pop Star* competition? 'Cause Gina Madison can blow just as well as Godiva, if not better."

Whiskey gave his brother a quick smirk as he popped a piece of grilled shrimp into his mouth.

"A'ight, I know Godiva's a sexy dime an' all, an' she got pipes like a sista, but I dunno if dat lily-white girl got what it takes to knock off a diva like Gina Madison, 'cause last week my girl was watchin' da shit on TV an' she said dey both sung a half-hour's worth of Anita Baker's songs, an' Madison sounded much betta than da white girl. An' my girl watch dat show every Thursday religiously."

"Everybody's entitled to dey own opinion, Alonzo, your girl included, but it's no way America is gonna let another black singer win a major singing competition. Shit, Fantasia already done won it all on *American Idol* just last year. Plus, Godiva is younger, prettier, and she got a mo' bubbly personality than Gina Madison. And don't ever forget the number one kicker—she's white! She's a young, blond-haired, blue-eyed dime piece wit' a bubble butt like a sista and, like you even said, the voice to match. Now Madison can sing her ass off, I know, but she's twenty-nine, short, overweight, dusty black and ugly. I love my black women, just like you, but hey, I'm also one ta keep it real. She ain't got a snowball's chance in hell to win *Pop Star* over Godiva."

"Damn, nigga! You pumpin' dat white bitch up a whole lot, ain't ya, bro? Shit, you reppin' dat ho like you dickin' her down or somethin'—is you? *Sheeet*, inquirin' minds wanna know," Alonzo said.

"Naw, dawg, I don't mix bidness wit' pleasure,

you know dat. Besides, David's my man. I'd never violate homie like dat."

"Yeah, okay. I betcha if dat broad offer up da ass, you ain't gonna turn it down, an' ya ain't gonna think twice 'bout ya boy David. Tell me I'm wrong."

Whiskey poured himself a glass of cold beer after downing the first one and grinned softly. "She is a keeper for damn sho, I agree wit' ya on dat, my man. An' if she wasn't David's girl, yeah, I'd fuck her." He swallowed a mouthful of the golden ale.

"Yeah, don't lie to me. I'm yo' li'l brotha, nigga. I know dat befo' too long you gon' be screwin' Godiva right under David's nose. Watch what I tell you."

Whiskey pushed his half-eaten meal to the side and waved the pretty waitress over to their table. "Check please, gorgeous." Then he tipped her a fifty and winked at her, to which she responded with a bashful smile.

Chapter 4

"Get This Money Right"

"Peola's famous top cop, Police Chief Mickey O'Malley vows to assist Daufuskie Island's fledgling police force with training and recruiting to crack down on the sea island's rising drug trade, which has made it a haven for both local and out-of-state drug traffickers. O'Malley's success as a police chief is well documented in Bryan, Chatham, Effingham, and Peola Counties, where his hard-edged, highly unorthodox style of policing has brought both praise and criticism his way.

"The controversial police chief stated, 'Criminals are criminals. It doesn't matter whether they're punk kids vandalizing churches with spray paint or millionaire drug cartels flying coke into our country from Colombia. They're all scum to me, and their crimes can't be tolerated for any reason. I live to lock these animals up and see to it that they're taken off the streets for a helluva long time, 'cause I don't want 'em in my town, my state, my region, or in my country, period.' "

Whiskey changed the remote from local Channel 11 to ESPN after the report on Mickey O'Malley's Sea Island drug war came to a close. It was painfully obvious that O'Malley was just as obsessed with ridding Daufuskie of dope-peddling riffraff as he had been with his native Peola. Even more ironic was Channel 11's commercial featuring the upcoming televised *Pop Star* grand finale pitting the sexy, well-liked blonde against her equally popular opponent.

Godiva was America's latest sweetheart, having joined Ciara and Ludacris on stage during a sold-out concert at the Georgia Dome, where she was greeted by a five-minute round of thunderous applause for her rendition of Ciara's hit song, "Oh." She was even invited to the Governor's Mansion in Atlanta.

Whiskey marveled at the dimensions of the girl's curves, which rivaled the thickest sista. He knew that she was Rae-Kwon's baby mama and currently the fiancée of his best friend, but from the eyes she would give him and the way she would put an extra wiggle in her walk each time he'd show up at the studio, he knew it was but a matter of time before he'd hit that phat white ass.

As he channel-surfed he could think of little else than how he'd go about murdering the chief of police. It could be perhaps his most challenging hit yet. He himself often paid underlings to take care of his murder-for-hire gigs when he either couldn't do it himself or felt that the job was too lightweight for him to consider carrying out himself. Those were usually small-time jobs—a few hundred dollars here, a kilo of coke there—but this was a big-time operation that needed time and patience to be taken care of properly, not to mention the resources.

O'Malley was a hater of drug dealers, and somewhat of a racist, having been born and bred up North in racially prejudiced Boston. He had totally wiped out illegal drug traffic throughout Peola altogether shortly after Snookey Lake and his ecstasy ring was brought to justice back in 1994. Only David Ambrosia's Bad Boyz II Syndicate made moves on the street, and that was because he had a good working relationship with O'Malley and several other high-ranking Peola police officers. Niggas on the streets of South Peola had wanted to rid themselves of the gung ho Irishman for well over a decade now. Yet, with Chief O'Malley's popularity and political power among the town's movers and shakers, it was a pipe dream at best.

Ever since Daufuskie Island was discovered to be more than simply another sunny Sea Island resort, O'Malley was stepping on the toes of much more organized and vengeful traffickers than before, including the seemingly straight-laced Ambrosia. There were corrupt cops and other equally unethical lawmakers on the take, unbeknownst to him, who were not about to let Peola's 2004 Man of the Year ruin a good thing. He was marked for death, and didn't even know it.

It was well into the evening when the mid-sized yacht, *Island Skipper*, pulled up to the dock at Daufuskie's Haig Point landing. The raucous humming chorus of crickets and cicadas filled the air as Whiskey and the other passengers left the cabin of the boat and stepped out onto the worn, wooden planks of the dock. Awaiting them was a cheesy, green-and-white tour mobile, which doubled as a Metro Bus of sorts for island residents after normal business hours.

The driver, an old black man with a curly, white beard and receding hair around his bald pate, kept the dozen or so passengers laughing at lame jokes and engrossed in conversation on everything from deviled crab ingredients to President Bush's unpopular war in Iraq .

When he'd dropped off the last old geezer at the Melrose Plantation, he drove along the lonely dirt road for over twenty minutes in silence before he decided to address the young man sitting three rows behind to his rear, staring out of the window in deep thought.

"How you doin' today, young man?"

"I'm a'ight. How 'bout yaself?"

"Oh, I'm blessed by da best. At sixty-four years old, I just thank da good Lord fa health and strength."

"No doubt. But where can I go ta get a drink and maybe see some cuties?"

The old driver cackled through yellowed, rotted teeth. "Well, sir, I'll tell ya what. 'Round here you got da Haig's Point Inn. Dey sells a lot o' beer and wine, 'specially a coupla bottle wines made right chere on da island by us Fuskie folks. Then ya got Melrose Bar and Grill where you can get some hard liquor, plus a nice meal. They gots some jazz on some nights and country western on some nights.

You can dance a li'l bit if ya wanna, but ain't no titty bars 'round here, if dat's what ya talkin' 'bout. Dese rich crackas ain't havin' no titty bars 'round here. Dey got too much tourist dollars ta make. Image, ya know? Now if ya go back to da mainland, I know ya can find mo' titty bars than a li'l bit."

Whiskey said from the back of the tour bus, "Damn! Ain't nuttin' a nigga can do down here but play golf and go crabbin', huh?"

"You gotta realize, young man, this island is for two kinds o' people—old black folk and rich, middle-aged white folk. Now you got black folk yo' age livin' on da island here an' there, but dey up to no good, mostly sellin' dat dope ta dem rich whiteys down on Bloody Point Plantation, Melrose and Haig's Point Plantation. But it done got so bad dat dey done gone an' brung a big city police from Georgia ta get rid o' all dis goddamn dope from 'round here, 'cause dese li'l bicycle-ridin' po-po here on Fuskie can't do nuttin' wit' dem gun-totin' niggas from down in Webb Place and Dunn Gardens."

"Hmm, dat's a trip, 'cause I'm stayin' wit' one o' my peeps out in Webb Place for a few days. Who knows, maybe I'll fuck around an' play a li'l bit o' golf myself."

Upon hearing from his young passenger that the drug-ridden trailer park was his destination, he wrinkled his already furrowed brow even more in deep thought as he drove along the scenic greenery of sprawling golf courses and exquisitely manicured plantation lawns surrounding majestic-looking Southern homes, dusk slowly falling on the sleepy sea island.

"Is dat a'ight wit' you?" Whiskey asked some-what sarcastically, sensing the old man's sudden discomfort.

The eyes of the driver met Whiskey's from the rearview mirror above. "Well, to tell ya da truth, I ain't gonna drive up in Webb Place fa nobody, not even my own chillen an' dem. You gon' have ta get out here on Silverdew Drive, young man. I's real sorry 'bout dis, but dat's how it's gotta be fa now, 'cause I's off-duty."

Whiskey tossed a small duffle bag across his broad shoulder as he made his way off the tour bus and onto the gravel-lined sidewalk below.

It was but a short twenty-minute walk through a winding footpath in an overgrown palmetto-dotted thicket before reaching the entrance of Webb Place. Nappy-haired little Gullah girls played hopscotch and jumped double Dutch among the run-down mobile homes as bare-chested teen boys threw a weather-beaten football back and forth along the dusty backroad of the heavily populated trailer park.

Whiskey walked up the wooden steps of an old eggshell-white doublewide and knocked several times on the door.

A tall, handsome boy with sharp facial features and dark, satin-like skin opened the door and im-mediately embraced him with a broad smile and hearty laughter, while welcoming him into the liv-ing room.

"My nigga! 'S up witcha, boy?" Theo offered Whiskey the freshly rolled blunt he'd been puffing on.

"Ain't shit, shawty. Still pimpin', steady hustlin',

stayin' trill wit' it, you know." Whiskey dragged deeply on the smoldering Dutch.

"My nigga, tryin' ta be like me an' shit. C'mon, lemme take you to ya room, so you can getcha self comfy-like."

Theo took a hold of Whiskey's duffle bag and proceeded down the long, carpeted hallway toward the room at the rear of the trailer. The room was mid-sized with an old cobweb-covered bureau dresser against a crayon-marked wall. A small electric lamp with a Power Ranger print lampshade sat upon the top of the dresser, illuminating the kiddie room in a soft yellow glow.

"You must be a fool for mufuckin' Power Rangers, huh?" Whiskey looked around at the Power Rangers posters, throw rugs, and action figures that adorned the entire area.

"Naw. What had happened was, I used ta fuck dis ho back in da day who had a li'l five-year-old— Da pussy was good. I moved da bitch and her son up in da crib, right? Well, da li'l nigga was a fiend fa Power Rangers, right, so I figured dat I'd hook his ass up wit' a Power Ranger-themed room an' shit, right. Man, dat li'l knucklehead loved dis shit. Too bad his mama had ta get caught cheatin' on me wit' da li'l nigga's daddy, so I kicked her hoin' ass up outta here. I just ain't never get around ta redecoratin' dis mufucka, dat's all."

Whiskey passed the blunt back to Theo after coughing loudly for several seconds after his last toke.

"Yeah! Dat's dat purple haze, boy. Whatcha know 'bout dat?" Theo took the strong-smelling weed-filled cigar from his guest's outstretched hand.

"Oh fuck, yeah, dat's da shit right dere. I know you got big clientele off dis smoke right here, don't cha?" Whiskey asked, unpacking his belongings on the bed.

"What? Does barnyard hog like slop? *Sheeet*, nigga, I gotta re-up 'bout every three or fo' days, no bullshit."

Just then a cute, freckled-faced, fair-skinned girl in her early twenties walked past the open door of the room and sashayed down the hall toward the living room. Then she entered the kitchen and disappeared from view.

"You coulda shut da fuckin' do', ya know, li'l high-yella heifa!" Theo moved out into the hallway to close the door of the adjacent room from where the music of Three 6 Mafia blared loudly out into the darkened hallway.

"Who's dat, Theo?" Whiskey asked, brimming with sexual interest.

"Oh, dat li'l chickenhead? Dat's my first cousin, Charmaine. Why? You tryin' ta spit some game at her?"

Whiskey smirked as he shot his Geechee friend a look of disbelief. "C'mon now, what do you think?"

"A'ight. Excuse me, pimpin'. *Sheeet*, pop ya mufuckin' collar then, playa-playa."

"She got a man?"

"She used to, but he went off to Parris Island to enlist in da Marine Corps two years ago. Now Bush got his black ass fightin' in Iraq ." Theo passed the blunt back to Whiskey as they both sat on the bed.

"How old is she?"

"She just turned twenty-two in June."

"Damn! She's just two years younger than me. Dat's a'ight. She a bad mufucka, I know dat much. She got chillen?" Whiskey finished off the last of the blunt before smashing it down into a nearby ash-tray, and the last thin wisp of smoke dissipated into the air.

"Naw, she ain't got no chillen, nigga. She ain't even never been pregnant, dawg! She know betta. *Sheet*, Charmaine goin' ta college at Savannah State. She just here visitin' for da summer, dat's all."

Whiskey stroked his neatly trimmed goatee, nod-ding his head thoughtfully. The cutie was both sexy and smart all at the same time. Plus, she didn't have any little snot-nosed brats hanging around. It seemed to him that she was ripe for the picking.

"A'ight, c'mon. Let's stop sittin' 'round here chat-tin' like a couple o' old-ass bitches an' whatnot an' go out on da back porch wit' her, if you tryin' ta put ya bid in, 'cause dat's where she likes ta chill out at all da time."

"True, true. A'ight, lemme get a dub o' dat haze up off you. Gimme da fattest bag you got on you." Whiskey attempted to hand his host a crisp twenty-dollar bill from a thick rubber band-wrapped wad of cash he took from the right pocket of his baggy jean shorts.

"C'mon, Whiskey, wit' dat ol' bullshit, nigga. Take dis bag o' reefer an' git da fuck on. You know I don't charge my peeps fa nuttin'. Now go 'head an' enjoy yaself 'cause I'm 'bout ta head to Benning's Point. I gotta drop off some X pills to some crackas at da lighthouse. Dey s'pose ta be havin' some late-night beach party or somethin'. I'm one o' da few black mufuckas dey invited. Shit, I'm-a go too. Ya never know, I might get a coupla dem white bitches ta suck on dis wood, ya know what I mean?"

"Well, if you servin' up dat X, you know fa sho da very least you gonna get is sloppy deep-throat action from dem white hoes. You know dey good fa givin' dat brain, but I need fa you ta bring me a small container o' kerosene or gas, a'ight?"

"What da fuck you gon' be needin' shit like dat for?"

"Nigga, don't worry 'bout it. Just make it happen, cap'n, a'ight?"

Theo nonchalantly flipped him off as he snatched a cluster of keys from the top of the dresser. "Whatever, dawg. I'll bring dat shit back on da rebound 'cause I'm on my way out da do'. Holla atcha a li'l while later."

Whiskey smiled, clasped hands with Theo in a brotherly show of affection, and followed his host to the front door. There they briefly engaged in further small talk before they both went their separate ways. Whiskey walked back down the hall to the room at the end and entered again to finish unpacking.

After that and a hot shower he emerged from the room rocking a pair of basketball shorts and a Dwayne Wade, Miami Heat jersey. His dark, silky hair was freshly braided and draped down his thick neck, and ended in miniature red-and-white dice at the tips. He briefly touched up his mustache and goatee in the partially broken mirror in the hall bathroom, afterward putting down the electric shaver and picking up a radiant platinum necklace that shimmered with polished brilliance against the black knit nylon of the jersey.

He smiled with satisfaction at the well-groomed image he beheld in the mirror before him. He blasted his open mouth with breath spray, smacked his lips, and applied a copious amount of Kenneth Cole's Reaction cologne all over his jersey before stepping out into the hallway and toward the living room.

Once there he turned toward the kitchen from which the delightfully melodious ballads of Alicia Keys filtered out from the screen door bordering the outdoor porch.

As he walked into the kitchen, he noticed a bottle of Armadale Vodka and a container of orange juice on the countertop and several empty glasses nearby. He helped himself to a glass and walked through the screen door and out onto the porch, where various moths, fireflies, and water beetles fluttered around a naked light bulb overhead.

Charmaine sat cross-legged in a huge, cushiony wicker chair, sipping on a screwdriver and reading a copy of Sister Souljah's book, *The Coldest Winter Ever.*

Whiskey took in the beauty of the female he gazed upon and was immediately smitten. With a pair of lovely legs and bulging cleavage straining against the sheer fabric of her paisley-printed blouse, she slowly twitched her manicured toes within the dangling stiletto, stopping to look up from her novel to peer at the man who stood in the middle of the floor silently admiring her good looks.

Whiskey salivated as he realized that Charmaine was even more attractive than he'd originally thought. As her soft amber eyes met his, he smiled and moved slowly over to her, extending his hand in an informal greeting while the sexy vixen wrapped her full red lips around the thin straw.

He felt his wood stiffen within his boxers. "'S up witcha, shawty? My name's Peter, but my peeps all call me Whiskey, ya know. So my man Theo is ya cousin, huh?"

Charmaine placed her book face down in her lap and reached forward, putting her delicate hand into Whiskey's for a light handshake. "Hi ya doin'? My name's Charmaine. It's a pleasure meetin' you finally. Theo been talkin' 'bout you for da last two weeks, an' so it's finally good to put a face wit' a name. Yeah, Theo is my first cousin, unfortunately—Naw, I'm just playin'. I love that boy; he's my heart."

"I heard you go to Savannah State. What you takin' up?" Whiskey pulled up a chair next to hers.

"Well, I major in pediatrics and minor in child development studies. I also cheerlead during da football and basketball seasons."

"What! Shit! Now I know why you got such a tight-ass body an' shit."

"Thank you! I'm flattered. Our team leader puts a lot of physical demands on all of us, so we gotta keep it tight at all times." She raised her drink to her lips and took another sip.

"I know dat's right. Well, whatever it is dat you doin', keep it up 'cause it's damn sho workin'."

"Yeah, yeah, yeah. I betcha say that to all the girls, don't you?"

"Only if dey's fine as you."

"Um-hmm. See what I'm talkin' 'bout. You ain't nothin' but a ho, ain't cha? Probably got a bunch o' baby mamas from Fuskie to Peola, don't cha?"

"Naw, sorry, miss lady, but I ain't got no chillens or baby mamas neither, so get it right. You tryin' ta hit some o' dis?" Whiskey displayed an overstuffed bag of strong-smelling cannabis.

"Nope. I don't smoke dat shit, sorry. Don't you know that one blunt is worse for your health than smoking five cigarettes? Think about that next time you fire up a J, okay?"

Whiskey grinned while shaking his head. He swigged down the entire contents of the glass before stuffing the twenty-dollar bag of bud back into his pants pocket. "Hey, whatever's clever. To each her own. I ain't mad at cha. I just wanna get ta know ya betta, dat's all, pretty girl. How 'bout catchin' a movie an' a li'l somethin' to eat afterward over on Hilton Head tonight?"

"I guess so . . . if you sure you ain't got nothin' else betta to do, like hangin' out wit' my cousin Theo."

"Theo's my man, fifty gran' an' all, but choosin' him over you would be outrageous. Plus, he got things to do tonight anyway."

"Whatever you say, Peter. I refuse to call you *Whiskey*, 'cause yo' mama didn't name you dat, did she?"

"Girl, you got too much damn mouth, you know dat? But I like a woman wit' a li'l spunk to her. It gives me a challenge. But I'm gonna getcha mind right, watch."

Whiskey quickly went into the kitchen and came

back with another round of screwdrivers for him and the young lady. He wanted to get into her pants before leaving Daufuskie by the end of the following week. Though she seemed like a tough cookie, those were, many times, the easiest to crack; it just took game.

After taking a long sip on her screwdriver, Charmaine took Whiskey's hand in hers. "Look, let's stop playin' games, okay. I'm turned on by you, and you are obviously turned on by me. We're both adults, consenting adults. Now just because I don't have any babies or fuck half the neighborhood doesn't mean that I'm some stuck-up, non-sexual being. I'm a very confident, self-assured gal, and at the moment, about as horny as a bitch in heat. So, while my cousin's away, let's take this opportunity to let nature take its course, okay?" Charmaine moved her slender fingers from Whiskey's hand to the swollen bulge in the front of his jeans and caressed his erection through the fabric of the denim.

Whiskey quickly and instinctively undid his belt, allowing his jeans to drop to the floor. His thick penis hung long and curved in Charmaine's smiling freckled face. Too drunk with lust to think of anything other than sexual release, Whiskey didn't seem to care that they were both on the front porch.

Charmaine hiked her skirt up while pulling her pink lace panties down around her thick, round thighs past her knees, calves and ankles. Then she pulled Whiskey toward her by his stiff member, guiding him into her moist, pink slit.

Whiskey pounded her in the missionary position. Charmaine moaned out in ecstasy, "Ohhh, yes, fuck me, baby. Ohhh, God, yes. Fuck this pussy hard, baby, ohhh yeah," her shapely legs trembling with delight as she reached an orgasm.

Whiskey, who usually used condoms, pulled out his rod, glistening with Charmaine's vaginal secretions, and shot a thick stream of semen across her lower abdomen and pubic hair before collapsing back onto the large wicker chair where he'd previously sat, totally exhausted from the intense lovemaking.

Chapter 5

"For da Soldiers"

Daufuskie Island was an area that most people knew as a resort spot, but natives of the sea island knew that Daufuskie could prove deadly to any outsider who took the sleepy, down-home Gullah culture for granted. Several of Whiskey's homeboys had been members of the infamous Fuskie Krew gang, which was a part of the much larger Geechee-Gullah Nation, a low country version of Chicago's People and Folks Nations gangs.

One time, a crackhead from Hilton Head's Spanish Wells community got behind on his dope bill, and to add salt to the wound, he turned out to be a rat for the island's cops. This bit of street betrayal severely cut into Whiskey's drug profits, which had been quite profitable after he'd partnered up with the Fuskie Krew to distribute crack cocaine throughout the Beaufort County region.

* * *

It was August of 1999, and Whiskey had contacted Joi Stevens, the crew's leader, and traveled down to Fuskie to meet with the violent gang leader. Over a traditional Gullah dinner of deviled crabs, fried oysters, and boiled hominy grits, they discussed the details of the murder that was to take place on Hilton Head.

When Reggie Dillon, a forty-six-year-old Beaufort County sanitation worker, sat in his trash truck near Hilton Head High, getting head from an underage girl, Joi calmly walked up to the driver's side window and pumped Dillon and his seventeen-year-old lover, Natalie White, full of hollow-tip slugs before roaring away in a black convertible BMWcoupe.

Joi was later caught and convicted of the double murder and sentenced to fifteen years at Daufuskie's Bloody Point Beach prison. He had been ratted out by a senior member of the crew, Marcus Finbarr, a.k.a. "Fin," who'd been given a major deal by low country authorities to act as an informant.

Whiskey knew of Fin's whereabouts on Hilton Head, and he had already decided in his mind to avenge his friend Joi. It had been six years since Joi Stevens had been imprisoned for the murders of Reggie Dillon and Natalie White. And over a dozen or more Fuskie Krew gang members had been thrown in prison for various crimes since then, greatly weakening the infrastructure of the one-time powerful crew.

Fin was now living among Hilton Head's wealthy socialites in the costly Sea Pines Plantation, a gated community, ferrying rich, retired geezers back and forth between Hilton Head and Daufuskie on his modest-sized tour boat for $150-a-pop weekly. And he supplemented this lucrative income with the under-the-table monies given to him by the sheriff's office of Beaufort County for dropping dimes on his old crew and their activities. Fin usually worked Monday through Saturday, eleven AM to seven PM, and conducted no ferryboat tours on Sundays, which was when he normally refueled, repaired, and tidied up his small yacht for the coming workweek.

After a quick touch-up to her wavy hair, Charmaine got dressed in a hot pink Baby Phat cotton corset with a crystal logo and a matching pink cotton tennis skirt with pink leather go-go boots. The couple took Theo's second vehicle, an old gray Camry, to the docks at Haig Point.

Whiskey showered again and dressed in what he'd worn before his back-porch tryst with Charmaine. Only, this time he would be traveling with a black Desert Eagle 9 mm handgun with accompanying silencer, both of which he stuffed down into his jean shorts. Hopefully he'd be able to track down the snitch right after painting the town with Charmaine.

After paying the reduced round-trip fee for island natives, Whiskey and Charmaine boarded one of the several river taxis that lined the sides of the dock. Steaming along at about thirty-three knots through the dark, choppy waters of the Cooper River, the red-and-white striped tower of Harbour Town's famed lighthouse welcomed them to the posh shores of Hilton Head.

As the river taxi drew closer to the busy, brightly lit pier, Whiskey noticed the many tourists dining outside under the colorful canopies of the assorted eateries in the warmth of the summer night. Lively jazz and solemn blues blared out into the streets from a live quartet playing in the courtyard filled with couples mingling and dancing along the cobblestoned street.

Once their passenger boat docked at the pier, Whiskey and his companion exited the vessel and caught a cab toward the island's downtown section, where they took a showing of Brad Pitt and Angelina Jolie's *Mr. and Mrs. Smith* at the Nickelodeon Theater. Then they ate at Osaka Japanese Steakhouse in Harbour Town .

As Whiskey sat in the lovely oriental-themed restaurant enjoying the cutlery-tossing skills of the Tokyo-born chef, he could think of little else than killing Marcus Finbarr. Fin had cost him thousands of dollars over the past six years, and it seemed as though the Fuskie Krew had little or no answers for Fin's consistent betrayals, which angered Whiskey more than a little.

They ordered a round of rice wine, which was probably the best served anywhere in the low country. After achieving the buzz they were both looking for, they tore into their succulent dishes of teriyaki chicken and fried rice and Sapporo shrimp appetizers before the pretty Japanese waitress, clad in a gorgeous red-and-white kimono, came over smiling with the bill.

Whiskey dropped two hundred dollars for the eighty-dollar meal and helped his lovely date out of her seat, telling the waitress to keep the change.

From there, the young enforcer paid the fare for Charmaine to be taken back aboard the awaiting ferryboat toward the neighboring Daufuskie Island. He explained that he had a small business matter to attend to on the mainland. She agreed to wait up for him, and they kissed goodnight.

As the passenger yacht sailed away into the moonlit distance, Whiskey moved toward the bottom end of the wharf, where Fin's yellow-and-white yacht, *Sally Ann*, floated against the algae- and barnacle-covered docks. The light below deck was a welcome sight to Whiskey's eyes, for it let him know that his quarry was right where he knew he'd be.

He went past tipsy couples giggling and cuddling along the moon-bathed boardwalk toward *Sally Ann*, floating at the end of the pier.

Once at the bottom of the winding, wooden stairwell, the pistol-packing figure glided deftly through the shadow-dappled wharf and closed in on the yacht up ahead.

As Whiskey got within a few feet of the boat, which was bobbing up and down in the surf, he withdrew the heavy 9 mm from his waistband and quickly screwed on the silencer. The infamous Desert Eagle, noted for its firepower and killing efficiency, was a well-known weapon of choice in the hood, drug dealers preferring it to the average 9 mm.

Whiskey slammed a fully loaded clip into the stock of the semi-automatic and carefully stepped down onto the deck of the vessel, slipping with cat-like stealth through the shadows and toward the cabin below. From the light of a small lamp on a nightstand near a meager cot, he noticed Fin tapping away on a laptop as he sat on a nearby chair pulled up to a coffee table, several empty bottles of beer strewn about.

Cautiously, Whiskey tested the door handle, turning it slowly counter-clockwise. It easily opened inward towards the room.

Fin was surfing adultfriendfinder.com, chatting with a number of delectable future booty calls. He had obviously settled on a hot-looking, dark-skinned, full-figured teen cutie from Bluffton called Hotchocolate16. The twenty-eight-year-old Fin sat bare-chested and in white Fruit of the Loom briefs. He had a container of Vaseline nearby, and an unmistakable look of unbridled lust on his heavy-bearded face.

"Nigga, get yo' mufuckin' hands up in da air an' turn yo' monkey ass 'round to me!" Whiskey leveled the pistol at the shell-shocked man, who sat wide-eyed before him.

The surprised Fin quickly raised his chunky arms skyward. "You got it, you got it, my man. What you want? Money, jewelry, dis boat? Whatever it is you want, baby, you can have it, a'ight. Just lemme go." The beady little eyes of the dumpy, pot-bellied Internet porn pervert with nappy chest hair darted back and forth, searching around the room, perhaps for a weapon or some other means of self-defense or escape.

"So you been livin' large out here on Hilton Head, huh? Livin' good out here on da backs o' ya homies dat you got locked up, ain't dat right? I betcha done got ya snitch check fa da month from five-O, ain't dat right? Say somethin', you fat, greasy mufucka!"

"Who da fuck is you, dawg? Do I know you?"

"Naw, you don't know me, but I know you. You's a snitch, which makes you a bitch-ass nigga o' da worse kind, dawg. So get yo' punk ass up an' get dis boat movin' ASAP!"

Fin rose up from the chair and walked toward the door of the small cabin, his assailant trailing him with the Desert Eagle pointed at the back of his head.

"'S up? Where you wanna go, playa? Coulda least let a nigga get dressed an' shit though."

Fin tried his best to keep cool. He'd been robbed on several occasions before and had obviously come out of those uncomfortable incidents alive and well, even critically wounding one unlucky would-be stickup kid. He saw no reason why he shouldn't walk from this latest predicament unscathed.

Whiskey roughly pushed the portly yacht owner up the stairs toward the huge steering wheel overlooking the wide bow.

"You gotta untie da line on the dock befo' we can take off. I'll be ready after you undo dem ropes, a'ight?" Fin said, walking into the captain's quarters.

"Oh hell, naw!" Whiskey pulled back on the chamber of the handgun.

Clack!

"You gonna do da rope-untyin' shit, punk bitch, not me! Now get yo' fat ass on dat dock an' untie dis bitch befo' I clap dis mufucka on yo' black ass!"

"A'ight, a'ight, man! Calm down! I'm gettin' to it, okay. Just gimme a chance to go up top. But, c'mon, I'm gonna need to get my clothes befo' I go out on da dock now. C'mon! You gonna draw suspicion like dat—a buck-naked black man walkin' 'round on da wharf an' shit, gimme a break!"

Whiskey silently agreed and forced the partially nude Marcus Finbarr downstairs to fetch his crumpled clothes piled up on the floor near the cot. After Finbarr got dressed, Whiskey made him untie the slipknots tying the yacht to the dock upon the lonely bottom pier, while club hoppers frolicked with merriment several feet above them along the cobblestone paths of Hilton Head's historic nightlife venue.

"A'ight, you got yo' wish. Now where we goin'?"

"Just drive dis mufucka toward Fuskie, a'ight. An' don't stop til I tell you to, a'ight."

"Looka here, playa, like I said, if you want money, I got you. I ain't hurtin' for no paper, so just take whatever it is you want, okay? I got 'bout five grand downstairs in da hole on da nightstand in a shoebox. All you gotta do is go an' get it, but don't go an' do nothin' stupid, 'cause if anything happens to me, lemme tell ya, you gon' be in a world o' trouble."

Finbarr carefully looked over his shoulder occasionally, while pulling the yacht away from Harbour Town's wharf and out into the night waters of the moonlit Cooper River beyond.

Whiskey quickly moved up close to his hostage's left ear, pressing the muzzle of the 9 mm hard to the back of Fin's sweaty head.

"C'mon, man, all dis shit ain't called for!"

Whiskey smiled wickedly and licked his lips. Then he said softly into Fin's bat-like ear, "Just drive this boat to where I tell you and shut da fuck up. Don't say shit else, or you's one dead ass, you understand me, boy?"

Fin silently obeyed Whiskey's orders and steered his yacht toward Daufuskie's Haig Point area, leaving white caps streaking the river in his wake.

Slowly the dark silhouette of Daufuskie Island came into view. Both men were silent as the yacht's engine hummed audibly, powering the mid-sized vessel steadily towards its destination.

As the old, rugged dock came into view, Whiskey kicked Finbarr square in his wide, saggy buttocks. "I'm tired o' playin' wit' yo' dumb ass now! Get dis raggedy-ass crab trap at da dock so we can get outta here!"

Fin groaned in pain and surprise. Cussing under his breath, he whipped the yacht into a higher gear, to add speed to the boat's approach to Daufuskie's dimly lit landing, and the engine roared, as white-capped waves broke on either side of the ship's upraised bow.

Once the boat pulled up against the weather-beaten pier, Fin quickly stepped down from the deck, closely followed by Whiskey, who pressed him forward, commanding him to fasten the vessel's ropes to the rickety wharf.

Then the two walked down the sun-bleached planks of the pier and into the humid, inky blackness of the Sea Island night.

"C'mon, snitch, walk y' ass down dis road right da fuck now!" Whiskey pushed Finbarr down the forest path.

They came upon a steep sawgrass-choked ravine bubbling over with thick quicksand sloshing about in an oatmeal-like swirl nearly twenty-seven feet deep. When Whiskey had Fin at the edge of the cliff, he leveled the muzzle of the pistol to the back of his head. "Dis is for all da soldiers who took da fall 'cause o' yo' snitchin' ass. Go to hell, where you belong, bitch!"

Fin tried to launch a desperate, empty-handed attack by lunging forward, but he was struck in the head, throat, and chest by gunshots.

Whiskey watched as Finbarr stumbled backward upon the soggy ground and clutched his chest, blood billowing out between his fat fingers. While he lay desperately, gasping for air, Whiskey walked over and stood looking down him, the man who'd single-handedly caused so much drama for him and his gangland associates for so long.

Slowly, he raised the 9 mm until its cold, hollow muzzle was level with Finbarr's head and squeezed the trigger twice, causing the heavy firearm to recoil violently with both muffled shots.

A crimson pool of gore gushed from Marcus Finbarr's shattered skull as he lay still, eyes staring upward and glazed over in a ghastly film, his mouth agape in a scream silenced by death.

Whiskey removed $227.00 from Fin's corpse before kicking the hefty body over the edge of the cliff.

He smiled with wicked satisfaction as the dead informant's body plummeted to its murky grave below. He quickly stuffed the cash into his pants and placed the weapon snugly into his waistband, and then proceeded back down the muddy backwoods trail toward the dock.

Once he got back to the pier he untied the ropes and boarded the *Sally Ann* and sailed for nearly a mile and a half across the Cooper River to the marshy shores of the uninhabited Bull Island. There he dropped anchor, doused the yacht in the gasoline that had been sitting on the floor of the cabin in a large red plastic container, and torched the vessel, simultaneously boarding a small outboard rig that had been attached to the yacht for emergency purposes.

Whiskey sped away, directing the outboard motor roaring on the rear of the shallow craft, toward Haig Point. Luckily for him, he'd honed his nautical skills amongst the Gullah folk long ago during his early years as a teenage drug runner, and this boating knowledge had served him well ever since.

As the boat swiftly hurdled the river's choppy waves, a mighty explosion reverberated in the distance. He turned briefly to catch a glimpse of the bright orange fireball glowing brilliantly in the night sky.

Once he'd arrived ashore at Haig Point Landing, he immediately phoned Theo on his cell phone to pick him up from the dock.

Within a half-hour a pair of headlights illuminated the pitch-black darkness surrounding the winding, dirt road of Daufuskie's West End. As the vehicle drew closer the thumping, Dirty South rhymes of Young Jeezy and Lil' Wayne became clearly distinct as the shiny metallic coppertone Porsche came to a halt in front of Whiskey.

"Damn, nigga, you been burnin' da midnight oil like a mufucka, ain't cha? Where Charmaine at?"

Whiskey opened the passenger side door and plopped down into the plush leather bucket seat. "Turn dis shit down, nigga." He lowered the volume on the radio in a quick display of irritation. "She should be home in bed by now. We went out earlier to catch a flick and get somethin' to eat afterward. We had a pretty good time." He checked the messages on his BlackBerry.

"I know you got some o' dat ass too, didn't ya? Yeah, I know you tapped Charmaine's li'l hot ass. Dat's my cousin and I love her, but I already knew she was feelin' you from da jump. See Charmaine ain't da type o' bitch dat'll fuck a whole bunch o' niggas, but I'll tell ya what, if she like what she sees, shit, she'll throw dat young, hot pussy on yo' ass befo' you can count to three, an' dat's real talk, pimpin'."

Whiskey simply grinned, steadily scrolling through his cellular message menu. "Yeah, you called it right. I fucked her red ass," he said nonchalantly.

"I knew it. Matter o' fact, you probably hit it soon as I walked out da do' 'cause dat's just how Charmaine is. Anyway, 's up wit' you out here all by ya-self at night? And how come you bringin' all o' dis mufuckin' mud an' shit up in my whip? Fuck you been doin'?—Wrestlin' gators or some shit back up in dem woods?"

Whiskey popped the glove compartment, fishing

around for something to wipe off his soiled red-and-black Jordans. He found a few paper napkins and began briskly wiping off his sneakers and the surrounding carpeted floor before tossing the muddied clump of tissues out the open window.

"Let's just say I took da time to handle a situation dat shoulda been handled a long fuckin' time ago."

Theo shook his head, knowing that his friend from Georgia had just murdered someone in the backwoods they were driving away from. "Who got dealt wit'?"

Whiskey placed his BlackBerry back into its belt clip. "Punk-ass nigga name Fin. Shit, you should know 'im. He right from here on Fuskie. He used to be a top balla wit' da Fuskie Krew, 'til he started snitchin' on his peeps for da po-po a while back. He da reason why half o' dem cats on lockdown right now, including my dawgs, Joi and Nicky Stevens—Dey locked up wit' my daddy and dem at Bloody Point—not to mention how much money dat fat, nasty mufucka cost us over da years. I had ta murk his ass, ya heard."

"I feel you, baby boy. You gotta handle yours, fa sho. It ain't no other way." Theo bobbed his braided head to Juvenile's hit, "Ha," as they cruised along the darkened, dusty backroads of the sea island.

"I hope you got rid o' da body an' all o' da evidence 'cause, once da Beaufort County sheriff's office finds out he's missin', dey gon' be lookin' for his ass all over da fuckin' place."

"Don't worry 'bout a thing, dawg. Yo' boy done covered all tracks. Don't forget, I been killin' mufuckas since I been sixteen an' shit, so I ain't new to dis type o' action."

"A'ight, I'll take yo' word for it, but just remember, once you leave an' go on back to Peola, dem alphabet boys gon' come 'round here kickin' ass first an' askin' questions second. Which means us Fuskie niggas gon' have ta deal wit' five-O, not you, a'ight. Just remember dat."

"If y'all Geechee asses woulda put dat nigga's ass to sleep a while back, I wouldn't have ta come all da way from Peola to do da job, so I ain't tryin' ta hear dat bullshit. Besides, enough cops is on da dope man's payroll down here in da low-bottom Cackalack to worry 'bout da few crackas trippin' off some ol' Robocop shit, so calm yo' nerves down a spell."

"Sounds good. If I didn't know you as well as I do, I'd say you's full o' shit. But I know you's a straight soldier dat's 'bout it-'bout it, so I'm-a let it go on dat note."

"Now dat's da type o' shit I wanna hear from ya, dawg, 'cause you already know I stay trill wit' it all day, every day. Now take me to da crib so I can lay da fuck down, 'cause I'm tired dan a mufucka."

Chapter 6

"Daufuskie Day"

The Daufuskie Day celebration was in full swing that following day at the Benning's Point landing. Theo, Charmaine, Whiskey, and perhaps most, if not all, of the residents of Dunn Gardens joined the rest of the sea island's local population down at the pier, where they intermingled with the multitudes of tourists from all over South Carolina and other areas of the United States who'd come to experience the rich cultural history, savory cuisine, and lively music and entertainment of the Gullah islanders.

Old, wizened ladies bedecked in head scarves and checkered blouses made a handsome profit hawking wares such as homemade quilts, wicker baskets, and colorful straw hats, while others drew a steady flow of eager customers to their tables with the lure of island fruit wine, canned preserves, and Daufuskie's famous deviled crabs.

The island's current civic leader, county chair-woman Heather Clay shook hands with an assortment of her constituents, occasionally stopping to pose for the cluster of photographers flashing cameras in her direction.

Whiskey slowly breezed past an animated Baptist choir belting out a string of gospel standards as fan-waving spectators clapped and sang along. He scanned the entire busy riverfront area. Several local cops could be seen moving back and forth among the crowd, keeping a watchful eye out for mischievous teens or the occasional rowdy drunk. Yet, to Whiskey's disappointment, O'Malley could not be found at all. To make matters worse, even if his would-be victim had been present, the sheer number of people attending the annual event would make the police chief's murder pretty much impossible to pull off. He had no choice but to go an alternate route with his deadly plans for O'Malley, if he indeed happened to be there or showed up at some point during the festivities.

As Whiskey walked along the crowded wharf with his two colleagues, Theo caught sight of several former high-school buddies he hadn't seen in years. He excused himself to greet them and to spend time getting reacquainted.

Whiskey and Charmaine watched Theo disappear among the multitude of people as they strolled past tables topped with mouth-watering Gullah dishes.

"Sorry 'bout last night. I waited up for you as long as I could, but you must have come in early this mornin' 'cause, as you already know, I ended up fallin' asleep." Charmaine bashfully peeked over her slender shoulder at him.

"Tsk, don't even sweat dat, shawty. I didn't think you'd be up by da time I got back to da Fuskie any ol' way. I had to take care of a whole lotta shit, trust me."

"At that time of night?"

"What are you? A private detective or somethin'? Lemme just say dis, I'm a real busy man, dat's all. Bein' a college student an' all, I'm sho you can understand dat, can't ya?"

Charmaine nodded, munching on a deviled crab she'd just bought. "Hey, it's whatever. Do you, I always say." Stuffed swell, she discarded the empty shell into a nearby garbage can after finishing the last two bites of the spicy crab cake. She wiped her greasy lips and fingers briskly then turned to her companion. "Damn! Was that deviled crab good. I'm gonna get me another one. Ain't you gonna get somethin' to eat?"

Whiskey surveyed the slow-moving throng of folks walking to and fro carefully. "Naw, I ain't hungry. I'll grab a li'l somethin' later on. Right now, I'm thinkin' 'bout somethin' else altogether."

"Penny for your thoughts." She placed her hand into his as they walked along.

Considerably more cops had arrived since they came, about a dozen to be exact—Daufuskie Island Police, Hilton Head Island Police, county sheriffs and a shitload of various surrounding low country cops representing their individual departments.

Whiskey had shot probably three people while in a crowd during his entire criminal career. It was from the window of a slow-moving car during his reckless gang banging days. But that was a group of unarmed civilians he'd shot into back then. He was now much wiser. Besides, it would be a little more than foolhardy to make an attempt on the life of an armed officer while surrounded by scores of pigs.

It was evident that O'Malley would show up sooner rather than later, but even still, Whiskey's hands were tied, at least for the time being. Undeterred by the failure of his original plan, he was determined to send a lasting message to his hometown's top cop that his presence on Daufuskie was not welcome, nor would his interference with the sea islands' drug empire be tolerated any further by the underworld.

Noticing the faraway look of concern on the face of her handsome lover, Charmaine snuggled up close to Whiskey while he stopped to buy a cup of homemade lemonade.

"Umm, that looks good. Can you buy me some too? It's gettin' a little bit too hot out here now. It wasn't this hot an hour ago, don't ya think?"

Whiskey shrugged and plunked down a few extra dollars on the table of the lemonade stand.

Charmaine happily grasped the cool Styrofoam cup of lemonade from the smiling vendor. She planted a juicy kiss on Whiskey's lips before sipping a long draught of the sweet yellow concoction. "Thanks. Ya know what, Whiskey? I'm damn horny right now, and I wanna go back to my cousin's house an' fuck. I'm gonna be goin' back to school in a couple weeks, an' you're gonna probably be leavin' for Peola even sooner. So in the meantime, between time, I'm gonna get all the dick that I can possibly get 'cause, once I get back to the books, it's gonna be all about term papers and exams. Gotta take advantage of my scholarship, ya know? Anyway, I want you to fuck me as hard as you can, 'cause I like it rough. I'm a freak for pain. It's sorta my fetish, if you will. Anyway, I'm sure you won't mind beatin' my li'l coochie up, will you?"

Whiskey chuckled as Charmaine's long, painted nails grazed his broad back up and down as they stood under the shade of a wide old oak tree. "Shit, you ain't said nothin' but a word, girl"—He pulled her to his chest, his strong hands cupped across her bodaciously plump booty—" 'cause I'll fuck da shit out ya, if dat's what ya want."

"Yeah, okay, we'll see, won't we?"

"C'mon, let's get up outta here. Theo's boys will drop him off at da house. He probably ain't gonna be home no time soon anyhow."

Charmaine smiled and quickly touched the front of Whiskey's suddenly bulging cargo shorts, and the couple weaved through the dense, sweaty crowd toward the Camry parked near the island's co-op, beneath a grove of pines.

It was somewhat irritating to Charmaine that even during their raunchy lovemaking, Whiskey's mind still seemed to be on other things.

After both lovers had achieved orgasms, they both collapsed on top the satin sheets, breathing heavily for several minutes.

Charmaine smiled and eased atop Whiskey's upper body. She rested her chin on his muscular chest, running her fingers back and forth through his curly, dark chest hair, whispering sweet nothings to him, to get him to concentrate on her. But all of her feminine wiles did little to change his mind even a little bit, which only made her more frustrated.

"Look, I came down here to take care of some bidness, a'ight. I mean, you got some good pussy an' all, but dat ain't da reason I came down to Fuskie. I got mo' important shit to do."

"Nigga, fuck you!" She raised up off of his sweaty body and stood near the bed. "Go on an' do whatever it is that you and Theo usually do, which is probably drugs or some other illegal bullshit. Go on. Git, 'cause I don't wanna be a part of whatever it is that you two usually get involved in, okay. So just get your shit an' go."

Whiskey himself got up off the bed smirking. "Bitch, please . . . you ain't shit but a ho any fuckin' way, so you can't talk 'bout nobody. What you need to do is shut the fuck up wit' all dat bullshit, for real."

"Look here, li'l boy, you don't know me well enough to go callin' me outside of my name, and if anybody's a ho, it's ya mama, bitch! I think it's best for you to get your shit and go."

"This here is Theo's crib, not yours, girlfriend. It's him who invited me here, and he's da only one who can tell me to leave his house, feel me? But you ain't gotta worry 'bout me gettin' in ya way or fuckin' wit' you while I'm here 'cause, as of right now, I'm done wit' ya, shawty."

Charmaine hurled a torrent of profanities toward the brawny young thug as he gathered up his crumpled clothes from the floor and went down the hall toward the bathroom. Then she buried her head beneath the fluffy pillows and cried her eyes out.

Whiskey enjoyed a refreshing shower right before packing his bags to leave the island for home. He'd at least accomplished one of the deeds he'd set his mind to follow through with during his trip to the Palmetto state.

Though it seemed unlikely that his plan to kill the vacationing police chief would materialize, he at least wanted to return to the Daufuskie Day celebration just to set his sights on the hated O'Malley, to be assured of his physical presence on Daufuskie.

As the island taxi which he'd phoned earlier pulled up along the dusty trail in front of Theo's mobile home, Whiskey gently placed three crisp hundred-dollar bills on the cluttered coffee table and stepped out of the rickety old screen door en route to the idling taxicab without saying good-bye to his weekend lover.

Charmaine parted the venetian blinds of her room and wiped her reddened eyes as she watched the white cab pull away down the dirt road amidst a cloud of dust. "Stupid fuckin' jerk!"

As she plopped backwards onto the sex-stained sheets of the queen-sized bed, she realized that she was a fool to give herself so freely. She now officially hated men.

Whiskey stepped out of the taxi after handing him a twenty-dollar bill. The temperature had dropped to a cooler seventy-two degrees, down from the much more humid eighty-eight degrees at midday, the late-evening sun dipping like a shimmering amber disk below the coastal Carolina horizon. He'd arrived just in time to see Mickey O'Malley, pale, portly, and with a broad gap-toothed grin, as he swiped at a shock of russet hair that fell down across his high forehead and into his squinting blue eyes.

Stepping up to the makeshift podium before him, the Irishman was greeted by a hearty round of applause that lasted several minutes.

Whiskey sneered with a growing anticipation for the chief, as he addressed the assembled onlookers in his familiar deep-voiced Bostonian accent.

O'Malley had put on considerable weight, and his rosy cheeks and red-tinged nose made him resemble a rotund leprechaun from the pages of a children's storybook.

However ridiculous the fat man seemed up on the podium cracking lame jokes in his loud yellow tropical print shirt, straw hat, and bargain basement shorts, Whiskey knew full well how formidable and unrelenting O'Malley could be when aroused to anger.

Besides bringing the people to laughter with his unique brand of humor, the chief of police received ear-splitting applause from the standing crowd, following his rousing speech declaring an all-out war on drugs and those who illicitly trafficked them on Daufuskie and throughout the surrounding low country regions, with the help of local authorities, including the Coast Guard.

As he stood along the outskirts of the boisterously cheering crowd, Whiskey realized that if something wasn't done quickly to prevent O'Malley from going forward with his objective, millions would be lost.

Whiskey checked out various spots to see if there would be any unsecured area where he could possibly pull off a quick hit-and-run shooting, but there was just no way to do that without being set upon by scores of angry boys in blue or getting shot himself. He grumbled angrily under his breath, gently toying with the trigger that lay nestled within his waistband.

While he stood staring intently at the podium up ahead, a slightly intoxicated Theo approached him, grinning and placing a beefy arm around his shoulder, sharing with him the hilarious details of his outing with his old homies. During their conversation, the matter of the kerosene came up. Theo apologized, stating that it had totally slipped his mind since he'd first requested it.

Whiskey voiced his anger at Theo for forgetting such an important matter and revealed to him the reason he needed the flammable agent in the first place.

Theo again apologized but then warned his visiting friend that the use of a Molotov cocktail to torch O'Malley's houseboat docked on the other side of the island would be a very risky move, especially since the Melrose Plantation Marina was gated and maintained by twenty-four-hour armed security.

As the waving policeman stepped down from the podium to be greeted by clapping politicians nearby, a roar of, "O'Malley for mayor! O'Malley for mayor!" went up from the crowd

Whiskey patted the bulge of the handgun's barrel in his shirt, glaring at the police chief with malice.

Then, without warning, a noisy scuffle broke out

amongst the crowd between two highly inebriated young men, drawing a group of uniformed officers over to the scene of the commotion.

While the officers subdued and arrested the drunks, Whiskey moved up closer to the chief, who'd become temporarily distracted by the incident himself. Quickly sizing up the Irishman, Whiskey knew better than anyone that to try something at this point, however tempting, would be just plain old stupid. He looked over his broad shoulder at a smiling Theo, who seemed to be enjoying the unexpected drama of the alcohol-fueled fisticuffs.

Whiskey walked away with Theo back toward the taxi stand, explaining to him the not-so-happy details of his and Charmaine's breakup, which Theo shrugged off with laughter as they both entered an awaiting cab along the curb of the crowded dirt road.

Whiskey felt no disappointment at not being able to hit O'Malley this time around, knowing that within the near future the hated police chief would be dealt with.

Chapter 7

"Dirty Dixie"

David Ambrosia sat fiddling with multiple switches in front of a large mixing desk, coaxing a hard-looking young gangsta rapper's street poems directly into the microphone over the booming speaker system reverberating loudly across the two-way speakers.

"C'mon, son, you gotta speak directly into the mic, a'ight? I need to feel the shit you talkin' 'bout, so spit that shit with some conviction 'cause you a thug, right? Well, make the listeners know that. That's what you are. A'ight, give it to me. One mo' time." He took a deep drag from a bubbling water bong sitting beside him on the wide desk, clasping hands with a smiling Whiskey, who'd just entered the studio.

Whiskey had just returned to Peola that morning, and after a brief breakfast, shower, and catnap, he decided to hop in his SUV and travel on Madison

Highway, taking Exit 54 toward west Peola, to get to Ambrosia's Spanish Moss Records located in Pemmican.

Usually, Ambrosia would have in-house disc jockeys develop mix tapes for the various hip-hop and R&B artists signed on his label. But this particular evening the multi-platinum music producer was to be found in his studio hard at work at what he did best, next to hustling.

"A'ight, that's what the fuck I'm talkin' 'bout, son. Spit that shit with some venom. I wanna hear Pac or Biggie, not Vanilla Ice. But, anyway, that's a wrap for today. Much, much, much better," Ambrosia said, voicing his approval of the rapper's renewed verbal bravado of his album's opening track into the mic.

The aspiring rap star, no older than maybe seventeen or eighteen, placed his headphones upon the wall stand and stepped down from out of the booth. He walked over confidently toward the producer, dapping it up, hugging and laughing as they spoke about the final edits to his debut album.

As they spoke business, Whiskey helped himself to the silver-embroidered bong, coughing heavily following each toke. He placed the bong back down upon the side of the mixing board and slowly walked about the cavernous studio, checking out the numerous gold and platinum record plaques on walls about the room. He chuckled out loudly for no reason, as the Holland-grown purple haze began to take effect.

Noticing an unopened bag of nacho cheese Doritos, he quickly took hold of it and gorged on its contents with marijuana-induced gluttony.

The artist, whose stage name was No Doubt, when introduced to Whiskey, quickly asked him to rate his performance.

"I think you got skills," Whiskey told him. "You's trill wit' yours, shawty. Just watch da hooks a li'l bit an' you'll be fine."

"A'ight, bet. So you feelin' my shit? For real though?"

Whiskey was extremely high at this point and somewhat uninterested in the teenager's rap album or career, but not wanting to diss him, he assured the grinning lyricist that he was a young Lil' Wayne in the making.

No Doubt left so pumped, he roared out the studio.

Whiskey and Ambrosia busted out laughin'.

"Remember when we in Cayman High back in the day, we used to get together with the Ballard brothers, some of them other cats from South Peola, and rock the mic on Saturdays at Da Juke Joint? So, c'mon, you already higher than a mufucka. Why don't you just step in the booth an' spit somethin' right quick?" Ambrosia said after a good laugh.

"Naw, I ain't free-styled in a while, you know. I ain't wit' all dat rap shit no mo'. I love listenin' to my Three 6 Mafia, my T.I., my Trick Daddy and shit, but I ain't 'bout ta step in nobody's booth, shawty."

"Okay, it's all good. Forget you then. Probably can't flow like you used to no how," Ambrosia said, taunting him.

"Aww, nigga, you a liar an' ya ass stink. You know I can still put it down if I wanna, but I just don't feel like it today. But I still got love for ya, though. C'mon, gimme a kiss," Whiskey said playfully.

"Yeah, your gay ass would say some shit like that, wouldn't you?" Ambrosia jokingly tapped Whiskey on the head. "Oh yeah, here take this. I almost forgot."

Whiskey stretched forth his hand to receive a personal check from his homie totaling thirteen thousand dollars and written out to Mr. Peter Battle.

"Ya know, Whiskey, when you took out Marcus Finbarr, you did a whole lotta folks a big favor, 'specially a lot of our soldiers on lockdown. So I'm gonna bless you with this as a thank-you from all of us to you."

"You didn't have to do dat, but shit, I ain't gonna turn down no money, dat's for damn sho." Whiskey folded the check between his meaty fingers.

"You ain't supposed to." Ambrosia poured three shot glasses of Gran Patrón Platinum for himself, his homie, and all his past homies. "Ahh, Patrón, the Cadillac of tequilas."

Whiskey took the glass of the high-end tequila and pounded it back in one gulp. "I was s'pose to be takin' care o' some otha bidness, but shit didn't go da way I thought it would at all. And a whole lotta cats was bankin' on me to take care o' dat work. It's a'ight though. You know how I do it—I don't quit 'til I finish da shit."

Ambrosia slowly leaned back in his custom-made Tony Montana-themed leather chair and smiled a toothy grin, swirling the glass of Patrón around in his diamond-encrusted ringed fingers.

He looked at Whiskey. "C'mon, Whiskey, why you tryin' to keep shit all hush-hush? This is me,

David, remember? We're boys, aren't we? Besides, I already know about your deal with a coupla renegade cops to Chief O'Malley. Ya know that I got contacts all across this mufucka. Son, what you think? Just 'cause I'm a white boy I can't be trusted or somethin'? Please . . . I got more hood in me than most brothas ever will have, an' you of all people know that. My late brother Lee was half black, remember, and my family grew up right outside Macon in a trailer park before moving here to West Peola. My mother was considered poor white trash by most people we knew. Even our stuck-up upper middle-class relatives disowned us because of my brother being bi-racial, and sometimes called my mom a nigga-lover to her face. It was me and my brother Lee who got out as teenagers and took our moms up outta that trailer park with hard work, both legal as well as illegal. So don't ever consider me nothing less than a brother from another mother to you, Whiskey, a'ight?"

"It's not you who I was concerned 'bout, David. It was your close bond wit' dat punk-ass O'Malley. You and dat mufucka seem to be pretty buddy-buddy an' shit last time I checked you. You even donated money to da police lodge. C'mon now, what was I s'posed ta think? It woulda been a conflict of interest tellin' you some shit like dat. Besides, it's a dirty game we're both playin' out here on dese streets. You really can't trust nobody. And trust me, no matter what you say, skin color does matter out dis bitch. Ain't shit changed since da old days. As a black man I got much mo' ta lose den you, pimp. You gotta feel me on dat one."

"True that, but I can help you, Whiskey."

Ambrosia leaned forward to pour his pal yet another glass of Patrón. "I have financial interests in the coke trade goin' down on Fuskie. Who in the game right now doesn't? Dudes realize that everybody can get a piece of the pie without killin' one another, which is just plain old good business sense. And now that you know that, you realize that just because I might pose for a picture or two with Mickey or attend an awards ceremony with the guy, it doesn't make me a fan or anything. That's just politics, a cover-up. Remember, Whiskey, always keep your enemies closer."

"Yeah, I guess ya right 'bout dat. Niggas do gotta switch dey game up every now and then."

Exhaling from the smooth heat of the tequila's trek down his throat, Ambrosia reclined into the leather seat and placed his half-empty glass down on the side of the mixing board. He touched his long pale fingers together as he settled into the leather and smiled at Whiskey from behind a pair of dark diamond-filled glasses.

"You're goddamned right, they should, 'cause it's just in everyone's best interests that we all consider doing business this way, that's all."

Taking yet another drink, he leaned forward. "So now that that's over with, how come you got Finbarr but not O'Malley? You did let certain people know that you'd have some of your homeboys handle the job, right? Well, why isn't he dead?"

" 'Cause incompetent Geechee niggas can't be depended on to do shit right, dat's why. And I couldn't get at him 'cause I happened to have come when dey was havin' dat Fuskie Day celebration. So cops was crawlin' all over da fuckin' place. A nigga

couldn't just bust caps off unda dem kinda circumstances, feel me? But, don't worry, he gonna get hit
sooner or later."

"I'll drink to that." Ambrosia swallowed his glass
of Patrón.

"Lemme walk wit some o' dat smoke, David."
Whiskey eyed the sandwich bag packed with large,
smelly marijuana buds lying next to the silver bong.

"Good shit, ain't it? It's purple haze. It has a THC
content of over eighty percent, real talk. I smoke
nothing but the best, you know that. But yeah, sure,
go ahead. Take it. It's all yours. Anyway, check it
out. We gotta get down to Fuskie tomorrow 'cause I
gotta meet with Snookey at the pen. He'll be glad to
see you, no doubt, and for more reasons than one
too." Ambrosia tossed the sealed bag of marijuana
toward Whiskey, who snatched it in mid-air as he
arose from his seat to leave.

"My nigga! What time tomorrow you tryin' to get
down dere?" Whiskey said, looking at the crystal
covering over the buds in the bag.

"Meet me here tomorrow at about noon. We'll
take my private jet to Hilton Head International and
then go by ferryboat from there. Got it?" Ambrosia
then poured another sip of Patrón before leaving.

"A'ight, white boy, I'll holla at you 'round noon
tomorrow." Whiskey smiled and tucked the smelly
marijuana into his pants pocket.

Bloody Point Beach Penitentiary stood amidst the
beige sand, driftwood, and deep blue surf of Daufuskie's largest beach like some old medieval castle
from a monster flick. Armed guards occupied the

towers above the prison yard, while others walked about stoically monitoring the daily activities of the large population of white-clad inmates. Who would think that these muscle-bound, tattoo-covered repeat offenders would give a fuck about CBS's *Pop Star* competition or *Billboard* top ten charts? Or getting rid of interfering police chiefs? No, these cats were more preoccupied with boosting their bench press or copping blowjobs from the prison's queers.

Both Whiskey and Ambrosia had done time before as juveniles, so the caged-animal atmosphere of B.P.B. prison was not unfamiliar to them.

As a long black limo pulled up to the tall wrought iron gates, the two young men emerged from the idling vehicle and entered the slowly opening gates. They were immediately searched and escorted into the facility by two heavyset guards. The guards followed closely with M-16's tightly gripped in their hands, ready for anything.

Once inside the lobby, Ambrosia nudged Whiskey and pointed to a small group of inmates sitting around a circular table near the far end of the room playing poker under a dangling ceiling lamp that illuminated every one of the card players' faces in the dim lobby.

As they approached the card table, everyone warmly embraced each other.

"My nigga. Hey, y'all, dis right here is my son, Whiskey, and my little homie, David, baddest mufuckin' cracka on dese streets right now." Snookey raised up and draped his powerful arms around Ambrosia and Whiskey.

The tall, muscular Marion "Snookey" Lake had packed on more than twenty-five pounds of muscle since he'd been imprisoned in 1994. Already a large man, he now looked absolutely colossal. Snookey was one of the most infamous street legends to come out of the Deep South, and was widely known for his ill-gotten wealth, voracious womanizing, and hair-trigger temper. It was rumored that the former New Orleans drug lord had murdered well over 175 people from 1983 to 1994, and according to his auto-biography, *Hate the Game, Not the Playa*, sixty-six by his own hand.

"Boy, c'mon here. Give ya pops a hug. I ain't seen yo' li'l ass in 'round 'bout, what, a year or mo'?"

"Naw, man, I seen you six months ago, Snookey. You done forgot already. C'mon, ya ain't dat damn old now."

"Six months? Dat's all? Well, when niggas on lock like us, we kinda forget shit somewhat, ya feel me?"

"So, Snookey, me and Whiskey tryin' to get down to some business, if you don't mind, 'cause we think you want to hear what we got goin' on." Ambrosia pulled up a chair near the wall and sat himself at the table amongst the hard-looking jailbirds, who eagerly awaited the white boy's speech.

A short, round fellow with horn-rimmed glasses and a neatly trimmed beard tapped his manicured nails incessantly against the top of the plastic folding table. He stood up and shook hands with both Whiskey and Ambrosia. "Gentlemen, I've heard many good things about you both. I'm Patrick Dutton. I do all of the computer troubleshooting around this joint. I'm sort of the prison techno geek, if you will."

Then a tall, distinguished-looking man of about fifty-four with a strong, square jawline, wavy salt-

and-pepper hair, and smooth, dark skin reached across the table over the cards to touch fists with the pair. "'S up? My name's Lawrence Tate, but these cats on the inside just call me Tate."

Whiskey knew from Ambrosia that Larry Tate was once a lieutenant on the LAPD who had gotten busted back in the eighties along with several other crooked cops who'd been found guilty of drug trafficking, money laundering, coercion, and murder, in cahoots with Colombian cartel boss, Sergio "Big Daddy" Mendez and his violent militia men. He now partnered up with the Lake Clan, running drugs throughout Bloody Point's west wing.

Next to the disgraced LA cop sat the leader of Daufuskie's Fuskie Krew, Joi Stevens, who pushed his chair back and embraced both men, especially Whiskey, with love. Tall, rangy, and nearly blue-black in complexion, he'd known both Whiskey and Ambrosia for many years, dealing narcotics and illegal firearms.

"Sup witcha, Joi?" Whiskey asked after embracing his imprisoned homie.

"Ain't shit. Just tryin' ta make dis money an' to get da fuck up outta da pen is all." Joi turned to Ambrosia and placed a stack of rubber band-wrapped bills in his hands.

Snookey pointed. "This is my man, Nicky. He's Joi's brother, as you probably already know, and this li'l skinny white boy right here is Peckawood. He is our own personal li'l snitch up here in da west wing, ya heard me?"

"I know all dese jailbirds, Snookey. I'm just ready ta get down ta some bidness here today, dang!"

Whiskey responded. "So can we cut all da reunion bullshit an' get started?"

Snookey Lake's face soured into a frown at the blunt words of his estranged son before he again resumed a calm, smiling demeanor.

"Yeah, Snookey, I agree wit' da kid. C'mon an' let's do dis," Joi said, " 'cause I can't wait to hear what dey talkin' 'bout."

Whiskey grabbed his chair and plopped down into it next to Ambrosia and Joi. Next to his old man Snookey, Peckawood and Nicky seated themselves simultaneously into the now crowded card table.

Correction officers stood guard over the impromptu business meeting, making sure that no one interfered or questioned the purpose of the gathering.

Snookey and the rest of the Lake Clan had the entire west wing on lock, buying protection and silence from the guards concerning their illicit in-house operations, and gaining special favors.

"Hey, look, we want y'all li'l mufuckas to know dat da C.O.'s ain't gonna bite cha, 'cause we break dese bitches off too damn good fo' dat hot shit. Ain't dat right, Marcus?"

The tall, wiry prison guard chuckled along with the wisecracking Snookey Lake and flipped him the middle finger all at the same time.

"Yeah, a'ight. It's like dat? Dat's why I'm gonna tell everybody dat you been suckin' on dis wood befo' you clock out every day, ya faggy-ass *beeaatch*!"

Everybody at the table busted out into raucous laughter at the kingpin's witty putdown of the broadly smiling guard, who continued to be peppered by the biting remarks of the suddenly jovial Snookey, who seemed to relish in the heavy laughter as well as the C.O.'s inability to counter his verbal assaults.

Then, just as suddenly as he'd begun the impromptu comedy session, he stopped dead silent, while the chuckling slowly died around him.

Staring directly at his seed and Ambrosia, Snookey spoke slowly, "Y'all makin' a li'l bit o' money back home, I heard. Been hearin' a whole lotta good shit 'bout y'all boys, 'specially Davey right here. Done gone an' got hisself a record label an' shit. I see some been learnin' a thing or two by watchin' da Snookey's hustle, huh. I'm proud o' ya, white boy. Now talk to me. What y'all got on ya mind?"

Ambrosia quickly dropped a tall stack of money upon the hard plastic tabletop and leaned his elbows forward on the table. "That right there is about, what, five grand? Yeah, five grand. That's my gift to da Lake Clan, especially you, Snookey, 'cause I wanna show you some love 'cause this one hustle is more important than any one deal you've ever closed."

Snookey leaned back into his chair, which was engulfed by his mammoth frame. He lit up a Salem cigarette and took a long drag on the menthol cancer stick. "Looka here, I know all about yo' hustle, da record sales, da singas and rappas, I know all o' dat shit." He exhaled a heavy cloud of smoke and stared at the youngsters through bloodshot eyes. "I know that you two didn't come down here to see us just fa GP, so lay it on us."

"Well, I'll just start off with thankin' y'all for gettin' with us today." Ambrosia smiled. "We've got a problem here on Daufuskie, as y'all already know. Whiskey came down here a li'l while ago to take care of O'Malley, but since it was during the time of the Daufuskie Day celebration, he couldn't peel his cap like he would've usually. But, of course, we're still gonna make sure that we get the job done 'cause O'Malley's costing all of us a lot of money, not just the Lake Clan."

The other inmates nodded in agreement with the white boy.

"So you all know that we gonna do da damn thing, but as they say, shit happens."

"Y'all betta, 'cuz we got over a million dollars worth o' coke s'posed ta be comin' in round 'bout December, so we don't need no mo' fuckups when it comes to gettin' rid o' this cop, period!" Joi said in a matter-of-fact manner.

"Ya know what, Joi? I feel your concern wit' da job bein' done correctly, I really do. But you know how I do shit. An' if you know dat, you know damn well dat don't nobody I set my sights on ta hit ever, ever get away. So you just remember dat befo' you come out at me wrong next time, playa," Whiskey said loud and clear.

Whiskey's sire flashed a broad grin that showed his diamond- and gold-encrusted teeth, in acknowledgment of his son's courage. "Dat's what da fuck I'm talkin' 'bout. Don't take shit off nobody, Whiskey, 'cause you's my son, an' I don't make no punks. But, for real though, it ain't hard to get O'Malley hit. I done got plenty o' cops touched back in da day when I was livin' in New Orleans. All I had to do was give a pipehead a coupla rocks, an' he or she would put dat pig ta sleep. So if y'all want help, in dat case it ain't nothin' but a phone call away."

Whiskey stared at his father unflinchingly. "I already got a coupla li'l hardheads ready ta put in work already, so I don't need nobody's fuckin' help."

"Yeah, okay. I'm tryin' ta help you out, li'l mufucka, 'cause you don't want just anybody doin' da job on a police chief. 'Cause, you betta believe, if you don't have a mufucka to take dat heat fo' you, you ain't never gonna see da light o' day again."

"Okay, now that is over with, obviously you cats got something or someone up your sleeve. Let's hear it," said an anxious David Ambrosia.

Whiskey shook his head. "Oh naw, David, ever since my methods been questioned an' shit, I wanna know how da Lake Clan can do a betta job at gettin' rid o' O'Malley. Dat's what I wanna know."

Joi lit up a cigarette. "Okay, bet. All we gotta do, for real, is to pay off one o' dese crooked cops on da island who work for the Daufuskie police department. I know a few o' dem dudes myself, an' dey got money tied up in dis cocaine bidness we runnin' from down in Miami. So work ain't gonna be hard."

"Yeah, I'm feelin' dat move mo' dan any other one," Snookey said. "Dat's what's up."

"Great. Let's get this cop on the payroll quick, 'cause we need this hit to happen now," Ambrosia said.

Peckawood said from the far end of the card table, near the wall, "Getting O'Malley hit ain't a problem, but murder-for-hire costs money, a lotta money. Now whoever we choose from the force to kill this sonofabitch is surely gonna cost us an arm an' a leg. Now I know for a fact the Lake Clan's gonna hold up their end of the cost, but how can we be certain that you guys are gonna be able to afford your part?"

David asked, "Y'all got enough paper to cover yo' end?"

"Look, y'all can pay some cop a shitload o' money to off dis cat, who just might snitch when it's all said an' done regardless, or y'all can pay me an' David sixty grand even, which we'll split 'tween us down da middle, an' I guarantee you da job will get done, 'cause dese dudes dat I use ain't nothin' but gutter-ass ex-cons who'd love nothin' more than to push a cop's wig back fa free. So you know what they'll do fa a coupla hundred dollars."

Ambrosia touched clenched fists with his friend in agreement. "I know you all feel Whiskey on this one. We all know that he's about his work, at least most of us at this table. Trust me, if this man says he's gonna do something, believe me, he's gonna."

Peckawood conversed softly with Lawrence Tuppince, as Ambrosia finished up his dialogue.

"Sixty gees is a whole lot just to kill some stupid cop, don't cha think?" Peckawood scoffed.

"Oh, yeah? Well, how much do you think dat police officer y'all thinkin' 'bout usin' woulda charged ya? I guarantee ya he'd go higher than sixty gran' to take his boss out. He'd probably hit y'all's pocket with anywhere from eighty-five to a hundred gran' easy, considerin' da stakes involved. I gotta take risks here my damn self, no matter who pulls da trigger. So da price stands at sixty thousand dollars, and dat's it and dat's all." Whiskey crossed his arms in front of him.

Joi snickered. "For sixty gran'? Shit, y'all betta bring back dat mufucka's dick and balls fa proof, dawg. You my man, Whiskey. You know you are, but hey, dis is bidness, and we gotta hire da best man fa da job 'cause niggas ain't payin' nobody dat kinda loot fa mistakes."

"Amen to dat, my brotha!" Snookey winked at Whiskey across the table. "I think fifteen thousand is more than enough. For sixty thousand dollars you'd betta kill da whole goddamned police force."

"Ya see, y'all mufuckas up here bullshittin', but as soon as Chief O'Malley gets the fundin' to beef up Fuskie's police department, y'all gonna be sittin' round' lookin' stupid 'cause he gonna put all o' dis big-ballin' shit y'all got goin' on down here to rest. Trust me, I know how dat Irish mufucka rolls," Whiskey said, his irritation growing. "'Specially you, Snookey, you know how hard O'Malley go. I know da connections y'all got down in Miami, Dade County, as well as y'all's Richmond, VA connects. Dem dudes ain't gonna keep fuckin' wit y'all if y'all let O'Malley make da block hot down here in Souf Cack. I damn well ain't tryin' ta blow over a million dollars worth o' Colombian flake comin' from Florida, nor a hundred gran' in heroin and crystal meth comin' down from Richmond an' Tidewater, VA. Dat's too much money to fuck up. Besides, da MS-13 already gettin' dey game plan together to cash in on dat money from Charlotte an' Orlando just as soon as O'Malley's drug task force shut down all dope operations down in da low

country. So y'all can sit here politickin' over nickels
an' dimes if ya want . . . 'cause, for real, in da long
run all o' y'all country-ass niggas gon' lose out
fuckin' wit' punk-ass Mickey O'Malley."

"Now that he's laid it to us like that, the kid just
might have a point there." Peckawood ran his pale,
thin fingers through his unkempt sandy brown hair.

Whiskey whispered with Ambrosia, while the inmates powwowed with each other at the table, trying to come to a final decision on the matter at hand.

"Look, y'all, I came here 'cause David asked me
to come. Either y'all dudes down, or you ain't, it's
dat simple. 'Cause I dunno 'bout David, but I got
better things to do than to hang around a jailhouse
all day long."

Snookey took one final drag off the cigarette before smashing it down into an ashtray beside him.
He cleared his throat to speak, his gaze fixed upon
both Ambrosia and his son. "A'ight, since you so
sho dat you can murk O'Malley's fat ass, we gonna
foot da bill dat you askin' 'cause I got too much
money tied up wit' my Florida and Virginia connects to let dis cracka fuck it up. You absolutely
right 'bout dat shit. But dis ain't a job fa no standin'-
on-da-corner, wannabe gangsta punks or no half-
baked, braindead dope addict neither. Dis shit gotta
be done right, and it gotta be done quick . . . 'cause
you my son and I fucks wit' you. But I ain't toler-
atin' no fuckups from you or nobody else, you understand? You either get da job done or don't even
go there, 'cause we ain't givin' you sixty thousand
dollars for nothin'.'"

"Look, guys, Whiskey is not only my friend, but
he's a pro when it comes to killin' cats. He's

disposed of quite a few rats, rivals, and overdue customers for me during the past several years, so I know what this guy is capable of. Trust me, your money will be well spent." Ambrosia looked over toward Whiskey, who sat back in his seat with his beefy arms folded across his chest and winked, all the while smiling confidently.

Lawrence Tuppince shrugged his shoulders and nodded his head in agreement with the other convicts at the table.

"A'ight then, you got yaself a deal, boy." Snookey shuffled the deck of playing cards in his hand.

The lanky corrections officer stood silent, except for a slight smile creasing the corners of his broad mouth when Peckawood eased a hundred-dollar bill into his back pocket as he kept watch over the illicit dealings.

"Hey, David, 's up wit' cha girl, Godiva? Word on da street is, since she been blowin' up on dat TV show, *Pop Star*, you been takin' notice. *Entertainment Tonight* last week aired a segment about da *Pop Star* finale, sayin' you was gonna sign her on to a contract after da competition. If so, I wanna piece o' dat action, 'cause da bitch can sing her ass off and she got star quality. I need to invest some o' dis dirty money in some good ol' clean bidness. Why not da music bidness?" Snookey asked.

Ambrosia laughed briefly. "Yeah, she's the hottest thing next to Beyoncé right now, and she hasn't even won the final competition on *Pop Star* yet. I was surprised that no other producer had signed the chick. But, hey, their loss is definitely my gain. And to answer your question, I totally would want to be partners with you in this music venture."

"Godiva? Music? C'mon, Snookey, quit playin', dawg. We got shit locked down with our dope hustle. Why da fuck we need ta put our money into R&B shit? Who da fuck you think you is? Berry Gordy?" Joi shook a cigarette into his palm from a newly opened pack.

"See, dat's da shit I'm talkin' 'bout. Y'all ghetto-ass mufuckas don't know shit 'bout no real bidness. All y'all know 'bout is how ta sling rocks an' then buy up a shitload o' whips, spinnin' rims, and gold chains an' shit. Ya know what da Italians I used to fuck wit' call dat? *Nigga rich*—Yeah, dat's what dem mafia boys used to say. Whenever dey saw one o' us step outta pimped-out truck with gold 'round dey necks and stylish clothes on, dem Italian crackas would bust out laughin'. Ya wanna know why?" Snookey asked. " 'Cause everybody know niggas love ta buy shit, but they don't invest in shit. 'Cept niggas who know da rules o' da game like me. Ya see, money launderin' is da backbone o' da game. If you ain't got a legit hustle ta hide ya dirty money behind as a smokescreen, you's one dumb mufucka. An' it can't be no obvious shit either. Laundromats, liquor stores, and car dealerships, da feds jump on dem joints like stink on shit, 'cause everybody done bought one o' dem in da hood. Even fast-food joints is hot nowadays, but if you put up money in some big-time classy shit like a five-star restaurant, or a fancy hotel on a resort island, or in dis case a nationally known record label dat's 'bout ta sign da next singin' sensation ta come along since Aaliyah, and she's a white girl too. Who in dey right mind gonna think dat a bunch o' dope-hustlin' cons down in a

Souf Cackalack pen is funnelin' drugs behind the scenes?"

Peckawood glanced at the still unsure Gullah prisoner, while leaning over to speak. "Joi, ya gotta consider this, man. We'd always have money comin' in, even if our drug spots get busted or we lose connects on the outside. David's got a nation-ally recognized record label that makes stars outta average singers and rappers, and now he's about to sign Godiva O'Sullivan. Shit, man, that gal's gonna take the fuckin' industry by storm, you just watch. Hell, she's on every television show and commer-cial now, not to mention hearin' just about every last one of her songs on the radio. And this kid hasn't even won the *Pop Star* competition yet. C'mon, Joi, we can't look a gift horse in the mouth, for Christ sakes!"

"Whatever."

"Anyway, I know my pops is familiar wit' da For-rester girls from Hilton Head. Them two bitches will murk dey own mama if da price is right, and dey top-flight when it comes to puttin' heads to bed. So get at me wit' da cash no later than August eleventh, an' we'll do da damn thang. It's July twenty-eighth right now, so time's a-wastin'."

"Sounds like a plan to me." Snookey raised up from his chair to embrace the two young men, and his fellow inmates followed suit.

Snookey walked his two visitors over toward the guards waiting at the exit door of the visitors' cen-ter. "So what y'all li'l hardheads 'bout ta get into once y'all leave here?"

"Shit, I dunno what David gonna do, but I'm gonna go clubbin' out at da Sand Dollar Lounge tonight. I heard T-Pain, Akon, and Young Jeezy gonna bring mo' bitches than a little bit out dat joint. I needs ta get my dick wet, so somebody's daughter gon' git stuck tonight."

"Well, as for me, I gotta meet with a few music executives in Manhattan tomorrow morning around nine. Then I gotta get back to Peola to take care of some paperwork and fly out around midnight or so. Unlike some people, some of us gotta really work for a living." Ambrosia jokingly nudged his friend.

Snookey strolled out toward the awaiting limousine with the two young men before stopping at the gate's entrance. "A'ight, handle ya bidness, ya heard me? Act like you know," he said, as the great iron gates slowly closed behind the departing visitors.

Chapter 8

"Big Dough"

A wind of change on August 29, 2005, a monstrous Category 5 hurricane dubbed Katrina, slammed into New Orleans with the force of a hellish sledgehammer, flooding up to eighty percent of the Crescent City with a devastating deluge and transforming it into a modern-day Atlantis that took away the lives of over a thousand residents, not to mention breaching several levees and causing $81.2 billion in damages, making it one of the greatest natural disasters in modern US history. Hurricane Katrina, which ranked as the sixth strongest hurricane on record, had the local residents scrambling for higher ground, including entire families stranded on rooftops, trees, and cars for a week or more.

The New Orleans Superdome became a haven for both the vulnerable as well as the predatory during the extended neglect from President Bush and FEMA, while looting and violent crime became so widespread that the National Guard and law enforcement officers from Louisiana as well as the rest of the US were brought into the city to restore law and order as the Red Cross went about their rescue and recovery business.

Mickey O'Malley immediately shifted his attention from the drug trafficking woes of Beaufort County's low country to the hurricane and crime-ravaged streets of New Orleans. On September 14, Chief O'Malley along with thirty of Peola, Georgia's finest officers arrived in the city for an extensive tour of duty. In his absence, lead detective, Courtney O'Malley, thirty-five-year-old daughter of the police chief, was appointed, to the dismay and irritation of many a veteran Peola beat cop. They'd considered their chief's act of nepotism unfair to the elder high-ranking officers who'd served on the department much longer than the attractive Harvard-educated youngster.

Singleton Beach was one of Whiskey's favorite hangout spots whenever he was visiting the Sea Islands. There the music tended to be upbeat, the food scrumptious, and the women willing and wanton. He enjoyed the festive atmosphere of the beach at night, particularly when the management hosted a special event such as the popular Beach Fest concert, which drew hundreds of low country youths of all ethnicities. As usual he'd paid for VIP tickets for the two-and-a-half-hour celebration.

As he enjoyed the final performance of the night by UGK from the back of the bar, a hulky Filipino-looking bodyguard approached and informed him that Godiva, who'd performed earlier to a standing ovation, wanted to have a drink or two with him backstage in her dressing room. After downing a tall glass of Rémy Martin on the rocks, he raised up off of the barstool on which he sat and followed the bodyguard through the dense crowd of young adults dancing barefoot upon the sandy beach, several huge bonfires burning brightly in the background all around them. He was ushered into a long blue-and-white RV, where the lovely, long-haired blonde sat cross-legged upon a leather couch, swirling a glass of champagne in her hand.

"Peter Battle, right? It's a pleasure to finally meet you. David talks about you all the time, so I decided to sorta introduce myself to you personally tonight after he told me you'd be here. So, would you like a drink? 'Cause there's plenty here." She giggled lightly before sipping her champagne.

"Yeah, that's what's up. I'll take a glass o' Moet, and please call me Whiskey, okay?" He pulled up a seat against the wall, beside the table that was laden with liquor bottles.

"Oh, my bad. Whiskey, you know what . . . have we met somewhere before? You look really familiar."

"Yeah, you used to strip at da Strokers Club up in ATL. A couple o' years ago you was da only white girl who stripped for 'em. Shit, I remember you used ta be one o' da top girls in da Strokers Club. Ya used ta be my favorite, dat's fa damn sho. I used ta drop a couple o' hunit on you alone. I ain't never had a lap dance like da ones you'd give a nigga."

She smiled broadly. "That's where I remember you from. You were the big baller who was always tryin' to get into my pants," she said, her voice slurring a bit from intoxication. "But, hey, you definitely weren't the only guy tryin' to fuck me, though. I'd say, I got hit on after every show. In fact, all the girls got propositioned by the customers. It just goes with the territory, I guess. Some of the girls would take a customer up on a sex-for-hire offer if the price was right. I even know a girl who had one particular customer pay her rent and her way through college. I never did have sex with customers, though, no matter how much money or how hot a guy looked. Stripping for me was strictly business. Besides, I heard more than a few horror stories about dates gone bad with customers."

"I feel you. But I coulda got you even wit'out givin' up no paper, 'cause I know you was feelin' a nigga fa sho. I almost had you twice, but you always backed out at da last minute, talkin' 'bout how you was already in a relationship, or some other bullshit story. You know you wanted me." Whiskey took a drink from the glass of bubbly he'd just poured for himself. "You lucky you my man's girl or else you'd be in real trouble wit' a pussyhound like me."

"Is that so? Well, guess what . . . David and I are engaged, yes, but married, no. Besides, I don't think you could handle li'l ol' me anyway, *Whiskey*."

"I'm gonna take that as the alcohol talkin'." Whiskey admired the songbird's shapely legs, which she seductively crossed and uncrossed periodically during their conversation. " 'Cause I know, and you do too, dat you talkin' crazy, don't you?"

During their discussion she noticed Whiskey checking out her bare legs and decided to give him a brief glimpse of her bushy blonde pubic hair, reminiscent of a Sharon Stone scene in the movie *Basic Instinct*.

Whiskey finished up the last swallow of champagne before filling his wine glass with more of the pricey booze and moving across the room beside Godiva.

"I was wondering how long it would take you to sit down next to me. I guess the fact that I'm not wearing any panties does the trick, huh?" She stared at him with a beckoning glint to her baby blue eyes. "You used to try really, really hard to get me in bed with you back in my Strokers Club days. Who knows, tonight you just might get your wish."

"A part of me wanna go dere wit' cha, but then again, wit' you bein' engaged to David, I dunno if I kin do dat. But I gotta tell ya, I'm a man first, and you makin' it real hard for me to get up and go outta dat do' wit'out puttin' dis dick up in you. I ain't lyin'."

"David? Gimme a break. Even though we're engaged, our relationship is more of a business arrangement than anything else. He met me two years ago when I was dancing nude at the Strokers Club, just as you and hundreds of other men over the years. Except, during the time we got to know each other, he discovered my talent as a singer, and with the *Pop Star* competition promising me a record deal after the grand finale, he is a great manager, a wonderful friend. Sure, I love David with all of my heart, but our sex life totally sucks. He's always on the go. New York on Monday, LA on Tuesday, and God knows where during the rest of the week. Tell me, do you think for one single minute that a young, hot-looking guy like David is not sleeping around on me during those many weeks away from me? Yeah, right! He's probably got a slut or two in every city just waiting for him whenever he arrives. I wasn't born yesterday, ya know. We might have sex twice a month, if am lucky. Besides, I like black guys in the sack anyway. My daughter's daddy is black, and nothing fills me up like a long, thick, beautiful, black cock. And you know what? I really think he knows that, deep down inside. He knows I have sexual needs that he's not meeting, so I feel that he'd rather have his best friend fuck me rather than me sleep with a stranger or groupie."

Whiskey licked his full lips, his wood stiffening within his boxers. "So what's up? You ain't gotta talk no mo'. I'm convinced, or sold, or whatever da fuck you wanna call it. I'm tryin' to scratch dat itch ya got, feel me?" He brushed away her golden locks from her soft neck, nibbling along its length, and kneading her large breasts delicately in his thick hands.

"Oh yeah. Don't stop. I want to feel you inside me."

Whiskey quickly removed his lengthy, heavily veined, uncircumcised member from within his jean shorts and drove it deep within Godiva's hot pink snatch, causing the blonde bombshell to gasp with pleasure as she wrapped her curly legs around his waist.

"Take dis big black dick. Ride it like you want it. Ride da dick, baby, ride it!"

"Oh my god, you're so fuckin' big. You're a stud, baby. Oh good god, yeah. Don't stop! It feels sooo good!"

"Oh fuck! Dat's what I'm talkin' 'bout. Fuck me back, baby. Put ya back into it!" He grunted, thrusting with primal gusto, causing Godiva to squeal out in sexual bliss as her body quivered through multiple orgasms.

Whiskey withdrew his penis from Godiva's sticky, wet pussy to shoot a heavy load of creamy, white goblets onto her abdomen and boobs.

Afterwards the two lovers cuddled together, sweaty and naked on the cum-stained couch, sipping on champagne, and listening to the festivities on the beach beyond.

Robbie Stevens, the younger brother of the incarcerated Joi, and Nicky resided on Wild Horse Road, in an old, weather-beaten mobile home that stood alone against a dense forest of tall pine trees and the rusty ruins of junked cars. The neighborhood was Spanish Wells, a predominantly black section of Hilton Head, known as "Da Wells" by drug-dealing thugs and addicts. Several snot-nosed brats romped about among the broken-down rust buckets as a scrawny, mixed-breed coon dog ran behind them, barking and playfully nipping at their heels as they zigzagged back and forth.

Whiskey exited his Jeep Cherokee and walked up the rickety steps and through the flimsy screen door to loudly announce his presence. Nicky emerged from the back, bare-chested and with blunt in hand to greet Whiskey.

"My nigga, 's up wit' cha, boy?"

"Ain't shit. I see you all back up in da cut and shit wit' cha li'l daycare."

"Aw, nigga, fuck you. You know fa sho all dem mufuckin' chillen ain't hardly mine. Just dese two right here, an' dat's all."

"A'ight, damn. Shit, I dunno, y'all Geechee niggas, like President Bush, don't believe in pullin' da fuck out."

"Keep talkin' shit and I'm-a tell ya mama she gon' have ta work a extra two hours on da ho stroll tonight."

Whiskey chuckled at Nicky's quick comeback and vowed to launch a counterattack when he least expected it.

Stepping through the threshold of the trailer, Nicky turned toward Whiskey and offered him the blunt as they entered.

"I know ya stankin' ass wanna hit dis mufucka, don't cha? Well, puff on it wit' caution, shawty, 'cause dis dat Sea Island funk, baby. Only thoroughbred niggas kin take dis shit."

Whiskey flashed his Gullah homie a quick smirk and snatched the blunt from his calloused outstretched hand.

Inside, cheap wicker-wood furniture stood out within the drab, musty interior of the mobile home. Broken toys littered the living room floor, along with several doggie chew bones and a big bag of bacon-flavored Alpo. The kitchen was untidy, smelled of stale malt liquor, and was dark, with the exception of the glowing red numbers displayed on the microwave.

"Damn, nigga! Don't you ever clean up dis raggedy mufucka?"

"I don't live here. Dis my baby-mama crib and shit. She da triflin' one, not me. I'm just over here to make sure everything is straight, while she make a run out to Savannah to pick up her sister." Nicky took a puff on the blunt again.

"Dat's some good shit, Nicky. Y'all da only dudes I know who got da bomb-ass homegrown bud. You gon' gimme a couple ounces o' dis Geechee weed to sell back home in Peola, a'ight? How much ya want for three ounces o' dis shit?"

"For you, lemme see . . . I'll let cha have five ounces for seven fifty. You a'ight wit' dat?" Nicky handed Whiskey the smoking roach. "Follow me to the bedroom. It's in da closet back here. Then I want you to meet my man Bubby. He lives over yonder cross da road a ways. He represent da Fuskie Krew, just like me. He also pushin' weight. Matter o' fact, he move mo' bricks 'round here den anybody."

Whiskey followed Nicky through the untidy living room, down the narrow hall, and into the cramped and humid back room. Not wanting to go any further, he stood at the doorway, while Nicky trudged through a smelly assortment of dirty laundry before opening the closet door and lifting a hefty sandwich bag filled with marijuana from between pairs of sneakers and patent leather pumps from the top shelf.

Like a gray flash, a cat suddenly raced from beneath the bed and through Whiskey's legs, momentarily startling the two men.

After Whiskey purchased the cannabis, the two young men hopped in Whiskey's Jeep and drove seven houses up the dirt road and pulled up into the cobblestone driveway of an impressive triple-wide mobile home that seemed more mini-mansion than high-end trailer.

The two friends were greeted at the door by Bubby, a handsome, narrow-faced gentleman in his fifties. He welcomed the guests into the spacious living room, which bore a sweet aroma of pink grapefruit potpourri, Floetry playing softly in the background.

Two highly attractive women sat upon the beautiful crushed velvet couch smiling broadly, periodically stepping to sniff the thin, neatly placed lines of white powder on a glass plate before them.

"You must be Whiskey. How you doin'? C'mon and have a seat. Y'all want some blow?" Bubby asked as his young guests sat down on the luxurious couch beside the smiling beauties.

Nicky took his host up on his offer and wasted little time joining the giggling girls in snorting up several lines of coke.

Whiskey said, "I'm good. Thanks anyway. My man Nicky tells me dat you rep Fuskie. You gotta be an OG. How long you been runnin' wit da Krew?"

"Shit, I'd say, I've been down wit' da Krew since seventy or seventy-one."

"Dat's wassup." Whiskey pounded fists with the older gangsta. "I been fuckin' wit' da Krew for a minute now, and dem boys like my family, know what I'm sayin'? Like family."

Bubby smiled slightly. "Nicky told me dat y'all go way back. Dat's good to know, 'cause anybody who's a friend of Nicky is a friend o' mine, and I don't have many. But da ones I do have, believe me, dey benefit from the association . . . greatly." Bubby bent down to snort a line with a tightly rolled hundred-dollar bill. "You down here for a while or what?"

"Naw, I'll be outta here by tonight or early tomorrow morning. I just came down to visit my pops, dat's all."

"Dat's what a son is s'ppose to do, ain't dat right, girls?"

The women both responded with a simultaneous, "Yes," smiling all the while with toothy grins.

"Ya see my girls Latrice and Mercedes over there? Dey some kinda fine, ain't dey? Dey been takin' care o' big daddy since two thousand, an' if you look 'roun' here at dis place I got, I'd say dese pretty gals is doin' a fairly good job at it, don't ya think?"

"Fa sho." Whiskey glanced over at the girls.

Mercedes winked an eye at him. "C'mon, sit down an' party wit' us, y'all. We can't possibly toot all o' dis powda by ourselves, now can we?"

"I gotta tell ya, I don't do coke. My mama was a coke addict, ya see. Flake, rocks, it didn't matter to her none, long as she got high. She'd rather chase dat white horse dan feed her own chillen. If it wasn't for my sister, LaTasha, we'd probably starve to death. I might drink like a fish and smoke hella weed, but I don't do no hard dope 'cause I seen what kinda damage it done to my mama. So now I just sell da shit, an' dat's it."

After a brief, awkward silence Mercedes, the more outspoken of the two girls, cleared her throat while dividing a small heap of cocaine with a playing card. "I'm so sorry, baby. We didn't know. I hope we didn't offend you. I apologize for everybody, boo, believe dat."

Whiskey slowly shuffled the deck of cards, focusing on her bulging cleavage as much as her apologetic words. "You ain't gotta apologize for nothin', sweetheart. Once we all get grown, we got da free will to do whatever. So please don't feel sorry 'bout da situation, 'cause she did it to herself."

Latrice sniffed a pinch of coke from a tiny spoon. "You ain't lyin'. We all reap what we sow, dat's for damn sure."

Nicky brought up the question of money. "Looka here, Bubby, remember dat crystal meth deal back in April when I drove a shitload o' dat product to Raleigh, North Carolina to close it with dem white boys up dere? Ya know, you only paid me eight hunit. When is you gonna pay me da rest o' da twelve hunit you owe me?"

"C'mon, Nicky, we've been through dis song an' dance befo', young man. I explained to you dat eight hundred would be da final and only payment fo' dat particular deal 'cause dat client only paid for that single delivery. Plus, you know as well as I do dat we don't do bidness wit' dem folks no mo', right. So don't ask me 'bout dat shit no mo', Nicky, okay?"

Whiskey noticed how uncomfortable Nicky looked behind Bubby's response, yet the Gullah youth did little afterward, except sit between the girls and look dejected and saddened.

Latrice placed a bejeweled hand upon Nicky's cheek and stroked his stubbly jaw slowly. "It's okay, baby, you know Bubby will make sure he takes care o' you. Don't he always?"

"Yeah, suga. Besides, you run all da coke bidness from Hilton Head all da way to Charleston for Big Daddy, don't cha? And whenever he make a big score, you know da first person he gonna call on ta go get dat paper."

Whiskey sprinkled a twenty-dollar bag of cannabis into the empty husk of a Dutch Masters cigar he'd just opened and folded it into a perfectly rolled blunt before licking the loose ends shut.

"I heard that you pretty good friends wit' Godiva, Whiskey. She was hangin' out wit' me an' da girls backstage after her concert at the Savannah Civic Center. She gets all o' her coke and weed from da Krew. She also mentioned how bad she wanna win dat competition, 'cause dat'll put her on da map. But she knows dat she'll need da votes o' da black community to help her out 'cause all o' da black folk is gonna place dey votes fa Gina Madison. In return, she say she gonna look out fa us country-ass ballers, ya feelin' me?"

"It's funny how white folks come callin' niggas when dey need favors, ain't it?" Whiskey answered Bubby through a cloud of exhaled marijuana smoke and noticed his smile cut upon hearing his answer. "Yeah, I know all 'bout Godiva. Matter o' fact, I remember when da bitch used to strip at da Strokers Club in Atlanta. I know all 'bout her big ambitions to be dat next Kelly Clarkson or Gwen Stefani. But tell me dis—Why should we help her? Why are you gonna go out on a limb to help dis white girl? How is it gonna benefit da niggas in da hood down here in da low bottom o' Souf Cack an' Georgia?"

"A'ight, bet. First off, I think I know Godiva just as well as you do, and guess what—I might even know a few things 'bout her dat you don't, such as her friendship wit' O'Malley's daughter, Courtney. Those two are so close, if you didn't know any better, you'd swear that that they were dykes. But wit' da boys in da hood helpin' out Godiva in her music career, she has already promised to put a bug o' two in her girl's ear to back off da hustlas down here and back home in Peola. Ya man David probably forgot to tell you that da IRS tryin' ta get at 'im fa tax evasion an' some mo' legal shit. Snookey done told David dat he'd use his team o' lawyers to handle his case and pay off Uncle Sam for 'im, which should be finalized by da end of dis December. But after da IRS trial is over, Davey boy gonna have to start over from scratch, and in order for him to get back up on his feet, he gonna need a whole lotta seed money, ya feel me? A whole lotta seed money and a hot artist to put Spanish Moss Records back on da map."

"Just like dat, huh? We help ol' girl win some dumb li'l televised contest, and dat karaoke will make everything all better, huh? Yeah, right."

"It don't matter none whether you believe me or not, 'cause da plan gonna go forward regardless. Yeah, you and me both couldn't give a flyin' fuck 'bout da goddam *Pop Star* competition, but plenty o' mufuckas do and a whole lot of 'em ain't nuttin' but a bunch o' kids. Kids wit' money all across dese United States who gonna buy up a shitload o' Godiva records once she wins dis contest over Gina Madison, which Snookey and dem already got locked down."

"I don't mean no harm or disrespect, but how da fuck you know Snookey gonna pay for all o' dis shit?"

"C'mon now, ain't you Snookey's son an' shit? You already know how Snookey do when it comes to bidness. Shit, half o' dem li'l rap niggas David got signed have relatives locked up down in Bloody Point Beach Penitentiary. Who you think put in da word to David to get dem li'l niggas inked to a contract?"

Whiskey steadily puffed on the blunt with a sense of nonchalance. "Dat's all good, Mr. Bubby, but how can you be so sho dat Godiva gon' live up to her part o' da bargain once she gets a record deal? After we big her up an' all, she sho as hell gon' blow up. Big time. Then where does dat leave us? Maybe back at da drawin' board, 'cause she ain't gonna need ya black asses no mo', ya feel me?"

"Dat ho know betta den dat. Shit, she ain't dat stupid." Latrice giggled.

"You know Godiva is Mayor Lattimore's niece an' Detective O'Malley's homegirl. Now Lattimore stays buyin' up coke from Peola's ballas from South Side, so he gonna get in da police chief's ear 'bout all o' dat hot police surveillance bullshit if Godiva say so. And she will, trust me. Godiva want this music career mo' den anything else. She already got CBS pullin' in a mufuckin' eighty-eight percent rating each an' every Friday dat da *Pop Star* show comes on. She knows she's on her way to much bigga an' betta things . . . if she gets da votes from all da black folks watchin' da show on Fridays. An' guess what, da niggas in dese country-ass ghettos gonna be her savior, 'cause wit'out dem makin' mufuckas call into the television studio, she might not beat Gina Madison, 'cause Gina's black, an' she knows dis. Godiva gonna win, and when she win da competition, we all know she gonna blow da fuck up. Bigger den Beyoncé, Britney Spears, Gwen Stefani, all o' dem otha bitches. She gonna do what the fuck da hood tell her to do, and dat's real talk."

"Shit, Godiva might look innocent to her fans an'

dem celebrity judges, but dat li'l white bitch ain't nuttin' but a ho, for real. She done fucked most every rapper in Atlanta. Shit, she fuckin' ATL Slim right now, unbeknownst to David Ambrosia. Or maybe he know da shit but don't give a fuck." Mercedes snorted yet another long line of powder up her left nostril. "ATL Slim ain't the only one layin' pipe in her ass. I heard she give da goodies ta No Doubt's li'l young ass too. Guess she just can't get enough o' dat black dick."

Whiskey looked over toward Nicky, who was still visibly upset over Bubby's nonpayment. "Thanks for all o' da hospitality an' everything, but I gotta say one thing. I think dat it was fucked-up dat Nicky ain't got da money you owed him. He a betta man den me 'cause I'd o' done something 'bout it, not just sit here an' pout like a li'l bitch. Anyway, it's been a pleasure meetin' y'all." He got up from the couch amidst the hard stares of Bubby and his two mistresses.

"A'ight, Nick, I'm out. Catch you outside in the whip whenever you get done in here." Whiskey flipped Bubby his middle finger as he exited the fancy furnished trailer.

"Yeah, it's been real nice meetin' you too, smart ass."

When Nicky exited the mobile home and got into Whiskey's Jeep, he was immediately accosted by his homeboy, who was thoroughly disgusted by his embarrassing display in the presence of Bubby.

As they drove away from Bubby Smith's property, Whiskey began to formulate within his mind how he'd get Nicky's overdue money.

* * *

On September 17, 2005, the wind and rain was coming down in great blustery sheets, obviously the remnants of Hurricane Katrina. It was 12:48 AM on Hilton Head Island on a night not fit for man or beast. Whiskey sat in his Jeep Cherokee bobbing his head to an old mix tape of Snoop Dog and Master P while he applied a pair of black leather gloves to his thick hands and slid on a dark ski mask. The steady stream of rain pelted the Jeep like a million tiny drumbeats, causing snaking rivulets to cascade down the front and rear windshields. He removed a metallic blue SIG-Sauer P220 .38 caliber double-action semiautomatic from the drawer and admired the beauty of the powerful handgun as it glistened beneath the street lamps in his gloved palm. He then took the ten-round magazine filled with hollow-tip shells and slowly but firmly shoved it into place within the handle of the pistol.

Turning the key slowly, the engine of the Cherokee revved with the powerful peals of thunder that followed the bright flashes of lightning, its angry electrical fingers zigzagging hither and thither and illuminating the night sky.

Once along the road leading to Smith's cobblestone driveway, Whiskey saw, through the swift sweeping movement of the wiper blades against the blurry windshield, a single light glowing a yellowish white from the living room. It seemed to him that perhaps the trio were yet still up and at it. Grasping the weapon and tucking it down into his waistband, Whiskey exited the dry comfort of his Jeep's cabin and emerged out into the chilly, driving rain of the late-night thunderstorm.

With no guard dogs to worry about, the black-clad gunman sprinted across the cobblestone driveway and past the parked sports cars and artistically sculpted hedges with the ease of a shadow. Once on the porch, he took a moment to remove the rain-soaked ski mask from his head and shook his long braids free of excess moisture. Then he wrung the knit hat free from water and stuffed it into the back pocket of his loose-fitting jeans, figuring that he would have little use for it. He peered through the transparent flower-printed cloth of the lime-colored curtains and saw the naked bodies of the three lovers mingled together in a steamy embrace of lust-filled moans and rhythmic gyrations, seductive jazz melodies bumping in the background.

Steadying himself, Whiskey kicked in the door, which fell inward with a hollow metallic crash and sent the nude women screaming with terror behind the long, lean frame of their sugar daddy, who sat in wide-eyed shock as the gun-wielding home invader burst atop the fallen front door and into the living room. Without speaking, Whiskey squeezed the trigger and blasted away at the nude man sitting before him. Bright crimson splotches of gore splashed against the paisley-print wallpaper as several slugs tore through Bubby Smith's chest and abdomen, causing him to flop awkwardly face first on the plush carpet below.

While the dead hustler's blood seeped out into the khaki-colored fabric and spread beneath the corpse in a sickly purplish red circle, Whiskey continued on his murderous rampage by permanently silencing the two screaming women with multiple gunshots to their heads and upper body. The heavy peals of thunder and the downpour made the sound of gunshots inaudible, not to mention that no one in their right mind would dare venture out during a thunderstorm of such a fearsome magnitude as this one.

After he dispatched of the three, he took his time combing through the interior of the well-furnished home in search of drugs and money.

After a twenty-minute scavenger hunt through the various rooms, Whiskey returned to his vehicle soaked but with a plastic trash bag bearing several sandwich bags filled with marijuana, as well as four ki's of Colombian cocaine and over $224,000 in cash. He double-bagged the contents and couldn't help but smile broadly as he checked out the goods.

Bubby was, in his estimation, an egotistical blowhard who had really done little to further the cause of the Fuskie Krew and seemed to care only about himself and his live-in tramps. No one would particularly miss his presence, and the police investigation that would begin within a day or so would end up going nowhere fast, due to the hood's unspoken code of silence when it came to cooperating with the boys in blue. Besides, he'd committed the murders during a driving rainstorm at the dead of night, and since he wasn't a citizen of the island, he would be miles away across state lines by the time the local cops launched their investigation. Nicky would be given the money owed him, and Whiskey would take the rest of the spoils with him back to Peola, where the real work would begin.

* * *

Three days later Whiskey treated several of his friends to a party at the level VIP room of the 95 South nightc. September 20, a night dubbed "Sexiest er Showdown III," a much ballyhooed event tha rew standing room-only crowds of booze-guzzling, cat-calling country boys intent on seeing an erotic pa-rade of naked female flesh. While his homies from around the way enjoyed the risqué entertainment, Whiskey calmly sat at the bar and sipped on a glass of Grey Goose and cranberry juice, joking around with the bartender and laughing at the hilarious antics of the drunks in the audience acting a fool over the shapely dancers.

Unlike most others, Whiskey rarely, if ever, felt any connection with a murder he'd committed or any remorse for the victim or victims after it was over. He'd witnessed violent death since his early teens. He himself had once shot a Pakistani taxi dri-ver in the face for calling his mother a whore and he was only thirteen. Scared straight programs, anger management counseling, church, and juvenile deten-tion halls did little to sway the young thug from be-coming South Peola's most lethal enforcer.

Whiskey swallowed down the remaining vodka and cranberry juice before sliding the empty glass to the side and picking up the newly prepared glass before him. He and the friendly old bespectacled bartender discussed the upcoming final competi-tion of *Pop Star* pitting soulful diva Gina Madison against the surprising young songstress, Godiva. The men at the bar acknowledged that Madison's popularity within the black community throughout

..ıe country would continue to serve her well, as it had from day one, and that the sex appeal of the blonde bombshell could easily score a major upset at the end of the night.

Ironically, as nearly a dozen exotic dancers took center stage all at once, each girl stepping forward under the dazzling spotlights to display their unique individual moves to the raucous approval of the men, and a multitude of greenbacks tossed at their feet, Godiva's sultry rendition of Mtume's "Juicy Fruit" came blasting through the massive wall speakers.

Just then someone tapped Whiskey on the shoulder.

Whiskey turned to see the smooth, handsome face of Paul Ballard. "'S up, shawty?" He got up and embraced his childhood friend. "So you up in da club checkin' out da hoes, huh, pimp?"

"*Ssshhhheeetttt*, nigga, mufuck dese skank-ass bitches. I'm up in here ta holla at you, my dude."

"Is that right? A'ight, you got da flo'. Talk to a nigga, pimpin'."

Paul instructed the attentive bartender to serve him up a stiff shot of straight Southern Comfort on the rocks and lit up a cigarette.

"You smokin' Salems again? Back in '02 you was on dem Marlboros hard. What happen? Dese joints better for you or somethin'?"

"Eat a fat dick, nigga." Paul handed the bartender a crisp twenty-dollar bill for a tall ice-filled glass of liquor. "Naw, when I was locked up in Akron, almost all o' da peeps in da pen smoked Marlboro, so I ain't had no otha choice. But once I got on da outside, I left dem joints alone."

"Why?"

" 'Cause dem mufuckas too damn harsh, dat's why."

Whiskey smiled and nodded in agreement. "I feel ya. If ya gon' kill ya lungs, shit, kill 'em softly. Ain't dat right?"

The young men shared a brief laugh then touched glasses in an impromptu toast to their long friendship.

"So you goin' to da telly wit' one o' dese tricks later on?"

Whiskey gulped his vodka and smiled slightly as he looked out over to the stage down below on the nude women writhing before the frenzied male mob. "Nope, I ain't pressed fa no ass, but I'ma probably buy some pussy fa a coupla my li'l homies just ta show dem dudes some big homie love, ya heard me?"

Paul twirled his glass around gently as he gazed into it.

"C'mon, son, why you actin' all weird an' shit? You said you wanted to holla at me, right? A'ight den, speak on it, baby."

"True, true. You know dat big-money Bubby Smith got shot right?"

"Naw, son. You bullshittin', right?"

"Whiskey, c'mon now. I might joke around 'bout a lotta things, but when it comes down to talkin' 'bout da death of a boss playa like Bubby, I don't bullshit."

"A'ight, da nigga dead. An'? Dat's what happens in da game. People get kilt. Dat's life. I ain't really know 'im like dat no way."

Paul slowly slipped a swallow of his drink and turned around on his stool to watch the strippers.

"I only met dude like one time when I was down Hilton Head, but otha den dat, like I said, I ain't really know 'im too good."

Paul finished the Southern Comfort in one hard swallow then called out to the bartender for another glass.

Whiskey also asked the bartender for another round of booze, tipping the old man nicely in the process. "When did he die?"

"Three days ago, dey tell me. Dem boys down in da low bottom say somebody jacked his ass up in his crib, punished him and his two bitches, shot dem people multiple times an' ransacked da place lookin' fa shit. Dey musta found it too, 'cause all o' his money and dope was missin' when da po-po found 'em."

"Fa real? Damn, somebody musta really wanted him dead. Dat's why you gotta watch da kinda niggas you let up in da crib. You can't trust everybody, ya know."

"True dat, but you know as well as I do dat news travel fast on the streets. 'Specially down dey in low-bottom Souf Cack, niggas talk."

Whiskey calmly took his fresh glass of Goose, staring steely-eyed at Paul. "So what you sayin', Paul? Please tell me 'cause . . . sounds to me like you beatin' round da bush an' shit. Spit it out, nigga. Say what you came up in dis mufucka to say."

"You know dude was one o' dem Fuskie Krew niggas, right? You know he was one o' da most top-earnin' OGs down in the low bottom, right?"

"So what da fuck? He ain't nobody to me. Shit, I could give a fuck less if somebody kilt dat nigga's whole mufuckin' family, dawg! And why is you comin' at me wit' dis dumb shit? What you think, I had something to do wit' dat bitch-ass nigga? I know betta den dat, Paul. You got me fucked up, shawty. Whoever givin' you ya info, tell 'em ta come see me, a'ight. You tell 'em dat."

"C'mon, son, calm yo' ass down. I ain't sayin' shit 'cause, fa real, just like you, I don't give a fuck. How long we been knowin' each otha, Whiskey, huh? Since the third grade an' shit, right. C'mon, I always gotcha back—Don't you ever forget that shit either, ya heard me? But ya boy Nicky Stevens down dey spendin' up some shit like he just won da Beaufort County lotto or somethin', flossin' ice, pushin' a fresh new whip, an' some mo' shit. When asked 'bout his sudden long paper, he hollerin' 'bout how one o' his homies from Georgia peeled Bubby's cap back. So guess what, ya man mus' not be so used ta gettin' money like he just got, 'cause he sho nuff on some ol' hot shit, runnin' his mouf like an ol' bitch. Now feds an' everybody else payin' attention to his big-mouf ass. As you know, we here in South Peola been bootin' up wit' da Fuskie Krew for years now. Dem boys is our bidness partnas an' our peeps. Shit, Bubby might o' been a bitch, but he still a Fuskie OG, dawg. We can't let dat news get back to Joi 'bout who actually murked his homie, 'cause if it does, den you know dem Geechee boys gonna do all dey can to get back at da killas. Not only would he lose an important bidness partna, but you betta believe dere gon' be a interstate war in the street. Now I dunno 'bout you, but I ain't tryin' ta go back ta da days o' da ol' drug wars we used to have wit' da Jamaican posses when we ran wit' da Wreckin' Crew back in Souf Peola."

"Okay, you got me. I guess you just can't trust everybody, no matter how well you might *think* you know 'em—dumb-ass Geechee nigga."

"Yeah, you damn skippy. You of all people should know betta, Whiskey. Ya see, we been ballin' outta control since we been thirteen and fourteen, so we used ta havin' big dough. So we know how ta act when we get a big sco', but niggas who only used ta gettin' short money don't know how ta handle da big time, so dey make da block hot when dey do get dey hands on some real money."

"Yeah, you're right, Paul. I let my guard down, thinkin' dat I was helpin' a friend get what he rightfully deserved. It's all good, though. I'll slow his roll, all right."

After a few more stiff drinks, the well-buzzed pair returned to the lighter conversation of the *Pop Star* competition.

"Everybody know Godiva gonna win it all. She younger and prettier than Gina Madison. I mean, I like Gina's singin' style betta, but hey, I'd rather fuck Godiva though. I heard ATL Slim used ta hit dat all da time. Matter o' fact, he s'pose ta have an old underground mix tape wit' a single on it called 'White Girl,' where he talk 'bout how much he used ta fuck her. I betcha she got some good pussy. Whatcha think, Whiskey?"

"Oh fa sho. She built like a sista, so you know she got it goin' on in da fuck-a-nigga-real-good department."

While clearing the counter of empty glasses and coasters, the bartender chimed in, "Shit, I sho wish I could find out fa myself."

"Yeah, a whole lotta cats in da rap game either done hit dat or tryin' dey damnest to hit it befo' she gets married. Then again as a housewife, I s'pose." Paul smashed the smouldering butt of the cigarette into a glass ashtray.

"Godiva's fine an' all, but so is Alicia Keys and Beyoncé. Shit, you know you'd cross land an' mufuckin' sea to get either one o' dem dime pieces. Tell me you wouldn't."

"True dat, true dat, but I'm on some ol' jungle-fever-type shit in my life right about now, feel me?" Paul said.

"Hey, do you, my nigga. Sounds to me like you been listenin' to too much o' dat ATL Slim single. What's it called?—'White Girl,' or some shit?"

Paul nodded. "Yo' daddy Snookey claims Godiva's his nephew's baby mama an' dat her real name is Brandi Welsh, is dat right?"

"Yeah, she got a daughter by my cousin Rae-Kwan, an' yes, her name is Brandi Welsh. Most o' da old hands who ran wit' my pops an' dem back in da day remember Brandi. She just look a li'l different now 'cause she let her hair grow down to her ass. Dat's why she calls herself Godiva . . . 'cause o' her extra-long hair. I used ta go an' see her strip back when she danced at da Strokers Club in Atlanta," Whiskey said.

"Oh! So she was a stripper, eh? I thought so. 'Cause there's a hook in da song 'White Girl' dat start off like,

'a nigga stay flippin', trippin' and dippin',
makin' dudes sick from da fuckin' lyrics he spit-
  tin',
but check it, life got 'em vexed 'cause his bitch,
  she be strippin'.' "

"He musta seen her perform at da Strokers Club too. C'mon, it's one o' da most popular strip clubs in da South, if not da whole damn country, an' trust me, Godiva, or Lady Godiva as she was known on da stripper stage, was probably da only white broad strippin' at da Strokers Club. And she was, in my opinion, one of the most popular an' well-liked dancers in da whole joint, so it's easy for one of several dozen mufuckas to have laid eyes on her before." Whiskey handed the bartender forty dollars, buying a round of mixed drinks for them both.

"I fucks with ATL Slim though 'cause, not only can son flow, but he stays baggin' only da baddest bitches, dawg. Now dat's pimpology fah ya ass, ya heard?"

"Damn, nigga, hop off his dick fa once." Whiskey took a sip from his glass. "Of course, if you got a three-and-a-half-million-dollar record deal and puttin' out a new rap video every otha day, females gon' flock to you like moths to a flame. It's all a part o' da game."

"Yeah, but Godiva ain't just any ol' no-name groupie. She's a star in da makin'."

"Shawty, ya man ATL Slim a bitch, fa real. My pops used to be locked up wit' 'im befo' he got transferred outta Bloody Point Beach Penitentiary to anotha prison somewhere else.

"He hood an' everything, representin' Atlanta

pretty good. He used to run wit' a gang called da Krazy Kountry Kripz, KKK, but when he called tryin' ta punk Snookey, he got dat ass whupped, damn near kilt, for real. So all o' dat shit he be spittin' on dem mix tapes, he ain't all thug, nor is da mufucka no playa like he say he is. So what, he got lucky an' fucked anotha celebrity. Dat ain't no real big feat or nothin'. Shit, I done had plenty o' famous chicks suck and fuck, an' I ain't no rappa or singa neither."

"Whiskey, man, you hatin' like shit, dawg. Give da nigga some props, man, c'mon."

"I just did. I said he was hood, but I ain't gonna suck his dick either. You talkin' 'bout dis dude like he God's gift to bitches or somethin'. Now dat right dere is some gay shit."

"Yeah, you hatin', bro. You sho nuff drinkin' dat *haterade*, ain't cha?" Paul slurred slightly from the deepening effect of the alcohol. Then he grinned. "Fuckin' a bitch like Godiva is a big plus fa a nigga's image. Ya see, it'll take you further along in da rap game. 'Specially fuckin' wit' a white bitch. Dat's just life. Why you think all da NFL and NBA stars got deyself a white woman on dey arm? 'Cause dey know she 'bout like a livin' Diners Club card or some shit. Hell, go back in ya history books an' check out Jack Johnson, America's first black boxin' champ. Shit, he was way ahead o' his time, 'cause he practically lived in white pussy. An' he ain't give a fuck 'bout what da white man thought 'bout it, 'cause couldn't no cracka whup his ass. And whenever he was in public or at home, he was strapped wit' da heat, ready fa any redneck feelin' lucky. Plus, he had money to burn, so mufuckas couldn't tell 'im shit. All dey could do was hate on 'im, and dat was 'round da early nineteen hunits. Now dat's what cha call *bossin' up*."

"Paul, you drunk, ain't cha?" Whiskey chuckled, then cleared his throat. "Godiva ain't trippin' off dat fake-ass wannabe trick daddy she engaged to. David Ambrosia a top-level record executive an' shit, so she might o' gave him a li'l bit o' ass back when she was strippin'. So what? And lemme tell ya somethin', Paul—At da end o' da day, a black woman gon' be da one ta have yo' back, nigga, don't you forget dat. Tonight dat liquor's talkin', but it's all right. I know you got mo' sense than dat."

Chapter 9

"We Own These Streets"

By October 1, Whiskey had a seventeen-year-old high-school dropout named Derek Myers pushing dope for him in both Hemlock Hills as well as the Badlands Manor projects. Paul Ballard had introduced Whiskey to a few crooked cops who would see to it that Whiskey's young drug courier would be able to sell his illegal wares without interference from other policemen or competing dealers along heavily trafficked strips of South Peola's drug-infested neighborhoods. They would also monitor his daily earnings, making sure that there'd be no underhand money or drug skimming, which often occurred whenever there was little or no supervision of the runners, particularly if they were of a tender age.

At 1:31 PM, Whiskey took the Peola commuter rail toward South Peola's Driftwood Station. By this time Derek Myers would be sittin' on the hood of his candy-apple red '65 Ford Mustang serving freshly cooked vials of beige-colored rocks to two, sometimes three, clients at a time as they stood in a winding line that stretched for nearly a block and a half, waiting to purchase their packages of fleeting baking soda-based nirvana.

Even though Whiskey frequented South Peola for business purposes, he had since lost the urge to mingle with the neighborhood thugs he'd grown up with. Most were a sorry bunch of losers who did little with their lives beside getting into trouble with the law and populating the surrounding projects with illegitimate children. A few others permanently crippled due to past involvement in gang warfare spent their days lounging around local pool halls, liquor stores, and barbershops, spinning colorful tales about gang banging experiences, all the while bumming loose change or cigarettes from anyone who'd give a listen.

Yet, the popular Hemlock Hills area barbershop, known to the folks in the hood as Eddie's, wasn't just a place to go to get a fresh shape-up or argue sports, but it served a slightly darker purpose as well. Edward Anderson, owner of the establishment, often used the shop as a front for a highly lucrative heroin and weapons ring that served all of South Peola and much of neighboring Savannah. Eddie also made a comfortable living as a loan shark, his ruthless techniques of punishing delinquent clients earning him the grim title, *Bonecrusher*.

Whiskey often ended up at Eddie's to have his beard trimmed neat and his silky hair taken out and freshly re-braided by Eddie's sister and co-owner,

Ramona Anderson. Today was just that kind of a day for him to pay Eddie's a visit.

After he'd gotten his beard trimmed and hair braided, he met with Eddie downstairs in the shop's supply room to pay for a shipment of a dozen Israeli-made AK-47's and around $6,000 worth of heroin. He had just recently made a connection with a death metal guitarist from Savannah, by way of Orlando, who along with his band mates was big on smack. The AKs would be the weapon of choice in the Mickey O'Malley hit, which had yet to be organized properly.

The visit to his old South Peola stomping ground would end as it usually did—with him stopping past the 1300 block of Fenris and Pelco Streets to collect his weekly pay from Derek. The teenager as always had done exceptionally well that week, serving the blocks of Hemlock Hills and Badlands Manor a wide assortment of the best dope in town.

After presenting his personal courier as well as the kid's police overseers their portion of the drug money, Whiskey boarded the subway train with a plastic shopping bag filled with several stacks of rubber band-bound bills totaling $27,000, which he would take back home to place into a fire-resistant lockbox.

Around 6:30 PM he left his sister's home to meet up with a realtor to have dinner and a few drinks at Big Mama's Place as they went over paperwork and photos of several West Peola area homes he might be interested in purchasing.

Basically, Whiskey had lived with his sister and nephews for the better part of two years, and though he and Tasha got along well, with the exception of her distaste for his choice of friends and baller lifestyle, he never wanted his involvement in the game to touch his family the way his father's drug dealing had claimed the life of his half-sister Dawn and his newborn nephew years ago. He knew that because he was so deep into the game that he'd have no choice but to distance himself in order to protect his sister and her kids.

Whiskey slowly flipped through the glossy printouts, intently staring at the lovely houses situated in several of West Peola's wealthiest communities.

As the middle-aged real estate broker rambled on and on in between bits of grilled swordfish steaks and sips of Parisian Chardonnay about the fine architecture and historical value of each house displayed on the photographs, along with the high-end amenities available in each, Whiskey feigned attentiveness to her, her words coming across as little more than vague babble. His heart was set on anything near the water, a lakeside rambler, a cozy beach house, or even a modest country cottage beside a woodland stream or lily-covered pond.

He quickly finished up his meal and assured his broker that he'd make his final decision by month's end as to which property he'd be buying and to begin the tedious process of signing the necessary legal paperwork.

From the time he'd arrived at the restaurant, and all through the meeting, his cell phone buzzed nonstop upon his waist. His two cop partners were attempting to speak with him about hooking up at Point Polite to talk business. (Point Polite was a popular park for nature enthusiasts, summertime picnics, and rich young lovers planning to make out in the backseat of the phantom.)

It was late, around midnight or so, when Whiskey pulled his Cherokee up beside the two police cruisers parked adjacent to the dark, silent picnic area and basketball court. He didn't trust cops and felt somewhat uneasy when he stepped out into the cool, breezy, autumn night to greet the boys in blue.

Hank Columbus was a wide, barrel-chested white boy with a square jaw, deep-set blue eyes, and a short-cropped military-style buzz cut. He spoke with a deep Southern drawl and couldn't have been much older than twenty-seven.

Maurice Tolliver was a six foot five former college basketball star who played shooting guard for the North Carolina Tar Heels. Born of Trinidadian parents, the deep-voiced, handsomely dark Tolliver had an eye for fashionable clothing and an obsession with grooming.

The two beat partners were like the odd couple, with Columbus enjoying all the niceties of redneck entertainment such as Monster Truck shows, NASCAR racing, and deer hunting, while the more refined Tolliver felt more at home flying out to New York to take in a Broadway show in Manhattan or playing a couple of holes of golf down on Hilton Head with members of his country club. There was one thing, however, that both men liked in common—illegal money, and lots of it.

"Well, well, look who's here finally. She musta been a pretty damn good fuck, 'cause we done called ya 'round 'bout a dozen times or so, I'd say. So did ya get your rocks off or what? You ol' horndawg, you," Columbus said in his heavy Southern drawl. "Then again don't answer that, bro, 'cause I haven't cheated on my old lady for a whole week and she's on the goddamn rag, for cryin' out loud. If I don't fuck something soon, I'm gonna have a bad case of blue balls. Say, ya think that hot sister of yours would be up for givin' a young studly white boy a shot o' ass?" he said, laughing out loud before spitting out a nasty, brown loogie as he chewed steadily on a plug of sun-cured tobacco.

Whiskey smiled broadly and flipped the cop the bird. "How 'bout you huggin' on dese nuts like ya mama done last night?"

The three men laughed at each other's expense for a few minutes longer. Then their conversation turned to business as they enjoyed a blunt that Maurice Tolliver had taken from the glove compartment of his police cruiser. Weed always seemed to be the perfect companion for any underworld business meeting, helping to sort of break the ice, particularly in uneasy contacts like this one.

"Ya boy Derek been ballin' outta control. I'll give 'im that much. He musta pulled in thirty-three gees just last month alone, but now that you've got the smack, I still think that you've got to have a tail on him, 'cause number one, this is too big of a deal to trust the boy, even Derek. Number two, he'll need protection just in case these cats wanna play hard ball an' the transactions goes south. So I'll make that ride down to Savannah to drop off the stuff to the metal heads, got it?" Maurice leaned up against his cruiser, his arms folded across his chest.

"He'll ride wit' Maurice in a unmarked car right after our duty shift is over 'round 'bout six in da

evening. Think he'll be ready ta go by then?"
Columbus took the blunt from his partner. " 'Cause
that kid's slower than winter molasses sometimes,
an' I don't know 'bout Maurice, but I ain't got no
time for 'im ta be draggin' ass tomorrow."

"He'll be ready, trust me. He been pretty reliable
fa me so far, an' dis'll be da first time he get ta go out
from Peola, since you been busy wit' Hemlock Hills
and worryin' 'bout Chief O'Malley's actions on
Fuskie."

Whiskey turned to meet Alonzo halfway along
the sidewalk. "Son, if you know so fuckin' much
'bout some dude steppin' on my toes out Badlands
Manor, why you ain't do nothin' 'bout it?"

"I *am* doin' somethin' 'bout it. I'm tellin' you
'bout da shit right now, ain't I? I got my own hustle
I'm handlin', but I got my ears to da streets all da
time, so I hear things, ya know? 'Specially things
dat need ta be heard. So now dat you know what
need ta be done, you just need ta make dese cats respect ya, gangsta. It's just that simple."

Whiskey shook his head in frustration as he
looked up toward the fading warm golden light of
the autumn Georgia sky. "I'm gettin' real tired of all
o' dis dumb shit, dawg. It's just aggravation as a
mufucka. Now I'm gon' have ta go out an' murk another mufucka 'cause niggas wanna violate an' shit.
Damn!"

"Calm down, Whiskey. You fucks wit' Hank and
dem, right? Well, let da police handle ya dirty work
fa ya. Ain't dat what ya payin' fa?"

"You got a point there. Dat would be a good look, though."

"You goddamned right, it'll be a good look. Why do you put yaself in unnecessary situations when you don't have to?"

"I'm gonna have ta get Hank's redneck ass ta do da job 'cause Maurice took Derek down to Savannah to drop off some heroin to some new customers o' mine. I don't like dat mufuckin' Hank too much, though. He too damn sarcastic for me. Talk shit too much. Makes me wanna punch him in the fuckin' face. But I guess he'll have to do for now," Whiskey said with disdain.

"Just think of it as bidness and bidness only, an' you'll be fine."

"Tell me some more 'bout dis Burt character, 'cause I ain't never heard 'bout him befo'."

"Like I said, all I know 'bout dude is dat he goes by da name Burt or Berk. I think it was Burt, though. He s'pose ta be up north, Newark, New Jersey, some say. He got a li'l crew pimpin' dat diesel an' shit out on da block from sunup to sundown, but it ain't nothin' da police can't handle."

"Ya know what? I'm gonna call Hank's hillbilly ass up in a minute so we can run up on this nigga tonight, catch his punk ass sleepin'."

"Tonight's as good a time as any to murk a mufucka. You can't miss 'im. My sources tell me he pushin' a hot pink Range Rover an' he's always wearin' pink camoflauge hoodies and whatnot. So he can't be too hard to find out on da block. Plus, he be lettin' his li'l dope boys rock da pink too. I dunno, he's from Jersey, so he must think he's Cam'ron an' shit, huh?"

"Yeah, he probably do think he's Killa Cam. Too bad I'm gonna have ta wet his pink outfit all up." Whiskey checked the number of a call that had just come in on his Nextel. "I gotta go, dawg. Got some bidness to tend to, a'ight. I catch you a li'l later on."

"A'ight, bet, but a footnote 'bout my man Burt. Word on da street is, he's an informant fa Mickey O'Malley. Seems like ol' boy got a li'l bit suspicious 'bout da activities of several of his officers, 'specially da ones assigned to South Peola or, as Peola police department calls it, da 'Red Sector.' Some of O'Malley's top aides even know 'bout Burt's dope hustle, but they'd rather look da otha way when it comes to dirt on his own men, know what I mean?"

"Sonofabitch! So this nigga's eatin' from every angle, huh? Yeah, Alonzo, you right, somethin's gotta be done 'bout dis mufucka. An' quick!"

The brothers spoke for a brief time before driving away in different directions and with different objectives in mind.

By the time Whiskey arrived at Eddie's Barbershop in Hemlock Hills, it was around 9:45 P.M. Only Bonecrusher Eddie and Officer Hank Columbus were there, sitting back in separate barber chairs and laughing hysterically at the buffoonish antics of the skit characters on Comedy Central's *Chappelle's Show*.

Once he stepped foot into the dimly lit barbershop, it didn't take the two men long to show him why his presence was needed so quickly. The urgent phone call to him earlier had come from Bonecrusher Eddie.

Outside the shop, along the narrow trash-strewn alleyway, at the very end near the street corner, were the bloody, mutilated bodies of Burt "Jersey Boy" Johnston and three of his runners.

The two had pounced on the dope peddlers during the middle of the day, around noon or so, according to Officer Columbus, who puffed and passed a thick blunt among his partners. He and Bonecrusher Eddie related the details of the entire event, from the early-morning stakeout in an unmarked cruiser, leading up to the shakedown and arrests of the suspects, which ended with the subsequent murder of the four men and the gory dismemberment of their corpses.

Whiskey listened to the story as the cop and the loan shark accomplice worked in the old storage room, cleaning up the blood spatter, torn flesh, and bone shards that had been shattered wither and thither across the floor and walls by the blood-stained chainsaws that sat on top of a bloodied table that had clearly been used for the gruesome task.

The severed body parts were then meticulously placed into several large, heavy-duty garbage bags that were then tossed into the dumpster out back, from where it would be removed first thing the next morning and then driven some one hundred miles away to be taken by a tugboat-pulled barge, to finally end up far from civilization in a smelly seagull- and crow-infested landfill on Skidaway Island.

Chapter 10

"It Ain't Easy Being Gully"

"I-I don't know what to say. I'm like totally blown away right now. Thank you all so much for coming out and supporting me, especially all you guys at home who called in to vote for me. I love y'all. I thank God for giving me this gift. I want to thank the producers of *Pop Star*, the judges, and every single contestant who had the guts to come out and audition since January eighth up until now. You're all so very special to me. Wow! I want to thank and give congrats to Ms. Gina Madison for a wonderful final performance here tonight. Give it up for Gina, 'cause, girl, you ain't no runner-up. You're a bona fide star in the making, and with pipes like yours, you're well on your way to the very top.

"I'd also like to extend a very special thanks to

my new producer and fiancé, David Ambrosia. I love you, sweetheart. And I want to say thank you for my lovely little girl watching at home. I know you couldn't be here tonight, baby, but I want you to know that Mommy loves you. And Mommy did it, baby, Mommy did it."

Seventy-five thousand strong roared their approval as a stunningly beautiful Godiva, adorned in a radiant form-fitting silver and sea-green satin gown shimmering with rhinestone embroidery, hoisted the star-shaped crystal and platinum trophy above her head after receiving well-wishing embraces from the show's host, judges, and dozens of defeated contestants surrounding her.

As was expected Godiva had surpassed Gina Madison by a walloping 180,000 phone-in and text-message votes to Gina's laughable 97,000 call-ins. But the masses that tuned into CBS's Friday night grand finale of *Pop Star* would never know the inner workings that launched the former exotic dancer into the stratosphere of superstardom.

About four months earlier on June 1, the IRS began to really step up its investigation of David Ambrosia's multi-platinum record label's books for tax evasion and fraud, among other financial discrepancies.

"Whiskey, I gotta let ya know, the feds are coming down on me real hard, brotha. So hard that I gotta either pay back all of the overdue money that I owe that IRS or go to jail. And you know that I ain't tryin' to do that. So, while I get up the cash to satisfy Uncle Sam, I'm gonna need somebody to run the business, ya know, handle the day-to-day activities of operating a record label. You can handle that, can't you?"

Whiskey was hesitant at first but quickly accepted his friend's offer, which was more of a cry for help than anything else. "You know I'm good for it, son. I got you," he said with reassurance.

Yet, on this special night for America's newest singing sensation it wasn't her smiling, debonair multi-platinum producer fiancé who'd rendezvoused with her at her lavish suite on the sixty-sixth floor of Atlanta's towering Westin Hotel after leaving the festivities at the Georgia Dome. Instead, his homeboy Whiskey agreed to see the lovely singer safely to her hotel room, since David Ambrosia had to meet with a group of important multimedia executives in Miami, Florida early the following morning in order to secure a summertime tour date for his suddenly famous lady friend for 2006.

It was a quarter past midnight when the tipsy twosome entered the fancy hotel room, which would serve as their love nest for a few hours until dawn.

Godiva threw open the large indigo-colored curtains to reveal a bird's-eye view of nighttime Atlanta, whose city lights twinkled brightly for untold miles below like a million fireflies. She then tossed her white ermine stole onto a nearby chair and plopped onto the king-sized bed, beckoning Whiskey with her finger, a naughty come-hither look in her gorgeous blue eyes. "I am sooo fuckin' wasted. How 'bout you? Are you nearly as trashed as I am?"

"Think I ain't? I musta kilt a whole fifth o' Crown Royal all by myself on top o' dat Rémy, so ya know

I'm twisted like shit." Whiskey crawled onto the bed beside Godiva and took her into his arms affectionately.

"My ex-husband used to drink Scotch and water almost daily, but I couldn't stand the stuff. It tasted like paint thinner. It was fuckin' horrible. Maybe that's why we divorced."

"Naw, yo' ex-husband probably didn't know how ta tap dat ass right. Dat's why you had ta get rid o' his tired ass. Dat's what I think."

"Well, I will say one thing—Once you go black, you never go back. I'm one white girl that can attest to that one!"

Godiva's voice, though slightly slurred by a full night's worth of victory binge drinking, was still seductively sweet and breathy and had just enough of a Southern drawl to give a man an immediate hard-on. Whiskey always enjoyed Godiva's velvety singing voice even more than Beyoncé's or Alicia Keys, who were his favorite singers of all. The pop diva had surprisingly powerful range and depth for a voice as lifting and syrupy-sweet as hers. She had a unique almost uncanny way of taking someone's song, even from classy artists such as Bob Marley or Billie Holiday, and making it her own.

But now here in the privacy of a luxurious hotel room America's newly crowned sweetheart was taking turns sipping Cristal while cupping Whiskey's hairy testicles within her milky white fingers and slurping up and down upon Whiskey's shaft like it was an ebony sugar stick.

Whiskey palmed the top of Godiva's head as she slowly bobbed back and forth on his throbbing erection. He ran his strong, dark fingers through her silky golden blond mane as he threw his head back and groaned in ecstasy. He began thrusting himself forcefully into her pouting, red-painted lips. He felt his balls tighten with building semen and abruptly withdrew himself from his lover's mouth. He then moved around behind her, ripping off her white lace panties and aggressively shoving his meaty eight inches deep into her gaping pink slit.

"Ohh yeah! That's right, fuck me, baby. Fuck me hard with that big cock! I wanna feel you deep inside me. Yeah!! Oohh, yeahh, don't stop!!"

Whiskey had conflicting thoughts mingling inside his head as he pounded the pop singer from behind. A small part of him actually hated himself for betraying his lifelong friend. Had he been cheated on by any female he loved, she would have surely paid the ultimate price, along with her lover. There was little chance of him ever being a cuckold without seriously maiming or murdering the offending party. Yet, Godiva's ravishing beauty, delectable curves, and irresistible sex appeal had eclipsed any second thoughts he might have had of spurning her advances out of respect for his homie.

"Damn, you got some good-ass pussy, girl. Fuck! Keep it right dey. Ride dis big black dick. Dat's right, ride dis mufucka 'til I skeet off!"

The two intoxicated lovers moaned and groaned together in a sweaty, orgasm-filled hour and a half of intense, animal-like passion before collapsing exhausted in each other's embrace upon wrinkled sheets.

After waking up from a brief catnap, a slightly hungover Whiskey showered and left a soundly snoring Godiva behind at the hotel. Not to be caught by snooping paparazzi, who would surely be waiting by the tens of dozens for Godiva to emerge from the Westin by the time the autumn sun peeked across the Atlanta skyline, he hopped into his whip at 4:57 AM and headed back to Peola.

It was almost ten when he pulled up into the driveway of his sister's North Peola townhouse. He entered the picket-fence home from the side and made his way down into the basement, which served as his personal space. His sister had long gone off to work, and his young nephews were by this time on a bus and on their way to school.

Before he could even get into the room and situate himself properly, his Nextel began buzzing loudly on his hip. It was the cops, Hank and Maurice, urging him to meet up with them at Big Mama's restaurant for a sit-down.

Whiskey showed up at the restaurant a little over an hour after the phone call feeling a bit grouchy from a night of boozing and marathon sex. The cops were seated at the far end of the crowded diner next to a large window, from where the Madison freeway with its bustling early-morning traffic could be seen and heard in the distance.

Whiskey took a seat at the table amongst the chuckling policemen, who carried on about the transvestite streetwalkers they'd busted the night before. With obvious disinterest in the ongoing dialogue, he ordered a cup of strong black coffee.

"Listen up, fellas, I know y'all ain't called me to talk 'bout a bunch o' fags y'all locked up. 'Cause, if so, I'm gon' drink my cup o' joe and I'm out da do'!"

"Calm down, calm down. We was just talkin' cop talk, that's all." Officer Columbus smiled brightly.

"You look like hell, man. Musta been one heck of a party last night, huh?" Columbus nudged Tolliver, and winked at Whiskey in an effort to pry the details of his adventure from him.

"I didn't know I was being interrogated dis mornin'." Whiskey took the porcelain cup of steaming hot coffee from the waitress.

"Naw, just fuckin' with you, that's all. Seriously though, we got a bit of a problem down on Hilton Head. A problem that if not handled ASAP could ruin the whole Chief O'Malley hit thing we've all worked so hard to put together." Tolliver placed a collection of photos down on the table in front of Whiskey. "Seems like this cat in the da pictures done gone an' bumped his gums to way too many folks down in da low country," the redneck cop drawled lazily. "Nicholas Stevens, a.k.a. Nicky, has been down there spending money like water since mid-September, sayin' that you broke him off proper-like after you killed a certain Bubby Smith, who was obviously the head honcho down there or somethin', I s'pose. This kid's been tellin' people how you killed this douche bag an' then basically burglarized his house afterward. Did you know 'bout that?"

Seeing the fury in the enforcer's tired bloodshot eyes, he shook his head and shrugged his broad shoulders.

"Hey, I feel ya pain, bro, but what can I say? Ya just can't trust everybody wit' a whole lotta cash, not even ya friends."

Whiskey slumped back into his chair and stared up at the slowly whirling ceiling fans above, exhaling a loud breath of disbelief and disappointment.

Then he leaned forward, placing his beefy forearms upon the table, and stared at the police officers, who sat staring back silently from their respective seats.

"Y'all know what? I gave dat fool every bit o' da twelve hunit mufuckin' dollas he was cryin' 'bout. Chump change! Then, to make it worse, I murked dis nigga Bubby fa two reasons and two reasons only. One, 'cause Nicky's my homie, ya know, or so I thought, and two, 'cause dude was just a li'l too stuck on himelf. And I can't stand dudes like dat. So, I goes over dis cat's house and he not only owed da boy money from a previous dope deal but he refused ta pay my man his bread. Plus, he disrespected 'im da whole fuckin' time in front o' me and his two hoes. So I took his ass out." Whiskey looked around the surrounding room to detect any eavesdropping on the part of the other patrons on the outside of their private booth.

Officer Columbus cleared his throat and smiled broadly. "Listen, Whiskey, I'm just as pissed-off about the situation as you are, but look, you got to keep ya voice down, okay. We in a restaurant, remember. But there's more. According to one of our contacts down in Hilton Head, he—Nicky I'm talking about now—was recently arrested outside of Bluffton, South Carolina for a simple DUI violation, but this idiot had a little over five thousand dollars worth of crack cocaine in the vehicle when they pulled him over.

"When they realized that ya so-called homie knew something about the September seventeenth triple homicide of Bubby Smith, Latrice Barton, and Mercedes Nolan, they took him in for questioning because, for the past few weeks since the murders, the Beaufort County sheriff's department been strugglin' to come up with clues to nail the dope man's killer. My sources tell us that he's being held in a Beaufort jail awaiting trial at the county court-house on January fourteenth of next year. I don't need to tell you that he's already copped a plea deal to rat you and everybody else out 'cause those back-water cops down there don't really give a flyin' fuck about some drug dealer gettin' offed. They see it all the time, and frankly they feel like those Geechees are doin' everybody a huge favor, really. But now that Chief O'Malley has been hippin' the depart-ments down there to the connections and delivery routes of the true movers and shakers of the dope game from Daufuskie Island all the way to Atlanta and Miami, having this guy take the witness stand in '08 would be disastrous, to say the least, for everyone concerned. And I do mean everyone. So regardless of how you may feel about this guy as a friend, he's got to be eliminated, period. I can't ex-press to you the severity of this situation, feel me? I know that he's your friend from way back an' all, but hey, he's damn sure not thinking about you or your freedom at this point, right. Hell, if saving his own ass means bringing down his friends and busi-ness partners for a lighter sentence, a new identity, and a big pay-off, then so be it. I know it, and so do you. So with that said, I know that there's no other choice but to stop this kid from testifying against us in January. It's just that simple."

"Yeah, dude, we gotta get rid o' dis asshole, Whiskey. There's no other way," Maurice said.

Whiskey slowly but angrily flipped through the dozen or more photographs showing Nicholas

Stevens in various stages of discussion with under-cover officers in reference to the Bubby Smith mur-der, also known down in the low country as the Hurricane Katrina killings. Feeling the bitter sting of betrayal, a wave of revenge overtook him.

By the time the three men got up from the their booth, it was already decided that Nicholas "Nicky" Stevens would become yet another victim of the brutal backroads of the dirty, dirty South.

Chapter 11

"You Rat, You Die"

All too often criminals seem to forget the unspoken but ironclad rules of the game when reaping the benefits from the ill-famed trade. Unfortunately, such negligence of the laws of the mean streets brought to an end the career of many a hustler by way of a prison cell or a coffin.

At 11:16 AM on the morning of November 2, 2005, Nicholas Jared Stevens was found dead in his jail cell. The cause of death couldn't be immediately determined. Since he'd been housed in a private cell with the Beaufort County jailhouse, no other inmate could be blamed for his death, and with a twenty-four-hour police vigil, it was perplexing to the county sheriff's department how a perfectly healthy prisoner in his twenties could simply up and die on them out of the blue. A heart attack, maybe? Not likely. A stroke, perhaps?

Forty-eight hours later an autopsy on Nicky

Stevens had confirmed that he'd been poisoned by an extremely lethal agent in either his food or drink the night before his untimely demise. This new revelation following the sudden passing of the county's most talked-about prisoner brought much unwanted press to the Beaufort County sheriff's department, which now had more than their share of questions to answer in the wake of this most embarrassing incident.

As the breaking news program interrupted a Thursday night college football battle between Palmetto State rivals, South Carolina and Clemson, Whiskey turned from tapping away at this computer to see his sister LaTasha descending the stairwell leading down to his basement apartment.

"What ya doin' down here, boy? Chattin' online wit' ya li'l cyber hoochies?"

"Naw, just checkin' out some o' dese houses my real estate agent e-mailed to me. I'm tryin' to decide which one I wanna get, 'cause dey all look nice, know what I mean?"

"Shit, if I were you, I'd take one o' dem beachfront homes, I guess, 'cause Mama used to take us to the beach every summer back in da day. Remember? We used to run up and down da boardwalk, bury each other in da sand."

"Yeah, an' get stung by dem fuckin' big-ass jellyfish."

"Whatever. You just couldn't sit ya li'l fast butt down and play in da sand. You had to wander off deep into da water. Shit, it's a wonder a shark didn't swim off wit' you." LaTasha leaned over her brother's shoulder to take in the photos on the computer screen. "You heard on da news 'bout Nicky

Stevens gettin' poisoned, right?" She pulled up a swivel chair next to him.

"Hell, yeah. It's all over da news on every channel, even cable. Dat's real fucked-up, 'cause dat nigga was my son right dere. Know what I'm sayin'?"

"Yeah, I was pretty tight wit' 'im myself. I went to school with his sisters Tammy and Angela. I know one brother locked up for God knows how long, and now the other brother's dead. Dat's too much. Dat's why I keep tellin' you and dat hard-headed-ass Alonzo ta leave dem li'l hoodlum niggas alone.

"Just last week Friday I had ta get Peaches mind right, call herself goin' out da do' on a date wit' some li'l thug who pulled up in front o' da house beepin' his horn and whatnot. *Sheeeeit*, I waited good 'til she grabbed dem keys off da table, and I calmly walked myself right outside with her and introduced myself to mister man before I politely bid his fake Ja Rule-lookin' ass good night. See, maybe next time he'll have better manners for da next young lady he take out on a date. As for my daughter, he can chalk dat one up as a loss cause he ain't welcome here no mo'.

"See, most all of o' dem dudes y'all call friends an' whatnot ain't nothing but a bunch o' thugs and criminals. No way, you know da police don't respect 'em. Shit, dey probably da ones who killed Nicky, 'cause ain't no way in da world dem police gonna not know how dat boy ended gettin' poisoned. Dat's a bunch o' bullshit, an' dey know it.

"But, hey, dat's the price you pay fa fuckin' 'round out here on da streets sellin' dat dope and shootin' folks. Ain't no good gonna come from livin'

dat gangsta life. I hope you an' Alonzo learn something from all o' dis. Ya do dirt, ya get dirt.

"Don't get me wrong, I'm real sorry 'bout what
done happened to Nicky, an' I feel so bad fa his family, but Nicky was out dere hustlin' and wildin' out
like da rest o' dem, so I knew it wouldn't be but a
matter o' time befo' he got himself locked up or
killed. It's a damn shame. He was so young, had his
whole life ahead o' him, and now he'll be a meal for
maggots. And for what? A li'l bit o' money? Some
jewelry? A fancy car or two? Y'all betta wake the
fuck up. Take heed and wake up."

Whiskey silently endured his big sister's scared-
straight speech, which usually followed the news of a
friend's or relative's arrest, hospitalization, or murder
from drug dealing. He was tired of hearing the same I-
told-you-so song and dance over and over again and
was ready to acquire his very own digs pretty soon to
avoid any further nagging.

The very next day he again met up with his police
cohorts who'd once more taken care of a potential
threat to the operation's smooth day-to-day affairs.
The crooked cops related to Whiskey how they had
gotten in contact with Beaufort Sheriff Oliver T. Drayton, a.k.a. "Doctor Buzzard," a known cocaine and
marijuana dealer among the area druggies, as well as a
renowned and feared practitioner of the mystical
hoodoo arts, the region's answer to voodoo.

It was rumored in and around Beaufort that the
tall, gangly country bumpkin was perhaps the only
white man to have been initiated into the magical
brotherhood of the Gullah people, and he utilized

his dark arts to direct malicious spells toward his enemies in the drug game who had little, if any, protection against such supernatural power.

Though the two Peola lawmen could've cared less about the supposed paranormal prowess of their Carolina counterpart, they did respect and appreciate the fact that Sheriff Drayton knew botany very well and used a deadly combination of arsenic, belladonna and several other poisonous Sea Island plants to concoct a toxic brew called Graveyard Dust. This was then placed into a tall glass of sweet tea and served with a dish of smothered short ribs and mashed potatoes to Nicky Stevens, who dozed off about a half-hour later, never to awaken again.

Point Polite was rather quiet this particular afternoon, and the temperature outside was a mild seventy with a bright blue sky accented with thin white cloud wisps along the horizon, where a golden orange sun slowly hovered.

Officer Columbus sat behind the wheel of his squad car, lip-synching to a Lynyrd Skynyrd CD he was playing, while gorging on a box of KFC, while the always dapper Tolliver stood beside the squad car, sharing the details of the Stevens murder with Whiskey.

Whiskey eased a newly rolled blunt from the pocket of his hoodie and sparked it up. "So what y'all sayin' is dat ya man kilt Nicky wit' roots? C'mon, son, you soundin' like my gran'mama, wit' all dat hocus-pocus hoodoo shit. 'Specially comin' from a college-educated mufucka like you, Maurice."

"Look, I didn't say that I believed in any of the spells, hexes, or any of that hoodoo Geechee magic crap that Sheriff Drayton practices, but that stuff does involve a certain knowledge of botany as well as chemistry, to determine which plants are going to heal or kill someone. He's done it before, and as you can see in the case of Nicholas Stevens, he's obviously done it yet again."

Whiskey passed the smouldering blunt to the policemen beside him and shrugged his broad shoulders in disbelief. "I dunno, man. Dat's some weird-ass Stephen King-type shit right dere. But how he gonna cover shit up, though? Everybody an' dey mama know my man done got poisoned. Now I heard da South Carolina District Attorney's office is gon' be lookin' into da case, so ya ol' hoodoo sheriff betta work some o' his strongest roots 'cause he sho nuff unda a microscope right about now. Him an' his whole fuckin' department. An' dat's not a whole helluva good look fa none o' us, ya feelin' me?"

Tolliver took in a final drag of the heavily packed blunt, smiling as he passed it over to his redneck partner, who snickered as if having knowledge of a joke that Whiskey was unaware of.

"Relax an' calm ya nerves, bro. We got it covered. Everythang's gon' be copasetic, okay. Now you just go on an' take it easy. We got dis." Columbus lowered the volume on his car stereo a bit. Then he tossed the empty box of greasy fried chicken bones over into a nearby metal garbage can. "We been dealin' wit Dr. Buzzard for well over, what, six years or so. An' he runs dat town wit' an iron fist, you hear me? An iron fuckin' fist. Everybody dat's anybody special in all o' Beaufort done bought pot or blow from 'im or else dey done went to him for some o' dem ol' hoodoo spells or whatnot, so you best believe ain't nobody down dere, white or black, rich or poor, young or old, is gonna rat out ol' Drayton. Everybody owe 'im somethin', for one thing, an' hell, most everybody else is too damn scared o' dat old bastard to dare run dere mouths to outsiders 'bout da sheriffs or his deputies. So you ain't got nothin' to worry 'bout, Whiskey, my man."

Whiskey took the blunt from Columbus's outstretched fingers and placed it to his lips. "Well, if y'all know dis so-called Doctor Buzzard like dat, den I guess everything's everything an' we can just keep movin' like always, huh?"

Columbus grinned. "Dawg, we're the police, remember? If there's anybody who can do the crime yet not the time, it's us, baby."

"Fa sho. Matter o' fact, I betcha if you was to, let's say, earn five bucks fa every dirty cop from, say, Key West, Florida all da way up north ta Boston, Massachusetts, *sheeet*, you'd be a fuckin' multi-millionaire," Maurice said.

Columbus pounded fists with his partner Tolliver.

"Shit, I'm damn near a millionaire now, white boy. Dunno what da fuck you talkin' 'bout." Whiskey chuckled.

"My bad, my bad, pimpin'. Please forgive me. Us li'l ol' po' white trash folk don't know too much 'bout ballin' and shot-callin'," Columbus answered.

Tolliver and Whiskey laughed heartily.

"Shut ya big redneck ass up an' pass dat blunt. How 'bout dat?" Whiskey playfully shoved Officer

Columbus away as he attempted to embrace him. "An' fire up another one, 'cause you keep some good kush on you, Mr. Officer, sir."

On November 11, Whiskey stood in a long, black-clad file of tearful, sniffling men and hysterically wailing women, who slowly shuffled past the open casket displaying Nicky Stevens waxen corpse. As he drew closer to the shiny metallic gray he felt somewhat uneasy. After all, the dead man lying before him was indeed a friend for life, or so he'd thought.

Looking down upon his deceased friend's cold form, Whiskey thought he looked mannequin-like in his navy blue double-breasted suit and gray tie. He quickly moved on past the casket as several women bawled out mournfully behind him. Whiskey slowly walked over to the Stevens clan sitting along the front pew and weeping heavily. He offered a few words of encouragement to them then walked away down the church corridor, toward his vehicle parked outside.

The melancholy atmosphere coupled with the host of grief-stricken relatives and friends of the dead dope boy was enough to drive Whiskey away from the crowded Baptist Church. It was very uncharacteristic for him to feel guilt or a sense of remorse after a hit on an informant. But since he grew up knowing Nicky as well as he did, there was just no way to shake the sorrow and shame that now enveloped him in its dark embrace.

Driving across the scenic bridge that connected Hilton Head Island with the rest of mainland South

Carolina, he could only think about the many times he'd spent nights over at Nicky's home enjoying the down-home Gullah cooking of Nicky's mother, Gertrude Ann Stevens, and the fun-filled sandlot football games played at Gator Field on Thanksgiving Day. The guy was like a brother to him, and he would still sorely miss him.

As he drove along the highway past rustic country homes and quaint old mobile homes, he listened to XM radio, silently recognizing that the deeper he got involved in the drug game, the more the bodies would pile up all over the low country regions of Georgia and South Carolina. And now with corrupt members of the Peola Police Department such as Office Tolliver and Columbus in cahoots with the area dope men, few ballers would be safe from the threat of death, not even himself.

Part II
Double Up

Chapter 12

"Blood Merger"

By December 14, David Ambrosia made another trip to Daufuskie's Bloody Point Beach prison to speak with the low country capo himself, Marion "Snookey" Lake. Although he had already secured a major record deal and a ten-city summertime tour for Godiva, he had taken a big-time hit from the IRS that left him nearly bankrupt, causing him to file Chapter 11 and to sell his record label to avoid prison. He had already asked Whiskey to run his business while he was going through his long, tiresome court proceedings of the past months, but had recently reneged on that idea when he found out about Whiskey's involvement with Tolliver and Columbus. He felt as though he could still manage the record label, now that his trials with the IRS had come to an end.

Now Ambrosia had arrived at the beachfront penitentiary to once more seek the aid of the drug lord. He sauntered down the hall, past armed guards, to the far end of the lobby to speak with Snookey.

Two corrections officers stood next to the seated Lake Clan leader, cracking jokes and chuckling, while he calmly sipped from a can of Mountain Dew at his favorite table in the corner.

Snookey patted an empty chair at the table, offering his young visitor a seat. He already knew why Ambrosia had come to see him. "'S up, Dave? How kin I help you today?"

Ambrosia pulled his chair closer to Snookey and cleared his throat. "You probably know all about my trouble with the IRS, right? Right, okay, check it out. After all the money I had to pay out to the IRS an' my attorneys, I've been pretty much wiped out financially. Now I'm not so much worried about the money as I am about getting my label back up and running. The feds are going to be investigating everything that I do from now on. I mean, every fuckin' thing. So, with that said, I'm here to request that you become a co-owner with me in the music business. I've got over twelve years in the industry, damn near as much as I've put into the drug game itself. You already know yourself that I'm probably the fuckin' hottest music producer in the States outside of Dr. Dre. My beats are like mad sick, and my artists all make hit records. All I need right now is a little seed money put into my business account from a separate source. Because, if I even think about funneling interests into my record label, Uncle Sam will ship my happy wigger ass off to a federal penitentiary quicker than you can say one, two, three."

"Partna-up wit' cha, huh? You know I'm good for

it an' all, but I can do but so much on lockdown here in da sticks, baby. If I'm gonna be ya partna, I feel like I gotta be a hands-on type o' nigga, ya know?" Snookey sipped on his drink.

David Ambrosia smiled weakly while shifting about in his seat. "Who says you gotta actually handle any of the technical legwork? All you have to do is put down the startup funds to get this party started again. Hell, you can use an alias. How about *Gullah Nation Records* or somethin'? Hell, I don't know."

Snookey snickered along with the C.O.'s at Ambrosia's title suggestions. Then he settled down and re-established eye contact with the music mogul. "Ya know, you just might be right, Davey boy, 'cause wit' dat dope money being laundered through yo' record company, it'll be da perfect smokescreen. 'Cause most o' da country know an' love you, 'specially back home in Peola. Spanish Moss Records? Are you shittin' me? Even wit' da tax evasion scandal, you still a music industry icon, an' a hometown hero nonetheless. So nobody will be the wiser 'bout what's goin' down behind da scenes, 'cept us cats in da game. You got me sold, white boy. Count me in."

"Now that's what I came down here to hear from you, Snookey. Because this is a win-win situation, dude. My fiancée Godiva's CD is due to drop on January twenty-second, and she begins touring with the rest of my artists during the summer. So you know that's sure money in the bank right there. Not to mention Godiva' friendship with new Peola Police Chief Courtney O'Malley. That can truly benefit every dealer, from Daufuskie to Miami. Because Godiva can pretty much get Courtney to do whatever she wants her to do, including have her old man Micky's sting operation halted down here in the low country."

The C.O.'s both smiled devilishly at each other before staring down at Snookey, awaiting the drug lord's answer.

Snookey slowly curled a thick diamond ring on his index finger back and forth, beckoning the crooked guards over to his side, where he chatted in a low tone with his badge-wearing cronies, occasionally glancing over at Ambrosia.

After several minutes of intense discussion, the three men returned back to facing the calmly waiting Ambrosia.

Snookey said, "A'ight, you got yaself a deal. Da Lake Clan gon' put up da chedda fa ya and gon' pull da strings in da industry to put yo' girl on da map. Wit' da help o' da game, we gon' all ride da wave of her success straight to da top. Ain't dat right?"

"You know me. I'm going to make it do what it do, baby."

The men then raised up from their chairs and embraced each other warmly before Ambrosia disappeared down the long hallway and through the large doors beyond, the two prison guards trailing close behind.

Outside the iron wrought gates of Bloody Point Beach Penitentiary, the hip-hop mogul opened the door to his pearl-colored Hummer limo and slid into the plush backseat, where he popped open a cold bottle of champagne and poured himself a glass of the bubbly light gold beverage. He sank back into the soft moss-green leather, content with the knowledge that, once more, he would not only be back in the business of producing hit records, but he'd also be back on top of his game and better than ever. With the help of the game, of course.

It had been a month since twenty-seven-year-old Brandi Welch, a.k.a. Godiva, had won the much-bally-hooed *Pop Star* competition finale, walking away with the BMW 325Ci convertible, $500,000 and a major recording contract with Spanish Moss Records. Yet, the singing sensation's best friend, Courtney O'Malley, seemed to relish in carrying on her poppa's obsession with eradicating Peola's un-desirables in his absence.

Daily police raids throughout South Peola's slums were the order of the day, many times harassing the innocent as well, simply for being relatives of tar-geted dealers. Aggressive racial profiling turned the projects into a veritable police state, bringing about the fear and loathing of Peola's finest to a new high amongst the ghetto's residents.

Whiskey and his numerous other area hot boys were furious at the cops with the latest rash of shakedowns, arrests, and even shooting deaths. It seemed as though Godiva had not spoken to her gal pal about the debt she owed to the streets, or either the policewoman simply didn't care.

Bright and early on November 28, seventeen Peola police squad cars roared up along Fenris Street in Hemlock Hills, sirens screaming and lights flashing. One by one, ghetto youth were shoved along the sidewalk and stuffed into the back of a black police Dodge Caravan while being read their Miranda rights.

"You little pricks are all gonna take a li'l ride downtown to my place. Got it? And once we're there, I'm gonna let a few of my guys, or should I say *homies*, kick it with you in our comfy little ol' interrogation room."

As the long row of frowning black teens shuffled past her, fuming silently on their way into the back of the van, Courtney quipped, "Doesn't that sound like fun?"

One older teen said, "Why is you sweatin' us, shawty? We ain't even do nothin'. *Tsk, tsk,* man, dis is some bullshit!"

"First of all, you will address me as Chief O'Malley or Ms. O'Malley, not shawty. Do you understand me, *asshole*?" Courtney swiftly kicked the handcuffed youngster in the buttocks, sending him careening against a row of garbage cans sitting along the muddied patch of earth below. "Get his ass up on his feet and get him outta my fuckin' sight."

Two female officers went over to the prostrate youth, lifted him up from the muddied filth, and led him on up into the back of the van.

Shortly before the assembled cops drove away with their shackled quarry, the police chief turned toward the crowd of ghetto residents gathered along the curb and smiled as she surveyed the silent faces of hatred all about.

"Let it be known that this is a new day in Peola, Georgia, people. No longer will thugs, hoodlums, and dopers overrun this fine town with their poison and crude manners. Nor will I or my department stand for any non-cooperation on the part of you citizens in regards to our follow-up investigations. Got it? And so help me God I'll do everything in my

fucking power to bring every single criminal scum-
bag to justice by any means necessary, just as my
dad instructed me to do. I'll be back here tomorrow,
and the day after that, and the day after that, and as
long as it takes, until you folks down here in South
Peola finally realize that it is us, the Peola Police Department, not you, who truly rule this city."

With those parting words, Courtney O'Malley
and her accompanying officers drove away from the
crowded streets with their dozen or so arrests.

Whiskey questioned Ambrosia as they sat in the
front office of Spanish Moss Records. "Man, what
da fuck is goin' on wit' cha girl Courtney?"

The hip-hop mogul shrugged his shoulders while
sighing deeply. "Man, I dunno what to tell you,
Whiskey," he said after handing over a stack of papers to the attractive Asian secretary, who stood
waiting patiently before exiting the spacious office
through the heavy glass double doors.

"I know for a fact that Godiva and I both met
with Courtney for well over two hours at her place
out in Canterbury Arms. The three of us discussed
over dinner what was expected of the department
in regards to having a blind eye and a deaf ear as far
as any drug trafficking conducted by our individual
organizations, namely Peola's Bad Boyz II Syndicate, which is our homies right here in town, as well
as your dad's Lake Clan, and also Joi Steven's
Fuskie Krew, which is a part of the larger Geechee
Gullah Nation that comprises of several other
cliques down in South Carolina's low country.

"So, as far as I'm concerned, everyone that I just

named is pretty much immune to any and all police harassment here in Peola, as well as down in South Cack. So relax, okay? I know how much of an asshole Courtney's old man was and is, but hey, she's her own person. She's already given us her word that she would take care of us.

"Now Godiva and Courtney go way back. They were friends since junior high, so Godiva knows her better than anyone of us. And she has promised me that Courtney O'Malley is a woman of her word who'd do anything she asks because they're more like sisters than mere friends. And my fiancée doesn't lie. She knows how the guys on the grind went to bat for her to gather up votes throughout minority communities across the country for her to win *Pop Star*. She hasn't forgotten, because she speaks about it every single day. She is grateful, and I myself will make sure that she does everything in her power to bless the streets back every chance she gets. So do me a favor, Whiskey. Work with me and give Captain Courtney O'Malley a chance, will ya?"

Though he nodded in agreement with his homie's assurance of the new police chief's compliance, Whiskey still had his doubts about the Irishman's daughter.

Just before midnight on November 29, Whiskey was slowly cruising East Peola's King Boulevard, in the direction of Burginstown Mall, to catch a movie and have dinner with a young lady he'd been wooing for the past week. The familiar sight and sound of a police Crown Victoria showed up in his rearview mirror, causing him to cuss out loud in anger and frustration as he pulled over to the shoulder of the busy street.

With words of assurance spoken softly to his suddenly nervous date, Whiskey turned to meet the bright glow of a flashlight pouring in the open driver's side window.

"Is dere a problem, officer?" He squinted as the bright light drew closer, illuminating the entire whip.

"License and registration please, sir," the cop demanded.

Whiskey's girlfriend asked with a sharp tone of irritation, "Is there a reason why you pullin' us over?"

"Ma'am, I suggest that you simply sit still and shut your mouth before you happen to piss me off more than I am already. Okay?"

The girl unlocked her seatbelt and leaned across her host, yelling out the window into the flashlight's cold white beam, "Well, that sounds like a personal problem to me, officer, because I know my rights. And you just can't go around stopping people without them knowing why they're being stopped."

The rude cop then demanded that both parties exit the vehicle. After a profanity-laced request for an explanation, the couple were promptly frisked and, following a routine search of Whiskey's vehicle, immediately arrested.

Two twenty-dollar bags of weed were recovered, along with a semi-automatic handgun with a full clip in the paper-cluttered glove compartment. The two were cuffed, read their Miranda rights, and transported back downtown to the Peola Police precinct for booking and interrogation.

During the uncomfortable and humbling ride downtown to the police station, Whiskey sat silently fuming, while his lady friend loudly ranted and raved about the treatment from the arresting officer, who egged the enraged girl on.

Whiskey and his now exasperated date were released from the city jail at 9:48 the following morning, after his brother Alonzo paid $1,000 bail, which Whiskey didn't have on his person at the time, carrying only several major credit cards in his billfold.

For over three hours, Whiskey had been grilled nonstop by a trio of straight-laced, no-nonsense detectives, who came down on him like a ton of bricks. Knowing the ways of the dope game like he did, the street-savvy baller remained mostly calm through the bulk of the questioning.

In the end he refused to answer any further questions until he spoke with his lawyer. That, however, turned out to be unnecessary, because no formal charges were ever filed, which meant that there would be no future court date concerning the late-night arrest.

As November gave way to December, Whiskey had had enough of Chief Courtney O'Malley's traitorous behavior and had devised a method to slow her roll. He met with Columbus and Tolliver. As Bonecrusher Anderson looked on from the high perch of one of his barber chairs that swiveled around slowly, the three men debated back and forth about blackmail and bribery.

"Looka here, y'all," Whiskey said, "I dunno what da fuck's wrong wit' y'all's boss lady Courtney, but she's trippin'. An' I'm talkin' 'bout some hardcore trippin', son. Now David my dawg an' all, but his fiancée seem to be mo' concerned wit' her music career right now dan tellin' her li'l Irish girlfriend to chill out with all o' dat Robocop type shit. So I'm gon' have ta go raw gutta my damn self, ya feel me? Since nobody seems to wanna stop dis bitch, I ain't got no choice.

"I got a couple o' pictures o' Godiva butt-naked on da stripper stage back when she used ta dance at da Strokers Club in Atlanta. I know good and damn well dat she gonna want da American public to know nothin' 'bout dat. Know what I'm talkin' 'bout? Not to mention, some more shit I got on her. So y'all two betta get dat li'l bit o' info out to ya boss if she so much of a friend to miss big-shot Godiva, 'cause, don't forget, if it wasn't fa my pops an' dem, dat bitch wouldn't be a star right now, ya feel me? So she need to get her shit together befo' da *National Enquirer* get a hold o' some nude pics, a'ight."

"Look, man, I know Chief O'Malley is just as hardcore as her father when it comes to nailing drug dealers, particularly those identified with your dad Snookey. Those two plain just hate each other, so you gotta believe that his little girl's not going to have much love in her heart for Lake Clan types either," Officer Tolliver responded dryly. "You know we got ya back in whatever you want done, don't we, Hank?"

"Oh, no doubt, Bub, no doubt. Hell, I don't like Courtney O'Malley either. I'd fuck her, but I don't like her." Columbus chuckled from having one can of Coors too many.

Whiskey lit the end of an apple-flavored Black & Mild cigar as he sat amongst his crooked pals. "Anyway, I spoke to my pops yesterday and he really want us to turn up da heat on dat Fuskie Island bidness, ya know? David done told me dat he don't want Godiva to get involved in none o' dis thug shit we got goin' on 'cause it'll fuck her career up at this early point. Shit, I ain't mad at 'im. Godiva is his meal ticket to get back on da map, know what I'm sayin'?" Cigar smoke rose lazily above Whiskey's corn-rowed head.

"That may be true," Tolliver said, "but what I don't like is that Courtney, er, Chief O'Malley, I mean, calls herself handling the bulk of Godiva's scheduling and day-to-day appointments, so she basically manages the girl. David seems to be fine with it also. And she has been in constant contact with her father down in the Big Easy about her dealings with local drug dealers here in Peola as well as continuing his operation down on Daufuskie Island."

"Yeah, she straight trippin', bro, but she don't know shit 'bout da hit dat's gonna go down on her dear ol' dad," Columbus chimed in with his distinctive Southern drawl.

Whiskey steadily puffed on the smoldering stogie as the other men chattered about the murder plot of Micky O'Malley when he arrived again on Daufuskie from his sojourn in storm-torn New Orleans.

"Don't Snookey got a bunch o' dem Geechee boys to peel ol' Mickey's wig piece back?" asked an intoxicated, red-eyed Bonecrusher Anderson, who was lying back in a barber swivel chair and clutching a forty-ounce of Colt 45 malt liquor in his thick hand.

"Fa sho, pimpin'. You know how Snookey roll. He got a couple o' like hardheads posted up ta put in work, know what I'm sayin'. But befo' we kin get shit on an' poppin', we gon' need ta pick da most gulliest, grimiest thugs from da island ta punish dis cracka, feel me?—No offense, Hank."

The brawny copy snickered. "No offense taken, bro. Hell, I ain't nothin' but a red-necked, beer-guzzlin' wigger, so trust me, Whiskey, I ain't hardly mad at cha."

"A'ight, bet. Anyway, Snookey wanted me ta come down to Fuskie ta get dese Geechee niggas' minds right, so dey kin do dis job da right way, feel me? My nigga, Doctor Buzzard, done wired me thirty grand ta take some time-off down on Fuskie, ya know?"

The hoodoo-practicing sheriff had built up quite a profitable narcotic ring over the past decade himself and could ill afford to allow the Irishman to destroy that, so he was more than happy to bless Whiskey with the "vacation money" he needed to take care of this pressing matter. I'ma need some time to whip dem dudes inta shape, 'cause dey real raw an' shit, an' dey ain't never had ta do nuttin' like dis befo'. So, yeah, I'm-a go down dere an' make it happen, cap'n."

Tolliver smiled broadly as he poured himself a clear glass of Jack Daniel's and Coke, swirling the potent, brown nectar around with the ice-filled glass before downing it in one grimacing gulp. "I really want this caper to go as smooth as possible. I still think that Godiva is more concerned with her up-coming concerts than with offing the sire of her best friend. So I've contacted some friends of ours who serve on the Beaufort County sheriff's department. You see, Whiskey, I too have spoken with the good Doctor Buzzard. He's already got two rogue cops working for us down on Daufuskie who will get as much info on O'Malley's fat ass as possible so that we can organize this hit properly. Get it?"

Everyone nodded in agreement to the crooked cop's words.

Tolliver continued as his interested friends looked on, "By early January, Mickey O'Malley will be back in South Carolina from New Orleans, so we've got to act fast because it's nearly December right now. There's this cat name Lonnie Newhart, a.k.a. Moose. He's a local high-school football legend down there in the sticks, but now he's much better known for flipping bricks than for touchdowns. It's this guy who'll be helping us in our efforts to eliminate Mickey O'Malley.

"Before O'Malley arrived down on Daufuskie, Moose was earning anywhere from fifty-five to sixty grand per week selling coke from Hilton Head all the way up to Richmond, Virginia, and down past the Florida Keys. It's rumored that he also ruled the low country with an iron fist, murdering over fifty-eight rival drug dealers in the fall of two thousand.

"My good friend, Lieutenant Gordon Nasser of the Savannah City police department, met Moose back in ninety-eight and has done brisk business with the guy ever since. I personally did my homework on the guy, and I found that he had connections with the Medellín and Cali Cartels in Colombia, not to mention various drug cartels out in Mexico, and even heroin smugglers from as far away as Afghanistan. The boy's a true baller, and trust me, he doesn't take kindly to some lard-ass mick cop ruining his coke business. Besides, he's also an ally of your dad. You did know that, didn't you, Whiskey?" Tolliver eyed Whiskey, who sat in a barber chair directly across from him.

"Who don't work for Snookey? Everybody dat's anybody out here on da grind done worked wit' my pops at one time or another. I don't put niggas on a pedestal just 'cause dey done made a li'l bit o' cheese from slangin' birds an' shit, 'cause if you 'bout yo' work out here on dese streets an' you ain't bullshittin', you gon' eat. All I'm tryin' ta do is get at dis bitch-ass O'Malley, so everybody kin breathe easier, sleep betta at night, and continue to serve dese fiends and make dis money like we always been doin', ya heard me?"

Tolliver glanced over at Columbus, who shrugged his shoulders nonchalantly as he channel-surfed the shop's overhead television with a small silver remote.

"All righty, then why don't you hook up with Moose when you get down there next month and the both of you work together on getting this operation off the ground. You'll be in charge of getting Fuskie Krew up to speed on the details of the big day, while Moose will stay in contact with the moles we've got paid off within the Daufuskie police department on the arrival and day-to-day movements of the visiting chief of police. Doctor Buzzard is going to ship thirty-three-thousand-dollars worth of assault weapons, clips, an' ammo to equip the Krew for the job at hand. I know that seems like a waste of money and way overdoing it, but you can never be too careful. Plus, this is a job that absolutely, positively cannot fail, because there's just too much at stake for failure of any kind. You do understand that, don't you?" Tolliver asked.

Whiskey nodded slowly while crushing his cigar butt into an empty soda can. "I feel you, but y'all gon' have ta work overtime ta keep this shit from gettin' back ta Mickey's baby girl, 'cause I know damn well y'all got mo' dan a li'l bit o' cops who consida deyself loyal to da department, feel me? And dat's all we need to blow da lid off da whole goddamed operation. So y'all dudes gotta make sho' dat everybody down wit' da program keep dey fuckin' mouths shut," Whiskey emphasized sternly.

Everyone gathered together in the interior of the barbershop nodded together in silent agreement to the young enforcer's statements, realizing the truthfulness of his words.

Chapter 13

"Sea Island Thugs"

"Shawty, gimme a hit o' dat dank, son," a young, bright-eyed ruffian said, reaching out with an outstretched hand to receive a thick blunt from a homie seated nearby, puffing away, as a heavy cloud of reefer smoke ascended above he and his fellows playing poker within the crowded living room of a Daufuskie Island mobile home.

As the heavy bass-laced tracks of Trick Daddy filled the smoky, gangsta-crowded living room, Whiskey stood near the refrigerator looking at an assortment of glossy assault weapons that Hilton Head's lovely sister assassins, Candice and Naomi Forrester, were showing him. He smiled broadly, stroking the silvery, metallic muzzle of a polished AR-15 rifle and fondly admiring its lethal beauty.

"She's quite a looker, ain't she?" Naomi unloaded a handful of ammo boxes from an opened suitcase sitting atop the kitchen table.

Looking up from his inspection of the weapon, Whiskey winked an eye at the attractive sisters smiling back at him as he checked out their hardware with growing satisfaction. "Oh yeah, y'all got some serious firepower right here. My mans an' dem gon' buy up all o' dis work up off you." He gently placed the AR-15 back down alongside the other smuggled guns on the table.

Candice unloaded another suitcase of smuggled items, this one being three dozen clips of different sizes to fit both handguns as well as rifles.

Naomi tallied up the total cost of the weapons on a small calculator as her sibling removed the empty gun magazines from their container. She tapped off a final price tally on the instrument's keypad then turned to Whiskey. "I'll say we'll let this stash go for, what, two thousand two hundred. Now that's really cheap for what you're getting, and of course it's only 'cause we know you and you're our peeps an' shit. Nobody else would walk away with all of these guns for that kinda chicken change. Plus, we wanna get rid of Mickey O'Malley just as bad as anybody else down here, ya know? Shit, we're losing money and clientele as a result of this dumb-ass cop's so-called war on drugs. Fuck that. My sister an' I want this punk bitch dead now. And we're now ready and willing to help you cats take care of that too."

"Gimme my moneeee!" yelled one of the boys sitting around the card-cluttered poker table. He gleefully pumped his fist in the air, before slapping high-fives all around with his malt liquor-guzzling partners.

Candice asked, "Why y'all need so many guns

though? I mean, I ain't mad at cha, though, but it's like y'all tryin' to kill a whole gang o' cops, rather than just this one dude."

"Don't start me to lyin', baby girl. Shit, I just do what da powers dat be tell me ta do, ya know? And dem powers tell me ta buy da very best state-o'-da-art weaponry fa dese li'l thug niggas down here, 'cause dem peoples I fucks wit' want hitmen set up all over Fuskie on da day o' da murda. So no matter where he turns or where he goes, he's gonna run into a hired gun, feel me?"

"I see. Yeah, Beaufort County ballers have lost well over a million dollars ever since ya man Mickey O'Malley brought his doughnut-eatin' Irish ass down here." Naomi dropped her calculator back down into her Dooney & Bourke leather handbag.

As the youngsters yelled and carried on boisterously at and around the smoke-surrounded poker table, Whiskey slowly began peeling off one "Benjamin Franklin" after another from a huge rubber band-wrapped roll of cash to pay for the deadly cargo that would be used to off the South's most hated lawman.

On December 8, 2005 David Ambrosia hosted a release party for Godiva's newly released album, *Party Favors*. Starting at ten PM, a steady stream of well-wishers and fans entered through the mahogany front doors of West Peola's posh 95 South nightclub.

By the time the lady of honor herself arrived an hour later, the place was packed with over a thousand fans, not counting the four thousand more huddling impatiently near the entrance in the night chill of the parking lot.

The famous VIP upper room was alive with the thumping music and beautiful people who all pushed and pressed their way through and around each other to get a few seconds to schmooze with Godiva. Cameras flashed, and champagne corks popped all around the room, as the incessant din of the chattering groupies raged in the background along with the booming sound systems.

Office Columbus, dressed down in a Southwestern denim-style outfit, came over to the bar where Whiskey stood and took a seat on one of the few empty stools available. He ordered a shot of Jack Daniel's on the rocks, and attempted to score with a slender, hippy dark-brown cutie with a weak pickup line, causing her to quickly turn her bare back to him in a blatant show of disinterest.

"Dat's all right, darlin'. After a coupla shots of Jack, you'll be ridin' home wit' me tonight. You just don't know it yet, is all. Hey, Whiskey, my man, how da hell are ya? Dem Gullah folks been treatin' you okay or what?"

Due to his preoccupation with the wide variety of sexy women clustering around Godiva, giggling like schoolgirls as they took snapshots of the smiling recording artist signing autographs in the middle of the crowd, Whiskey barely acknowledged the redneck policeman with a nod as he took a sharp swallow of gin and grapefruit juice.

Columbus took the shot of liquor slowly to his thirsty lips. "Maurice told me dat you done gone an' got dem fine-ass Forrester sistas to help wit' da O'Malley thing, huh. Sweet."

Whiskey glanced at the off-duty cop with irritation and put up a thick finger to his lips. "C'mon, son, watch ya mouf up in here. You don't know who listenin' ta dis conversation. I know you know betta dan dat, pimp."

"My bad, my bad. I didn't feel anybody could hear us over these goddamned loud speakers in here. Besides, everybody's so caught up wit' Godiva over there dat I seriously doubt dat anyone's payin' da slightest bit o' attention ta us."

Whiskey wrinkled his brow in dismay. "You just can't be too careful out here nowadays, Hank. You of all people oughta know dat."

"A'ight, a'ight, you've made your fuckin' point, okay? Calm down, dude. Anyway, it seems like li'l miss superstar over there is so stuck on herself dat she ain't even bothered ta tell her bosom buddy Courtney O'Malley to lay off da boys in da hood even a li'l bit. Not to mention da fact o' her an' ya boy David Ambrosia refusin' ta return our phone calls an' whatnot, which is pissin' off just about everybody dat had anything ta do wit' dis bitch gettin' on da map."

Whiskey took another sip of gin and juice. "I spoke ta David twice down in Fuskie and he told me dat he already talked to Courtney 'bout da fava her girl Godiva owe us fa helpin' her win da *Pop Star* competition and he said to me outta his very own mouf dat da bitch was callin' off da dawgs from sweatin' our dope spots out in South Peola. An' peep dis, David even wired a li'l bit o' change, fifteen hundred to be exact, to help wit' payin' da young bucks who gonna be down wit' dat thing, feel me? So I dunno why he ain't hittin' y'all back on da phone."

Suddenly a recognizable figure emerged from the dense crowd to take a seat at the bar among them. It was Maurice Tolliver dressed to the nines in a finely tailored rust-colored Emporio Armani suit. "What's up, what's up, people?"

Columbus chuckled. "Ain't shit. Just kickin' it up in here wit' our buddy Whiskey, an' a whole lotta pretty li'l bitches."

"I see. I just got back from LA, Compton to be exact. I've got family, but in Inglewood. But that wasn't really why I went out West. David Ambrosia hipped me to the job that you pulled off for his guy, DiVante Lovett, a while back. Well, to make a long story short, this cat was so impressed by the thoroughness of the hit on your part that he pretty much promised to help David or you out anytime you may need him in the future. So that was an opportunity that I felt we would benefit from, especially right now. As you already know, DiVante's the leader of one of South Central's largest gangs, the Reapers, second in size only to the Crips, but even more violent, from what I'm told.

"Anyway he's more than willing to contact a few of his business associates down in Charlestown to take advantage of a suddenly booming crystal meth trade taking shape down here in the Atlantic coastal states. Both he and I believe that by investing in this crystal meth craze we can recoup some of the millions that fat fuck O'Malley cost us over the past few months. What do you guys think about that idea?"

Columbus raised a glass of Jack Daniel's on ice in a toast to his partner's entrepreneurial skills.

"Maurice, do you care dat we here in public? I just got through warnin' Hank 'bout dat dumb shit. C'mon, dawg, y'all makin' us hot, don't ya think? Besides, I ain't worried 'bout doin' no bidness right about now, 'cause we kin do dat whenever. Shit, Charlestown ain't nothin' but a stone's throw away from Fuskie, but ain't nobody gon' be able to do a goddamned thing as long as Chief O'Malley has anything to do with it. I think we gotta stay focused on gettin' rid o' da Irishman befo' we kin even think 'bout makin' money or slangin' any kinda new product out on da streets."

On December 19, interim police chief Courtney O'Malley called an emergency meeting with twenty-two of her most decorated officers. One by one, the top brass of Peola's tightly run police department came marching through the training academy doors to take a seat at one of the simple sawdust desks lining the clean, waxed tile floor. Corporals, sergeants, lieutenants, captains, and three majors shuffled over to their desks and sat silently.

Officer Maurice Tolliver had received his corporal bars on December 3 after several months of recommendations by his peers on the force, including Hank Columbus. Though he felt no desire whatsoever to attend this early-morning supervisor meeting, he had no choice, since it was mandatory for every officer with stripes. He made sure that he sat near the rear of the large gymnasium-size room. He fiddled briefly with his BlackBerry before putting it away upon the chief's arrival.

Courtney O'Malley was a busty, freckled-faced

redhead with bright green eyes, which stared out fiercely at the assembled police officers seated before her as she stood at the podium. "Good morning, ladies and gentlemen. I'm so very glad that each and every one of you could make it here this morning. There is coffee and doughnuts out in the hall for you guys after we get finished up here this morning, okay? And for you healthy types, there's green tea and trail mix.

"Well, now that all that's out the way, I want to let you all know why I brought you here. It has come to my attention that certain members of this department are taking drug money and narcotics from raids on known stash houses, as well as taking bribes from area traffickers. Can you men and women of this esteemed department fathom, if even for a nanosecond, betrayal of this magnitude?"

A few cops shifted about uncomfortably in their seats, while others mumbled softly among themselves.

"Oh yeah, it's disgusting, I know. But don't worry, people, I will not sit back idly while a few pathetic renegade officers bring disgrace to this proud department and this town. My father has devoted his life to the development of the Peola Police Department and providing the citizens of our community with a safe haven from the ills, which unfortunately affect many of our nation's largest cities. That was his number one priority, as it is now mine in his absence.

Several high-ranking majors and captains seated in the front row nodded their heads in agreement with the young chief.

"I say we lock every last one of 'em up whenever

and wherever we find 'em and throw away the god-damned keys," one brash young sergeant announced.

Scattered handclaps broke out throughout the room.

Courtney O'Malley smiled as she brushed away a frock of fiery red locks from her face. "You, sir, are absolutely correct. I feel the same way, as do most of us here." She noticed Tolliver dozing off at the rear of the room. "Isn't that right, Corporal Tolliver?"

Stirring himself abruptly, the newly decorated sergeant said, "Uh, yes, yes, ma'am, that's right. We're going to do everything possible to bring any criminal in this town to justice. Including any police officer who breaks the law, ma'am."

Mild laughter escaped the lips of a few cops in the audience, and the chief of police grinned at the sergeant's mild embarrassment.

"Well, Corporal Tolliver has been on an extended vacation on the West Coast, so I'm sure his drowsi-ness stems from jetlag and hopefully not boredom," she said, bringing some amusement to the other-wise serious-minded meeting.

"However, ladies and gentlemen, we are dealing with a grave situation here, one which our fine de-tective branch has been investigating since early Oc-tober of this year. We brought in several persons of interest over the past few weeks to answer some pertinent questions and to provide us with some possible leads in this ongoing case we're building. Among the perps who were interviewed were some this town's top drug traffickers, largely from the projects of South Peola, such as Paul and Marion Ballard of the Bad Boyz II Syndicate, Edward An-derson, also known as Bonecrusher down in that part of town, as well as a handful of lesser-known hoodlums.

"As is the norm among these criminal scumbags, even after hours of intense interrogation here at the precinct, we ended up having to let each one of them go with even less info than when we had when we first brought them in for questioning. So I've arranged to have extra officers monitor the open-air drug markets throughout South Peola, as well as place hidden cameras and listening devices in strategic areas around these drug hot spots.

"I intend to bring these rogue cops and their drug-dealing allies to justice no later than the end of January, people. That's next month. So let's get our shit together and catch these assholes ASAP."

As the final few handclaps died down, a distinguished-looking lieutenant, tall and straight, with impeccably pressed uniform and highly shined brass, stood. "Chief O'Malley, it is my understanding that there might even be reason to believe that certain prison gangs here in Peola's penal system and abroad who have considerable influence outside as well as behind bars often bankroll criminals to execute a variety of illegal acts, from drug trafficking, weapons smuggling, money laundering, and even murder. One of the names that draws an immediate red flag is that of Marion Lake, now residing in a South Carolina prison down in Beaufort County's low country. Even though he's now imprisoned, he is still a force to be reckoned with."

The chief of police gritted her teeth at the very mention of her father's long-time nemesis. She cleared her throat and steadied herself by grabbing a firm hold of the podium. Then she adjusted the microphone to her liking. "Thank you, lieutenant. This is indeed a crucial observation on your part, and one that will not go without a thorough investigation in the very near future. I assure you, Mr. Lake has been a menace to society ever since he began his criminal career in pre-Hurricane Katrina New Orleans. I know, because my father has collected a virtual library of criminal files on him alone, much of which he himself inherited from his boss, the honorable Leon Rossum.

"Don't worry, Marion Lake is going to remain a locked-up loser for a long, long time, if not for the rest of his pathetic life. I'll personally see to that, and I'll also make sure that any prison-run crime rings either here in Akron Corrections or elsewhere will be eliminated completely. You can take that to the bank."

The officers stood and gave her a rousing round of applause that lasted for several minutes.

"If I have my way—which I almost always do, just ask my dad—I'll see to it that Marion Lake is transferred back to the Leavenworth Federal Pen where he resided before he was allowed to move back down to the South. Give me a few weeks and I'll make some phone calls to a few friends of mine down in the South Carolina Governor's Mansion, and Mr. Lake will be Kansas-bound and well out of our hair."

Courtney O'Malley spoke for another ten minutes then thanked her top brass for attending the meeting and formally dismissed them from the gymnasium.

As the officers all arose simultaneously from their seats, Officer Tolliver slipped through the crowd and out the door as his coworkers gathered in the adjourning hall to chit-chat while having coffee and such. He had an important phone call to make.

Christmas morning in the Battle household was a laughter-filled, festive affair, with Tasha's three young sons gleefully ripping open present after present under the snow-white, ornament-adorned Christmas tree standing in the middle of her living room. While the boys compared notes on who received the best gifts, their mother and older sister Peaches began adding the finishing touches to a holiday meal, its delicious, mouth-watering aroma filling the entire room.

Whiskey, Alonzo, and their cousin, Lil' Shane, proceeded downstairs to the basement apartment to get high and converse.

"Dawg, y'all niggas wouldn't believe da kinda paper we pullin' out in Hemlock Hills off o' da crystal meth shit. Dem rich white kids been buyin' da shit up like hot cakes up in West Peola. I been buyin' da meth in bulk from some cats down in Beaufort who work for ol' Doctor Buzzard. From what I hear, he gettin' it from a bunch o' MS-13 eses from DC. But, hey, who knows, and who gives a fuck? As long as me and my niggas stay gettin' dat money, know what I'm sayin'? I say we makin' over fifty thousand or mo' a week movin' meth. Just last week I musta got my dick slobbed on by mo' den seven white hoes at da same mufuckin' time, just fa givin' dem bitches ten grams o' meth, pimp. Since then, I stay wit' no less than ten grams o' meth 'cause I know I'm gon' get coochie from da fly snow bunnies up on da West Side, feel me?"

Tasha and Peaches yelled for the three men to come for dinner.

Alonzo took one last deep drag from the strong-smelling blunt and exhaled a thick cloud of smoke.

"A'ight, tell ya what, lemme get five hunit grams o' dat crystal up off you tonight 'cause I wanna have first dibs on introducing dat shit to dem caked-up crackas down in South Cack befo' anybody else beat me to it. 'Cause once we get rid o' Chief Mickey O'Malley's bitch ass, it's on. Da way dat bitch Courtney goin', dat hit might never happen. My man Maurice told me dat Courtney O'Malley is crackin' down on all o' dat crooked-cop shit, so now da police who used to do bidness wit' us is runnin' scared. So I dunno 'bout all dat kill-O'Malley shit dat's s'posed to take place."

Lil' Shane choked, hacking hard from the overwhelming potency of the purple haze that had just entered his lungs.

"Ain't nobody worried 'bout dat broad. She know what's up. David gon' get her mind right." Whiskey winked at his brother and cousin as they ascended the old wooden staircase, which creaked and groaned under their combined weight. "C'mon, let's eat, y'all. Ya don't wanna get Tasha pissed."

Later that night, the trio drove down to the Hemlock Hills projects. Within the trunk of Lil' Shane's black Bentley Continental GT was a cache of fifty grams of crack, five kilos of powder, fifty kilos of heroin, three pounds of marijuana, and several machine guns.

During the drive out to South Peola, Lil' Shane and Alonzo discussed Godiva's well-known promiscuity. According to the dealers, Peola's infamous detective Tyrone Warner was none too happy that Mickey O'Malley had snubbed him in favor of his daughter for interim police chief.

As a result, the fourteen-year veteran of the Peola Police Department despised his boss's feisty young daughter, Courtney, who felt similar hatred for him. He knew of the tight-knit friendship his new chief had with superstar songstress Godiva and had knowledge of David Ambrosia's criminal activities as well. He then had the offices and recording studio of David Ambrosia wiretapped to record anything that might incriminate Ambrosia or his artists.

Within minutes the familiar sight of Hemlock Hills' rusted wrought iron gates came into view. Alonzo reached into the breast pocket of his North Face jacket and retrieved a neatly rolled blunt. As the sleek black automobile pulled up against the curb in front of Eddie's Barbershop, Alonzo lit the end of the blunt and inhaled deeply as he exited the vehicle.

Dozens of drug-dealing youths raced to the car, opening the trunk and removing the illicit contents.

One cornrow-wearing thug stepped over to Alonzo and placed a briefcase filled with neatly lined rows of cash onto the hood of the Bentley. "Bonecrusher told me to give you da money for da products. He said he'll be here in a few minutes after he get back from da bank," the thug said, stepping back slightly.

"I ain't goin' no place, pimpin'. I just got here."
Alonzo passed the blunt to his brother Whiskey.

Whiskey puffed on the *L*. "Y'all hear anything
from David an' dem?"

"Naw, dawg, he been too busy settin' up Godiva
with TV interviews and late-night performance
spots to fuck wit' us li'l folks out here," the thug answered.

"I think I know David a li'l bit betta than you,
pimp, an' I know fa sho dat he got our back, believe
dat," Whiskey commented.

Alonzo and Lil' Shane smiled as they leaned up
against the Bentley and saw the buzz of activity on
the corners near the barbershop. A steady stream of
cars, expensive models from the upper-crust communities of West and North Peola, pulled up one,
no more than fifteen or twenty minutes apart, to
buy their narcotics of choice from the ghetto youths,
who approached the curbside window.

Lil' Shane and Derek Myers oversaw a group of
unemployed high-school dropouts and newly released ex-cons that numbered around sixty strong.
The men of various ages wore different color jackets
to identify what type of drug they peddled—green
for marijuana, white for cocaine, yellow for crack,
and so forth. This ingenious method netted the two
ballers ninety-one grand a day. Two Peola police
squad cars always remained along the outskirts of
the projects, acting more as sentries for the dope
boys than monitoring them for the chief of police.

Whiskey took the blunt from his little brother's
hand and put it to his lips. Dope boys raced back and
forth along the street across from the barbershop

slangin' their wares to one eager customer after one another.

"Ain't it a thing o' beauty, big brotha?"

"Fa sho. We taught dem two li'l knuckleheads well. Almost too well. Hell, dem li'l mufuckas makin' mo' money dan we did at their age. You realize dat?"

Alonzo grunted. "Shit, yeah, 'specially wit' dat crystal meth shit. I musta counted ten cars already dat pulled up to da curb just to buy meth alone. Dem boys on da come-up, no doubt."

"I'm gonna get Derek to go wit' me when I head back ta Fuskie. I might git him ta peel ol' Mickey O'Malley's cap back. Whatcha think 'bout dat?"

Alonzo took back his blunt and dragged on it deep and long before finally exhaling. "Da li'l nigga is a Bad Boy II Syndicate member, ain't he? Right, so you already know he ain't no stranger to pullin' a trigga. It sho as hell wouldn't be da first time."

"Ya think so?"

"C'mon, son, stop playin' wit' me. You know dat you gotta murk somebody just ta join up wit' da Syndicate niggas." Alonzo dropped the smoldering roach down on the pavement, crushing it underfoot. "Godiva and David need ta send money or whatever they need to provide us wit' to get rid o' Mickey O'Malley. I don't give a fuck if he's her best friend's pops. If it wasn't for niggas out here an' in dem jail cells all across da nation gettin' their peeps to vote for Godiva on dat cheesy-ass karaoke show which, for real, niggas in da hood didn't give a fuck about, she wouldn't be all high an' mighty right now. She betta not ever get it twisted, neither her man. Dat li'l favor came wit' a price tag attached. Dem two mufuckas owe us, son, big time."

Whiskey shook his head slowly. "C'mon, calm down, man. You know David as well I do, don't you? You know yourself David always been a man o' his word, right? Shit, he da one founded da Bad Boyz II Syndicate. Dese li'l nappyhead dope boys runnin' 'round out here gettin' paper 'cause o' David Ambrosia, nigga. An' dat's real talk. So I'm gon' say it again regardless o' what y'all cats say or think 'bout my man David. I know David. I know dat his word is his bond, an' dat's it an' dat's all."

Alonzo watched as Lil' Shane and Derek Myers directed their drug runners from the sidelines like two winning football coaches, to secure sales from the procession of vehicles pulling up nonstop.

"A'ight then. If you so sure dat David is 'bout it-'bout it, then so be it. Keep talking to 'im. From now on you'll be da middleman between Hollywood and da hood. How 'bout dat?"

Whiskey grinned lightly. "Oh, so now I'm an errand boy, or better yet a secretary, huh?"

"Hey, you da one sayin' how close you are to David. An' didn't you fuck Godiva befo'? So you would be da perfect bridge between us and dem."

"Look, I ain't tryin' ta be nobody's official messenger or nothin'. I've been doin' too much already."

Alonzo quickly checked messages on his cell phone before flipping it shut. "Just make sure your friends do what's right, that's all, a'ight?"

"You trippin', son. I dunno what's gotten into you, thinkin' David is somehow untrustworthy, but you need ta let it go."

"Naw, Whiskey, you da one who's trippin', pimp. You might o' spoken to David and Godiva lately, but da rest o' us ain't seen hide nor hair o' dem people since she won it all on dat TV show two months ago. Dem two mufuckas ain't thinkin' 'bout us niggas out here. They used us to get what they want, an' now they gone. Dat's what I think."

Whiskey hopped up onto the wide hood of his cousin's Bentley. "Who you really need to be worried 'bout an' suspicious of is Chief Courtney O'-Malley, not David or Godiva. It's dat bitch who ain't followin' orders an' shit. Godiva done told da bitch how key ballas on da outside an' in da pen helped her get on da map an' how she needed for her to back off all da hustlas here in da city, an' she gave Godiva her word dat she'd lay off wit' all o' dat Robocop bullshit. But so far she's been nothin' but a lyin', fake-ass bitch. Ya boy Maurice called me, lettin' me know how dis bitch is gettin' ready to go after her very own officers who been workin' with da hustlas down here in South Peola. Plus, she somehow got word dat our pops been runnin' things outside from inside da pen, and now she fixin' ta ship him back out to Kansas. Leavenworth, to be exact."

"Whaaaat!!? Nigga, you gotta be bullshittin' me."

"I wish I was, but I ain't. I'm gonna tell Snookey 'bout it when I get back down dere later on this week. 'Cause we gotta beat dis ho to da punch befo' it's too late."

Alonzo clenched his brother's hand in a brotherly embrace. "Fa sho. But I tell you what—Ain't nobody gon' fuck with our father without gettin' touched, son. I mean dat shit."

Whiskey playfully threw a few short jabs at his younger sibling's taut midsection. "I know what you're thinkin', Alonzo, and I'm tellin' you, don't do it."

"Don't do what?"

"You know what da fuck I'm talkin' 'bout, nigga."

"So I guess we gon' just sit back an' let some dumb bitch send our father back out to Leavenworth, an' it's cool, right?"

Whiskey placed his muscular arm around Alonzo's shoulder. "Wrong. Trust me, li'l brotha, we ain't gotta kill Courtney, 'cause she's already dead. She just don't know it yet. An' you can kill a person in more ways than one, always remember dat."

Chapter 14

"Peola's Finest"

At approximately 8 AM on December 28, 2005, Peola Police Chief Courtney O'Malley sat behind the huge mahogany and granite desk in her father's office, slowly sipping on a hot mocha latte as she awaited the arrival of Detective Tyrone Warner.

At 8:07, he entered her office and approached her desk, reaching across and shaking hands with his boss. She offered him coffee and doughnuts from on a small wooden table beside her, but he politely refused and sat down on the leather chair in front of the desk.

"Good morning, Detective Warner. I'm so glad that you could take some time out of your busy schedule to meet with me this morning. It won't take long, I assure you."

"It's not a problem," the lean detective said. "I've been wanting to speak to you as well."

"Oh really? Well, that's just swell. By the way, remember the report I placed on your desk concerning the placement of monitoring devices in the South Peola drug spots?"

"Oh yeah, what about it?" he asked calmly.

"You haven't done anything at all about it, that's what, and I want to know why."

"I'll get around to it in time. I've got a shitload of cases that I've got coming up, so there you have it."

The police chief rose up from her desk and walked around it to the front. "You know what, Detective? There's three things that really irritate me. One, I hate balding guys who insist on going with a comb-over, when it's clearly obvious that it fools no one and just looks plain ridiculous. Second, I hate really fat people who try to squeeze in spandex, because that's just wrong. And, finally, I hate it when people don't follow orders—especially those who work for me, *capisce*?"

The detective leaned forward, a mild smirk creasing the corners of his lips. "Miss O'Malley, no disrespect to you, ma'am, but as I said to you just a minute ago, I have been swamped with paperwork that's been stacked up on my desk since early September. I've got narcotic, homicide, and rape cases, so it's not that I disregarded your request. I just simply lost track of it in lieu of everything else that I've had to deal with. I'm telling you, chief, I've got a fuckin' full plate."

The police chief hopped up onto her desk. "All right then, I'll accept that as fair enough, but I need for you to put the rest of your work on the back burner for now and focus on placing those closed-circuit cameras in the hot spots we spoke of earlier."

"I'm all ears. What exactly do you want me to do with these monitoring devices, chief?"

"I'd like for you to place cameras all over the projects of South Peola, namely Hemlock Hills, Badlands Manor, and the Geneva neighborhood drug spots, and believe you me, there's quite a few of them scattered all over the place."

"All right, that's not a problem, but an operation such as that would take weeks, if not months, to complete, considering the sheer size of the area itself we have to cover."

Courtney O'Malley raised her coffee mug up to her lips to savor another sip of her latte. "Oh, don't worry about that, Detective. I've already been in contact with several area contractors, as well as Bell South, who've both expressed interest in working with us to cover those areas with cameras."

"Chief, if I may interject, I believe that this counter-surveillance project of yours may be easier said than done. First of all, even with police escorts, these areas could prove dangerous to any contractor working within them, especially when the local dealers catch on to what they're really up to."

Courtney O'Malley ran her pale, slender fingers through her curly red hair and sighed softly as she stared up at the ceiling for a few seconds.

"Detective, I may not have the amount of years as you in law enforcement in general and in this department in particular, but I will say this—I've learned this business from the best goddamned police officer in the world, and that would be none other than Mr. Mickey O'Malley, who just also happens to be my dad. He always said to me, 'Honey, in this line of work you can never let the bad guys feel as though they can intimidate you, because then they've won.' And then he'd say to me, 'So never let them win.' So, with that said, do you even think for one minute that the threats or street machismo of a few idiot kids are going to weaken my resolve? If so, think again.

"As a matter of fact, Detective, I've been hearing some rumors from my sources close to the streets who inform me that there's been some buzz recently concerning my father's work with the authorities down in Daufuskie Island. Obviously, the local drug traffickers are none too pleased with his presence there or his training of their police force. I want you to pull the files on every last drug dealer, gang member, pimp, etcetera down in Beaufort County, South Carolina. I've already contacted the sheriff's department down there, and they've okayed our investigation. I want answers, facts, and leads on this ASAP, because my father could be in danger, and I'm not having it."

"You got it, kid. I'm on it as of today." The detective rose from his seat to shake the chief's hand.

"Good. You have a great day now, Detective. I'll be speaking with you later in the week."

"Not a problem, Chief. Take it easy."

Chapter 15

"Daufuskie Day"

The Forrester sisters, Candice and Naomi, had helped load the magazines with ammo before handing the firearms over to the island youth as they headed toward the parked cars along the side of the darkened county road.

A call on Corporal Tolliver's cell phone from Candice informed of the impending murder about to take place miles away from him, far across the state line that divided Georgia and South Carolina.

Tolliver felt a surge of adrenaline rush through the bloodstream as he ended the brief phone call. He then contacted his police partner in crime, Hank Columbus, who yelled out in excitement, nearly toppling the naked honky-tonk floozy from the cheap hotel bed they'd been sharing for the night.

"C'mon, niggas! Let's ride!" Eight ski mask-wearing gunmen yelled as they boarded two hoopties, an old slate-gray '81 Buick Skylark, and an off-white Ford El Camino that coughed and sputtered with noisy resistance before finally turning over to a humming start. Three 6 Mafia's smash hit, "Stay Fly," blasted out from the Pioneer speakers in the Skylark with enough bass to vibrate the very dirt road on which it stood, while the thugs riding in the El Camino pumped out Bun B and Ying Yang Twins's "Git It" as their choice of mood music.

As the two vehicles proceeded along Daufuskie Island's moon-dappled, forest-lined dirt road toward Mickey O'Malley's Haig Point bungalow, cellular phone calls between underworld conspirators in both the Peach and Palmetto states buzzed for over thirty minutes, briefing everyone involved about the events unfolding on the tiny sea island sandwiched in between Savannah and Hilton Head.

"Operation Cop Killer," as it was informally known among the crooked cops of the two regions in on the murderous plot, was now officially underway at last.

It was 11:18 PM when Tolliver first received word of the hit from Candice Forrester. Now at 1:37 AM, he would again receive word again.

Only two hours and some change later, the Mickey O'Malley hit, supposedly bought and paid for by David Ambrosia along with incarcerated crime boss Snookey Lake, had gone terribly wrong.

The hoodlums attempted a late-night home invasion of the Irishman's residence instead of staking out the house over the course of the night and waiting for him to emerge during the pre-dawn hours in sweats to run a few miles with Lucky, his Golden Retriever.

They would then kidnap him as he jogged along

the narrow hunting trail beside Bennett's Road, bounding and gagging him, then dispatching him with several gunshot blasts to the upper body. He of course would then end up buried in one of the sea island's many saw grass-covered quicksand spots.

But unfortunately for the low-country big ballers, none of that ever materialized, as had been discussed for weeks in advance. The ghetto youth, stoned out their minds from heavy consumption of cheap malt liquor and marijuana, underestimated the wily old police chief, whose many years of experience on the force had equipped him with the self-defense skills to survive just such an ordeal.

Though O'Malley lived alone at the end of a scenic but lonely country surrounded by a dense wooded area, the small cottage was fully equipped with expensive state-of-the-art surveillance cameras and security alarms, which instantaneously alerted him to the immediate threat looming on his property. Not to mention Lucky's persistent and frenzied barking in the dimly lit living room.

The first three armed toughs fired upon the front door with a furious volley before recklessly storming the bullet-riddled doors, only to be quickly mowed down one by one by the spewing barrels of flame from the police chief's service revolver.

Keeping the handgun in front of him, O'Malley cautiously slid out the darkened interior of the hall closet and against the smooth walls of his living room. He noticed the still, bloodied forms crumpled along his living room floor.

Three of the boys lost their nerve and opted to flee instead of face a similar fate.

Two of their hardier partners squeezed off a few

rounds at the open door, which brought no return fire.

Until they attempted to approach within five feet of the wooden steps leading up toward the entrance.

A gruesome headshot immediately felled the nearest ski mask-clad invader, who died before he dropped lifelessly onto the Irishman's pumpkin patch, his skull shattered. The other tried to crouch down behind an outside tool shed but was taken out with two shots to the chest. He fell up against the front of the shed, his fingers squeezing the trigger of the Uzi and rattling off a series of shots that zipped harmlessly into the chilly night sky. Then his hand dropped limp onto the damp ground and released its hold on the weapon.

Three of the young men made their way to the El Camino, only to be apprehended by over a dozen Dausfuskie Island police officers hopping out of numerous siren-wailing squad cars that surrounded the nearby intersection.

It was over. The plot to kill Mickey O'Malley had come to an unexpected and disappointing end. This major setback would indeed bring more than just a little unwanted attention to everyone involved with the conspiracy to off the visiting police chief. More than likely, they'd face the stiffest of legal penalties. Which would mean that heads would have to roll gangland-style for the mistake.

Chapter 16

"When the Shit Hits the Fan"

The local newspapers ran bold headlines of the attempted murder of Peola police chief Mickey O'Malley. By the end of the week following New Year's Day 2006, the sensational news story had spread like wildfire all across the Deep South. Television, radio, and newspapers ran updates around the clock on the incident.

There was more than a little evidence of involvement from rogue officers within the Daufuskie department as well as those departments on the outside, and as a co-conspirator in the botched attempt David Ambrosia's name would come up several times during the week that followed.

David Ambrosia would soon prepare a live response via satellite in a passionate press conference in which he would deny any involvement in the bloody home invasion and reiterate his close friendship with the police chief and his daughter.

Meanwhile, the local chapter of the FBI, led by Agent Mohammed—he had brought Snookey Lake to justice many years earlier—uncovered damaging evidence that David Ambrosia had indeed dealt with known drug dealers throughout the South as well as various street gangs from Los Angeles. The unsavory media attention formed a dark cloud over what had been America's premier feel-good story.

Godiva was enraged by news of the attempted murder of her best friend's father and immediately broke off the June '06 wedding.

Whiskey himself received a late-night e-mail from Godiva. It read:

> Hey Whiskey, it's me, Godiva. Look, I just gotta let ya know that I'm no longer engaged to David, nor am I going to remain a part of the Spanish Moss Records Incorporated family. I no longer want any affiliation with them at this time. It is not in the best interest of my music career to continue on with the partnerships that had been forged previously, including those with your dad Snookey and his affiliates.
>
> I do understand fully what you guys did for me during my time as a contestant on the *Pop Star* competition, and though I have been really, really busy performing all over the country, I have spoken to Courtney as you well know about keeping five-O off your back and out of sight.
>
> But I don't agree to killing anybody. Certainly not Chief O'Malley, who is not only my best friend's dad, but also is like my own dad.

I still love David, but I can't allow him to ruin my career like he's ruined himself.

Courtney has promised me that she will be my manager and agent from this point on, as she has a master's degree in business management and an accounting degree from the University of Georgia. She will handle everything concerning my career, including security. So at this time I'm separating myself from everyone. I'll contact you soon, my dear, all right?

Luv ya!
Godiva

Chapter 17

"Is This the Thanks I Get?"

Over two dozen Gullah hoodlums and their homies were rapidly arrested, tried, and convicted of masterminding the plot along with the famous Marion "Snookey" Lake to kill Police Chief O'Malley. By mid-January a majority of the drug dealers and gangstas of South Carolina and Georgia's low country regions were either already behind bars or on trial.

Chief Mickey O'Malley and his daughter launched their very own witch-hunts, which in tandem with the investigation already being handled by the feds, turned up several more conspirators to the attempted murder case that came to be known in the media as "The Daufuskie Cop-Killer Trials."

Few from the hood managed to avoid police scrutiny. Not even Peola's elite.

On the morning of January 18, 2006, thirteen Peola police officers stormed David Ambrosia's swank, Italian-style villa out in Pemmican, West Peola. Corporal Tolliver and Officer Columbus were among the policemen on the scene as their fellow officers escorted an angry and disheveled Ambrosia in handcuffs toward an awaiting squad car sitting along the curb just outside of the fourteen-foot-tall brass gates surrounding the twenty acres of lush, rolling hills, pine forests and meandering streams that was the music mogul's property.

As his uniformed captors escorted him to the open back door of the Crown Victoria, Ambrosia, dressed in a heavy London Fog coat over his silk Emporio Armani pajamas and leather house slippers grumbled something incoherent to his handlers as they eased into the backseat and closed the door behind him.

The feds had reason to believe that David Ambrosia had funded his studio and recording label with seed money he'd borrowed from key street gangs such as his very own Bad Boyz II Syndicate and underworld heavyweights like Snookey Lake, DiVante Lovett, and Joi Stevens, to name a few. In return, he would allow these criminals to launder money through his business, conduct drug trafficking operations to high-end celebrity clients, and even contract out murder-for-hire at times.

Thirty minutes later the police convoy ended up in front of the Peola police precinct, where several cops emerged from their vehicles with their famous suspect in tow.

Ambrosia walked along between two solemn-looking officers, saying little besides a nasty comment or two about Courtney O'Malley. He was quickly processed and led downstairs to a small private jail cell, where they removed his cuffs before slamming the shiny metal bars shut.

Ambrosia walked over and grasped two of the bars in front of him, squeezing angrily with clenched fists. He pressed his handsome face against the cold bars and watched the guard walk away down the hallway, jingling a heavy ring of keys.

Less than an hour later, Whiskey and Alonzo showed up at the front desk of the precinct. The pretty, young fair-skinned girl behind the desk with the light gray eyes showed pleasant surprise as the brothers approached.

Fresh out of the academy, she'd once dated Alonzo back in high school, and tried to catch up on events before signing them in on the register.

"All right, boys, I'm sorry to inform you, but Mr. Ambrosia is currently being held without bond. I'm sorry, but I can have an officer lead you downstairs to the holding cells to visit with him if you'd like."

Within minutes the brothers were standing outside David Ambrosia's jail cell. David was chatting away on his Blackjack before noticing his childhood friends standing in the hall. He ended the call and stuck his hand through the narrow bars and grasped the palms of both men in the strong handshake.

"Dawg! I'm soo fuckin' ticked-off right now! You have no idea how pissed-off I am behind all of this bullshit!" Ambrosia snarled.

Alonzo leaned in closer to the cell door. "I kin imagine how you gotta feel, my dude. But you already know how we do shit, right? We gonna get you outta dis mufucka in no time. We brought bail money down here, but dat li'l bitch done gone an' held you wit'out bail. Did you know dat shit?"

"Nope. Didn't know anything about that. But it's all good though, because I've already hired Mark J. Burton the third and Carolyn Myers-Pierce, so I'll be outta here soon enough."

Alonzo asked, "Who the fuck are they?"

"Dude, you gotta be kiddin' me. You don't know? Those two are only the best lawyers money can buy, that's all. Who do you think got Katrina Ricks off scot-free back in ninety-one? Everybody in the country remembers that trial that was held up in Washington, DC back then, because the feds had been trying to nail Katrina for a while. She was a fuckin' street legend in DC for years before her trials. Anyway, she was facing life for murder, and guess what? She livin' overseas now with her daughter, or so I've heard."

Whiskey said, "Oh yeah, you talkin' 'bout dat ballin'-ass broad, Southeast Trina, right? Yeah, I remember dat shit like it was yesterday. Dat trial was all over da news every fuckin' day."

Alonzo placed his hands into the pockets of his baggy jeans, hanging his head reflectively. "Look here, David, Godiva done used us and used you too. Da bitch ain't nothin' but a strip club ho, for real. You betta off without her dumb ass, but like ya said, it's all good though, 'cause she gonna get hers befo' too long. You betta believe dat. And as for you know who, we got dat fa ya, my man. Don't worry, a'ight?"

David Ambrosia noticed Alonzo looking over at a nearby guard standing silently across the hall.

"Don't worry about that guard, dude. I've already slipped him a little something that will keep him quiet as we kick it down here for a minute.

"Whiskey, I gave that woman all of my energy and helped get her to the top of the *Billboard* charts. Did you know that? Well, that's a fact. Also, I've booked a year's worth of television performances, radio interviews, and a ten-city tour for her, and this is how she repays me? Her and that bitch, Courtney O'Malley. Well, check it, before I got into the music industry, I was a hustler, and the code of the streets prompts me to take care of a situation once and for all after I get up outta here. I promise, my sweet, sweet Godiva is going to have the shortest career of any singer in history. You guys heard of Janis Joplin before, right? Or maybe Kurt Cobain?"

The brothers nodded their heads simultaneously.

"Yeah, well, once I get myself together and get out from behind this jail cell, which won't take long, my former artist and fiancée is going to join them in the great studio in the sky."

Whiskey and Alonzo drew even closer to hear Ambrosia.

"It's one thing to cheat on me with other guys—Didn't think I knew that, did ya?—break off our wedding engagement, fire me as her manager, jump ship from my record label. I even forgave her for taking on a spiteful bitch like Courtney as her new manager. But one thing I can't forgive is setting me up to be arrested and sent to prison. She knew all about the events; now she's playing the innocent role. She knows that there was a cost. She owed certain individuals in the game when me and Snookey pulled strings to get her to win votes. We had people all over the United States to tune in to that program and vote for her. That took the influence of some of the nation's top shot-callers, both in prison and on the street, to make that happen. Yet she thought nothing of even sending a thank-you card to those who helped her get to where she's at currently, largely because of her association with Courtney, who obviously had much more influence on her than I even realized.

"When you guys came in to see me, I was speaking with your dad. He was pissed. He caught wind of Courtney's plan to transfer him back to Leavenworth Penitentiary, and do you know what he said to me? He said that Joi Stevens said to him that it's a Gullah saying, 'If you kill da head, da ass gotta dead,' which means now that Courtney is riding the crest of Godiva's major success. We gotta do it, y'all. We gotta hit Godiva."

The three men agreed silently as to the necessity of the job at hand, and as the brothers left Ambrosia behind, they both seemed ready to begin the orchestration of an urgent call to duty for the boys in the hood.

TO BE CONTINUED . . .

Assorted comments on the content of *The Dawkins Letters*

'I found The God Delusion *quite a depressing read because a) the arguments did seem banal and not in any way inspiring b) many of the criticisms of religion I could only help agreeing with.... I couldn't quite believe that someone so clever would use such biased and naïve arguments. I thought I was missing something. You've helped me see through it....'*

'Robertson is a prat. And not only a PRAT, but a dangerous PRAT. A complete loser. I've never read such a dogmatic, vicious diatribe as this. WHEN WILL THEISTS LIKE ROBERTSON actually provide some EMPIRICAL EVIDENCE of their own – something we can really scrutinize and say – 'Hey! You know, there could be a God, judged on this evidence'.'*

'Bravo David Robertson, Not only did you take the time to read The God Delusion You also took the time to write a long article about your reaction, and now you join this discussion.'*

'Wow, this is an intelligent and well-crafted view of RD's book. I can see that it really got to most readers of this site as well, seeing as it was posted 2 days ago and already has a comment pagination level of 5, and most of the comments are just stating that the writer of this entry is wrong and a dumb stupid-head. I love it when things get stirred up. Please keep it up!'*

'I'm impressed that some of the people here bother to debate this Robertson nincompoop. He is clearly out of his mind and beyond reason and logic. If you do debate him, stop respecting his delusions, however eloquent he puts them, and please approach him with the scorn and contempt that he deserves. Dawkins refuses to debate this sort of weirdness because it gives the person with the sick mind the impression that there really is something to debate'.*

'I'd like to say thank you for your articulate responses to all of these (sometimes hostile) questions. I am definitely an atheist but I really appreciate some good, healthy, well written debate.'*

'Of the four books, rather astonishingly only one attempted a serious rebuttal of TGD and imparted a clear view of its writer's *beliefs – and that was David Robertson's. I found this the best of the four books.'*

The Dawkins website review of The Dawkins Letters

'I've just finished reading your Dawkins Letters... Absolute masterpieces... All of them!'

M. in Botswana.

'I came across your Dawkins Letters and I was blown away. You have my utmost respect for your rationale and for raising points of the God Delusion – and general atheist demands, such as "Go on! Prove God exists!" – and showing where the fallacies lie. You are a superb writer and have a fantastic gift of keeping the reader enthralled. Thank you so much for your brilliant collection. If others jibe at you and call you crazy, please ignore them.'

An Atheist from South Africa

'I am a 23 year old student doing my PhD in Biochemistry at the University of Oxford. I have just finished reading your Dawkins Letters. I have to say that you have a done an amazing job. Not only have you stripped down Dawkins' "theories" (as you convincingly show, he has no support whatsoever for many of his assumptions), but you also prove that one can be passionate about ones beliefs in a respectful, tolerant way.'

An agnostic from Oxford.

'Well, what a breath of fresh air. I must admit, since The God Delusion was published, I've felt somewhat gloomy and don't have the ability to refute Dawkins' statements. I think I was in awe of him because of his supposed ultra brilliance, but yet felt he was mistaken somehow. Your book is great. I woke up this morning feeling as though a weight has been lifted from my mind.'

A Christian in USA

THE DAWKINS LETTERS
CHALLENGING ATHEIST MYTHS DAVID ROBERTSON

CHRISTIAN
FOCUS

Copyright © David Robertson 2007

paperback ISBN 978-1-84550-597-4
epub ISBN 978-1-84550-652-0
Mobi ISBN 978-1-78191-027-6

10 9 8 7

Published in 2007
Reprinted in 2007 (three times), 2008, 2010, 2013 & 2018
by
Christian Focus Publications, Ltd.,
Geanies House, Fearn, Ross-shire,
IV20 1TW, Great Britain.

www.christianfocus.com

Cover design by Moose77.com

Printed and bound by
Nørhaven, Denmark

THE DAWKINS LETTERS
CHALLENGING ATHEIST MYTHS DAVID ROBERTSON

Contents

INTRODUCTORY LETTER TO THE READER

Dear Reader,

The book you are reading is a collection of open review letters written in response to Professor Richard Dawkins in the winter of 2006/7 concerning his book *The God Delusion*.[1] Richard Dawkins is a brilliant and well-known British scientist. He is the Charles Simonyi Professor of the Public Understanding of Science at the University of Oxford and one of the best popularisers of science. However, in recent years he has become better known as Britain's most famous atheist. His most recent works have taken an increasingly strident and militant anti-religious position, his previous book being *A Devil's Chaplain*, which is a collection of essays many of which attack religious beliefs,[2] being followed by this, his most important work.

The God Delusion has hit the American and British markets at a time when religion is never far from the front pages. For those who grew up in the 1960s thinking that they were witnessing the death throes of religion it has been something of a revelation and concern that the 'march of progress' seems to have been impeded by

1. Bantam Press (2006)
2. Weidenfeld and Nicholson (2003)

a resurgence of 'irrational' religion and superstition. There is considerable worry that 9/11 and the rise of Islamic fundamentalism is being matched by a rise in Christian fundamentalism. In Europe this is seen by many as being a significant motivating factor in the 'War on Terror'. In the US there appears to be the beginnings of a backlash against the perceived power of the Christian Right. It is into this climate of hostility, religious confusion and fear that Dawkins' clarion call to atheists to 'come out' and organise is addressed. It is a message that is being welcomed by many and is causing considerable interest. *The God Delusion* has been on the New York Times bestseller list for several months and is well on its way to becoming a million seller in Britain. This despite a significant number of hostile and negative reviews (by no means all of them from religious protagonists). It is a powerful, well-written book which despite its many weaknesses is having a considerable influence.

It is also generating a response. Alister McGrath and his wife, Joanna, have published *The Dawkins Delusion?*[3] in response. Many articles, newspaper columns and reviews have already been written. So why add to them with this small book? There have been a number of academic responses to the various accusations made by Dawkins and I am sure that there will be more. However, for many the damage will have been done and those who do not read academic books will still be left with the impressions and the myths. On the other hand there will be those who from a religious perspective, have a kind of knee jerk reaction and respond to Dawkins' vehemence in kind. Whilst this may appeal to those in their own

3. *The Dawkins Delusion?* SPCK (2007)

constituencies, it is unlikely to do anything other than reinforce the impression that religious people are deluded. And of course there will be many who think this should just be left alone and ignored. After all, is anything ever settled by argument? I suspect that you are not in the latter grouping, otherwise you would not be reading this book.

Given that there have been and will be many responses, why add to them with this collection of letters? I guess the answer is simply that many people will not have the time, inclination or money to read about every single subject that Dawkins addresses. My aim is to present one person's response to Dawkins and to do so from a wide and personal perspective. My aim is not to convert, nor to insult, nor even to defend. Rather it is to challenge some of the basic myths that Dawkins uses and encourages in his book, in order that you may think and consider these things for yourself. If you are interested in reading about or even discussing these immensely important subjects further, then at the end you will find a reading list and some suggestions.

A word about the style of these letters. Some will consider that they are too angry, others that they are not angry enough; some wonder whether humour is appropriate, others will ask, 'what humour?!' It will be helpful to remember that these are personal letters, not an academic discourse, nor an exercise in English grammar.

I am deeply grateful to those who have read and commented on the letters (the wounds of a friend are faithful!). In particular I would like to thank Dr Elias Medeiros, Bill Schweitzer, Dr Grant Macaskill, Dr Iain D.

Campbell, Gary Aston, Dr Deuan Jones, David Campbell, Dr Sam Logan, Will Traub, Dr Cees Dekker, Nigel
Anderson, Dr Phil Ryken, Iver Martin, Alex Macdonald,
Alastair Donald and Dr Ligon Duncan. Whether scientists, philosophers or theologians, British, American or
European you have all provoked, encouraged and stimulated. I am especially grateful to my editor, Dr Bob Carling,
whose patience and suggestions have been invaluable.
The final responsibility for what is written, including any
errors or misjudgements, is, of course, mine.

I am not a scientist, and I am not a well-known Oxford scholar with an international reputation. There are
many people who will be able to go into detail and answer Dawkins' many accusations in greater depth than
this book even attempts. Some of my own personal background comes across in the letters but perhaps at this stage
it will be helpful for you to know that I am a 44-year-old
minister in a Presbyterian Church in Scotland. Having
been brought up on a farm in the Highlands of Scotland,
I studied history at the University of Edinburgh and then
theology at the Free Church College. I have been a minister for 20 years, 14 of them in the city of Dundee. I am
a Christian minister with a deep interest in what Dawkins
calls the cultural *zeitgeist* – the way our culture is going.
I am a frequent visitor to the USA and Europe with a particular interest in bringing the Good News, the Gospel,
to our post-Christian society. I believe that the Gospel is
something that is relevant and vital for all people in all cultures at all times and it has been my privilege to see people
from many different backgrounds come to know, love and
have their lives changed by Jesus Christ.

As a deeply committed Christian I am disturbed by the attacks that Dawkins makes on God and the Bible, and astonished that his attacks are taken so seriously. I believe that he is appealing not to people's intelligence and knowledge but rather to their ignorance. This series of letters is presented to the reader in order to challenge some of the atheist myths that Dawkins taps into and feeds. Each letter deals with a chapter of the book and each highlights at least one atheist myth. I call them atheist myths because they are beliefs that are widely held or assumed without necessarily having been thought through or evidenced.

If you are a Christian then I presume you are reading this because you want to think about some of the issues involved and like me want to reflect on how your faith fits into modern society. If you are not yet a Christian (or you are unsure, or a follower of another faith) I hope that you will benefit from reading these letters. My prayer is that you will be stimulated, challenged, provoked and most of all drawn to consider the claims of Jesus Christ.

Finally, I would like to thank my congregation St Peter's Free Church, for their love, support and understanding over the years. Likewise I thank my wife and best friend, Annabel, and our children, Andrew, Becky and Emma Jane who are constant reminders to me of the grace and goodness of God.

This book is dedicated to the glory of God and in memory of the many millions who lost their lives in the wars and injustices of the Failed Atheist 20th Century.

David A. Robertson
Dundee 2007

LETTER 1 –
THE MYTH OF THE HIGHER
CONSCIOUSNESS

Dear Dr Dawkins,

I hope you will forgive me writing to you but I have just finished reading your book and it was very frustrating. There was so much in it that I could identify with and yet so much that was to my mind just simply wrong. I would love to discuss it with you, or with those who are your disciples, but I'm afraid that I am not an Oxford Don, I don't have the access to the media you do, and I am not part of the Establishment. And of course you have stated that you do not discuss with 'fundamentalists' or those who believe in revelation or supernaturalism. Given that the subject about which you are so vehement is the whole question of supernaturalism and whether there is a God or not, do you not think it is kind of loading the dice to discuss this only with those who already share your presuppositions?

And then there is the problem of what you call 'the Higher Consciousness'. You argue that those who share your views have been raised to a greater level of consciousness. Your book is written to make atheists 'loud and proud' that they have had their consciousness raised, whilst also seeking to raise the consciousness of those of us who have been left behind. This reminds me of the story of the Emperor's New Clothes. The Emperor is told by a couple of 'tailors' that they have produced a set of new clothes for him which can only be seen by the enlightened and wise (those who have had their consciousness raised). Of course not wanting to appear stupid he and all his courtiers state that they can see the wonderful and stunning new clothes. It is only when the emperor is wandering naked through the streets and a small boy cries out, 'The Emperor has no clothes', that the people realise the truth. I think your notion that atheists are those who have had their consciousness raised, and that they are *de facto* more intelligent, rational and honest than other human beings, is a myth on a par with the Emperor's New Clothes.

Of course I realise that many people who buy your book will already be converts – they already share your faith and will be looking for reassurance or confirmation. You are preaching to the choir. This is rather obvious even from the people who write the blurb on the jacket cover, admittedly not normally unbiased objective judges. Stephen Pinker, Brian Eno, Derren Brown and Philip Pullman all wax lyrical about your book – but then this is hardly surprising given that they are convinced atheists already. Pullman wants your anti-faith book to be put into every faith school (which is a little surprising, given that you make such a fuss about children being indoctrinated – unless of course atheist indoctrination is OK). Eno says it is 'a book for the new millennium, one in which we may be released from lives dominated by the supernatural'. Heady stuff. But best of all is Derren Brown who affirms *The God Delusion* as his 'favourite book of all time'. It is 'a heroic and life-changing work'. He hopes that those who are 'secure and intelligent enough to see the value of questioning their beliefs will be big enough and strong enough to read this book'.

Well, I have read it. I did expect to be challenged. You are after all one of the world's top three intellectuals' (as the book jacket reminds us). Of course *The God Delusion* was well written, very entertaining and passionate. But at an intellectual and logical level it really misses the mark. Most of the arguments are of sixth-form schoolboy variety and shot through with a passionate anti-religious vehemence. What is disturbing is that your fundamentalist atheism will actually be taken seriously by some and will be used to reinforce their already prejudged anti-religion and anti-Christian stance. Your 'arguments' will be repeated *ad nauseam* in newspaper letters, columns, opinion pages, pubs and dinner tables throughout the land. You will forgive me saying this but it seems remarkably similar to the kind of thing that 'intellectuals' were putting out in 1930s Germany about the Jews and Judaism. Just as they claimed the Jews were responsible for all the ills in Weimar Germany, so according to your book religious people are responsible for the majority of ills in today's society.

Along with John Lennon you want us to 'imagine' a world with no religion and no God. A world that you claim would have no suicide bombers (despite the fact that the most suicide attacks have been by the secular Sri Lankan Tamil Tigers), no crusades, no 9/11, no Israeli/Palestinian wars, etc. By the way, John Lennon was one of my heroes and I loved *Imagine*. Then I grew up and realised that it took a great deal of imagination to take seriously a song which spoke of imagining a world 'with no possessions too', written by a man who lived in a mansion and had an abundance of possessions, whilst there were millions dying from lack of resources. It seems to me that your vision/imagination is almost as unrealistic as Lennon's.

I want to write a letter in response to each of your chapters. As you correctly point out each of them deals with issues that are fundamental to our existence, meaning and well-being as humans. But let me finish off this first letter by looking at a couple of other things you state in your own introduction.

You claim that your book is for those who have been brought up in a particular religious faith and now either no longer believe it, or are unhappy in it and want out. You want to raise the consciousness of such people to the extent that they can realise that they can get out. Do most people not already know that it is perfectly possible to leave a religion and not suffer any significant consequences? Of course if you are in an Islamic society that is not true (but your book is not really directed at Islam) and I realise that for some in the US admitting you are an atheist is political suicide, but overall most people are free to change their beliefs. I was brought up in a religious home and knew from a very young age that not only was it possible to leave, but that for many people it would be considered normal. I fought my own battles so that I could be free to think for myself. But it was not only, nor even primarily, against the religious teachings of my parents or others (and I did fight against them), but also the patronising expectations of teachers, media

16

and others who just assumed that the only reason anyone would be religious was because of parental influence, brainwashing and a weak mind. You know the real relief came when I realised I could be a Christian *and* think for myself *and* seek to make a difference in the world; and that I did not have to buy into all the quirks and cultural nuances of religious groups, nor the fundamentalism of the secularists who just knew that they were right.

I cannot think of a single career option in Britain where being an atheist would place you at a disadvantage (unless you are thinking of becoming a member of the clergy – although current form suggests that even there you could get away with it!). However, there are many people for whom admitting they are 'religious' is a severe block to their career and life. Those who seek to be Christian politicians, singers, businessmen, teachers and social workers often face significant prejudice and irrational fear. It is sometimes advantageous to deny one's faith or even to leave it. Being a Christian is more often than not a stumbling block to one's chosen career path, rather than being an atheist.

Of course there are those who belong to cults that exercise a form of mind control tantamount to brainwashing, but surely even you would not argue that every religious person is in that category? You seem to think that anyone who is religious is actually at a lower level of consciousness and needs to be set free by becoming an atheist. Of course you offer no empirical evidence for this. Like much of the book, it is a presupposition (even a prejudice) that does not appear to be founded on anything other than you would like it to be so. Have you ever thought that there might be many others who are in the opposite position – brought up in an atheistic secular society and discovering that they can actually believe in God? Would you give them the freedom to do so? What would you do if your daughter turned out to be a Bible believing Christian? Would you disown her? Would you even allow her that choice? Or have you done your best to inoculate her against the virus of religion? I remember one young man, highly intelligent, who came to a Christianity Explored group. When he was asked his religious position he said, 'I'm an atheist, but I'm beginning to have my doubts'. I laughed. A backslidden atheist! I thought that was quite neat. Maybe there are a lot more of them than you think. You ought to be careful about the raising of consciousness – maybe people will become tired of your modernist certainties and instead find refuge in the clear fresh air of Jesus Christ!

I also smiled when I read your complaint that atheists were persecuted and misunderstood. You contrast the current situation of atheists with the situation of homosexuals a couple of decades ago and suggest that just as 'gays' had to 'come out' so also 'brights' (the rather hopeful and somewhat arrogant newly coined name for atheists) need to come out of the closet and establish their place in society. I had not noticed that atheists were particularly silent or poorly represented in British society (or even American). In Britain all our government institutions, media outlets and educational establishments are primarily secularist. The National Secular Society get a far bigger exposure than the vast majority of Christian churches – despite the fact that most secular societies could fit their members into a phone box. Even when the Prime Minister was asked a relatively innocuous question about whether he prays, his media minder Alasdair Campbell felt compelled to point out, 'we don't do God'. Atheism and secularism are, without doubt, the prevailing philosophies of those who consider themselves 'the elite'.

You were given the immense privilege of having editorial control of your own TV series *The Root of all Evil*. Can you tell me when an Evangelical Christian was last given the opportunity by a national TV channel to produce a film demonstrating the evils of atheism? Do you not think that in an open and democratic society when you are allowed to make a 'documentary' attacking whole groups of people they should at least be allowed some right of reply? Of course, that is not going to happen, because, as you well know, those who are primarily in charge of our media outlets are those who share many of your presuppositions and prefer to make programmes which present Christians as either weak ineffective Anglican vicars, or tub-thumping American Right Wing Evangelists who want to hang gays. It is propaganda – not truth, not reason, not debate and most certainly not fair.

At a meeting of BBC Executives in 2006 it was reported[4] that the policy of the Corporation is that secularism is the *only* philosophy to which others must eventually come. Other philosophies and belief systems can be tolerated but they must never be allowed any real say in the BBC. Apparently some had the audacity to suggest that perhaps the BBC should recognise that secularism is *a* philosophy and not *the* philosophy. I hope that you will support such pluralistic open-mindedness.

4. *Daily Mail* (24 October 2006); *Prospect* Magazine (November 2006)

The atheist revival is now being challenged from all sides. Having had a century of elitist domination and control many in the Western World are beginning to wake up to the fact that the secular emperor has no clothes. The 20th century can truly be called the Failed Atheist Century. Can I recommend that you read an excellent book on this subject, written by one of your Oxford colleagues, Niall Ferguson, *The War of the World: History's Age of Hatred*?[5] He shares your evolutionary secularist presuppositions, but his account of the 20th century is a stunning indictment of the failure of secularism and 'science' to bring peace on earth.

Your book comes across as a desperate attempt to shore up atheism's crumbling defences. Ironically it reminds me of some in the Church who, faced with what seems to be overwhelming odds and staring defeat in the face, issue evangelistic tracts, articles and books which are designed to shore up the faith of the faithful rather than being aimed at the conversion of unbelievers. *The God Delusion* fits nicely into that category. I am sure you will delight your disciples, establishing what they already believe, but I very much doubt you will make any impact on others who are less fixed in their opinions and who really are seekers after truth. What I do appreciate is that, unlike the irrational and the lazy who want to deny its existence, you admit that there is such a thing as truth. You may laugh at the idea that the truth is ultimately found in Jesus Christ. But I remain an optimist. I believe not only in truth but also in the power of God and his Holy Spirit to bring enlightenment to even the darkest mind. So there is still hope for us both.

Yours, etc.

David

5. Allen Lane (2006)

LETTER 2 –
THE MYTH OF GODLESS BEAUTY

Dear Dr Dawkins,

Thanks for posting my letter on your website. That was very unexpected – almost as unexpected as the response from some of your fellow atheists, as evidenced on your message board. Although some were intelligent, thoughtful and expressed their disagreement in a constructive and stimulating way, a surprising number reacted with all the vehemence of religious believers whose sacred holy book was being blasphemed. I thought I had seen vitriol before, but this lot would take some beating. Anyway it's not fair to judge a belief system by those of its advocates who are eccentric, extreme and in need of some kind of therapy. Please remember that when you discuss Christianity.

I have also found it very interesting watching your 'tour of the USA'.[6] It struck me that there are a number of similarities between your tour and some revivalist TV evangelist rallies. You have mass rallies to the converted (which you totally control). You mock those who disagree with you and refuse to engage with them in any constructive way. You demonise those who do not share your point of view. You (or your advocates) exult

6 See www.richarddawkins.net

21

at your book being in the New York Times Bestseller list and encourage people to go out and buy copies for friends and even, in the latest campaign, copies for politicians. Fans are also encouraged to watch the latest YouTube of 'Dawkins Destroying Dumb Fundies'. I can even obtain special edition jacket covers and website banners. It's highly entertaining -- in the same way that 'Reality' or even 'God TV' can be, but it hardly constitutes rational argument and discussion.

Anyway, let us leave aside this rather commercial and politicised behaviour and not indulge in the view that because the methods are suspect, the message must be false. Let's go to chapter one of your book. It's a great beginning, well written, well argued, informative and, much to my surprise, very persuasive. This is probably my favourite chapter. There is so much I can identify with and even say 'Amen' to! However, whilst I can accept and am convinced by some of the premises you state, I am less than convinced by some of the conclusions that you draw.

A Sense of Wonder

This is a key concept and you deal with it brilliantly. Many of us have been there. I remember as a boy being transfixed by the stars as I walked home across the Morrich Moor in the Scottish Highlands. I lived on top of Nigg cliffs where I often sat looking out over the Cromarty Firth (an inlet leading to the North Sea), being utterly amazed at the beauty and variety in nature: the seagulls, the blue sea, the purple heather, the yellow gorse, the seals and even the occasional dolphin. It felt like paradise (even with the old World War 2 gun emplacements still deeply embedded in the cliffs). If you don't feel a sense of wonder in such an environment you ain't got no soul. You have obviously had the same experience – as I suspect most human beings have. But you interpret it differently.

You think that to believe that God has created and is responsible for such magnificence is somehow to demean the beauty and explain away the sense of wonder. I must admit, that thought was not something new to me. I tried really hard to think the same thing. It seemed to me also that the 'gods' of religion were somehow trivial compared to such beauty and grace. And here's the rub. They are. But neither could I replace them with humans. Darwin's quotation, which you cite, is an example of human arrogance at its worst:

> Thus, from the war of nature, from famine and death, the most exalted object which we are capable of conceiving, namely the production of the higher animals, directly follows.

Is that really it? Is mankind the most exalted object that we are capable of conceiving? I remember a good man saying that if Jesus Christ was not real he would worship the man who invented him! Was I to be faced with the choice of man-made idols or human beings as the apex of creation? Neither was satisfactory. But where did this beauty come from? Why did I feel it? No one gives a better answer than Solomon, the wisest man who ever lived: 'God has made everything beautiful in its time. He has also set eternity in the hearts of men; yet they cannot fathom what God has done from beginning to end' (Ecclesiastes 3:11).

I tried really hard to be an atheist, or at least an agnostic, but I just couldn't get there. One New Year's Eve I even prayed to a God I was not sure even existed: 'Oh God, if you are there, show me and I will serve you the rest of my life.' There was no voice from heaven. No flashing light. And as far as I could see the prayer remained unanswered – until one Sunday I decided that after all I would go to Church. I went to a small Scottish Presbyterian church beside the sea, down from those same cliffs. As I listened to the sound of the plain singing of the psalms of the Bible and heard the waves of the sea splashing against the walls of the Church, it struck me what a fool I had been. Of course God existed. Nothing else made sense. You cannot explain beauty or evil, creation or humanity, time or space, without God. Or at least you can, but to my mind the materialistic, atheistic explanation is emotionally, spiritually and above all intellectually inadequate. Indeed, it takes a great deal of faith to be an atheist.

By the way, I should point out that there is an interesting connection here between religion and science. Across the cliffs, on the other side of the Firth, is a small village called Cromarty. About 150 years ago there lived an extraordinary man called Hugh Miller. He was a genius. He had your gift for writing and he was also one of the founding fathers of modern geology. His book *The Old Red Sandstone* and *In the Footprints of the Creator* are still classics. He was absolutely convinced that the geological evidence was for an old earth. Miller was an elder in the Free Church, editor of its newspaper and a strong political advocate for the Highlands peasants who were being cleared from their homes (in yet another example of the Selfish Gene principle at work). He loved science and found in it, not a contradiction of the Bible, but a complementarity.

You cite Carl Sagan from his *Pale Blue Dot*.[7] It is worth quoting in full again.

7. Ballantine Books (1997)

How is it that hardly any major religion has looked at science and concluded, 'This is better than we thought! The Universe is much bigger than our prophets said, grander, more subtle, more elegant?' Instead they say, 'No, no, no! My god is a little god, and I want him to stay that way.' A religion, old or new, that stressed the magnificence of the Universe as revealed by modern science might be able to draw forth reserves of reverence and awe hardly tapped by the conventional faiths.

That is brilliant. I would shout Hallelujah if it were not for the fact that this would immediately caricature me as a tub-thumping evangelical! The modern Christian church in the West has, on the whole, to hold up its hands and admit guilt. *Mea culpa*. We have too often reduced God to a formula, belief to a system and worship to a happy-clappy, feel-good floor show. Our God *is* too small. But that is because he is *our* God and not the God of the Bible.

Not long after becoming a Christian I came to understand and appreciate the writings of John Calvin and others who followed his particular line of biblical teaching. I loved it. They portrayed the God of the Bible as magnificent, powerful, deep, glorious, sovereign, worthy of praise and the creator of this amazing, vast and complex universe. They did not put him in a box, indeed they argued that by very definition God could not be boxed. Which is what led men like the 19th-century Scottish theologian Thomas Chalmers to enquire and think 'outside the box'. Chalmers even wrote a best-selling book entitled *Astronomical Discourses* which discussed the possibility of life on other planets.

When I first became a Christian I thought I had it all worked out. I had God in a box. I had Jesus. But as I grew and matured I realised that instead of me being in charge of the paddling pool, all I had done was dip my big toe into the ocean of God's knowledge, love and being. The boxed small God does result in an antagonistic view to anything (including science) that will not fit into that box. But the unboxed God, the God of the Bible, allows us – no, encourages us – to explore his creation, to climb the heights and scale the depths. I think of the award-winning, brilliant biochemist who heard me waxing lyrical about the wonder of God in the stars and spoke to me afterwards. He told me that in his work, studying some of the smallest observable things known to man, he too was seeing the wonder and glory of God.

Some of your followers have been trying to contrast science and Christianity with the rather foolish challenge, 'science has given us cars/toasters/spacecraft, etc. What has religion ever given us?' It is foolish because they are making a false dichotomy between science and Christianity as though science is one belief system and Christianity another. No. The difference is not in terms of science but in terms of philosophy and belief. The danger of the position that you are advocating is that you want to drive a wedge between science and religion to suit your own philosophy (of course in that you are joined by some religious fundamentalists). But your position is philosophical, not scientific. To put it more plainly, the reason that you are an atheist is not because you are driven there by scientific fact, but because that is your philosophy. You use science to justify it but then many religious people also use science to justify their position. The question is not science but rather the presuppositions that we bring to science.

Let me leave this section on wonder by suggesting that you could do a lot worse than read one of the greatest philosophical minds that America has ever produced – Jonathan Edwards. If any human being grasped something of the grandeur of God, it was Edwards. Take this from his work *The Nature of True Virtue*:

> For as God is infinitely the Greatest Being, so he is … infinitely the most beautiful and excellent. All the beauty to be found throughout the whole creation is but a reflection of the diffused beams of that Being who hath an infinite fullness of brightness and glory. God is the foundation of all beauty and glory.[8]

A Sense of Religion

Now let's turn to your use of the term 'religious'. I agree with most of what you say here. It is all about how we use and understand the term 'God'. I accept fully that too many Christians have been guilty of selective quotation, and circulation of urban myths, in order to prove that this or that famous person was either a Christian or had a deathbed conversion. Your evidence concerning Einstein seems absolutely convincing and it means that I will have to be careful about using such quotes as 'Science without religion is lame, religion without science is blind.' Although I am convinced that you are right about this and indeed about many 'religious' people who only use the term 'god' as a synonym for their own 'religious' feelings or sense of wonder, yet I am not convinced that this sense of wonder is something that is just a product of our natural being/environment.

You state that naturalists believe that everything is physical. I think of one highly intelligent chemist who

8. 1765. Republished by Banner of Truth (1974)

when challenged on this admitted that love, hate, beauty, spirituality and so on were all in the end 'just' chemical reactions. This seems to me a profoundly depressing minimalist view of the universe and of human life. Of course, if you could prove it and evidence that there was no personal God then I guess we would have to live with it. But you cannot. Your view, that the universe is only physical, is a hypothesis and one that is largely based on wishful thinking. In fact, your position is a kind of 'science of the gaps': there are certain things you observe, you cannot really explain them scientifically and you do not want to resort to explaining them spiritually (because you have a basic philosophical presupposition that nothing exists except matter), so rather than leave any gaps (through which you fear a small god might slip) you basically expand your scientific knowledge so that it becomes a theory of everything – and you conveniently shut out anything that does not fit in that box. Ironically, the very thing that you accuse Christians of doing with God, putting him into a box, is something that you are in danger of doing with science, creating a human construct based upon your anti-religious presuppositions which, whilst designed to shut out God, actually ends up boxing in science.

Whilst I agree in general with the section on the use of the term 'god' there are a couple of remarks that do not hold up. For example you state that, 'the notion that religion is a proper field, in which one might claim expertise, is one that should not go unquestioned'. Here your hatred for religion has gone slightly over the top. Given that the majority of the world over the majority of history has been, and still is, religious, one would have thought that it is a reasonable field for study and that there are some who can claim some degree of expertise in it. Indeed, your dismissal of any who do is a neat trick that will allow you to critique religions and religious books without having to resort to any kind of academic scholarship because after all religion is not a proper field. This, then, allows you to get away with simplistic statements such as 'pantheism is just sexed up atheism'. Given your earlier definition of atheists as being naturalists who hold to the notion that there is only the material you will find that there are many pantheists who are not atheists. They believe in numerous spirits, gods and non-material things.

I also find that you have an interesting use of quotations. You cite letters from an American Roman Catholic and the president of a historical society. I am sure they are not the only letters sent by those who disagreed with Einstein's views but they are the ones you selected. Why? Because they allow you to imply or assert that Christians are either ignorant or full of 'intellectual and moral cowardice'. It is the classic *ad hominem* argument: look how stupid these Christians are, therefore God cannot exist. I, as a Christian, do not agree with either the tone or the substance of those letters, and I know of very few Christian scholars who would (but you already covered your bases with that one by declaring there is no such thing as Christian scholarship!). In particular, the oft-cited, but biblically false assertion, 'as everyone knows, religion is based on Faith, not knowledge'. I would argue the opposite – faith without knowledge is blind and stupid. Biblical faith is in a person. If you do not know about that person you cannot have faith in him.

How would you feel if I took some of the more ludicrous and ignorant comments from some of the atheists on your website and used them as an example of how atheism rots the brain? It would not be fair or honest.

One final thought. You claim to be a religious non-believer. That to me is the worst of both worlds. I hate religion. I think that Marx was in some sense right – religion has far too often been used as the opiate of the people. In the name of religion a great deal of evil and harm has been done. Ironically I believe that religion *per se* has brought us a great deal of harm. But I do believe. I believe in the God of the Bible. I find that his revelation of himself in both the creation and Scripture is wonderfully liberating and best fits the facts as far as I can see them. You may aspire to be a religious non-believer. I am delighted to be a non-religious believer.

All the best,
David

LETTER 3 –
THE MYTH OF ATHEIST
RATIONALITY AND TOLERANCE

Dear Dr Dawkins,

I would like to apologise if I am in any way misrepresenting your position. It is not intentional. I disagree with what you say and it would therefore be pretty pointless to write about what you are not saying. However, I am becoming more and more convinced that your position is primarily a philosophical and religious position, rather than one you are driven to by science. That also appears to be the position of many of your fellow atheists on your website, whose reaction to the criticism has been akin to some religious fundamentalists I know.

You have a central thesis, that science proves, in so far as it is possible, that God does not exist and that belief in him is a delusion. But you surround that thesis with a whole army of smaller arguments, such as the nature of religion, supposed errors in the Bible, hypocrisy in the Church, etc. These have the effect of, apparently, reinforcing your main argument whilst at the same time allowing your supporters to complain, when these surrounding arguments are challenged, that the challenger's views are irrational and stupid because they do not address the central thesis.

Some Christians want to argue in the same vein – of course God exists and anyone who denies otherwise is ignorant, irrational, etc. Thus we end up with the dialogue of the blind and the deaf. Which is pretty dumb. What I am trying to do in these letters is deal with all the secondary arguments in the order that you bring them up in the book. As we deconstruct these, we can see that many of them are either red herrings, irrelevant or just simply wrong. We are then left with the central kernel of your argument, which, shod of this scaffolding, is seen to be naked and without any significant support. The atheist emperor is seen to have no clothes.

A number of years ago when I was a student at the University of Edinburgh I was involved in a debate with members of the Feminist Society. It left a profound impression. Amongst the other 'rational' arguments used to prove that men were no longer needed was the classic 'the nuclear bomb is the ultimate phallic symbol and therefore all men are less than nice people' (I paraphrase slightly for the sake of decency!). At one point they even threw flour and eggs at me and my colleague, yelling that we were MCPs (Male Chauvinist Pigs) just because we stated that there was a role for men on the earth. It would all have been good fun if it were not for the fact that some of them really believed the hyperbole and nonsense they were spouting. I wonder whether they had had a bad experience of some man or other and this was then being projected on to all men and into some kind of radical feminist philosophy.

I had a sense of *deja vu* whilst looking on your website. I'm afraid that many atheists seem to work from the same premise – their own experience, as indeed many Christians, including myself, also do. However, I am sure you would recognise that whilst experience is an important factor it cannot be the determining factor in ascertaining what is objective truth. Many have had a bad experience of religion in some form or other; therefore they project that on to every religion or religious person. And when someone like you comes along and provides what seems to be a cast-iron intellectual justification they seize it like an alcoholic seizes the bottle. Not only are their feelings justified but also they are suddenly part of the 'higher intelligence' or 'greater consciousness'. The trouble is the argument you use and how you approach your subject.

I have received several complaints from some of your followers that I have not addressed the central question in my two previous letters, namely the existence of God. 'Go, on,' they say. 'Prove it.' They then complain that I have talked about the issues you talk about. What they do is a simple and false equation. They state there is only the material and that the only thing that can be called proof is a material proof. In effect, they are asking me to prove God as a chemical equation. 'If you can't do this,' they say, 'there is no God.' This is the ultimate in circular argument. But it fails at two levels. First of all its presupposition and assertion/assumption, that everything is chemical or the result of chemical reaction, is itself an unprovable assertion. Second, it is not an assertion that fits with the observable facts around us. Indeed, it requires a great deal of special pleading before one can honestly come to the position that religion is just a chemical reaction, beauty is just a chemical reaction, evil likewise and the sense of God also. Furthermore, the logical consequences of such a belief are disastrous. We end up with the absurdity of man as God – the most highly evolved chemical reaction.

As I have already indicated, most of your book does not seek to prove its central 'everything is chemical' hypothesis, quite simply because it is not provable. So in order to protect and prop up the faith of your fellow atheists and encourage them to 'come out' you do two things. First, you defend atheism from the charge that it leads to various negative consequences. And second, you go on the attack – ridiculing, mocking and denigrating the beliefs of those who do not share your presuppositions. You realise that this opens you to the charge of being aggressive, arrogant and even harmful to your own cause. Thus, you seek to defend your methodology to other atheists. Indeed, there is a fascinating subtext in your book – the in-house debate within atheist circles. In the Church of the Blessed Atheist it seems as though there is a doctrinal dispute that could result in a split. On the one hand there is the Respect party (the 'niceies'); on the other the Ridicule party (the 'nasties'). Both factions believe that religion is evil and that anyone who believes in God is a superstitious anti-rationalist. The Respects argue that you have to be nice to people to win them. The Ridicules regard this as cowardice, having more to do with keeping the peace, rather than standing up for the truth.

If I belonged to your religion I would be inclined towards your side. And so would the apostle Paul who argued that if the resurrection was not true then Christians should 'be pitied more than all men'

(1 Corinthians 15:19). As would the prophet Elijah who mocked and ridiculed the prophets of Baal as they prayed, danced and cut themselves in order to arouse their God – 'At noon Elijah began to taunt them. "Shout louder!" he said. "Surely he is a god! Perhaps he is deep in thought, or busy, or travelling. Maybe he is sleeping and must be awakened!' (1 Kings 18:27). Even Jesus was fairly scathing towards those who peddled religious untruths and myths.

It is in this context that the last part of your first chapter argues over the question of respect. Your main point is that you think it unfair and illogical that just because something is deemed to be religious it should be treated with kid gloves. You cite with glowing approval your friend the late Douglas Adams: 'Religion ... has certain ideas at the heart of it which we call sacred or holy or whatever. What it means is: "Here is an idea or notion that you're not allowed to say anything bad about; you're just not. Why not? – because you're not."' I agree with the main substance of your argument – just because someone cites their view as religious does not *de facto* entitle it to respect. Where both you and Adams miss the point is that you fail to acknowledge that every society, whether overtly religious or not, has its shibboleths. There are some things that one is not allowed to question at least not without losing one's job, position, etc. And that is as true in a secular society (perhaps even more so) as it is in a religious one.

This is seen in another example you bring up, that of Christian groups on campuses suing their universities because the universities are harassing these groups for their perceived anti-homosexual stance. As it happens, I am writing this alongside a copy of *The Times* (18 November 2006) which on its front page reports on a similar situation in the UK. Edinburgh University for example has banned the Christian Union from teaching a course about sex and relationships because it promotes 'homophobia'. I have seen this course (entitled *Pure*) and it does no such thing (unless you are prepared to make the completely unwarranted and bigoted assumption that if one does not agree with something one automatically is phobic about it and hates the people who do agree with it). *Pure* encourages the biblical teaching that sex should be within the context of marriage and that marriage should be between one man and one woman. Likewise the Christian Union in Heriot Watt University has been banned because its core beliefs 'discriminate against non-Christians and those of other faiths'. The 150-strong CU in Birmingham was suspended for refusing to alter its constitution to allow non-Christians to preach at its meetings and to amend its literature to include references to gays, lesbians, bisexuals and those of 'transgender' sexuality (one wonders what the logic was for leaving out polygamists, bestialists or paedophiles?). The point is simply this – not whether you agree with their particular view of sexuality but whether they are to have the freedom to express that view. Some secularists in the US and the UK seem prepared to take this matter of sexuality and use it the way that Douglas Adams describes. You are not allowed to question it or to have a different viewpoint and when you ask why, you are just told – that is the way it is. I would hope that you would accept that Christian Unions have the right to determine what they believe themselves, as I would Atheist societies, and that nothing should be imposed on people because 'that is just the way things are.'

Going off on another bypath meadow that you set up, you assert that conflicts in areas such as Northern Ireland, Bosnia and Iraq should be seen as religious wars and not ethnic ones. Whilst I fully agree that religion is sometimes the cause of the most appalling behaviour in people, it is more often the case that religion is the excuse rather than the cause for ethnic divisions and wars. I have met people, for example, from both sides of the divide in Northern Ireland who were involved in 'the Troubles'. Not one of them thought that they were rioting or killing for 'God'. It was for their 'community', their 'tribe' – God was just a useful person to bring in to up the *ante*. The IRA, for example, were a Marxist group who were Catholic only in the sense of belonging to an ethnic community. I remember speaking to a group of young men on their way to Ibrox stadium, the home of Glasgow Rangers, bearing a banner stating 'For God and Ulster' (for readers wondering what this has to do with football and Glasgow – don't bother – it's too stupid even to begin to explain). I asked them if they believed in God. 'Don't know – but we're Protestants!' 'Do you go to Church?' 'No (expletive deleted). We go to Ibrox why would we need to go to Church?' Yet doubtless you would cite such political and ethnic Protestantism as another example of religious conflict. Likewise the Sunni and Shia war in Iraq and the conflicts in the former Yugoslavia are primarily ethnic conflicts with religious tribal gods being called in as reinforcements.

And again there is an inconsistency in the atheist argument being used here. On the one hand, you claim that the gods are social constructs of the various tribes/people groups of humanity. On the other you claim that religion is the cause of the various splits and ethnic infighting. Which is it? Do people invent religions so that they can fight one another, or do religions create peoples who will, because of their religion, hate and fight one another? You can't have it both ways – unless you are someone who accepts the Bible's teaching that human beings are inherently selfish and prone towards war, and that they are equally idolatrous, seeking to create 'gods' in their own image – and that the two often come together.

I am grateful to you for your somewhat amusing and sad exposé of the Danish cartoons fiasco. I too have the photo of the Islamic lady with the sign round her neck proudly proclaiming, 'Behead those who say Islam is a violent religion.' And I also deplore the absolute cowardice of the press in Britain who refused to publish the cartoons out of 'respect' and 'sympathy' for the offence and hurt that Muslims suffered. You and I know that the real reason they did not publish was nothing to do with respect and everything to do with fear. *The Independent* newspaper, for example, had no difficulty in publishing the most blasphemous attack upon the Christian God but would not publish these cartoons. The BBC would not show the cartoons but had no difficulty in broadcasting the *Jerry Springer* caricature and assault upon Jesus Christ, thereby showing little 'respect and sympathy' for the hurt and offence that Christians had to put up with. The British media know that there is a core difference between Islam and Christianity: while there may be a few Christians who threaten boycotts or pickets, there are none who are going to seek to kill those who blaspheme our God, whereas they know full well that any derogatory mention of Mohammed will result in serious death threats and violence. At least you have the grace (and the courage) to acknowledge that Islam is a physical threat, 'on a scale that no other religion has aspired to since the Middle Ages'.

Having said all that I am a little concerned that you use this defence of free speech to justify your caricaturing and ridiculing of religion and in particular Christianity and Christians. It is not that you do not have the right to criticise but rather that with that right also comes responsibility – a responsibility to tell the truth, to listen to others as well, and not to inflame those who might listen to you. The trouble is that your ridicule, combined with an atheist fundamentalism and the bitterness and irrationality of some of your own supporters, leads to persecution and intolerance. The only atheistic states (Stalin's Russia, Mao's China, Pol Pot's Kampuchea and Hitler's Germany) in the world have been the most vicious and cruel that the world has ever seen. Atheistic secular fundamentalism is in my view more intolerant and coercive than almost any religious position.

On the other hand, I would suggest that biblical Christianity is the most tolerant and practical worldview that exists. Why? Because we don't need to impose our views by force (indeed we are forbidden from doing so). We don't need to shut out knowledge because all truth is God's truth. And we don't feel ultimately threatened.

We are not interested in political power (or at least we should not be) because we know that our weapons are not the weapons of this world. We respect every human being because they are made in the image of God. Like you, we believe that we should stand up for our views. I am not going to accept Mohammed as a prophet just because some religion tells me to. I must and will, however, respect and love Muslims as fellow human beings in need of God.

And one last thought. One thing that really annoys some atheists is when Christians promise to pray for them. Why do we pray for you? It is not the kind of 'smite the Amalekites' prayer (although sometimes the temptation is enormous!). Rather we pray that God will work in your life, reveal himself to you and draw you to himself. Not so that we can be proved right but rather because it is, believe it or not, the best possible thing that could ever happen to you. Therefore, to pray for you is a supreme act of love because it asks for the best for you. And Jesus tells us that we are to love our enemies. So I do pray for you and for all those who have been deluded into thinking that there is only the material, and that their Creator does not exist. Forgive me.

Yours, etc.
David

LETTER 4 –
THE MYTH OF THE
CRUEL OLD TESTAMENT GOD

Dear Dr Dawkins,

At last we are getting to the meat of your case against God
– 'The God Hypothesis'. I wonder in what sense you are
using the term 'hypothesis'. Is it that of a supposition?
A provisional explanation? Or a theory to be proved or
disproved by reference to facts? I suspect that your viewpoint is that mankind, having a 'religious sense' has invented a god or gods to fill in the gaps of our knowledge.
In Christian terms this results in Moses, Jesus, Paul, Augustine, Luther, Calvin giving us the 'God hypothesis' to
explain what would otherwise be inexplicable. The story
then continues – along comes Darwin with another hypothesis and, lo and behold the God hypothesis is disproved. Eureuka! God is a delusion. Humanity has moved
onto a higher consciousness and the only thing left to do
is write a book which tells people that is the case, and encourages the enlightened to 'come out' and organise po-
litically so that the virus of religion and the old ways can
never be used again. The world is saved. Hallelujah!

Except that is not the way it works. And your attack
on the 'God Hypothesis' does not work. Not least because

in this chapter you really refuse to discuss it. You define the God Hypothesis as, 'there exists a super human, supernatural intelligence who deliberately designed the universe and everything in it, including us' and you tell us that your proof that this is not so is that, 'any creative intelligence of sufficient complexity to design anything, comes into existence only as the end product of an extended process of gradual evolution'. And that is basically it. You spend the remaining 41 pages telling us almost nothing about the God Hypothesis. We learn about secularism and Thomas Jefferson, atheism and American politics, TAP, PAP and NOMA, the Great Prayer Experiment, Little Green Men and why you disagree with Stephen J. Gould, Michael Ruse and other evolutionary appeasers. It is a rambling incoherent chapter, the worst in the book, and is probably the reason that your book has received such a critical slating. *Prospect*, a magazine which largely gives you a sympathetic platform, put it very strongly:

> It has been obvious for years that Richard Dawkins had a fat book on religion in him, but who would have thought him capable of writing one this bad? Incurious, dogmatic, rambling and self-contradictory, it has none of the style or verve of his earlier works.

You begin with a quite vicious and specious attack on the God of the Old Testament. Your first paragraph is one that you enjoy reading to people and it generally gets a round of applause. To me this indicates that you are touching a raw emotional nerve in many of those who hear you. They have a deep-seated hatred of the God of the Bible. I found this paragraph very offensive – so offensive that

I will not repeat the whole of it here. Now your standard retort is that you are not offending me, you are offending a god who does not exist. (Cue applause from the fans.) But I'm afraid that you *are* offending me. First, you are implying that I believe in this cruel, capricious and evil god. And second you seem to be working on the basis that as long as you are not directly insulting me, then I cannot be offended. But if you attack my family, my friends, my community I *am* offended because part of my identity is tied up with them. I'm sorry but part of being human is that 'no man is an island' (unless as Nick Hornby points out 'his name is Madagascar'!). My identity is bound up with the God of the Bible and especially Jesus Christ. Therefore, when you attack him you are attacking me. So please don't patronise.

However, I am not a person who believes that the unforgivable sin is to offend. Maybe I deserve the offensive remarks. If what you say is true then they would be deserved. But, your caricature of both the God of the Old Testament and the Jesus of the New is just that – a caricature. Like all such there is an element of truth within it but it is so distorted that it becomes unrecognisable. When I read the Old Testament I find a wonderful God – a God of mercy, justice, beauty, holiness and love, a God who cares passionately for the poor, for his people and for his creation. And, amazingly, it is the same God in the New Testament. I realise that there are difficulties and problems but these are largely caused by your exaggerated caricature. If you take the foundational teachings about God in both the Old and New Testament then you come up with a much more realistic picture.

For example, one of your complaints against God is that he is a jealous God. This is true, but not in the sense of the 'green eyed monster'. God is jealous in the way that a man would expect his wife to be jealous if he started sleeping with other women, or jealous in the way that I am protective of my children. It is about protection, care and honour, not the negative envy. It is difficult to believe that you are not aware of that distinction. My main complaint here is that your description of the God of the Old Testament is not one that the Old Testament itself sets forward. Does this fit with your description?

> The Lord works righteousness and justice for all the oppressed. He made known his ways to Moses, his deeds to the people of Israel: The Lord is compassionate and gracious, slow to anger, abounding in love (Psalm 103:6-8).

And there are numerous similar passages. It is only by a very selective citation out of context, ignoring all the passages and teaching about God, that you could come anywhere near the caricature you espouse.

Now of course, as you acknowledge, whether this God is good or bad is irrelevant if he does not exist. Why would we bother arguing about an imaginary being? So that begs the question why you begin the chapter with such a vicious attack upon someone you consider to be an imaginary being? Could it be that it is a cheap shot expressing hatred against a being who might exist? Or that you know the main substance of your argument will appeal to those who have experienced some sort of religious abuse? Is it not the case that you are really aiming at a polemical and emotional response rather than a rational one?

At this point you then go on to discuss polytheism, Oral Roberts, and the Roman Catholic teaching about saints. I am still trying to work out what this has to do with the God Hypothesis. However you do make one point which is now being repeated *ad nauseam* by atheists across the country – that Christians are atheists when it comes to Zeus, Thor and Ra. Atheists just go one god further (cue more gasps of admiration, laughter and cheers). Once again this cheap point fails to take account that there might actually be myths, false gods and delusions. Nor does it recognise that Christians could believe in Christ *because* of the evidence, not in spite of it. Your point has no more validity than a man who announces that a Rolex cannot be real because he once bought a fake watch, or a woman announcing that love does not exist because she once had a bad experience. It is a rhetorical device that does not actually deal with any of the issues involved.

Another argument that you try to counter is one that I often use. When someone tells me they do not believe in God I often ask them to tell me about the God they do not believe in. They will then come out with the kind of statement that you do at the beginning of the chapter and I will tell them that I do not believe in that God either. You rightly point out that this argument is not valid for someone who is claiming that there is no God whatever his character because there is no supernatural (a faith posi-tion, which is of course itself indemonstrable). However, you spend a considerable amount of your book attacking particular versions of God and therefore you open your-self to this rejoinder. Most of us do not believe in the God you so passionately attack. And the *ad hominem* examples you use of eccentric and unbalanced religious people are not what most Christians would identify with. If you stuck to the philosophical debate about whether there was a God at all your book would be a lot shorter (and a lot less popular with your followers). It is your attack on a distorted and perverted version of Christian teaching about God which provides you with the most entertaining smokescreen for your lack of substantial argument on whether God exists in the first place or not.

This leads us on to NOMA ('non overlapping magisteria'). This is the view that science and religion are two separate spheres and that science can neither prove nor disprove the existence of God. The most famous exponent of this view is Stephen J. Gould who in his book *Rocks of Ages: Science and Religion in the Fullness of Life*[9] neatly summarises this as, 'science gets the age of rocks, and religion the rock of ages; science studies how the heavens go, religion how to go to heaven'.

You don't like this. And you certainly don't like theologians. If science cannot answer a question then why bother asking theologians – they are as much use as a chocolate teapot. You write: 'I simply do not believe that Gould could possibly have meant much of what he wrote in *Rock of Ages*.' Are you really suggesting that he is so cowardly that he is prepared to lie in order to have some kind of reconciliation between religion and science? That is a serious charge. And one that is not immediately obvious from reading *Rock of Ages*. I find it a fascinating book with a great deal of valuable insights within it. Take

9. Ballantine Books (1999)

the following for example: 'But I also include among my own scientific colleagues, some militant atheists whose blinkered concept of religion grasps none of the subtlety or diversity.' He also points out that there are people, 'who have dedicated the bulk of their energy, and even their life's definition, to such aggressive advocacy at the extremes that they do not choose to engage in serious and respectful debate.' It's no wonder you don't like him!

However, I would like to take a middle position between your position and that of Mr Gould. He argues for complete separation of the two magisteria (science and religion). You argue for complete annihilation of the religious. I would suggest that there are two magisteria, science and religion which actually do overlap, albeit not totally. There are things that science cannot and possibly never will be able to prove, and there are things that religion does not comment on. Gould's example is correct – the Bible says nothing about the age of rocks and science can tell us nothing about the Rock of Ages – Jesus Christ. However there are places where the two link. For example, if someone claims a miracle that they have been healed from cancer, then science is able to judge whether or not the cancer has gone.

You tell us that the existence of God is a 'scientific hypothesis like any other' and that if God so chose he could reveal himself. He has. And He will. You tell us that 'even if God's existence is never proved or disproved with certainty one way or the other, available evidence and reasoning may yield an estimate of probability far from 50%'. Really? Why such a confident assertion? Besides which science has moved on since you made that unqualified

and unsupported assertion. *The Times* newspaper reported (20 November 2006) that the actual figure was well
over 50%.

> The mathematical probability of God's existence is just over
> 62%. So says a German science magazine. *P.M.* [*Peter Moos-
> leitner's Magazin*] tried to settle the issue by using mathe-
> matical formulae devised to determine plausibility and prob-
> ability. Researchers started with the hypothesis 'God exists',
> then tried to analyse the evidence in favour or against the
> hypothesis in five areas: creation, evolution, good, evil and
> religious experiences. The scientists applied the formulae to
> calculate how statistically probable different answers were to
> questions such as 'How probable is it that the evolution of life
> took place without God?', and 'How probable is it that God
> created the Universe?' Their conclusion will be cheering to
> many, although not, perhaps, Richard Dawkins.

Hoisted by your own petard.

By the way, I am fascinated that you think that there
is something to be said for treating Buddhism not as
a religion but as an ethic or philosophy of life. Would
you therefore accept the philosophy that says that
handicapped people are born that way because they
were bad in a previous life and they are just getting their
karma?

Now we move on to the 'Great Prayer Experiment'.
This is a complete red herring. By definition the God of
the Bible is not mechanical and prayer is communicating
with him as a person. It is only if you accept the slot
machine view of prayer (put your prayer in and out will
come the answer you want) that any such experiment
could be conducted. Given that the Bible does not teach
that God is a divine slot machine who answers our prayers
mechanically the whole experiment is a nonsense. So

I am left once again with asking why you even mentioned it?

Speaking of which what do the position of atheists in the US and your dislike of evolutionary appeasers like Michael Ruse have to do with the God Hypothesis? Do you not think such in-house debates in the Atheist church should be conducted – well, in-house? Or am I right in thinking that your book is actually written as a polemical tract for atheists, a rallying call to political action, rather than a serious discussion about the existence of God? Hence the question in the midst of a chapter meant to be discussing the God Hypothesis, 'What might American atheists achieve if they organised themselves properly?' (p. 44).

Before we leave this depressing chapter we have to deal with another tired old argument (put out in almost every atheist forum). When it is pointed out that an atheist cannot disprove God, the standard text book response is now 'yes – no more than we can disprove the Celestial Tea Pot god, the tooth fairy or The Flying Spaghetti Monster'. (I loved the notion of a schism occurring resulting in the *Reformed* Church of the Flying Spaghetti Monster!) Do you seriously think that the evidence for the God of the Bible is on the same level as the tooth fairy? You have not, for example, written a book on the Tooth Fairy Delusion. The evidence for God is on a completely different level. I suspect you know that but again in your rhetorical style the sound-bite put-down works so much better. Let me put it another way – if the only evidence that existed for Jesus Christ was the same as that which exists for the Flying Spaghetti Monster then I and millions of others would not believe in him. So how about dealing with the evidence that we assert and staying away from that which only states your own presupposition – that there is no God?

And finally something on which we can agree: 'A universe in which we are alone except for other slowly evolved intelligences is a very different universe from one with an original guiding agent whose intelligent design is responsible for its very existence.' I live in a universe created by a personal God, the God of mercy, logic, justice, goodness, truth, beauty and love – the God whose purposes and intentions are good. You live in a universe which appeared from nowhere, is going nowhere and means nothing. Perhaps in the next chapter you will give us some reason for this soulless, cold and depressing belief.

Yours, etc.
David

LETTER 5 –
THE MYTH OF THE
SCIENCE/RELIGION CONFLICT

Dear Dr Dawkins,

We are getting closer to your 'proof' that God is a delusion. But before you come on to your 'big argument' you try in this chapter to deal with some of the arguments that theists put forward for the existence of God.

Your understanding of Christian theology is shockingly bad. For example you argue, 'If God is omniscient he already knows how he is going to intervene to change the course of history using his omnipotence – but that means he can't change his mind about his intervention which means he is not omnipotent.' I can hardly believe that a professor at Oxford wrote such a juvenile argument! If you really want to go down that line here are a few more for you. Can God create a stone heavier than he can lift? Can God make a square circle? These may be amusing 'problems' for a teenage class in metaphysics but as a reason for believing that God cannot exist? As Mr McEnroe would say, 'You *cannot* be serious!' A Sunday school teacher once asked the children in her class, 'is there anything that God cannot do?' Not having a particularly good grasp of theology either, she was horrified when

51

a small boy held up his hand and answered 'yes'. She challenged him by asking him what. 'Lie' was the short, succinct and accurate reply. Saying God is omnipotent is not saying that he can do what is immoral or inconsistent with his own nature.

Your discussion of Anselm's Ontological argument is short and largely one with which I would agree. Anselm's view that the greatest thing we can conceive of must exist because otherwise it would not be the greatest thing we could conceive of is a neat philosophical argument but it is only that. However, you spoil your discussion of that with a list of nonsensical satirical 'proofs' from 'godlessgeeks.com' (glad to note that you choose your sources so carefully!) and a vicious attack on the atheist backslider Anthony Flew.

Professor Flew was until recently one of the world's most influential atheists but has apparently had a change of heart and now accepts that there must be a designer. Your attack on him in a footnote in this chapter (and in some of your public speeches) comes across as 'bitchy' – unnecessarily implying that advancing old age must have something to do with his conversion from atheism, that he is not really a great philosopher (contrasted with Bertrand Russell who was a great philosopher and won the Nobel Prize) and that his flawed judgement is shown by his acceptance of the Phillip E. Johnson award for Liberty and Truth. Could you not allow for the possibility that he may have changed his mind? – not because of senility or because that all along he was never really a great philosopher, or because he is seeking the Templeton Prize, but rather because of the evidence and the facts? I guess any atheist who changes his mind needs to know that he will face the wrath of Richard, but please put the claws away. It is very unattractive.

You then deal with three of the major arguments for God – beauty, personal experience and the Bible.

Beauty

You state this argument really badly. For me it is one of the arguments that is central to proving the existence of God. You reduce it to someone asking, 'how do we account for Shakespeare, Schubert or Michelangelo?' But it is much more than that. It is not so much the fact that there is beauty – but why do we as human beings have a sense of beauty? I am sure you will account for that by stating that it is a chemical reaction in our brains caused by millions of years of evolution. But that seems to me at best a partial explanation. Beauty is part of consciousness and it remains one of the great unanswered questions in evolutionary philosophy – where does consciousness come from? When I see the beauty of a sunset over the river Tay, or hear Beethoven's sixth, or walk along the banks of the Mighty Mississippi then I cannot grasp or believe that this is just instinct or impulse that ultimately comes from nowhere. The words of Solomon fit so much better, 'He has made everything beautiful in its time' (Ecclesiastes 3:11).

Is it not a bit of a cheap shot to state that Raphael or Michelangelo only produced their great work because they were paid to? And imply that if they were living today they would be producing the *Evolution Oratorio*. Out of interest where are the great atheist composers, artists, etc? I have no doubt that human beings who are not believers can produce great works of art – but that is because they are *Imago Dei* – created in the image of God. Their creativity is a reflection of the creativity of their creator, whether they acknowledge it or not. The ugliness of much modern art is that it has lost its connection with the divine and the wonder of beauty. Can I suggest that you read Hans Rookmaaker, *Modern Art and the Death of a Culture*[10] for a fascinating and enlightening discussion on this topic? Meanwhile the argument from beauty remains one of the most powerful arguments for God. The fact that you neither understand nor agree with it hardly constitutes a rational argument against it.

Personal Experience

You also seem to be having enormous difficulty with this argument reducing it to those who hear voices (whether audibly or within their heads) or see visions. You cite one of your 'cleverer' undergraduates who was ordained at least partially because of an experience he had of hearing the devil whilst camping on the Scottish Isles. This was apparently a 'Manx Shearwater' bird. Yet this 'clever' man was stupid enough to see it as a call to the ministry! Which puts him on a level with others you mention – those who have experienced a pink elephant (have you met any such?), the 'Yorkshire Ripper' Peter Sutcliffe hearing Jesus telling him to kill women, President George Bush being 'told by God' to invade Iraq (again what is your source for this information?) and people in asylums thinking they are Napoleon or Charlie Chaplin! According to you the only difference between those locked up in asylums and religious people is that religious

10. Apollos (1994)

people are more numerous. Now, of course there are people who hear voices and see visions which are nothing more than simulations. But does that mean that every such experience is such? I am very wary of people telling me that God has told them something – more often than not they are at the fringes of belief and often do have mental health problems. Nonetheless, I would never be so arrogant as to assume that that is the case for everyone.

Furthermore, you completely misstate the argument from personal experience. The vast majority of Christians do not believe because they have heard a voice or seen a vision – indeed I am struggling to think of anyone I know in that category. Yet personal experience does play a major part (after all it is the experience we know best). C. S. Lewis once wrote that he was a Christian because, 'I arrived where I now am, not by reflection alone, but by reflection on a particular recurrent experience. I am an empirical theist. I have arrived at God by induction.'[11] That is where most Christians are at. We believe because we experience and we think and reflect upon that experience.

There are many other kinds of personal experience which at the very least point us towards God: answered prayer, a sense of God ('truly God is amongst you'), experience of the miraculous, experience of the truths and truthfulness of the Bible and the experience of being filled with the Spirit, to name but a few. From my own experience, I can recall clear, specific and direct answers to prayer, an overwhelming sense of the presence of God, and the Word of God being used to speak to my

11. Cited in C. S. Lewis, *The Authentic Voice*, William Griffin, Lion (1986)

mind, heart and soul. I am sure you and your followers will manage to diss and explain away all these things and I for one would not argue that I believe in Jesus Christ solely because of any one of them. But the accumulation of these experiences in addition to the truth of the Bible, and the observation of history, creation and society, add up to a very powerful personal apologetic. And not one that can just be dismissed by talking about those who hear voices in their heads. All I have seen teaches me to trust the Creator for all I have not seen.

The Bible

As you also cover this in chapter seven I will resist the temptation to comment too much on what you say in this section. However, there are a couple of points that really do need to be addressed. You begin with a critique of C. S. Lewis' claim that as Jesus claimed to be the Son of God he must have been a Lunatic, a Liar or Lord (Mad, Bad, or God). You write, 'a fourth possibility, almost too obvious to need mentioning, is that Jesus was honestly mistaken'. But that is precisely what Lewis addresses. He makes the point that if Jesus was honestly mistaken in his claim to be the Son of God, it is equivalent to a man who is honestly mistaken in thinking he was a poached egg – it is the lunatic part of the equation. Lewis himself answered this objection when he wrote in 1950: 'The idea of a great moral teacher saying what Christ said is out of the question. In my opinion, the only person who can say that sort of thing is either God or a complete lunatic suffering from the form of delusion which undermines the whole mind of man'. Your book is entitled *The God Delusion*. Lewis presents us with a simple choice. Either you are right and Christians are all deluded people following a deluded Jesus, or the boot is on the other foot and in fact the deluded ones are those who reject Jesus and follow the myths and 'reasons' of the atheist belief system.

You then go on to declare: 'In any case, as I said, there is no good historical evidence that he ever thought he was divine'; which being translated meaneth 'there is no evidence which I have read in *Free Inquiry* or my other atheist "how to" books'. Just what historical evidence have you evaluated? Please note that using *Free Inquiry*, A. N. Wilson and Robin Lane Fox as your sources on biblical material is like me suggesting that those who want to find out about evolution should only go to the *Answers in Genesis* website! The historical evidence for the claims that Jesus made is quite clear. The Gospels make it explicit. And it was after all the reason he was crucified – because he 'blasphemed' by claiming to be God.

You also illustrate the truth of the saying that 'a little learning is a dangerous thing'. For example, you cite as conclusive proof that the gospel of Luke is not historical the fact that a census took place in A.D 6 after Herod's death. And yet there is evidence that the census in A.D. 6 was the second such census and that the first probably took place in 5 B.C. The problem is not that there are not significant questions and problems in the Bible (there are). The problem is that you, with all the certainty of the fundamentalist delighting in proving his opponents wrong, seize upon the flimsiest of evidence and, without any further investigation, make sweeping statements that this proves the Bible wrong.

In this regard I am astounded at how out of touch you are with modern biblical scholarship. You write: 'Ever since the 19th century scholarly theologians have made an overwhelming case that the gospels are not reliable accounts of what happened in the history of the real world.' Unless you are adopting the phrase 'scholarly theologians' as a euphemism for 'those who happen to agree with me' your statement is just plainly and demonstrably false. Can I suggest that you ask your Oxford colleague Alister McGrath, Principal of Wycliffe Hall, why he is ignoring this overwhelming case? Perhaps you should read his *Christian Theology: An Introduction*?[12] I am sure it would be enormously helpful and prevent you making the kind of gaffes that you pour out here.

Your position reminds me of a debate that was held in the Dundee Contemporary Arts Centre concerning the *Da Vinci Code*.[13] During the course of the evening the most heated opposition came from a couple of people who made the same claim that scholars no longer accepted the Gospels as historical accounts. When one man was challenged on this and told that he was being 'so 20th century' (although he was in actual fact being so 19th century) he struggled to name one modern scholar who took that position. Eventually, he came up with the name Bultmann, whose main work was done in the first half of the 20th century. On the other hand I can think of at least 20 major biblical scholars at 'real' Universities today (not Mickey Mouse tin hut Bible colleges) who would argue for the basic historicity of the Gospels. At the very least, any statement which claims the scholarly

12. Blackwell (1993)
13. Corgi (2004)

position is that the historical evidence for the Bible is the same as that for the *Da Vinci Code*, is at best ignorant and at worst downright deceitful. Indeed it is so breathtaking in its audacity that it reminds me of Goebbels' maxim that the bigger the lie (and the more it is stated with absolute conviction) the more people are likely to believe it.

Religious Scientists

You also attribute a somewhat strange argument to theists: 'The Argument from Admired Religious Scientists'. I say 'strange' because I have never heard anyone say that they believed in God because such and such a scientist believes. However, what we do say is that the atheist attempt to set science against religion is one that is fatally undermined by the considerable number of scientists who are also believers. And I guess that is what bothers you and why you are so disparaging about the ones you identify. You neatly dismiss all pre-Darwinian scientists by claiming that it was normal for people to profess belief and that they would come under pressure if they did not. Indeed such is your disdain for your fellow scientists who are believers that you even hint that those who continue to profess faith may be doing so because of social or economic factors. Furthermore, you state that they are so rare that 'they are a subject of amused bafflement to their peers in the academic community'. So Asa Gray (American Botanist), Charles D. Walcott (discoverer of Burgess Shale fossils), T. Dobzhansky (Russian Orthodox evolutionary biologist), R. J. Berry (Professor of Genetics at University College London), Owen Gingerich (Professor of Astronomy and History of Science at Harvard) and Francis Collins (Head of the Human Genome Project) are all 'sources of amused bafflement'? I think nothing illustrates your arrogance and almost pathological hatred of God and religion more than this dismissive, patronising and 'who's not for us is against us' view of your scientific colleagues.

Incidentally, I noted with interest your footnote contrasting the 'administrative' head of the American branch of the Human Genome Project with 'the brilliant and non religious buccaneer' of science, Craig Venter. It is an interesting contrast, not least because of the descriptive language you employ. But what fascinates me most is the different way that the different worldviews impacted how they wanted to use their science. Whereas Francis Collins, the Christian, wanted to keep the Human Genome Project in the public domain and the information available and accessible to all, your 'brilliant and non religious buccaneer' wanted to privatise the whole project to make money. His company, Celera, aimed to file patents on many of the genes and, had they been successful, would have only allowed the data to be available to those who paid large sums of money. I think that is an apt metaphor for the difference between two very different worldviews. On the one hand there is an alliance of science with those who seek to use it for the public good of all (and not just private profit), who recognise its limits and who believe that they are accountable to God for what they do with his gifts. On the other there is an alliance of science with a godless morality and materialism which seeks to use knowledge for personal gain and private profit. I think we have been down this scientific materialistic route before – I believe that Stalin, Mao and Hitler all thought that their societies should be governed with such 'science' and morality. I am sorry if that offends you and I am not trying to equate your 'nice' atheism with the nasty but I honestly believe that this is where your atheistic hatred of God will eventually lead society. Indeed, it is one of the reasons that I believe in the God of the Bible – because without that biblical worldview I have no real explanation of, nor defence against, the evil of which humans are capable.

Let me finish by pointing out that you missed out the most important argument of all for the existence of God – the person and work of Jesus Christ. By far the number one reason I believe and trust God is because of Jesus Christ.

> In the past God spoke to our forefathers through the prophets at many times and in various ways, but in these last days he has spoken to us by his Son, whom he appointed heir of all things, and through whom he made the universe. The Son is the radiance of God's glory and the exact representation of his being, sustaining all things by his powerful word (Hebrews 1:1-3).

The presence, power and perfection of Jesus Christ is no delusion.

Yours, etc.
David

LETTER 6 –
THE MYTH OF THE CREATED GOD
AND THE UNCREATED UNIVERSE

Dear Dr Dawkins,

Finally we arrive at the centre of your book and its main argument. The title of your fourth chapter is a bold claim: 'Why there almost certainly is no God'. In it you propose to prove, insofar as it is possible, that there is no God. I found this chapter astonishing. Allow me to explain why. I had expected that your case against God was to be a cumulative one – a bit like your view of evolution. Faced with the mountain of Divinity and the universal belief of humankind in a God or gods, I expected you to climb Mount Improbable gradually, building a case slowly and leading us by a cumulative process to the view that there is no God. However you go for the big leap. You think you have the killer argument and you can go straight to the Holy Grail of atheism and then have a gentle slide downhill afterwards, picking off the remaining theistic arguments because you have already proved there is no God.

What is this killer argument? The one that even Nietzsche could not find? Your argument goes like this. Evolution is true. Evolution explains the illusion of design. The design argument is the main argument for

God. Therefore there is no God. And the reason that the design argument does not work? The point that you think almost 'certainly' proves there is no God? The core and heart of your intellectual justification for your emotional atheism? It is astounding. (I almost feel at this point that there should be a drum roll...) The argument is: 'Who designed the Designer?'

In your own words:

> Once again, this is because the designer himself (herself/it-self) immediately raises the problem of his own origin.
>
> Indeed design is not a real alternative at all because it raises an even bigger problem than it solves: who designed the designer?
>
> But whatever else we may say, design certainly does not work as an explanation for life, because design is ultimately not cumulative.
>
> As ever the theist's answer is deeply unsatisfying because it leaves the existence of God unexplained.
>
> To suggest that the original prime mover was complicated enough to indulge in intelligent design, to say nothing of mind reading millions of humans simultaneously, is tantamount to dealing yourself a perfect hand at bridge.

It is clear that this point is very important to you and the foundation of the rest of your arguments. When I read it I was genuinely shocked. Not because of its originality, killer force or overwhelming logic, but rather because of its banality. 'Who made God?' is a question I would expect from a six-year-old. 'Who made God then?' is the accusation I would expect from a sixteen-year-old. I am genuinely surprised to find the world's most famous atheist (now that the philosopher Antony Flew[14] has

14. Life-long atheist philosopher Anthony Flew recently announced that he was persuaded by evidence of intelligent design that there was a supreme being. His conversion was to Deism not necessarily to Theism.

defected) and an Oxford Professor to boot, using it as *the* intellectual foundation for his atheism. This is the argument that is going to change the world? This is the key?! Forgive my incredulity and perhaps even the slight mocking tone but you are very quick to mock some of the stupider theistic arguments. Using the 'Who made God?' argument is the atheist equivalent of the argument from degree.

The answer to the question who made God is simply 'nobody'. God is not made. God is the Creator, not the creation. God is outside of time and space. (This is not to say that he is not also in time and space and that there is not plenty evidence for him there.) God creates *ex nihilo*. That's what makes him God. He does not craft from what is already there. He creates time, space and matter from nothing. I realise for you that is nonsense because the core of your creed is that evolution means that everything starts from the simple and becomes more complex, therefore because that is the case (and any designer would have to be incredibly complex) God cannot exist. But even if we grant that this is true for biology, biology is not everything. As Joe Fitzpatrick argues, 'Dawkins is methodologically confused, taking a principle of biological science and making it into a universal principle.'[15] To argue as you do is to take an incredible leap of faith and to beg the question. Who says that everything, including God himself, has to come from something? Christians and other theists do not argue that God was created. That is precisely the point. He did not come from anywhere. He has always been. He did not

15. In the Catholic Magazine *Open House*, (January 2007)

evolve, nor was he made. If there is a personal Creator of the Universe then it makes perfect sense to regard him as complex, beyond our understanding and eternal. When you state that you can disprove God because there can *de facto* never be anything that was uncreated you are engaging in a circular argument. We do not believe in a created God. We believe in an uncreated supernatural power. I'm afraid you disprove nothing when you argue against the existence of a created God.

Let us assume for the moment that evolution is true, why would that disprove God? Let us assume that the Intelligent Design movement is wrong – why would that disprove God? It would disprove one argument that some theists use but there are many other arguments. Moreover, there are many Christians who do not accept the ID science and who continue to be believers in the God of the Bible. You mention with particular praise Kenneth Miller, of Brown University and author of *Finding Darwin's God*.[16] He strongly disagrees with Michael Behe, one of the leading ID scientists, and with the whole ID movement. By your logic he should then be an atheist. He is not. He is a theist. I am sure you would not call him stupid but you do accuse other theists who are also 'good' scientists of 'compartmentalising'. To my mind this is patronising and the equivalent of accusing them of a fundamental dishonesty. To you, they have the evidence to prove there is no God (who designed the designer?) but they do not have the moral courage or the mental capacity to embrace the logical conclusions. Except of course these conclusions are not logical. As McGrath puts

16. HarperCollins (2000)

it, 'There is a substantial logical gap between Darwinism and atheism, which Dawkins seems to prefer to bridge by rhetoric rather than evidence.'[17]

In order for there to be natural selection there has to be something to select. Where did that come from? This is where Aquinas' 'theistic proofs' – the Unmoved Mover, the Uncaused Cause and the Cosmological arguments – come into their own. In terms of the origin of matter there are only three alternatives:

1. Something came from nothing. At one point there was no universe, there was no material, there was no matter, no time, no space. And out of that big nothing there came the Big Bang and our vast universe, tiny planet, evolution and the human species. Such a notion is beyond the realms of reason and is a total nonsensical fantasy.
2. Something was eternal. In other words matter has always existed. There is a lump of rock, or a mass of gas or some kind of matter which had no beginning and will probably have no end. And at some point that matter exploded and we ended up with the finely tuned and wonderful universe we now inhabit.
3. Something was created – *ex nihilo* – out of nothing. And that Creator has to be incredibly powerful, intelligent and awesome beyond our imagination.

I cannot see any other logical alternative. Can you? I found it fascinating that when you were challenged about this you argued that we don't know where matter came from but

17. *Dawkins' God*, Blackwell (2004) p. 87

one day scientists will find out. Despite this rather touching faith in the potential omniscience of scientists, I'm afraid that will not do. The existence of God is not dependent on the argument from design as regards evolution; it *is* dependent on the fact that there is any matter at all, and that we live in a universe which is so finely tuned that life is possible at all. Why is there something rather than nothing? And why does that something manage to produce you and me? That is not a question which you can just brush aside or express no interest in.

Let's move on to this second stage. It is not only the fact that matter exists at all, but that it is so ordered that life can exist. As a young boy I was brought up in an area which had very little light pollution and so during the winter nights I often walked under the stars, risking injury by continually gazing upwards. The stars awe, amaze and fascinate me. Nowadays I can visit the local observatory in Dundee where I am greeted by an inscription above the door: 'This observatory is given that you may observe the wonders of the Creator in the heavens.' Above the door of the 'old' Cavendish Laboratories in Cambridge – where J. J. Thompson discovered the electron and Crick and Watson determined the structure of DNA – there is an inscription: 'Magna opera Domini exquisita in omnes voluntates ejus' (Great are the works of the Lord; they are pondered by all who delight in them, Psalm 111:2). This theology does not seem to have hampered the sciences in Cambridge, which has still managed to produce more Nobel prize winners in science than any other institution, including Oxford – 29 Nobel prizes in Physics, 22 in Medicine and 19 in Chemistry!

To stare at the stars is for me one of the major if not *the* major reason for believing in God. I found it difficult to believe that this vast universe existed by itself, or as the result of an accident. As I have grown in years and in knowledge, it has been a real delight to discover that my natural instincts in observation are in accord with what science has also discovered. Whereas I struggle with most books on evolution because of a lack of knowledge (your books have actually been the most accessible and interesting), I really enjoy cosmology. Recently I have been reading Owen Gingerich's *God's Universe* and Francis Collins, *The Language of God* which beautifully explain why the Universe is the best evidence for the existence of God. After going into detail about the wonders of the Big Bang, Collins cites with approval the astrophysicist Robert Jastrow from *God and the Astronomers*:[18] 'For the scientist who has lived by his faith in the power of reason, the story ends like a bad dream. He has scaled the mountain of ignorance; he is about to conquer the highest peak; as he pulls himself over the final rock, he is greeted by a band of theologians who have been sitting there for centuries.' I thought you would like that!

Jastrow also writes, 'Now we see how the astronomical evidence leads to a biblical view of the origin of the world. The details differ, but the essential elements and the astronomical and biblical accounts of Genesis are the same; the chain of events leading to man commenced suddenly and sharply at a definite moment in time, in a flash of light and energy.' Stephen Hawking points out that if the rate of expansion one second after the Big Bang

18. W. W. Norton (2000)

had been smaller by even one part in ten thousand million million, the universe would have recollapsed before it ever reached its present state. If it had been greater by one part in a million then the stars and planets would not have been able to form. Is that not spine-chillingly incredible? Constants like the speed of light, the force of gravity and electromagnetism all need to work precisely together for there to be life. Apparently there are fifteen such constants. Wonderful and incredible.

If you hold the position that matter is eternal, which you must as a rationalistic atheist, then you are left with this vast improbability of the fine-tuning of the Universe. And it is an improbability that cannot be explained by evolution because there is nothing to evolve. The question is how did we get the conditions for evolution? I guess you could argue that we were very, very, very lucky – to the point of one in ten thousand million million. That takes an enormous amount of faith. Like the example you cite from the philosopher, John Leslie, who talks about a man sentenced to death standing in front of a firing squad of ten expert marksmen. All of them miss. There could be some way of explaining such 'good fortune', but it is such an improbable event. Multiply that a million times and you have the improbability of the universe as we have it. So, in order to avoid that, what can you do? Well you can invent the multiverse, the view that there are billions of universes co-existing like bubbles of foam and the chances are that at least one will end up with some form of life. You even cite Lee Smolin's view that daughter universes are born from parent universes and that they in effect evolve thus eventually getting to a stage where life is possible. This is really special pleading and indicates desperation to try and explain the universe we have without God.

You keep telling us that science is about what we can observe, that it is about fact and empirical evidence. The multiverse notion is a 'sci-fi' nonsense for which there is no evidence whatsoever. One almost gets the impression that you would accept any theory as long as it did not involve the possibility of there being a God! This becomes especially evident when we move on to the last chapter – there you take this speculation even further citing David Deutsch's *The Fabric of Reality: Towards a Theory of Everything.*[19] Deutsch speculates that there is a vast and rapidly growing number of universes, existing in parallel and mutually undetectable – except through the porthole of quantum mechanical experiments. You write, 'In some of these universes I am already dead. In a small minority of them, you have a green moustache.' And you have the nerve to mock those of us who believe that the Creator of the Universe could raise the dead! Are you really so desperate to escape God that you have to have faith in a universe where there are green moustaches? Why stop there? Why not suggest that the Wachowski brothers' film *The Matrix* is correct? The world we live in is not really real – we only think it is because we are wired up to a giant computer which feeds our minds with the illusion of reality. Maybe there is some giant computer program somewhere that is feeding our mind with the illusion that we are really reading this?!

19. Penguin Books Ltd (1998)

You like to suggest that your position is a logical one caused by the fact that Darwin has raised your own consciousness and you seem to think that those who do not agree with you are not so highly evolved (at least in consciousness). Your position is *the* scientific one and you set up the debate so that it is always the forces of reason and science against the blind irrationality of faith. I'm afraid that that just does not square with the facts. In fact, although you state that science is the reason you do not believe in God you offer no substantive scientific reasons as to why we should not believe in God. Your arguments for atheism as a belief system are primarily arguments which are non-scientific. And you need to stop misrepresenting those of us who believe in God as doing so because we are looking for a 'God of the gaps' – someone who will fill in until 'science' gives us the real answer. The reason that we believe in God is *because* of the evidence, *because* of science (knowledge), *because* of what we see in the universe. As Francis Collins declares, 'There are good reasons to believe in God, including the existence of mathematical principles and order in creation. They are positive reasons, based on knowledge, rather than default assumptions based on a temporary lack of knowledge.'[20] I'd take the awe of understanding over the awe of ignorance any day.

Let me leave you with a couple of other quotes:

The best data we have are exactly what I would have predicted, had I nothing to go on but the five books of Moses, the Psalms, the Bible as a whole. (Arno Penzias, the Nobel-prize-

20. *The Language of God*, p. 93

winning scientist who discovered background radiation that proved the Big Bang.[21])

It would be very difficult to explain why the universe should have begun in just this way, except as the act of a God who intended to create beings like us. (Stephen Hawking, *A Brief History of Time*.)

I am personally persuaded that a super intelligent Creator exists beyond and within the cosmos, and that the rich context of congeniality shown by our universe, permitting and encouraging the existence of self-conscious life, is part of the Creator's design and purpose. (Owen Gingerich, *God's Universe*.)

... the extreme difficulty, or rather the impossibility, of conceiving this immense and wonderful universe, including man with his capacity for looking far backwards and far into futurity, as the result of blind chance or necessity. When thus reflecting I feel compelled to look to a First Cause having an intelligent mind in some degree analogous to that of man; and I deserve to be called a Theist. (Charles Darwin, cited in the book you mention – Brown's *Finding Darwin's God*.)

In bringing up the argument of the origin of matter and of the universe you have in fact scored an enormous own goal. Instead of proving that there almost certainly is no God, you have demonstrated that there almost certainly is. It might be a good idea to find out who he is, stop burying your head in the sand and stop shaking your fist at a God you say cannot exist because in order to exist he would have to be more complex than you. He is.

Yours, etc.

David

21. Malcolm Browne, 'Clues to the Universe's Origin Expected', *New York Times*, Mar. 12, 1978, p. 1, col. 54, cited in Jerry Bergman, 'Arno A. Penzias: Astrophysicist, Nobel Laureate', http://www.asa3.org/ASA/PSCF/1994/PSCF9-94Bergman.html

P.S. – there is much in this chapter that I have not interacted with including another attack on the Templeton Foundation and further criticism of another backsliding, compromising scientist – Freeman Dyson. But there are a couple of quotes that I cannot resist. First, you point out that, 'It is utterly illogical to demand complete documentation of every step of every narrative, whether in evolution or any other science.' I agree. Can I suggest that you also apply that to theology and the Bible? Why do you demand that we have to have evidence and documentation for every detail of every event described in the Bible? Of course we are aware that there are 'gaps', but why do you demand that unless we fill them and give you 'the complete picture', then what we have must be classed as false?

Second, you declare, 'When pressed, many educated Christians today are too loyal to deny the virgin birth and the resurrection. But it embarrasses them because their rational minds know it is absurd, so they would much rather not be asked.' Wrong. An educated Christian believes in the God of the Bible who created this whole amazing universe. To raise the dead or create a virgin birth seems to me to be, if not quite chickenfeed in comparison, at least very probable and doable and certainly not illogical. Besides which, I would regard it as a whole lot more logical to believe that an eternal omnipotent God could raise the dead, than to believe that the explanation for our universe involves there being multi-universes in which I exist or am already dead – with or without my green moustache!

LETTER 7 –
THE MYTH OF THE
INHERENT EVIL OF RELIGION

Dear Dr Dawkins,

There is an English nursery rhyme – *The Grand Old Duke of York*. You know how it goes

> *The Grand Old Duke of York*
> *He had ten thousand men;*
> *He marched them up to the top of the hill;*
> *And he marched them down again.*

I kind of feel that this is where we have now arrived. You have led us up to the top of the hill to prove why there is no God. Having in my opinion failed, in the rest of your book you now march us back down again, having a swipe at your favourite religious targets on the way. Chapter five on the roots of religion is your attempt to answer why religion is so prevalent in every society throughout the world. 'Though the details differ across the world, no known culture lacks some version of the time-consuming, wealth-consuming, hostility-provoking rituals, the anti-factual counter productive fantasies of religion.' Chapter eight follows up on the title of your Channel Four TV series, 'The Root of all Evil?' I find your analysis in these two chapters hard to respond to because they depend upon the failed thesis that God has been proven not to exist and, because your treatment of religion is imbalanced, distorted and reflective, not so much of objective analysis but rather your own subjective anti-God feelings.

There have been numerous attempts to explain why religion is so prevalent. Some neuroscientists have argued that there is a 'god centre' in the brain; some psychiatrists argue for the placebo effect of religion whereby people are comforted and have their stress reduced; Marxists argue for the view that religion is a tool of the ruling class to subjugate their people; and Freudians will argue that religion is part of the same irrational mechanism in the brain that makes us fall in love. That latter point reminds me of studying, as a student at the University of Edinburgh, E. P. Thompson's *The Making of the English Working Class*,[22] in which he explains away the Methodist revival by suggesting it was an expression of repressed sexuality. Even then I found it a forced and somewhat amusing explanation.

Your own preference is to suggest that religion is a misfiring by-product of natural selection. Somehow, we have developed a survival mechanism which means that we tend to be obedient to our ancestors. Children naturally have trusting obedience which, whilst it is good for survival, makes them very gullible to 'mind viruses' such as religion. This is where another of your pet theories comes to the fore – the notion of memes. This is an attempt to link Darwinian evolution with the development of ideas. As regards religion, it means, as McGrath points out, 'people do not believe in God because they have

22. Gollancz (1963)

given long and careful thought to the matter; they do so because they have been infected by a powerful meme'.[23] But this idea falls down on at least three levels. First, there is no empirical evidence of such a theory – this is once again a 'science of the gaps' just making things up as you go along in order to fit everything into your all-encompassing evolutionary theory. Second, if it were true then your own ideas, including Darwinian evolution, would be considered memes as well. Third, as Simon Conway Morris, Professor of Evolutionary Paleobiology at the University of Cambridge, points out, 'Memes are trivial, to be banished by simple mental exercises. In any wider context, they are hopelessly, if not hilariously, simplistic.'[24] And I would go way beyond that. They are dangerous. If you regard religion as a virus what should be done with a virus? It should be eradicated.

Which leads me to jump to chapter eight – 'What's Wrong with Religion?' You state that you do not like confrontation and that you 'regularly refuse invitations to take part in formal debates'. I'm afraid this will not wash. Your book is highly confrontational. You surround yourself with those who agree with you before being aggressive about those who do not. In fact, you set up debates and this chapter with a basic myth/meme that is a largely influential one in our culture today. It is the view that religion is essentially something evil and that atheism by contrast is good. Whilst it would only be a fool who denies the fact that some aspects of religion and some religious people have caused a great deal of

23. Cited in McGrath, *Dawkins' God*.
24. From Simon Morris, *Life's Solution: Inevitable Humans in a Lonely Universe*, Cambridge University Press (2003)

harm in the world, it is equally foolish to make the kind of irresponsible sweeping statements that you do here – in order to foster the myth that religion is in essence harmful. This is an atheist half-truth which is erroneously but widely accepted. The *Guardian* newspaper in December 2006 carried a survey of British people, which made clear that a majority of people thought religion was harmful and divisive. Of course all religions were lumped together as one. It is the equivalent of the doctrine of the axis of evil – the world is divided into the good guys and the bad guys. You share that simplistic, fundamentalist view.

But you don't like being called a fundamentalist. A fundamentalist is someone by your definition who believes 'in a holy book'. A fundamentalist would never change their mind: 'we believe in evolution because the evidence supports it, and we would abandon it overnight if new evidence arose to disprove it. No real fundamentalist would ever say anything like that.' Really? I believe that the Bible is true. I believe that Jesus rose from the dead. I believe that God is the Creator of heaven and earth. I believe that all human beings are created equally in his image. And I would abandon these beliefs tomorrow if new evidence arose to disprove them.

I think there are several reasons why you are called a fundamentalist. First, you are passionate about what you believe. Anyone who is passionate about what they believe is often labelled a fundamentalist. Now of course you argue that the hostility you 'occasionally voice towards religion is limited to words'. You are not going to bomb anyone or behead anyone or fly planes into skyscrapers. But on page 318 you directly contradict yourself when commenting on the old adage 'Sticks and stones may break my bones, but words can never hurt me.' You declare, 'the adage is true as long as you don't really believe the words'. What's sauce for the goose is sauce for the gander.

If you are concerned about the impact that words used by religious people may have then you must apply the same criteria to yourself. When you go around describing religion as evil and as a virus you should not be surprised if there are those who hear your words and put them into practice in a way you would not like. Nice middle-class Professors from Oxford do not kill (unless you watch Inspector Morse) but then neither did nice middle class Professors from Nuremberg in the 1930s. Atheists don't bomb or burn? Try telling that to the members of the 77 churches in Norway which were burnt down when some over-zealous young atheists took on board the teaching about how dangerous and evil religion was. Clearly you have also forgotten the clarion calls of some of the great atheist thinkers of the recent past. Bakunin and Lenin for example both argued that religion was a virus which needed to be eradicated – they both advocated and implemented the killing of believers as a social obligation. In this they were only developing the philosophy of Nietzsche:

> I call Christianity the one great curse, the one great intrinsic depravity, the one great instinct for revenge for which no expedient is sufficiently poisonous, secret, subterranean, petty – I call it the one immortal blemish of mankind....

Another atheist writer in advocating attacks on those who believe in the Judaeo-Christian God writes:

Any intelligent Antichrist methodology at that point will involve a consolidation of strength, public education in the ways of science and logic for our individual members, and actions taken against the remaining believers. The new society must first stabilize itself and come to a point of economic self-sufficiency and growth in social, intellectual, economic, technological and cultural areas. Once this is achieved, the executions of diehard Christians and Jews should bother no one. (Taken from the 'Church Arson' website.)

Of course, it would be entirely wrong to take the actions and words of a handful of atheist extremists as being indicative of atheists in general (just as it is wrong of you to take the actions and words of a handful of 'Christian' extremists as indicative of Christians) but please bear in mind that your vehemence and language can have consequences that are as serious as the consequences of the vehemence and language of some 'religious' fundamentalists.

Second, you do not debate – which gives the impression that you know you are right and that there is nothing really to discuss. It also reinforces the impression that you operate within a very closed worldview. In this sense your website has more fundamentalist believers than many religious ones I know. Another sense in which you can be described as fundamentalist is the way that you attack anyone who dares to disagree with you and how you gleefully jump upon books that support your point of view. An example of this is when you hammered Mother Teresa as a woman with 'cock-eyed judgement' not worthy of a Nobel Prize and 'sanctimoniously hypocritical', on the basis of one hostile book you read.

Third, you caricature, mock and misrepresent those who disagree with you. This is easy to do when you do not debate with them but it is not fair. As C. S. Lewis pointed out, 'Such people put up a version of Christianity suitable for a child of six and make that the object of their attack.'[25]

Chapter eight for example is full of the worst examples of this kind of 'reasoning'. You cite the case of Abdul Rahman who was sentenced to death because he converted to Christianity. And this in the modern liberated Afghanistan we have set up, and that our soldiers are currently dying to defend. Then you equate the Afghan Taliban with 'the American Taliban'. This is disingenuous and dishonest. Whilst there are many aspects of the association between right-wing politics and some evangelicalism in the US which I cannot stand, it is clearly wrong to compare them with the Taliban in Afghanistan. No-one (even from the extremes) is calling for the State to execute those who convert to another religion, no-one is arguing for women to be banned from education or that all American women should be covered up. To the ignorant, the link between the Taliban and Christianity is a neat tie up and a further justification for their opposition to Christianity. But that is only to the ignorant. You are not ignorant and you know this.

Another example you use of extremism is Pastor Fred Phelps of Westboro Baptist Church, of 'God Hates Fags' infamy. 'It is easy to write Fred Phelps off as a nut, but he has plenty support from people and their money.' You even cite as evidence for this the fact that since 1991 he has been able to organise one demonstration every four days. Is the fact that one self-publicising head-banger manages to organise a handful of people every four days to carry

25. C. S. Lewis, *Mere Christianity* (1952)

obnoxious banners proof that religion is dangerous? Are you really blaming Mother Teresa, the Pope, Billy Graham, one thousand million Christians throughout the world and even 'yours truly' for every lunatic who expresses their mental and emotional imbalance in religious terms? That is as rational as my suggesting that because Dr Josef Mengele was a scientist, all scientists are to blame and therefore science should be banned. The point is simply that anyone could produce a list of fringe mentally imbalanced people on any subject. That does not invalidate the subject.

You have a good reason for equating Christianity with the unbalanced fringe. It suits your purpose to agree with them as to what Christianity is. That's why you interview extremists. You set up straw men and then it makes you look so much more reasonable. But that is the tactic of the fundamentalist who is out to prove that he alone has the truth, rather than the scholar or the seeker after truth. A number of years ago I went to a meeting where the speaker was a theonomist, the late Greg Bahnsen. The majority of what he said was excellent but then he made a quantum leap trying to prove that the Old Testament Mosaic civil code, including the punishments, should be applied by the state today. I, like most of the Christians there, was horrified at his misapplication of the Bible. But there was a group of people there who supported him and agreed with his interpretation of the Bible – the people from the Secular Humanist society. You need religious extremists to prove your point and they need you. It's a kind of mutual fundamentalist admiration society where both of you justify your extremism by citing the opposition. A plague on both your houses.

You know this so you attempt to justify the link by pointing out that, 'even mild and moderate religion helps to provide the climate of faith in which extremism naturally flourishes'. Do you think that it would be fair of me to point out that even mild and moderate anti-religious rhetoric helps to provide the climate of hatred and certainty in which extremism naturally flourishes? Again, you can only get away with this by using your own definition of faith and refusing to acknowledge the good that is done by religious people because of their religion. You define faith as believing something without evidence – a definition which is just something that you have made up in your own head and has nothing to do with Christianity. My faith is based on evidence. The minute you disprove that evidence I will change my faith. But although you lump together all faiths and all faith as the same, for polemical and political reasons, you are actually creating a grave danger.

Take the question of Christianity and Islam. It suits you to lump them both together (including the extremists). Patrick Sookhdeo's article, *The Myth of Islamic Tolerance*,[26] which you cite, is an excellent discussion of the differences between Christian theology and Islamic theology. The danger is that in your equating Christianity and Islam (because of the wilful blindness caused by your hatred of religion *per se*) you would end up handing Islam a victory – at least in Europe. Secularism cannot handle nor deal with Islam – it does not have the spiritual, moral or intellectual

26. The *Spectator* (30 July 2005)

fibre to do so. If you were to destroy Christianity (which is your aim), what that would leave is a spiritual and moral vacuum in Western Europe that would be filled by either a new fascism or Islam. Then you would find out for real the fact that all religions are not the same.

Despite all the above it is still a truism for many that 'religious' necessarily means 'evil' and is seen as the cause of division. I would suggest that, as so often is the case, the reality of the situation is more complex. Miroslav Volf, in his work *Exclusion and Embrace: Theological Exploration of Identity, Otherness and Reconciliation*,[27] examines the complex ways in which human beings tyrannise one another and the subtle way in which religion is subverted by the human desire to define the self against the other. In other words the problem is not that human beings are basically good and that religion turns them bad, but rather that human beings will use anything, including religion, to justify their own selfish behaviour.

Before finishing, let's return to the question of where religion comes from. Why are people so religious? As you point out, evolutionary psychologist Paul Bloom tells us that we are naturally dualists believing that there is a difference between mind and matter. Bloom even suggests that we are innately predisposed to be creationists. Dorothy Kelman points out that children are intuitive theists. I would actually agree with this and respectively suggest that this evidence contradicts another atheist myth – that people are only religious because they have been brainwashed as children. In actual fact, the default position for humans is to be religious. It takes the 'education' of

27. Abingdon Press, USA (1994)

secularists to get them to a 'higher consciousness' (in other words to disbelieve what they would naturally believe).

Can I make a tentative suggestion to you? That the reason why human beings worship is that there is someone to worship? That the reason we have a sense of God (as opposed to other animals – when did you last see rabbits holding a prayer meeting or cows a worship service?) is because God has given us that sense? That the reason we are spiritual is because we have a spirit? As C. S. Lewis argued, 'Creatures are not born with desires unless satisfaction for those desires exists. A baby feels hunger: well, there is such a thing as food. A duckling wants to swim: well, there is such a thing as water. Men feel sexual desire: well, there is such a thing as sex. If I find in myself a desire which no experience in this world can satisfy, the most probable explanation is that I was made for another world.'

You cite the following in your attack upon those of us who are deluded by our belief in God: 'Self deception is hiding the truth from the conscious mind the better to hide if from others.... There is a tendency for humans consciously to see what they wish to see.' Perhaps the boot is on the other foot. What if there is an Atheist Delusion – where we delude ourselves that our natural God consciousness within is not real? That the evidence is not really evidence at all? And that God does therefore not exist? Would not the Psalmist's description be right? 'The Fool has said in his heart, there is no God' (Psalm 14:1).

Yours, etc.
David

Dear Dr Dawkins,

As a young boy I watched with fascination *The World at War* on our TV screens (the whole series is now available on DVD and is regularly repeated on the History Channel). One scene in particular has stuck in my mind. A group of French Jewish men, women and children were herded into a large barn by Nazi soldiers. The barn was set on fire and the Jews were given a simple choice – they could come out of the barn and be shot or they could stay in and be burnt to death. It horrified me then and it horrifies me now. In fact, it so disturbed me that when I took the opportunity to do Sixth Year Studies at school, I determined to look at Weimar Germany and then went on to study history at the University of Edinburgh in order to try and answer the question, 'why?' The same question that was displayed on the poster hanging in my bed-sit, superimposed over the soldier being shot in the back and the young naked girl running across a bridge screaming as napalm burned into her flesh. This question of morality is thus of great importance – not only for me but I suspect for most people.

You address this issue of morality in chapter six and in particular the question as to why we are good. As far as I can understand it, your case seems to be as follows: you define goodness as altruism and therefore point out that we tend to be altruistic towards those of our own kin because we are genetically programmed to care for those who are most likely to have copies of the same genes that are in us. In addition to this there is reciprocal altruism – the 'you scratch my back and I'll scratch yours' theory. Kinship and reciprocal altruism are the twin pillars on which a Darwinian explanation of morality is based. To these you add reputation (we want to be seen to be 'good') and then the notion that altruistic giving may be seen as a form of superiority – a way of buying self-advertising. You also explain 'kindness' or 'sympathy' as a blessed Darwinian mistake. And that's it. That is the Darwinian explanation of morality. There are so many problems with this approach.

First, it does not seem much of a morality. It is still primarily focused on the Selfish Gene. It is all about me, me and mine. As a Christian I believe that the Bible teaches that human beings *are* fundamentally selfish and self-centred – however the Bible is not content to leave us there. There is something better. Christ came to challenge and to deliver us from the self-centredness which you glorify as the basis of morality.

Second, it is deterministic. There is no concept of free will, choice or responsibility. We are only 'good' because we are programmed to be that way. If my will is not free then you cannot blame me if I only do what I am genetically programmed to do. The trouble with such an approach is that it legitimises all kinds of behaviour; from the drunkard claiming it is in his genes, to the rapist saying that he is only doing what he has been programmed to do. On the other hand, if I am free and responsible for what I do, then I cannot be genetically programmed. I do not doubt that there are genetic factors in all aspects of human behaviour but I cannot believe that every human being and their actions are governed by such determinism. A crucial part of being human is having the ability to choose.

Third, your secular morality is not, as you admit, absolute: 'fortunately however morals do not have to be absolute'. As you indicate it is changeable according to the whims of society. Indeed, if we are, as your favourite philosopher Bertrand Russell puts it, 'tiny lumps of impure carbon and water crawling about for a few years, until they are dissolved again into the elements of which they are compounded', there seems to be no basis for absolute morality. You recognise this: 'it is pretty hard to defend absolute morals on grounds other than religious ones'. Why is this important? Because if there are no absolutes then there is no ultimate standard to judge by. And if there is no ultimate standard then we are left with anything goes, might is right, or the whims of a changing and confused society.

And finally, your absolute Darwinian philosophy cannot logically and consistently argue for morality because, to put it bluntly, there is no good or evil. As you so brilliantly describe it in *The Blind Watchmaker*: 'In a universe of blind physical forces and genetic replication, some people are going to get hurt, other people are going to get lucky, and you won't find any rhyme or reason in it, nor any justice. The universe we observe has precisely the properties we should expect if there is at bottom, no design, no purpose, no evil and no good, nothing but blind pitiless indifference.' That then is the atheist basis of morality – no justice, no rhyme nor reason, no purpose, no evil, no good, just blind pitiless indifference. It is little wonder that atheist philosophers have been desperately hunting round to try and establish some basis for a godless morality. Despite the best efforts of atheistic philosophers such as Peter Singer, Princeton Professor of Bioethics and a leading atheist polemicist, this basis is severely lacking, being little more than a utilitarian 'greatest good for the greatest number' without ever defining what 'good' is.

I think you recognise that this is the Achilles heel of atheism and so you go on the attack – ridiculing Christian morality. It has to be admitted that there are many things that have been done in the name of religion, including Christianity, which are inexcusable and that the behaviour of many professing Christians leaves a great deal to be desired. However, you should be careful before denouncing the whole of Christianity on the basis of the behaviour of those who are Christians and fail to be perfect, or of those who, whilst claiming the label Christian, have no more faith than yourself.

Your major case against Christian morality is the Bible itself (we will come on to that in your next chapter) but in this one you throw up a couple of red herrings.

First, at the beginning of the chapter you cite a number of letters which you have received from people you say are Christians. These contain expletives, threats of violence and grotesque language. Why did you cite these at the beginning of a chapter about morality? Because it is again your favourite *ad hominem* tactic. Look how stupid/ignorant/violent/immoral these Christians are and therefore Christian morality is the same. There are two easy counters to that. First, by definition these people cannot be Christians, followers of the one who told his disciples to turn the other cheek, not to threaten violence, not to use foul language and to love our enemies. Second, what would you think if I cited the following from your own website:

> XXX David Robertson is a self-righteous narrow minded, up his own XXX thick as pig XXX moronic retard! Watch out David, the sky fairy is late for his second coming and will be angry with you. Why is anyone debateing with this moron? He doesn't know how to! He has the intellectual capacity of road kill.
>
> May your XXX come to life and kiss you. I'm impressed that some of the people here bother to debate this Robertson nincompoop. He is clearly out of his mind and beyond reason and logic. If you do debate him, stop respecting his delusions, however eloquent he puts them, and please approach him with the scorn and contempt that he deserves.

Prat. Bigot. Moron. In fact there are pages and pages of this stuff. It is quite clear that your website acts as a kind of therapy centre for some people but do you think it would be fair for me to say that therefore all atheists are as rude, ignorant and angry?

The second argument you use is to point out that Christian morality cannot be up to much if it requires the threat of hell or some kind of punishment in order to make people behave. You cite Einstein: 'If people are good only because they fear punishment, and hope for reward, then we are a sorry lot indeed.' Einstein is right in at least one thing. We are a sorry lot. Here is a simple test for you. Would you like the police to be removed from Oxford? Do you think that students at your University should be threatened with punishment if they cheat? Or should they be given higher degrees if they do better than their peers? Surely if your students are only studying and not cheating because they fear punishment or have hope for some reward they are a sorry lot? Of course you see the fallacy of the argument. The Bible recognises that human beings are complex and that we need a system of checks and balances to help us – but here is the rub, the Bible's teaching is not primarily moralistic. It is much more radical than that. If it were the carrot and stick approach only, then the Bible would just be recognising the situation for what it is – rather than seeking to change it to a better world.

Let us look then at the Christian case for morality and why, for some people, it is the most important proof for God.

1. It explains evil. The question is not 'why are people good?' but rather 'why are people evil?' Your view of morality seems to stem from your nice middle-class English background. It is a hopelessly optimistic and unfounded view of human nature – that human beings are essentially good and indeed are getting better all the time. Remember the question that I went to University to study – how could a decent civilised nation like the German people allow themselves to get into a position where they eradicated six million Jews plus many homosexuals, gypsies and Christians? It is easy in those circumstances, aided by decades of

Hollywood conditioning, to believe that the world is divided into the good guys and the bad guys, and just simply to suggest that the Germans were bad, or Hitler was an insane demon. But my studies led me to the conclusion that the Germans were human and that Hitler was all too human. Indeed, there was an enormous fuss a couple of years ago when the film *Downfall* was shown in Germany because it portrayed Hitler as a human being. The Bible tells us what we would already know if only we opened our eyes, that human beings are screwed up. As Freddy Mercury, late of Queen, sang at the first Live Aid, 'If there's a God up above, a God of love, Then what must he think, of the mess that we've made, of the world that he created?'

2. It explains the universe. Have you ever read C. S. Lewis' 'Right and Wrong as a Clue to the Meaning of the Universe' in his *Mere Christianity*? He, more than anyone, sums up why the moral law is such a powerful proof for the existence of God. He wrote, 'Human beings all over the earth, have this curious idea that they ought to behave in a certain way, and cannot really get rid of it. Secondly they know that they do not in fact behave in that way. They know the Law of Nature; they break it. These two facts are the foundation of all clear thinking about ourselves and the universe we live in.' Lewis points out that there are two clear evidences for God – the first is the universe he has made. The second is the Moral Law which he argues is a better bit of information because it is 'inside information'. One of the major objections that many people will have to the notion that God created the universe is that things

seem so cruel and unjust. But, as Lewis asks, how do we get the idea of cruel and unjust in the first place? What is there in us that makes us aware of right and wrong?

3. It explains me. In looking at the horror of the Holocaust it was the most humbling and awful experience to realise that not only were the Nazis human but I was too. The same evil that came to such horrendous fruition in the Nazis was also, at least in seed form, present in me. Reading books like Gitta Sereny's excellent *Albert Speer; His Battle with Truth*[28] was a sobering experience. As one G. K. Chesterton masterfully put it in a letter to *The Times*: 'Dear Editor: What's wrong with the world? I am. Faithfully yours, G. K. Chesterton.'

But let us return to the atheistic view of morality. I accept fully that you are not a Social Darwinist. You know that that would be wrong. Although I am intrigued as to how you know. But leaving that aside, my fear is that once society as a whole accepts your basic presuppositions (that there are no absolutes in morality, that morality changes and that human nature is genetically determined) then it is a downward slippery slope to the kind of atheistic societies that the world has already seen (such as Stalin's Russia and Mao's China). I am not arguing that all atheists are immoral any more than I am arguing that all professing Christians are moral. All of us live inconsistently with our creeds. However, in Christianity there are brakes, checks and balances and it does not appear immediately obvious that this is the case with atheism. If there is no absolute right or wrong then how can we state that anything is right or wrong?

28. Random House (1995)

Take the case of abortion which you discuss in chapter eight. You point out a fascinating fact that 'strong opponents of abortion are almost all deeply religious'. This is a fact that has always puzzled me. Surely any scientist would know that there is nothing that the baby has outside the womb which she does not also have inside the womb. Why then is it considered a human right to be allowed to kill a baby in the womb but not outside it? And there is another question in this debate which fascinates me. In India over 500,000 female fetuses are aborted each year because they are female. Naturally women's groups are objecting to this form of selective abortion. But why? Why would pro-abortionists want to interfere with a woman's right to choose not to have a girl? Is it not after all the woman's body? Besides which, in the eyes of pro-abortionists, it's not a girl but a 'potential' girl. The inconsistencies are ironic.

Of course, once we move away from the simplistic and unscientific 'a woman has a right to choose to kill the baby in her womb but not outside of it', then we can end up with all kinds of difficulties. Peter Singer argues that 'mentally impaired babies have no greater rights than certain animals'.[29]

Bill Hamilton, to whom you owed a great deal in the writing of your book *The Selfish Gene* – and whose writing you stated was passionate, vivid and informed – was an excellent Darwinian biologist whose views were certainly of a different kind of morality. He once said that he had more sympathy for a lone fern than he did for a crying child. He argued that males were largely doomed

---

29. *Independent Extra* (13 September 2006)

to compete and that the purpose of sex was to clean out the gene pool by filtering out the useless and the weak. The low status male would be better off dead. Everything in nature according to Hamilton could be explained as the outcome of competition between genes. He argued for a radical programme of infanticide, eugenics and euthanasia in order to save the world. He believed that modern medicine was doing harm by allowing the weak to survive and thus preserving their genes. His two concrete examples of these are caesarean sections and the glasses worn by John Maynard Smith! Spectacles were a symbol of decadence within the gene pool and as for caesarean sections – women should be allowed one and then only to save the mother's life – after that they should be paid not to have any more children.

Hamilton's view of modern medicine was so eugenically based that he believed that the only acceptable forms of medicine were painkillers and surgery. He declared that genocide was the result of over-breeding and that he would grieve more for the death of one giant panda than he would for a 'hundred unknown Chinese'. He also argued that the handicapped should be killed at birth. In arguing for what he termed 'inclusive happiness' he stated, 'I have little doubt that if trying to survive on Robinson Crusoe's island with my wife I would indeed with my own hands kill a defective baby'. In this, he and Singer would be as one.

It may be that the extreme social and political views of Hamilton are in fact an exception and that it would not be right to tar all biologists with the same brush. That is true. It is not biologists who are the problem but some biologists who also happen to be atheists and who do not accept the notion of an absolute morality. And whilst Hamilton may have been on the extreme there have been plenty others who have worked out the logical conclusion to their atheistic materialism. Some of the leading evolutionary biologists in the 20th century have been people who, because of their atheistic philosophy and misunderstanding of science, adopted extreme political views. Konrad Lorenz was an enthusiastic Nazi. J. B. S. Haldane was a committed Stalinist and R. A. Fisher used to argue that civilisation was threatened because upper class women (i.e. 'quality') did not have enough babies.

At this point, perhaps, someone might point out that I am doing the same thing to you that I accuse you of doing to others – namely picking some extremes and using them to condemn the lot. The difference is this. Whereas you cite people who are on the wacky fringes of Christianity the people I am speaking about are key and central figures. Can you imagine how atheists would have reacted if the Archbishop of Canterbury, the Pope or Billy Graham had come out arguing for infanticide, banning caesarean sections, or encouraging the 'superior' classes to breed more than the common people?! We would never have heard the end of it.

Meanwhile, you cite such fringe characters as Fred Phelps of Westboro Baptist Church and ignore the substantial history and philosophy within the grounds of atheistic secular biology of those who have advocated such extreme social views. What was most disturbing about Nazism was not whether its main thinkers were 'nice' people, but rather its philosophical foundation and the basis and justification it gave for cruelty and injustice. That is the same for Social

Darwinism where the elimination of the weak and the destruction of the handicapped are the very antithesis of Christianity and the real enemy of humanity. I repeat again, for the umpteenth time, that this is not to state that all evolutionary atheists are *de facto* fascists, but it is to say that the logical consequences of evolutionary atheism can easily lead, and has led, to such a position.

The Christian view of morality is not, as most people suppose, that the Bible gives us a set of laws to live by. Real Christians are not moralists – thinking that if only we offer a reward here, a bit of punishment there, then 'decent' human beings will behave better and somehow earn their own stairway to heaven. We know that we can neither legislate nor use religion to make us good. Real Christians realise that the Bible's teaching is that there is an absolute morality – from which we all fall short. And no amount of religion, good works or pious acts will ever be able to make us right. That is where grace, salvation, the cross and all the wonderful truths of the acts of God in Christ come into their own. God was in Christ reconciling the world to himself. That is why the Gospel is Good News. Not because it gives us a set of laws to live by, or religious rites to perform, but because it deals with the biggest problem in the world – the problem of the human heart. It is for that reason that every year I religiously watch *Schindler's List* to remind me of why I am a minister of the Christian Gospel. I don't just want to explain the Darkness. I want to defeat it.

Yours, etc.
David

LETTER 9 –
THE MYTH OF THE IMMORAL BIBLE

Dear Dr Dawkins,

In chapter three you had a go at the Bible but now you really stick the boot in. The belief in the Bible as instruction or moral example 'encourages a system of morals which any civilised modern person, whether religious or not, would find – I can put it no more gently – obnoxious.... Those who wish to base their morality literally on the Bible have either not read it or not understood it, as Bishop John Shelby Spong, in *The Sins of Scripture*, rightly observed.'

I have studied the Bible for over 25 years. For 20 of those it has been my job to do so. I have tried to do so with an open mind and a desire to know what it really says. At times it has puzzled me, caused me to question and has presented me with seemingly insurmountable difficulties. I hope that you would grant me as a professional in this field of study, the same respect I grant you as a biologist. Your understanding of Scripture is extreme in its condemnation and seems governed more by your atheism than by any knowledge or understanding of the text. Yet you prejudge the whole issue at the beginning of this chapter by again implying that those who do not accept your point of view are not civilised, moral or intelligent enough to understand the Bible. This is yet again another one of those 'Emperor has no clothes' moments. You imply that only those who see the Bible as immoral are intelligent and moral. There is almost nothing I can say to people with such presuppositions but let me at least try to help those who are inclined to accept at face value your distorted and sour-grape-picking version of the Bible.

In your attack on the Bible you mention Noah's Ark, Sodom and Gomorrah, The Levite concubines in Judges, Abraham lying, the almost sacrifice of Isaac, Jephthah's daughter, the Golden Calf, Moses attacking the Midian-ites, all in the Old Testament (and for good measure you throw in Pat Robertson and New Orleans, although quite what that has to do with the Bible escapes me). In the New Testament your objections seem to be that Jesus was rude to his mother and had dodgy family values, and the doctrine of the atonement. In addition to this you try to dismiss the positive teachings in the Bible of 'do not kill' and 'love your neighbour' as actually racist, meaning 'do not kill Jews' and 'love only fellow Jews'. You go so far as to state that, 'Jesus would have turned over in his grave if he had known that Paul would be taking his plan to the pigs.' It's all wonderful knock about stuff for your fans, equivalent to the kind of comedy that George Carlin, whom you cite, is famous for. But, it is a long way from what the Bible actually says.

First, anyone who reads the Bible in its context cannot take seriously the suggestion that Jesus only came for the Jews and that 'love your neighbour' only meant the Jews. The very parable that Jesus told to illustrate that truth was one which involved a non-Jew. Your re-writing and re-reading of these verses is out of context, dishonest and deceitful special pleading which says a whole lot more about your prejudgements than it does about the Bible. You base much of your thinking here on what you call a 'remarkable paper' by John Hartung, an associate professor of anaesthesiology and an anthropologist. This paper, entitled 'Love Thy Neighbor: The Evolution of In-Group Morality', includes an acknowledgement of you and your wife and more disturbingly a sympathetic review of Kevin MacDonald's *A People that Shall Dwell Alone: Judaism as a Group Evolutionary Strategy*.[30] It is all getting disturbingly close to the 'evolutionary' view of religion and Judaism that the Nazi academics and scientists taught. And it is a million miles away from what the Bible actually says.

Second, Pat Robertson, New Orleans, and the various twisted theologies of some exponents of Christianity have nothing to do with the teachings of the Scriptures, which should be judged on their own merits.

Third, you need to learn the basic principles of reading the Bible. You must always read it in context – that includes historical, literary, theological and biblical context. To read out of context is to misread. Then you must recognise that much of the Bible is descriptive rather than prescriptive. In other words, it is telling us what went on rather than what should have happened. In fact, this is one of the things that helped convince me of the truth of the Bible. Most of the main characters, even the heroes, come out quite badly. They are painted warts and all. If this was myth why would someone write about such things as David committing murder and adultery, or Abraham lying about his wife?

30. Greenwood Press (1994)

Atheists are fond of arguing against what they consider to be 'literal' interpretations of the Bible. Like some fundamentalists you consider those who are not literalists as just cowards. But it really does depend on what you mean by 'literal'. When I am asked if I read the Bible literally I can never answer directly because I need to know first of all what the questioner means. If he means do I take every word at its literal meaning then the answer is no, of course not. When Jesus said 'I am the vine', he did not mean that he was green and produced literal grapes. To read any literature in such a way, never mind such an extensive collection of books as the Bible, would be plain stupid and false to the book itself. The Bible has at least five different genres: prophecy, poetry, history, letter and law. On the other hand, if by literal you mean 'at face value' then yes, I do read the Bible literally. You ask 'by what criteria do you decide which passages are symbolic, which literal?' The answer – context, genre and common sense. I really do not expect to be dressed in white and playing a harp in heaven (aka the Book of Revelation) but I have no doubt that Jesus literally rose from the dead. It was not symbolic of anything, it was written not as poetry but as verifiable history, and it is a fact that is repeated several times. It is quite clear what the Bible means when it speaks about the resurrection. Mind you, if you seriously believe that when Jesus taught the Old Testament refrain 'love your neighbour', he meant only Jews, then I guess you can make the Bible say whatever you do or do not want it to say!

One important principle is that of progressive revelation. This is the idea that the Bible, written over a period of more than 1000 years, progressively reveals God to us.

Little by little the curtain is opened and the light comes in. Therefore, some aspects of earlier revelation are superseded by the later.

Another significant principle is one that you state yourself when trying to defend the horrific statements of such enlightened and liberal atheists as H. G. Wells and Thomas Huxley. The latter declared, 'No rational man, cognizant of the facts, believes that the average negro is the equal, still less the superior, of the white man.' Yet, in order to defend them, you declare, 'It is a commonplace that good historians don't judge statements from past times by the standards of their own.' Exactly. Please apply that to the Bible as well.

I believe the Bible is the Word of God; as such it is true, without error and communicates all that God wants it to. That does not mean it is without problems but I would like to suggest that if you read it bearing in mind the basic principles above, then 90% of the problems you cite will disappear. However that leaves the other 10%. It would be foolish to deny that there are major difficulties within the Bible. There are parts of it that make me feel distinctly uncomfortable and that I struggle with. But who am I to sit in judgement upon the Bible?

Not long after becoming a Christian there were parts in the Bible that greatly disturbed me. I read a book that purported to deal with most of those difficulties; however it did not really help much. But I made a decision that it was stupid and arrogant of me as a young Christian to think that I alone could understand the Bible, and to attempt to sit in judgement upon it. It was not that it was wrong to question but rather that I had to be patient, humble and thoughtful.

After more than 25 years studying it I have come more and more to appreciate the truth, wisdom, beauty and relevance of the Bible. This is not because I have to, or I am paid to – in many ways it would have been so much easier to give in and go with the flow; it would certainly have made for an easier life. But I could not, in all intellectual honesty, give up. As a result, I have found the Bible to be more reliable and relevant than anything. I find it amazing, when I teach even parts that seem more obscure and difficult, that it addresses the needs, desires and lives of ordinary people living in the 21st century. I would venture a guess that many of the 'atheist' converts from religion are those who have never really drunk deep from the well of Scripture. For me, to paraphrase the words of B. B. King, 'the thrill has not gone'.

You clearly have difficulty with the atonement as well. 'I have described atonement, the central doctrine of Christianity, as vicious, sadomasochistic and repellent. We should also dismiss it as barking mad, but for its ubiquitous familiarity which has dulled our objectivity. If God wanted to forgive our sins, why not just forgive them?' Whilst I am grateful that you at least recognise, unlike some professing Christians, that the atonement is the central doctrine of Christianity, it is sad that you are obviously missing out on the best part of the whole Bible. The cross has always been a stumbling block both for the religious and those who consider themselves to be wise. Polly Toynbee, a *Guardian* columnist, was scathing about this when she reviewed *The Lion, the Witch and the Wardrobe*.[31] She vehemently declared that she did not need anyone to die for her sins.

31. 'Narnia represents everything that is most hateful about religion', Polly Toynbee, The *Guardian* (5 December 2005)

For most people, the notion that we have done anything so bad as to deserve death *is* repellent. But that is because we do not have an adequate understanding of evil and sin. And we have no real awareness of the depths of depravity in our own hearts. Once you grasp that then the doctrine of atonement – the idea that the Son of God died in my place and paid the price for my sin – is a truth that is wonderful. It's the best part of the whole Bible. What would be repellent would be if Rousseau's reputed last words were true; he claimed that God would forgive him because 'c'est son metier' (that's his job). So, no matter what we do or how we behave God will forgive us. Such cheap forgiveness is neither just nor biblical.

The most interesting and disturbing part of this chapter is the section headed 'The Moral Zeitgeist', which examines the changing moral cultures. Here you are expounding a fairly common belief that atheists hold – that things are getting better all the time. Humanity is evolving from a primitive morality to a generally improved moral consensus. This of course is highly questionable and the evidence you offer for such chronological (and indeed Western) snobbery is scanty. Is it really the case that the moral *zeitgeist* is improving in Britain and the US? Are women really being treated better? Has racism and prejudice been done away with? Is our current sex-obsessed, materialistic and shallow society better than it was one hundred years ago? That is not immediately self-evident! Of course there have been vast improvements but sometimes one wonders whether it is one step forward and two steps back. I suspect that only a nice middle-class Western moralist could be so confident and glib about the greatly improving moral situation with humanity. I had thought that such liberal utopianism had received a mortal blow after the First World War and was killed off after the Second. But apparently not. You are once again teaching that the human race is evolving to moral perfection and that the only thing that is preventing us from realising this is the evil of religion.

You cite as examples of the improved moral *zeitgeist* increased female suffrage and a change in attitude to race. You mention that even Washington, Jefferson and other 'men of the Enlightenment' held slaves (curious that you are prepared to excuse this practice in these men because it was 250 years ago but you condemn it in the Old Testament 2000 years ago). Most shocking of all you point out that H. G. Wells in his *New Republic* in answering the question as to how the New Republic would deal with the 'inferior races' such as the black, the yellow man, etc. stated, 'Well, the world is a world, and not a charitable institution, and I take it they will have to go.' He made it quite clear what he meant – the extermination of inferior races. You state that this position would now be unacceptable in society and more astonishingly you claim that this is because of 'improved education and in particular, the increased understanding that each of us shares a common humanity with members of other races and with the other sex – both deeply unbiblical ideas that come from biological science, especially evolution.' When I read that I had to stop and take a deep breath. Did he really write that? Does he really have the audacity to think that he can get away with such a big lie?!

The Bible taught a long time ago (Genesis 1) that both men and women were made in the image of God. The

Bible also taught that all human beings, of whatever race, were descendants of Adam and that all were made in the image of God. To describe these ideas as unbiblical when they are foundational to the Bible is bad enough. But then to suggest that it is evolution which has led us away from the evils of Wells *et al.* is breathtaking. The Church was teaching long before the end of the 19th century that all human beings were made in the image of God. Last year I visited a Black University in South Africa where one of the photos on the wall was of a Black South African who had come to study in Glasgow and returned as an ordained Presbyterian minister in the 19th century. It was not the Church nor the Bible that was teaching that 'inferior races' should be destroyed. In fact, you cite Huxley's racism (*Emancipation – Black and White* – published in 1865) as typical of the *zeitgeist* of the time. Yet Huxley was arguing against the *zeitgeist*. Society, led primarily by Christian activists and thinkers working on biblical principles, had come to the conclusion that slavery was wrong. William Wilberforce, the British parliamentarian, made his first abolition motion in 1789. Motivated by his Christian biblical understanding that all human beings were created in the image of God, he presented no fewer than 11 abolition bills to the House of Commons until finally, in 1807, the slave trade was abolished. After further campaigning slavery itself was abolished in 1833. Britain then sought to persuade other slaving nations to reject slavery – the government bought Portuguese and Spanish abolition for over £1 million and French in exchange for military aid. The British navy enforced this abolition over a period of 50 years spending £40 million seizing 1,600 ships to liberate 150,000 slaves.

Twenty years before Huxley, in the 1840s, my own church, St Peters in Dundee, was holding anti-slavery meetings and acting as a focus for supporting the anti-slavery movement in the US. And yet Huxley was arguing that this biblical morality was unscientific. He believed what he believed not because of the *zeitgeist* but because of his science. It was such Social Darwinian evolutionary thinking that fed the manic utopianism of Wells and others. I am grateful that the *zeitgeist* of atheistic evolut-ionary biologists has improved more recently but please do not put us all in the same boat.

Which brings me on nicely to the six pages you devote to Stalin and Hitler. I can understand why atheists want to dissociate themselves from the like of Stalin, Mao and Pol Pot – after all they were the leaders of the only officially atheistic states so far, and their human-rights record was, shall we say, not exactly great. The only argument I have heard atheists use is that, well, really, Stalin was not an atheist because he behaved unreasonably and unreason-able people cannot be atheists! It's the ultimate in circular arguments and there is no point in trying to break into the circle.

However Hitler is different. You want to cite Hitler as a Christian, although even you know that is going a bit far. As already indicated this is one subject that I have studied extensively. The basic facts are as follows: Hitler was brought up as a Catholic; when he came to power he did so in a situation where the Catholic Church and the Lutheran Church were still significant social forces within German society; he was quite happy to use the Christian churches and Christian symbols when he could; ironically it was those who taught as you do – that religion should be privatised and that the Church should stay out of politics – who provided the biggest reason for non-opposition to Hitler. Thankfully men like Dietrich Bonhoeffer and others were prepared to ignore that advice and do what they could to resist evil. Bonhoeffer even put into print an accusation that Hitler was anti-Christian, and attacked the 'Blood and Soil' ideology of the Nazis ('He may call this ideology Christian, but in doing so he becomes Christ's enemy.'[32]) For this bravery, based again upon his Christian faith, he paid the ultimate sacrifice.

If we really want to know what Hitler thought, his actions and above all his private words are the most compelling evidence. And I am grateful to you for citing Hitler's *Table Talk*, which tells us conclusively what Hitler thought about Christianity: 'The heaviest blow that ever struck humanity was the coming of Christianity.' Even more interesting is the following from Traudl Junge, Hitler's personal secretary:

> Sometimes we also had interesting discussions about the church and the development of the human race. Perhaps it's going too far to call them discussions, because he would be-gin explaining his ideas when some question or remark from one of us had set them off, and we just listened. He was not a member of any church, and thought the Christian religions were outdated, hypocritical institutions that lured people into them. The laws of nature were his religion. He could reconcile his dogma of violence better with nature than with the Christian doctrine of loving your neighbour and your enemy. 'Science isn't yet clear about the origins of humanity,' he once said. 'We are probably the highest stage of develop-ment of some mammal which developed from reptiles and

32. Bonhoeffer *Discipleship*.

moved on to human beings, perhaps by way of the apes. We are a part of creation and children of nature, and the same laws apply to us as to all living creatures. And in nature the law of the struggle for survival has reigned from the first. Everything incapable of life, everything weak is eliminated. Only mankind and above all the church have made it their aim to keep alive the weak, those unfit to live, and people of an inferior kind.[33]

That just about says it all.

You ask at the end of this chapter, 'Why would someone go to war for the sake of an absence of belief?' I assume by that you mean an absence of belief in God. The answer to your question is twofold. First, it could be that the reason people go to war *is* the absence of belief. If, like Stalin or Hitler, you believe that there is no God to answer to, that 'might is right' and that power comes at the end of a gun, then you are much more likely to indulge your selfish genes and go to war to get what you want. The second answer to your question is in the quote above. Hitler clearly did not go to war because he believed in God or because he wanted to spread Christianity. He hated Christianity. On the other hand he did believe that religion was a virus (where have I heard that one before?) and that the Jews especially were vermin who should be eradicated in order better to preserve the species. It was all perfectly logical, Darwinian and godless. Perhaps the atheist *zeitgeist* has moved on. But meanwhile, until it is proven otherwise, I would prefer to stick with the tried and tested morality of the Bible.

Yours, etc.

David

33. *Until the Final Hour* p. 108

Dear Dr Dawkins,

You ask, 'Isn't it also a form of child abuse to label children as possessors of beliefs that they are too young to have thought about?' This question is the whole purpose of your chapter nine. Your view that children should not be taught religion you illustrate with a horror story of the kidnapping of an Italian Jewish boy in the 19th century; abuse by the Catholic Church; an interview with Pastor Keenan Roberts who sets up Hell Houses to educate children; testimonies from people brought up in Christian homes who are now atheists; a wee go at the Amish; a six-page attack on Emmanuel school in the North East of England and an appeal against the labelling of children on the basis of their parents' religion. You finish by arguing that religious education should be about learning the Bible as literature. All in all, those who are atheists will share your horror at what you call this religious child abuse and others may be influenced to think that perhaps you will have a case. But let me suggest that there are yet again major flaws in your argument.

You underplay the role of sexual abuse in order to demonstrate the horrors of the psychological abuse caused to children. You openly admit that you were a victim of child sexual abuse in your English boarding school from a teacher 'whose affection for small boys overstepped the bounds of propriety'; something you describe as 'an embarrassing but otherwise harmless experience'. This leads you to talk about the horrific child abuse cases that have come to light regarding the Catholic church, and then to make the extraordinary statement that 'horrible as sexual abuse no doubt was, the damage was arguably less than the long-term psychological damage inflicted by bringing up the child Catholic in the first place' (a comment which you inform us was made to an audience of Dublin intellectuals and received spontaneous applause). And it is not just the Catholics you have a go at – although you do seem to have a particular disdain for both them and American evangelicals. You also mention the Exclusive Brethren, a 'more than unusually odious sect'. Later on you come to the Amish and in a few disparaging sentences suggest that modern society is guilty of allowing Amish parents to abuse their children.

All this is of course leading to an inevitable and shocking conclusion. If the situation is as you say and religion is a virus then the logical thing is to protect children. You cite with evident approval the psychologist Nicholas Humphrey:

> Children, I'll argue, have a human right not to have their minds crippled by exposure to other people's bad ideas – no matter who those other people are.... So we should no more allow parents to teach their children to believe, for example, in the literal truth of the Bible or that the planets rule their

lives, than we should allow parents to knock their children's teeth out or to lock them in a dungeon.

We are almost coming full circle here. You began with the story about the kidnapping of Edgardo Mortara, who was taken away from his parents because a servant had baptised him as a Catholic and his parents were Jewish. The Catholic authorities were prepared to 'save' the boy from the Jewish upbringing that they believed would cause him harm. You are rightly horrified by this and yet you have now moved on to an almost similar position.

I have taught and will continue to teach my children that the Bible is true and you are now accusing me of doing them more harm than if I sexually abused them. Perhaps in the Brave New World of the Atheist State the religious thought police will be sent round to ensure that my children are being taught 'correct' thoughts. If it is right for the State to take children away from parents who would sexually abuse them, and if you believe that bringing a child up in the Christian faith is more abusive, then logically you must believe that the State should have the right to remove children from such abusive situations. If you follow your logic through then the story of Edgardo Mortara will be the story of many more children, whose parents do not accept the atheist *zeitgeist* of the new moral order. As Marilynn Robinson, the brilliant and perceptive author of the best novel of the past century, *Gilead*, points out:

> And how might it have been worse? If the child had fallen, as in the next century so many would, into the hands of those who considered his Jewishness biological rather than religious and cultural. To Dawkins's objection that Nazi science was not authentic science I would reply, first, that neither Nazis nor Germans had any monopoly on these theories,

which were influential throughout the Western world, and second, that the research on human subjects carried out by those holding such assumptions was good enough science to appear in medical texts for fully half a century. This is not to single out science as exceptionally inclined to do harm, though its capacity for doing harm is by now unequalled. It is only to note that science, too, is implicated in this bleak human proclivity, and is one major instrument of it.[34]

The notion that keeping children away from religion will somehow save the world is a fanciful one which ignores logic, common sense and human history. As regards the latter, I am reminded of an asylum seeker in the Netherlands whom I met last year. She is an educated doctor from Azerbaijan. She has experienced the horrors of religious ethnic cleansing – having been forced from her country by Muslim fundamentalists. You would expect that having experienced the evil effects of some religion she would have been supportive of your point of view. But when I discussed it with her she completely disagreed with you. 'We spent 70 years,' she told me, '70 years when we were not allowed to be taught about God. We lived in an atheist state where only atheism was taught. They even tried to ban God from our homes.' The results were all too clearly seen in the atheist Soviet Union. The philosophy and ideas you put forward in this chapter have been tried already and, as already pointed out, they have been a spectacular failure.

It does scare me a little that the basic position you outline in this chapter is one which labels me both as

34. Review of *The God Delusion* in *Harper's Magazine*, November 2006, reproduced online at http://darwiniana.com/2006/10/23/marilynne-robinson-on-dawkins/

abused and abuser. I was brought up in the Brethren. There are aspects of it I did not like and I met some strange people and heard some strange things. However, I also met some wonderful people and was taught some wonderful things – not least that I should use my own mind. It was doing precisely that which caused me first of all to reject the faith I had been brought up with and secondly to return, not to Brethrenism, but to Jesus Christ. My childhood was largely a happy one within the context of a loving family and an open community. Yet you think I would have been better off being sexually abused by some boarding school master than being brought up having been taught about Jesus Christ. And you accuse me of being worse than a paedophile because I happily teach young children that God loves them, that they are important and have a purpose and a place in his world. Is it little wonder that people think that your logic is a bit twisted by your secular fundamentalism and are they not right to be more than a little frightened by the consequences of such a perverse view?

Speaking of schools your American readers must be wondering why you spend six pages attacking one state school in the North East of England. What kind of evil and horrendous place is this that it results in you, the Bishop of Oxford and almost all the English intelligentsia uniting to condemn and attack it? Emmanuel College is a state school. In Britain we do not have a formal separation of Church and State and therefore many state schools are meant to be based upon a Christian ethos. A considerable number of schools in England are Anglican and it is still the case that most schools have at least one act of public

Christian worship per week. However, much of the state system in Britain is in crisis – the fact that the decline in standards has arisen at the same time as the decline in Christianity and the rise of secularism may or may not be apposite. Many of the poorest are being left behind in run-down schools with very poor academic records. The government, for better or for worse, has tried to encourage rich benefactors to invest in State schools in poorer areas known as 'city academies'.

One person who has invested is Sir Peter Vardy, a millionaire businessman and a Christian. One of the three schools he has supported, to the tune of £2 million each, is Emmanuel College, Gateshead, in the North East of England. So why are you, and so many of your friends, so bitterly opposed to this school? Why in a book about 'the God Delusion', and a chapter about religious child abuse, do you devote so much space to attacking this school and calling it an educational scandal? Because the head of science, Stephen Layfield, is a Christian and wrote a paper on the 'The teaching of science: a biblical perspective'. In this he commits the cardinal sin of daring to question evolution. Now he may or may not be wrong – and I am sure that if the basic principles of science are taught then his pupils will soon be able to discern the truth. But are you really justified in labelling Emmanuel Christian School as a place where child abuse is taking place? Are you right to label it a 'creationist college' which brainwashes students to accept the biblical view uncritically?

I decided to find out and not surprisingly the truth is somewhat different. The policy of the College is to teach the arguments for and against evolution, intelligent design, etc. Students are encouraged to take a critical approach and not to accept things without subjecting them to scrutiny and discussion. Teachers and students are encouraged to state their own views. Of the nine science staff three would hold to a young-earth creationist position, three to a theistic evolutionist position and three are non-Christian evolutionists. Does this sound like a school that is designed to ignore current scientific thinking? As far as I can recall it reflects my own experience of school where my chemistry teacher was an atheist, my physics teacher was a Christian and my biology teacher was a young-earth creationist. They were all good teachers who did not seek to impose their views. So why are you so bitterly opposed to Emmanuel?

This is made even more puzzling when we look at how well Emmanuel is doing. In March 2006 Emmanuel received its third 'outstanding' rating from Ofsted – one of only twelve schools in the country at the time. August saw exam results that placed the College in the top five comprehensive schools in England. This is not a school in the elitist green suburbs of Oxford. It is a school in one of the poorest areas of England and its 1250 pupils are receiving an excellent education in a good school. Surely, as a liberal humanitarian you should be delighting in this success – even if the head of science has views which you consider to be wrong. Your attitude to this is puzzling and smacks more of the fundamentalist ethos than a liberal humanitarian view which sees education as a good in and of itself.

It is worth noticing that the campaign against this highly successful school was begun by the National Secular Society. Why? Why have they not begun a campaign to raise all our schools to the level and standards of Emmanuel? Why are they not shouting from the rooftops at the scandal of the declining education system in our country, especially for the poor, instead of attacking a school that is actually working? It is because they are more concerned for their ideology than they are for people. I even know one official of that society who, whilst publicly campaigning against any sort of Christian influence in state schools, sends his own children to a private Christian school because 'they get a better education there'. Hypocrisy.

Speaking of hypocrisy you mention Dan Barker, a former fundamentalist minister who continued to preach for a while even after he became an atheist, who says that he knows 'many other American clergymen who are in the same position as he was but have confided only in him, having read his book'. I do not dispute this. There are many theoretical Christians who are in reality practising atheists in the Church. This is especially true when religion can be seen as a way to make money or make a living. If someone no longer believes then of course they should not continue to take a salary from an organisation they no longer support, teaching doctrines they no longer believe in.

Coming from a working-class background I did not go to boarding schools and I do not have the money to buy my children the 'best' education. I am more than happy to send them to state schools but I do not want them to be indoctrinated by the minority of secularists and atheists who seem to think that their philosophy is the only one which should have any credence. I have noticed that although atheists talk the talk about education, when it comes to walking the walk, they do not generally build schools or put their money where their mouth is. Instead they prefer to seize, cuckoo-like, the work, money and initiatives of others so that they can then use these to teach on the basis of their own philosophy.

My own country, Scotland, was famous for its education system, a system that provided opportunity, education and advancement for all who were prepared to take it. It was a system that was based upon Christian principles and operated on the notion of where there was a church there should be a school. All our major Universities were founded on Christian principles and in general that system has served us well. It is no coincidence that as the basic principles of Christianity have been driven out of school and culture Scotland has become a significantly dumbed down culture and we are rapidly slipping down the international educational league table.

I do not want a Stalinist system which bans Christianity from school and home. Nor do I want an American secularist model that leaves the wealthy and middle class to send their children to private schools (often based on Christian principles) whilst often allowing the poor to rot in an under-funded state system based on a poor philosophy of education. Teaching children on the basis of Christian principles of love, mutual respect, inquiry, truth and justice is not abuse. Denying children the opportunity to a decent education because of the bias of your philosophy – that is abuse. And accusing parents who seek to bring their children up in the love and peace of Christ of being child abusers is contemptible.

There is however one area where I can agree with you. You lament the biblical illiteracy of our current society. I agree. Totally. Mind you, it is only such ignorance which means that you can get away with many of the claims you make about the Bible in your books. Anyone who is biblically literate would soon recognise that your representation of the Bible is distorted and out of context. What may shock you even more (it certainly depresses me) is how biblically illiterate many professing Christians are. If Christians knew the Word better and were better taught, we would not have much to fear from the resurgent atheism you are trying to encourage. The Bible is so much more than an interesting literary and cultural collection. It is the living and enduring Word of God. Heaven and earth will pass away but the Word of God will endure forever.

Let's move briefly on to chapter ten. This is a somewhat strange and disjointed chapter which skirts over the notion of religion as some kind of consolation, the Christian attitude to death and ends up with the theories of quantum physics. You seem to think that those of us who believe in God are in effect children who have not grown out of the need for an imaginary friend. Apart from the patronising aspect of this, the question arises to me that if the God of the Bible, or the God of the Catholics or the God of anyone is as horrible as you state, how can belief in him be a consolation?

As regards death, you imply that if we really believed what we said then we would all be happy about dying. Of course, if we all went delirious to the grave you would then be citing this as evidence of the power of religion to brainwash! One of the reasons I believe is precisely because of death. It would be so easy and such a relief in some ways to believe that once I died that was it. Imagine no afterlife. No one to answer to. No heaven. No hell. Nothing unknown. Just death, stillness and nothingness. To believe that would for many people be bliss. It is little wonder that some of your converts describe such a belief with religious fervour. And yet I have tried that route. And it just does not work. It does not work because it does not ring true. It does not work because there is something inside me that tells me there is more to life than this life. It does not work because the whole universe screams out the majesty and glory of God. It does not work because I have a mind which tells me that I am neither an inanimate object nor just a collection of molecules on their way to nothing. It does not work because I know that my body is more than a throwaway survival machine, just as I know that the world is not flat and life is not meaningless. The atheist answer to death is found in Camus' *L'Etranger* (*The Stranger*). It is hopeless. The Christian answer is vastly different. It is Christ.

In reviewing your book I think we have come across two competing philosophies. They actually don't have all that much to do with science except insofar as both will cite the discoveries of science as evidence. Your philosophy of logical positivism means that your science replaces God. It is your worldview. It is your life. It is your faith. No wonder that you are so religious in defending it and so keen on rooting out heretics and wishy-washy appeasers! In chapter ten you talk about 'removing the Burka' meaning removing the limited view we have of Middle World (I think Tolkien should sue!). You suggest that now we see only partially but soon science will enable us to see clearly. I was blind but now I see. It's almost Messianic in its fervour and biblical in its language: 'For now we see through a glass, darkly; but then face to face' (1 Corinthians 13:12, KJV).

And this last chapter is where you finally and completely blow away any pretension that your view is based upon empirical, observable, testable evidence. Throughout the book you have been using the existence of the material as the lens through which we are to judge everything. You flavour this with what you deem to be commonsense experience and especially probability. And yet in chapter ten you move way beyond that. You cite Steve Grand, a computer scientist who specialises in artificial intelligence: 'Matter flows from place to place and momentarily comes together to be you. Whatever you are, therefore, you are not the stuff of which you are made. If that doesn't make the hair stand up on the back of your neck, read it again until it does, because it is important.' Grand also goes on to argue that if you remember an experience from your childhood you should remember that you were not really there. 'What we see of the real world is not the unvarnished real world but a model of the real world, regulated and adjusted by sense data – a model that is constructed so that it is useful for dealing with the real world!' This is brilliant stuff which seems to fit with the spiritual, and perhaps even with the biblical notion of the soul, but it is a million miles away from the empirical evidence that you keep demanding. In fact most of it is highly entertaining guesswork – trying to explain and fill in the gaps that science cannot answer. I call it ABGism – Anything-But-God-ism.

Your final sentence declares, 'Even better, we may eventually discover that there are no limits.' Of course you don't mean that. Because you draw the line at God. You cannot believe in a God who created the universe (that's a limit). You refuse to believe in a God who raised Jesus from the dead (another limit). And you ridicule the notion that this God could communicate with human beings through his Spirit and his Word (another limit). You are only prepared to accept no limits in terms of human knowledge. Indeed you want to replace God with humanity. You want us as the Higher Consciousness, to become like God. I believe that a long time ago there was someone else who once offered humanity the key to all knowledge. We fell for it then and have ever since been paying the price. I pray that we will not fall for that one again.

Yours, etc.
David

THE FINAL LETTER
TO DAWKINS

Dear Dr Dawkins,

It's been an interesting couple of years. Your book has sold millions and spawned lots of imitators and responses. Indeed it could be argued that the whole New Atheist publishing phenomena was kickstarted by *The God Delusion*. Congratulations. And thanks for giving my own wee response such a reaction. I loved Paula Kirby's review, commissioned by you, and posted on your website. The review was almost as long as my book. Although I thought it did not engage with the arguments and showed the usual New Atheist inability to listen, at least Paula provided me with some good advertising material, calling *The Dawkins Letters*, the best of the 'flea' responses. Thanks!

As we are republishing these 'flea' letters again, I thought I would add another one and take the opportunity to reflect on where all this is going. I have to admit that you have been successful in several areas. Firstly, you have managed to take control of the New Atheist movement – the respectful, reasonable, logical (insofar as that is possible) 'old' atheism of Bertrand Russell and Anthony Flew has been well and truly replaced by the 'Ridicules' –

as letter three in this book prophesied. Because of this the New Atheism is emotional, illogical, triumphalist, fearful and overflowing with bile – as I have found many times in my travels.

I have journeyed all over Britain (and to a lesser extent Europe and the USA) debating and discussing – in the past two years I have been involved in almost 100 such events. Many of these I have approached with fear and trepidation. After all, as one of your supporters in Cambridge, dressed resplendently in the atheist t-shirt with a big 'A' emblazoned on the front, asked, 'Who do you think you are?' I am a 'nobody' in your eyes – just a mere 'flea' seeking to make a living off your genius! I have no formal training in philosophy or science. I am not the Archbishop of Canterbury or the Chief Rabbi. (Interesting that you are prepared to debate them but you refuse to debate people such as William Lane Craig and other Christian apologists – why?) I don't believe that you are scared of losing. Is it because you are so convinced of your own rightness that engaging with anyone who thinks differently is beneath you? Does that not justify my charge in the earlier letters of atheist fundamentalism? Or maybe it is something much simpler – just good old-fashioned snobbery and pride. I suspect you really do think it is beneath you to discuss or debate with such plebes. After all if you can dismiss Frances Collins, head of the human genome project, as an 'adminstrator' and Professor John Lennox of Oxford University as an 'Irish mathematician', why should you bother with a Scottish Presbyterian Plebe?!

Speaking of Lennox, I loved the series of three debates that you held with him, first in Alabama and then in Oxford. I guess the Professor took you by surprise in the first one. He was articulate, intelligent and gracious as he wiped the floor with you. It was a tour de force. You were better prepared for the second one, but the third was the most interesting, because sadly you reverted to type. What I mean is this: in the first debate when John Lennox mentioned the resurrection of Jesus you could hardly contain your contempt. In the third 'debate' (although it was no such thing – it was apparently meant to be a conversation between two great minds), right from the beginning you launched into personal abuse, sneering and contempt. There was no attempt to engage. No attempt to dialogue. No attempt to win hearts and minds. It was, as we say in Scotland, just 'sticking the boot in'. It was cheap, sordid and nasty. Why? What had Professor Lennox ever done to you other than demonstrate that Christians can be reasonable, rational and Oxford professors as well!

This is the second area where you have succeeded. By displaying such a contemptuous attitude you have managed to provide plenty empirical evidence that the New Atheism is not based on reason or logic, but rather on experience and emotion. I have seen this so many times. Let me mention a couple. There was the time at the now sadly demised Borders in Cambridge when my talk was interrupted by an atheist who was furious that I had mentioned the emotionalism of the New Atheism. In order to demonstrate that I was wrong about this he shouted at me, somewhat emotionally, until one of his friends told him, 'Sit down you fool, you've just proved his point'! It reminded me of the Islamic fundamentalist waving a placard stating 'Behead those who say Islam is violent'!

Another incident occurred on your website – indeed in the aforementioned lengthy discussion on Paula Kirby's review of this book. I received a death threat. Yes – it was intended as a joke. But it was a joke in appalling taste and quite disturbing – in that it involved personal details and information. What was even more disturbing was that it took you over a week to agree to remove it, as I had requested, whilst the one person who had the courage to object to it, removed his own objection. It's funny, if you had received a death threat on a 'Christian' website, even a joke one, I am sure you would have evidenced it as yet another example of where 'moderate' religion leads to. Did you need a bullet proof jacket in Alabama? Or were the Christians really nice to the lion?

Another side of this is that it is generally remarkably easy to debate the New Atheists. Why? Because you are so convinced that you are de facto right and that the only logical and intelligent position is atheism, that you regard anyone who disagrees with you as being either stupid or evil. The result is that the New Atheists tend to approach each debate with the same arrogance and the same arguments. If I had a penny for every time I heard the 'Flying Spaghetti Monster' argument, or the 'You don't believe in Thor or Zeus, atheists just go one God further', I would be a rich man! I recall debating a professor of philosophy in the United States. I expected to take a hammering, but as the debate went on I felt like the King in *The Lord of the Rings*, who when defending Helms' Deep asked Sauron and the

Orcs, 'Is that all you have?', as they hurled themselves against the castle wall. In that instance the forces of darkness did have something extra – a massive bomb that blew up the castle wall. But each time I have been in debate and waiting for the bomb – it has never arrived (including with the said philosophy professor). Why is that? It is not because I am particularly clever – far from it – but rather because the intellectual reasons for atheism are so weak. After one debate in London, a woman who thought she was an atheist, came along to the church the Sunday afterwards and became a Christian. Why? She graciously thought that both the speakers were intelligent, articulate and humorous. That observation was certainly true of my charming opponent however, as she also observed, it was the content that was different. She recognised at the end of the day that the atheist position is just simply empty. It lacks content and credibility. Basically the New Atheism is a jazzed up version of the 'I don't believe, I won't believe" children's argument. The demand for 'evidence' is just a smokescreen, because you have already predetermined that there can be no such evidence. Why do you think a non-material God can be proven in a materialistic/ naturalistic test tube like experiment? The New Atheists are like the man who sets up a football goal that is ten centimetres wide, asks you to score a goal with a ball that is a metre wide and then proudly proclaims that you can't play football because you don't score!

A third area where you have been successful is in getting religion discussed. The problem I had had as a Christian minister was not usually antagonism, but rather apathy. Most people did not really care that I was a Christian, as long as I kept it to myself and treated it like being a member of the knitting club. But then you came along, and sold millions of books discussing God and Christianity. The atheist bus campaign was also a real boost. It was great to be able to point at a bus where the atheist sermon was – 'There is probably no God, so stop worrying and enjoy life', and ask people what they thought of it. Apart from the banality of the message (try telling the mother who has just lost her child – there is no God so just enjoy life!), it was just a spectactular own goal. Thanks for the £250,000 free publicity. In fact, in reacting to the stubborn refusal of Christianity to die, in using 9/11 as an excuse to lump all religions together, you have only succeeded in preaching to the choir/flock and opening up the door for us to present a much better message. *The Economist* magazine in its millennial edition in 2000 published an obituary for God. In 2007 they published what appointed to a 16 page apology, entitled 'God is Back: God returns to Europe'. The bottom line is that we are very grateful to you for stirring up the apathetic and creating such wonderful opportunities for us to present the wonderful good news of Jesus Christ.

And I am particularly grateful as I recall the many who have had cause to think again, and those who have gone all the way from darkness to light. There are so many examples, but perhaps the following letter, amongst the hundreds I have received, will give you pause for thought?

Dear Mr Robertson,

Many, many thanks for having written such a wonderful series of letters in response to the redoubtable Richard Dawkins' book.

Thanks because those letters (as published in your book) have proved enormously useful to me at the present time: useful and inspirational. I hope that I can be frank with you. Before the publication of the Dawkins book, I would have quite happily (even proudly) labelled myself as an atheist – perhaps with shades of the intellectual agnostic: I am (or was until I retired) a deeply rational computer scientist, convinced that what I saw and felt as consciousness was little different from what I saw as computer program. Admittedly different in complexity, but not in fundamentals.

I was happy that I had my perspective on the world of spirituality well-sorted: there was no God, no heaven, no hell, no soul, no afterlife – and no reason to feel concern about those things.

And then I committed the atheists' cardinal sin: I started to think and read more broadly! Perhaps more sinful than that, I started to read more widely on religious matters, and I decided to drop (or at least, to shelve) my preconceptions about the world-view of those who wrote from the perspective of faith. You'll forgive me, I trust, if I confess that my preconceptions were indeed that those of faith hadn't, couldn't have fully thought through their intellectual position on faith: how could they? But then I decided to read and think on the basis that perhaps – just perhaps – they *had* fully thought through those positions. I decided to give faith a chance!

What prompted me to take what was for me a radical (and I must admit, a scary) step was the feeling I had after reading Dawkins.

Like many, I came to Dawkins through Selfish Gene – and found it an enormously useful piece of work. I then followed his texts, and followed his increasingly obvious atheist position – first with gentle amusement, then with enthusiasm... But then increasingly with distaste. *The God Delusion* was – at least for me – simply a step too far.

I found it a profoundly uncomfortable book. Dawkins is an atheist; I had enthusiastically labelled myself as an atheist... But I simply could not find it in myself to align my world-view with that of somebody who could write in such a vitriolic fashion about a subject that millions (billions!) feel to have had a positive impact on their lives.

If I was an atheist, I was (at least in some regards) like Dawkins. But I am not like Dawkins, so perhaps I wasn't an atheist?

I began to read, committing myself to take what those writers said on face value when they talked about their relationship with God... And the more I read, the more I began to feel my familiar foundations of thought crumble – and then gradually be rebuilt in a different (and more interesting) shape. Your book is not the final step along this path for me; but it has been an enormously encouraging book at this stage.

Anyway now that I have got on to quoting letters within letters, I think it is time for me to go. But I do have a question. Where do you get this idea that we are only interested in money? Do you really think that Alister McGrath, John Lennox and yours truly are really just 'fleas' trying to make a living off your back? Do you think that you are that important? Or more ludicrously, that Christian publishing is that lucrative? You may disagree with us but at least do us the courtesy of respecting our motivation. Mine is simply that I believe that Jesus is no delusion and that he is the answer to the deepest problems that the world faces. Besides which, although I accept that it was not your motivation, it is a bit rich for someone who has made millions out of rehashing old arguments about a God he says does not exist, to complain about money making! One of your fellow atheist 'horsemen' had agreed to debate me in London, the only trouble was that his agent demanded $50,000 plus first class airfares (later reduced to $20,000 because it was a 'charity'). Highly flattering but totally ridiculous (my 'fee' was a second-class rail fare from Dundee). Who would think that atheists were so insecure that they will only debate for money or prestige? Speaking of which, can you please agree to debate someone like William Lane Craig? I realise that I am beyond the pale and you do not want to make my CV look better, but you should at least debate some of the people you keep writing so disparagingly about. Otherwise it does look a little like cowardice. And of course, if you change your mind, I am more than happy to let your Goliath slay this particular David.

At the end of the first edition of this book I suggested some further reading. For the sake of those who read this, let me add a few more. Tim Keller's *Reason for God* and *The Prodigal God* are two outstanding works, providing an intellectual rationale for Christ that is second to none. John Lennox's *God's Undertaker – has Science buried God?* is the best book on science and God that I have ever read. A new book that has just come out is also excellent – Edgar Andrew's *Who Made God?* a fascinating rebuttal of your central thesis. There is also Roger Scruton's *On Beauty*, an interesting book that demonstrates again that human beings need beauty because we are all created in the image of the Beautiful Being. And finally there is Tobias Jones's *Utopian Dreams* in which Jones discovers that Christianity rather than secularism is the source of community and love. A brilliant work full of perceptive insights. Meanwhile it remains my prayer that you and all those who read this, will come to know the One who is Love and Justice, before you meet Him.

Yours etc
David

PS. I have also added an appendix which serves to illustrate how God can even use an atheist website to bring people to Himself. Read and enjoy Richard's testimony. I especially love the part where he describes coming out of the two dimensional black and white world of unbelief, into the glorious technicolour liberty, joy and beauty of life in Christ. Once you have tasted that the Lord is good, you will never want to go back to the drabness of life without Christ. C.S. Lewis put it beautifully – it's as though we are children playing with a bucket and spade in a mud pit, when we discover that there is a whole beautiful beach for us to enjoy ourselves. I wish you all the best and pray that you will indeed come into the Light.

SALVATION CAME THROUGH RICHARD DAWKINS

What a relief it was to become an atheist.

I had become worn out and frustrated by my fruitless search for God. I had studied holy writings from three different continents. No God there. I had tried prayer and 'positive thinking' as if they were the same thing. I had wrestled with the problems of theodicy without even knowing that the word existed. I felt that I had sought God everywhere – in the cosmos, in my neurones, in my bank account. Everywhere. Or so I thought.

Then I read *The Blind Watchmaker* by Richard Dawkins.

What an immense relief it was to discover that my search for God and Meaning was bound to be frustrating and disappointing, could only lead me up blind alleys, because God simply didn't exist. How obvious. Evolution explained everything. The notion of God (the supreme alpha-male) was a side-effect of the evolution of the human brain. Attributing 'agency' was an effective survival strategy. The God that you attributed agency to was uniquely dependent on the culture into which you had been born. Religion was an exercise in social manipulation and power.

Believing information received from non-verifiable sources (revelation) opened the door to all kinds of horrendous excesses from Inquisitions and witch-burning to flying planes into towers and fathers committing 'honour killings' and a president lying to bomb and massacre innocent people in Iraq.

Man had invented God in his own image. God was the ultimate comfort blanket. Science was leaving no space for the 'God of the gaps'. Talk of Eternal Life was in fact just a morbid obsession with death. Even monkeys had invented The Golden Rule. Science and Reason alone revealed Truth. An 'Omnipotent God' was an impossible notion anyway. Religion was 'the opium of the people.' Love, self-sacrifice and charity were just the misfiring of evolutionarily selected survival mechanisms. Everything could be explained. There was just simply no need for the God delusion any more. Hallelujah!

Many years later, in November 2006, I discovered the internet site RichardDawkins.Net, and my very first internet Forum/Discussion group. What a joyous experience that was for me at the beginning!

Discovering other people's ideas on atheism, being able to interact with them, making friends of some of them, and from time to time being presented with some scientific discovery or irrefutable philosophical reasoning – this was what life was all about.

One of the favourite sports on RDNet was insulting and mocking Christian authors who had the gall to write books refuting Dawkins' *The God Delusion*.

One thread on the site was devoted mainly to David Robertson's *The Dawkins Letters*. I mention this, because it was this same David Robertson who spoiled all the fun for me. He replied at great length, with considerable politeness and restraint to a very long 'review' of his book *The Dawkins Letters*.

My first reaction was, 'Poor guy, why is he wasting all his time doing this?'

My RDNet friends had the answer for me, 'Attention-seeking'. (Ironically, I was to discover that they weren't entirely wrong. Except that DR wasn't seeking to draw attention to himself…)

In spite of the abuse, DR kept coming back. He kept answering the criticisms. Several of us started wondering, 'What is wrong with this guy?'

The 'royal decree' on DR was that he was a 'dishonest, unpleasant, unbalanced; un-Christian fruitcake', so why did we all persist in engaging him in discussion? Not only did he argue with us, from time to time he wished us well and quoted Scripture!

But (and it's a big 'but') many RDnetters accused David Robertson of being a liar. This surprised me, but I didn't dare say so on the site. I couldn't risk being excommunicated as a troll.

'Get over thyself.'

'Get thyself a life.'

Those were our commandments.

I read and re-read DR's lengthy comments. I found all the evidence I needed to prove that he was probably a deluded fruitcake, but none to substantiate the accusations of being 'mean' or 'evil' or best of all 'a liar.'

The poor deluded 'WeeFlea' asked in all humility for someone to point out precisely where and how he had

137

lied. I got brave and posted, saying, 'Whatever else we may think about DR, I'm sure he does not wilfully and knowingly tell lies.'

My friends, of course, shot me down in flames.

So I tried to accept that the lies were there, but that I was intellectually incapable of perceiving them.

Then came that terrible moment, when the site administrator published an article about some deluded Russian prophet who had tried to commit suicide in a particularly clownish way when his prediction for the date of the end of the world failed to come true.

Even as I was reading the article, I started having forebodings about the kind of comments that I was likely to find afterwards. And my worst suspicions were confirmed.

Much laughter. Considerable mocking and jeering. And there were even a couple of posters who regretted that the fallen prophet had failed in his 'attempt' to put an end to his life. They made a joke of wishing somebody dead.

I expressed my shock and disappointment in a couple of posts. And then I went too far. I wrote and signed my own RDNet death sentence when I said:

> '...and apart from all that, don't you guys realise that you are giving David Robertson and his ilk stuff to use against us as atheists? Already they accuse us of being soulless and unfeeling! I am sure that David Robertson would never, ever laugh and gloat over a suicide attempt by an atheist.
>
> Can you imagine him saying "Serve him right, dumb atheist! That's where rejecting Jesus gets you! He deserves nothing better. Psychotic, godless fruitcake!"'

Now there are many fine and highly intelligent, articulate members of RDNet. A small number of them timidly came out and defended me. But one of the most respected of them, a doctor, contented herself with quoting me and adding 'LOL'.

After a few faltering attempts to justify my position I decided that RDNet was not where I wanted, or needed, to be. The cognitive and affective dissonance was just too much for me.

So there I was. Alone again. No God. Rejected by atheists.

Now I have another confession to make here. Whenever David Robertson posted a long comment on RDNet, I had developed the guilty habit of printing it out, and sneaking onto the balcony to read it with my morning coffee.

So one morning, I took out my copies of his posts and re-read them. What did I have to lose? I found nothing of apparent interest. DR was clearly stubborn, persistent, polite, but still deluded.

As I was reading, my thoughts turned to the honey bee and the invisible, ultra-violet landing pads on the petals of certain flowers that guide the bee to the pollen and the delicious nectar that awaits the happy apidae. The fact that I can't see these landing pads doesn't mean that they don't exist. Just as the fact that the bee can't see the colour red doesn't mean that he can fly through a tomato.

I have my five senses and a brain that works in a particular way to process what my five senses pick up. But that doesn't prove that anything that can't be captured by my five senses doesn't exist.

If ever, in a science fiction journey, I came across a universe where living beings had ten senses, well, I could only have half as much fun as they did.

The wonderful philosophical explanations and arguments that I read on RDNet had fascinated me, filled me with awe and admiration, and I even understood some of them.

But they always left me with the uneasy feeling of, 'Well, yes, that's what brains do. Ducks quack; the French complain, and the human brain processes information. However sophisticated my reasoning processes, they will still be limited to the capacity of my brain. But does that mean that anything that cannot be perceived by my senses and processed by my brain, therefore, doesn't exist?' I started ruminating about all this during that fateful weekend.

But ruminating is not all that I did.

I committed the unforgivable sin: I started posting on the FCoS Forum. The Free Church of Scotland. A veritable den of theists. I defected. I spoke about being a sad atheist, about my desire to be able to believe.

Then, on Saturday, April 12th 2008, in reaction to my posts, FCoS's 'resident fruitcake' asked me two questions which were to change me life:

'Why don't you believe in God?' and

'What could make you believe in God?'

My knee-jerk reaction to the first question was, 'That's a dumb question.' And to the second, I had two instinctive and spontaneous answers:

1.   I don't know.
2.   Certainly not proof and evidence.

At that moment, the words that I had learned many years previously and that had always provoked a terrible sensation of longing in me, came into my mind:

'We can love Him, because He loved us first.'

And my universe exploded.

Lights came on, prison doors opened, and scales fell off my eyes, the whole 'Amazing Grace' thing.

As I considered my perception of life, the universe and everything, it was literally as if I had been looking at a two-dimensional image in black and white, and in an instant everything became three dimensional and Technicolor!

A short time later, I went back to my DR documents and was amazed to discover that the words that almost leapt out at me from the pages were the Biblical references that had so embarrassed me before. Not David Robertson's words – the Word of God.

The ensuing 48 hours were very intense, as my brain started processing tons of previously stocked information in a different way.

The Bible, that I had previously studied so much that I couldn't read an 'And it came to pass...' without having a migraine, became exciting. Meaningful.

Today, I feel no resentment towards my RDNet correspondents.

After all, it was among the atheists that I found salvation. An insistent, obtuse Scottish clergyman kept 'coming back for more'. Not only defending his arguments, but boldly confronting atheists with the Word of God.

A voice crying in the wilderness? Perhaps. But even in the wilderness, perhaps somebody is hiding behind a rock, listening. I was.

'For the word of God is living and full of power'
(Hebrews 4:12)

It is so good to be loved without having done anything to deserve it. It is so good to raise my eyes from the science laboratories and the books of philosophy and start to behold the glory of God. Science and philosophy are wonderful manifestations of the enormous capacities of the human mind.

But the Word of God is Truth, and truth is what it took to set me free. My journey in faith begins.

Watch this space.

FINAL LETTER TO THE READER – WHY BELIEVE?

Dear Reader,

Thanks for reading this far (or if you are the kind of person who starts a book backwards – thanks for beginning here!) I promised that I would provide a reading list and some other resources and so space-permitting I will do so. I also want to answer a question that has continually been asked me over the past few weeks and one I promised I would answer. But let's do the books first.

I have read over 100 books and articles relating to the subjects covered in these letters. It has been an exhausting but stimulating journey. Some material has stretched my mind until it hurt – especially the quantum physics! I take comfort in the fact that as Richard Feynman pointed out, 'If you think you understand quantum theory … you don't understand quantum theory'. Perhaps the most helpful books have been the following. (Please note that 'helpful' does not necessarily mean an endorsement of everything in every book. I am assuming that those of you who have managed to read this far are grown up enough to realise that we can sometimes learn a lot from people we disagree with. The books below are books I have interacted with – there is only one book I would regard to be absolutely trustworthy, the Bible!).

Obviously *The God Delusion*[35] is the book I am interacting with. If you already have the book then you will know what I am referring to. If you don't, I cannot honestly recommend that you should get it. It really is as bad as I have tried to demonstrate and I would be reluctant to put any more money into it! If you are interested in science then Dawkins' other books are much more palatable. In terms of the science/religion interaction I would recommend:

Alister McGrath, *Dawkins' God: Genes, Memes and the Meaning of Life;*[36] *The Twilight of Atheism*[37] and *Science and Religion: An Introduction.*[38] (I have not yet read *The Dawkins Delusion?*[39] by Alister McGrath and Joanna Collicutt McGrath as, at the time of writing it had not been published; however, I have little doubt that it will be up to McGrath's usual excellent standard.) Kirsten Birkett *Unnatural Enemies: An Introduction to Science and Christianity*[40] is a beautiful little primer on the whole subject and her *The Essence of Psychology*[41] is equally worthwhile. Stephen J. Gould's *Rocks of Ages: Science and Religion in the Fullness of Life*[42] is a mine of information as well. Malcolm A. Jeeves and R. J. Berry, *Science, Life and Christian Belief*[43] has been very helpful to me. For those interested in the history of science and religion David N.

35. Hardback: Bantam Press (2006); Paperback: Black Swan (2007)
36. Blackwell Publishing (2004)
37. Rider & Co (2004)
38. Blackwell Publishers (1998)
39. SPCK Publishing (2007)
40. Matthias Press (1997)
41. Matthias Press (1999)
42. Ballantine Books (1999)
43. Apollos (1998)

Livingstone, *Darwin's Forgotten Defenders: The Encounter Between Evangelical Theology and Evolutionary Thought*[44] is fascinating. For a 19th-century populist writer who is as good as Dawkins in communicating his message, but has the distinct advantage of being a Christian, have a look at Hugh Miller: *The Footprints of the Creator: or, The Asterolepis of Stromness*[45] or *The Testimony of the Rocks: or, Geology in its Bearings on the Two Theologies, Natural and Revealed.*[46]

Some other populist science books that I have found helpful include Steve Jones, *In the Blood: God, Genesis and Destiny;*[47] Steven Hawking, *A Brief History of Time;*[48] Matt Ridley *Genome: The Autobiography of a Species in 23 Chapters;*[49] and especially Paul Davies *The Mind of God: Science and the Search for Ultimate Meaning,*[50] and *The Goldilocks Enigma: Why is the Universe Just Right for Life?*[51] Whilst Paul Davies is not a theist I have found him to be very fair and he does not dismiss theism – indeed he puts forward an excellent case for it. His books stretched my mind and in so doing reinforced my faith.

There are a number of scientists who are committed Christians and who have written about the interaction between their work and their faith. John Polkinghorne's *Quarks, Chaos and Christianity: Questions to Science and*

44. Eerdmans (1987)
45. University of Michigan University Library (1858)
46. Available from http://www.openlibrary.org/details/testimonyofther ocks00millrich (1857)
47. HarperCollins (1996)
48. Bantam (1995)
49. Fourth Estate (2000)
50. Penguin (2006)
51. Allen Lane (2006)

Religion[52] is stimulating and thought-provoking as well. Owen Gingerich's *God's Universe*[53] is a small but well worthwhile book from a senior Astronomer. R. J. Berry's *God and the Biologist*[54] gives a theistic evolutionary viewpoint. My personal favourite (even though I do not agree with everything in it) is Francis Collins' *The Language of God: a Scientist Presents Evidence for Belief*.[55] It is one of the most interesting and faith-affirming books I have ever read.

Although many scientists would not agree with the Intelligent Design Movement (including many who accept that there is evidence for intelligent design) no-one should comment on it without reading Michael Behe's *Darwin's Black Box: Biochemical Challenges to Evolution*.[56] Likewise there are scientists and many Christians who adopt a young-earth creationist position. The best defence I have read of this is Douglas F. Kelly, *Creation and Change*.[57]

There are so many books that could be mentioned on Christianity, theology and morality. C. S. Lewis' *Mere Christianity*[58] and also his *Surprised by Joy*[59] remain wonderful explanations of many aspects of the Christian faith. Lee Strobel's *The Case for Christ: a Journalist's Personal Investigation of the Evidence for Jesus*[60] makes a good

52. Crossroad Publishing Co., USA (2005)
53. The Belknap Press (2006)
54. Apollos (1996)
55. Simon & Schuster Ltd (2006)
56. Simon & Schuster Ltd (1996)
57. Mentor/Christian Focus Publications (1997)
58. Fount (1997)
59. Fount (1998)
60. Zondervan (1998)

case. McGrath's *Christian Theology: An Introduction*[61] is the most reliable standard text book, whilst if you want a really reliable and in-depth systematic biblical theology it would be hard to beat Robert Duncan Culver's *Systematic Theology*.[62] John Stott's *Issues Facing Christians Today*[63] is a superb example of how to apply the Bible to modern life. On the other hand, *Godless Morality: Keeping Religion Out of Ethics*[64] by Richard Holloway is an example of how far the Church can wander away from the Christian faith, whilst Richard Bauckham's *God and the Crisis of Freedom: Biblical and Contemporary Perspectives*[65] contains an excellent chapter dealing with Holloway's book. John Wenham's *The Enigma of Evil: Can We Believe in the Goodness of God?*[66] is a tremendous discussion about some of the major issues as is Miroslav Volf's *Exclusion and Embrace: Theological Exploration of Identity, Otherness and Reconciliation.*[67] And I have always enjoyed reading F. F. Bruce – *The New Testament Documents: Are They Reliable?*[68] and his *The Hard Sayings of Jesus.*[69] Personally I have gained a lot from Augustine's *Confessions* and his *City of God.* Calvin's *Institutes* and anything by Jonathan Edwards will always repay the effort.

On the whole question of the 20th century being the failed century of atheism the best place to begin is Niall

61. Blackwell Publishers, 3rd edition (2001)
62. Mentor/Christian Focus Publications (2005)
63. Zondervan Publishing House, 4th edition (2006)
64. Canongate Books Ltd (2000)
65. West-minster/John Knox Press, USA, 1st edition (2002)
66. Inter-Varsity Press (1985)
67. Abingdon Press, USA (1994)
68. Inter-Varsity Press (2000)
69. Hodder Christian Essentials, Hodder & Stoughton (1998)

Ferguson, *The War of the World: History's Age of Hatred*.[70] Eric Hobsbawm's *Age of Extremes: The Short Twentieth Century 1914–1991*[71] is a standard work in the same vein. If you have any doubt about the atheism of Stalin or Mao then I would recommend Simon Sebag-Montefiore's *Stalin: The Court of the Red Tsar*[72] and Jung Chang's *Mao: The Unknown Story*.[73] On the rise of Nazism and Hitler's atheism have a look at Daniel Jonah Goldhagen, *Hitler's Willing Executioners*,[74] Gitta Sereny, *Albert Speer: His Battle with Truth*,[75] Ian Kershaw's *Hitler*[76] and Traudl Junge's *Until the Final Hour: Hitler's Last Secretary*.[77] To see how a Christian dealt with the evil of Nazism read Dietrich Bonhoeffer's *Discipleship*[78] and *Letters and Papers from Prison*.[79]

Two other works mentioned are Patrick Sookhdeo's article *The Myth of Moderate Islam*,[80] and Hans Rookmaaker's book *Modern Art and the Death of a Culture*.[81]

However, these letters have not just come out of science, theological, philosophical or history books. There are many other things that need to be added to the mix. I should also mention films that I have found to be stimulating

70. Allen Lane (2006)

71. Abacus (1998)

72. Phoenix Press (2004)

73. Jonathan Cape (2005)

74. Abacus (1997)

75. Picador (1996)

76. *Hitler 1889-1936, Hubris*, Penguin (1998); *Hitler 1936-1945, Nemesis* Penguin (2000)

77. Weidenfeld & Nicolson (2003)

78. Augsburg Fortress (2003)

79. Pocket Books, enlarged 1st Touchstone edition (1997)

80. The *Spectator*, 30 July 2005

81. Apollos (1994)

and informative: *The Matrix, Downfall* and the recently released *Amazing Grace*. In terms of human nature and describing the problems that modern society faces *Crash* is thought-provoking and disturbing. *The World at War* is the best TV/DVD series made on the subject.

Music and poetry are two of the greatest gifts given to humans. Leonard Cohen, John Lennon, B. B. King, U2, Mozart, Emmylou Harris and Johnny Cash are the soundtrack of this book! Poems such as Leonard Cohen's *All There is to Know about Adolf Eichmann* say in a few words what I say in many!

In terms of novels I would recommend the following in particular: Dostoevsky's *The Brothers Karamazov*, the final part of C. S. Lewis' science fiction trilogy *That Hideous Strength* (which brilliantly warns us about the dangers of a godless scientific materialism), Nick Hornby's *About a Boy*, Albert Camus' *L'Etranger*, Douglas Coupland's *Girlfriend in a Coma* and Marilynn Robinson's beautifully written and wonderfully perceptive *Gilead*.

There are also numerous articles/reviews and booklets that I have read. One I would certainly want to recommend is a sermon published as a booklet by Alec MacDonald of Buccleuch and Greyfriars Free Church in Edinburgh – *Why I am not an Atheist*. Go to the Free Church website (www.freechurch.org) in order to get a copy.

Speaking of which, the Web is an excellent source of information, although please be careful about using *Wikipedia* and *Google* as shortcuts to actually finding out and thinking about things for yourself. (I have lost track of the number of times I have read 'scholars' who prove that this part of the Bible is false or that part is wrongly translated, usually by people who have never read a word of Greek or Hebrew in their life but suddenly 'know' because of something they have read on the web!) Some of the other websites I have used are the Faraday Institute – (www.st-edmunds.cam.ac.uk/faraday/index.php, an excellent source of material from Cambridge on the faith/science interaction), Christians in Science (www.cis.org.uk), Cees Dekker (www.mb.tn.tudelft.nl/user/dekker/index.html), Redeemer PCA (www.redeemer.com, a constant source of stimulation and encouragement as is John Piper, www.desiringgod.org). And of course I must not forget Richard Dawkins' own website (www.richarddawkins.net).

Prospect magazine, *Time,* The *Spectator,* *The Times,* The *Guardian* and The *New York Times* online often have excellent articles discussing many of the issues raised in these letters.

The originals of these letters and some of the responses to them can be found on the Free Church website (www.freechurch.org). The initial letter was posted on the Dawkins website and got such a vitriolic response that none of the others was posted there. I have however enjoyed corresponding with a number of atheist thinkers who in general have been a great deal more gracious and helpful. Most of our discussions tend to get bogged down in presuppositions. Atheists presuppose there is nothing outside matter. They tend to be logical positivists who demand proof but then set unreasonable limits as to what they will accept as proof. They reject totally the concept of revelation. Like atheists, I too presuppose that matter is real but I do not presuppose that matter is the *only* reality and I cannot *de facto* reject the concept of revelation out of hand. Indeed, that is one thing I have become more certain of – that despite the testimony of God in the creation ('For since the creation of the world God's invisible qualities – his eternal power and divine nature – have been clearly seen, being understood from what has been made', Romans 1:20) it is all the more necessary for the Spirit of God to work in our lives so that we may see. After all, did Jesus not say that unless a man was born of the Spirit he could not even see, never mind enter, the kingdom of God (John 3)?

In a sense I am grateful to Richard Dawkins for writing his book. It has made me think and has stretched my mind. Occasionally the book has angered me, and I am sorry if that sometimes has come across in these letters. (Perhaps I should point out that no atheists were harmed in the making of this book!) More often than not it has saddened me – I thought that Bertrand Russell was the most depressing atheist I had ever read but Dawkins beats him hands down – take for example this from *River Out of Eden: a Darwinian View of Life*:[82]

> We are survival machines – robot vehicles blindly programmed to preserve the selfish molecules known as genes. Our genes made us. We animals exist for their preservation and are nothing more than throwaway survival machines. The world of the selfish gene is one of savage competition, ruthless exploitation, and deceit.

What a desperate, sad and ugly world.

I am not surprised that Dawkins was 'mortified' by the fact that *The Selfish Gene*[83] is the favourite book of Jeff

82 Phoenix Press (1996)
83 Oxford University Press, 3rd revised edition (2006)

Skilling, the disgraced CEO of the Enron Corporation, and of course I realise that Dawkins is not a Social Darwinist. However I do not see how his social and political position is logically consistent with his philosophical position. My passion against what Dawkins is teaching is not driven out of some desire to protect or defend God. If God was a human construct then he would not be worth defending. If he is for real then he can defend himself. I am reminded of the famous Baptist minister C. H. Spurgeon who once retorted to a comment about him defending the Bible: 'Defend the Bible? I would as soon defend a lion!' No, my passion is simply that I have no doubt that if atheist philosophy gets an ever-increasing grip on Europe or the USA then we are really heading for another Dark Age.

For those American readers who think this may be true of Europe but can hardly apply to the USA let me remind you that the Church is only ever one generation away from extinction in any one area. I am not convinced that the USA Church is as strong as people suppose. Certainly, it looks as though the numbers are there but I suspect that much of it is very fragile and just as the European Church was largely unable to stand up to the assaults on the Bible that took place at the end of the 19th century, so the American Church, unless it wakes up and really does get back to the Bible, will soon find itself collapsing like a house of cards in-face of the onslaught of New Age spirituality, the cults, materialism and the newly confident militant atheism of Dawkins *et al*.

When I began this series of letters I had no idea where it was going to lead. I approached *The God Delusion* with a certain fear. Partly this was because whilst at

University, I spent one year studying the English Civil War. I remember one black week when in reading the brilliant Marxist historian Christopher Hill I came across a statement to the effect that the English Puritans had engaged in the biggest brainwashing exercise in history. The thought crossed my mind: 'What if that is true? What if I too have been brainwashed? What if belief in God is just a delusion?' Twenty-five years later I sat down to read Dawkins' book. I tried to be as open-minded as possible. I approached it with twenty-five years more knowledge, knowledge of things that would strengthen my belief, and knowledge of things that would cause me to question my belief. Believe it or not the top three things that have caused me the most doubt have been some of the more difficult passages in the Bible, the Church and the God Channel. I have never really had any problem with the God vs. science dichotomy, which has always struck me as a false dichotomy – something that Dawkins illustrates almost more than anybody. And I still believe. Indeed I believe more than ever. If anything Dawkins' book has not only confirmed to me the barrenness of the wastelands of atheism but has caused me to be even more thankful to God for his glory, his truth, his universe, his Word and, most of all, his Son.

I have been challenged myself many times by atheists as I have been writing these letters: 'Prove it. Prove that God exists.' And I have told each of them that when I came to the end I would attempt to answer the question. I do so in the knowledge that it is impossible to prove God, not because he is unprovable, but because of our presuppositions. For example, if you believe that miracles don't happen then miracles will never be accepted by you as proof. When I went through that period of doubt 25 years ago it was the blackest period of my life, not because I could not see the attraction in not believing, but rather because I could. But what I knew then and what I know now will not allow me to turn away from God. It may be comforting to be an unbeliever (especially if you have been traumatised or let down by some religion or religious group) but what good does that do if your unbelief is not true? What if it is not the Christians who are deluded but the non-believers?

What then do I know? Why believe that Christianity is true? I can only list the following – all of which have been mentioned and discussed in the ten letters.

1. The Creation. By that I mean the heavens and the earth, from the smallest atom to the vastest galaxy. It all shouts to me of the glory of God. As I write I am sitting in my parents' home in the Scottish Highlands overlooking the Dornoch Firth. The night is still and clear and in a moment I will go and clear my head and gaze up at the stars.

> 'The heavens declare the glory of God; the skies proclaim the work of his hands. Day after day they pour forth speech; night after night they display knowledge. There is no speech or language where their voice is not heard. Their voice goes out into all the earth, their words to the ends of the world. In the heavens he has pitched a tent for the sun' (Psalm 19:1-4).

I include science in this category. I think it is very foolish for Christians or others to seek to prove or disprove God on the basis of a current scientific theory or on empirical evidence alone. But science within its own constraints as the observation of what God has made is a marvellous and often faith-affirming thing.

2. The Human mind and spirit. Why are we conscious? Why are we special? And life. Where does it come from? How can we get life from non-life?

3. The Moral Law. How do we know what good and evil are? Why do we have a sense of that at all? And what is evil? Unlike Dawkins I cannot believe in the innate goodness of human beings. I see too much evil and no explanation fits what I observe as neatly and realistically as the teaching of the Bible. More than that I find that the Bible also brings us the answer to evil – and I have never yet come across any philosophy which does so.

4. Beauty. We have already looked at this in letter two. Why is it that human beings have an awareness of beauty? It could just be a chemical reaction but to me it makes a whole lot more sense to believe that God has made everything beautiful in its time. We see the beauty of the Creator in the Creation. Without God is beauty anything more than a meaningless myth? With God beauty is more than a hint of eternity.

5. Religion. Yes there is so much in religion that is wrong and in many ways I hate religion. Generally I think it is a human imitation that more often than not blocks the way to God rather than opens it. And yet it is an imitation of something that is real. As Augustine

said, 'Our hearts were made for you, O God, and they are restless until they find their rest in you.'

6. Experience. I believe because I have tasted that God is good. Of course we can be deluded in our experience (that is why we need to reflect). And we can be wrong in our knowledge. But it would be a strange kind of person who did not take into account their experiences as part of the whole package. Not long after I became a Christian I was visiting a 'hippy' home where amidst all the music and drugs paraphernalia there was a poster stuck on the wall. Its words have remained with me ever since: 'All that I have seen teaches me to trust the Creator for all that I have not seen'. Sure – answered prayer, that sense of God's presence and that joy in worship may all have been illusory. But then again it may all have been real.

7. History. Again as I have continued to read and study history it has broadened my horizons and enables me to see in the words of the old cliché that it is 'His Story'. The history of mankind makes a whole lot more sense when it is set in the context of the history of God.

8. The Church. I mentioned earlier that there are things in the Church that more than anything else have caused me to doubt. When you see Christians behaving in a way which would shame Satanists, when you see preachers being pompous, hypocritical, money and glory-grabbers, then it is enough to put you off Christianity for life. But I have also seen the other side. I have seen the most beautiful people (some of

whom had been quite frankly ugly before their conversion) behave in the most wonderful, inexplicable
ways. Inexplicable that is except for the grace and
love of God. The Church at its best is glorious, beautiful and one of the best reasons to believe.

9. The Bible. Again I mentioned problems that I have
   had and occasionally still have. But I can truthfully
   say this – that every year I read the Bible through at
   least once, that every day I try to read it and every
   week I study it in order to proclaim it. It has been
   a source of challenge, comfort, truth and renewal.
   I have no doubt that God speaks to me through
   it (and I don't mean the kind of loopy ignoring of
   context or more esoteric interpretations). In fact,
   I am so assured of this, experiencing it continually,
   that I have very little time for Christians who are
   always looking for 'extra words' – as though the Bible
   were not enough. For me the thrill is still there.

10. Jesus. I guess that any one of the above nine rea-
    sons would not be enough on their own – although
    I think their cumulative effect is overwhelming. But
    this is the icing on the cake. Actually no ... this *is* the
    cake. Jesus is the reason I believe and will continue
    to believe. 'In the past God spoke to our forefathers
    through the prophets at many times and in various
    ways, but in these last days he has spoken to us by
    his Son, whom he appointed heir of all things, and
    through whom he made the universe. The Son is the
    radiance of God's glory and the exact representation
    of his being, sustaining all things by his powerful

word' (Hebrews 1:1-3). All things were created by Christ, and for Christ. In him all things hold together (Colossians 1:17; Hebrews 1:3). It is in Christ that 'are hidden all the treasures of wisdom and knowledge' (Colossians 2:3). We hear about Jesus. We believe him. We receive him as Lord. We continue to live in him, 'rooted and built up in him, strengthened in the faith as you were taught, and overflowing with thankfulness' (Colossians 2:7). We are warned: 'See to it that no-one takes you captive through hollow and deceptive philosophy, which depends on human tradition and the basic principles of this world rather than on Christ' (Colossians 2:8). Would I really want to trade Jesus Christ for the Selfish Gene? No thanks. 'For in Christ all the fullness of the Deity lives in bod-ily form, and you have been given fullness in Christ.' Why would I swap the fullness of Jesus Christ for the emptiness of a universe and life without God?

And why should you? The wonderful thing about Jesus Christ is that you cannot inherit him, he cannot be bought and you cannot earn him. He simply comes as a free gift to all who would receive him. I leave you with some words from another man who had his life changed by Jesus and I pray that you too will see, believe and be changed.

In the beginning was the Word, and the Word was with God, and the Word was God. He was with God in the beginning. Through him all things were made; without him nothing was made that has been made. In him was life, and that life was the light of men. The light shines in the darkness, but the darkness has not understood it ... The true light that gives light to every man was coming into the world. He was in the world, and though the world was made through him, the world did not recognise him. He came to that which was his own, but his own did not receive him. Yet to all who received him, to those who believed in his name, he gave the right to become children of God – children born not of natural descent, nor of human decision or a husband's will, but born of God (John 1:1-5 and 9-13).

If you want to know more, just ask. Pray to God, seek his face and his forgiveness and he will never turn you away.

This book has been part of a conversation. One that is ongoing. It's not just about talk; it's about truth, life, meaning, beauty, justice and eternal love. And You. Join in.

Yours, etc.
David

David Robertson
St Peter's Free Church
4 St Peter's Street
Dundee
DD1 4JJ
Scotland, UK

Website – www.stpeters-dundee.org.uk
(we have set up a section to discuss
the issues raised in these letters)

If you have any questions or comments about this book please feel free to contact David at david@solas-cpc.org

Christian Focus Publications

Our mission statement –

STAYING FAITHFUL

In dependence upon God we seek to impact the world through literature faithful to His infallible Word, the Bible. Our aim is to ensure that the Lord Jesus Christ is presented as the only hope to obtain forgiveness of sin, live a useful life and look forward to heaven with Him.

Our Books are published in four imprints:

CHRISTIAN FOCUS

popular works including biographies, commentaries, basic doctrine and Christian living.

CHRISTIAN HERITAGE

books representing some of the best material from the rich heritage of the church.

MENTOR

books written at a level suitable for Bible College and seminary students, pastors, and other serious readers. The imprint includes commentaries, doctrinal studies, examination of current issues and church history.

CF4•K

children's books for quality Bible teaching and for all age groups: Sunday school curriculum, puzzle and activity books; personal and family devotional titles, biographies and inspirational stories – Because you are never too young to know Jesus!

Christian Focus Publications Ltd,
Geanies House, Fearn, Ross-shire,
IV20 1TW, Scotland, United Kingdom.
www.christianfocus.com
blog.christianfocus.com